Fran...

SWEET Valley High®

FLAIR
Collection

including
COVER GIRLS
MODEL FLIRT
FASHION VICTIM

BANTAM BOOKS
TORONTO • NEW YORK • LONDON • SYDNEY • AUCKLAND

Visit the official Sweet Valley Web Site on the Internet at:
http://www.sweetvalley.com

SWEET VALLEY HIGH FLAIR COLLECTION
A BANTAM BOOK : 0 553 81281 5

Individual titles originally published in USA by Bantam Books
First published in Great Britain as individual titles in 1997
Collection first published in Great Britain

PRINTING HISTORY
Bantam Collection published 1999

Conceived by Francine Pascal

Produced by Daniel Weiss Associates, Inc,
33 West 17th Street, New York, NY 10011

Bantam Books are published by Transworld Publishers Ltd,
61–63 Uxbridge Road, Ealing, London W5 5SA,
in Australia by Transworld Publishers,
c/o Random House Australia Pty Ltd,
20 Alfred Street, Milsons Point, NSW 2061, Australia,
and in New Zealand by Transworld Publishers,
c/o Random House New Zealand,
18 Poland Road, Glenfield, Auckland, New Zealand.

Made and printed in Great Britain by
Cox & Wyman Ltd, Reading, Berkshire.

FLAIR
Collection

COVER
GIRLS

Written by
Kate William

Created by
FRANCINE PASCAL

BANTAM BOOKS
NEW YORK·TORONTO·LONDON·SYDNEY·AUCKLAND

To James Ryan

Chapter 1

Elizabeth Wakefield pushed a strand of her long blond hair behind her ear as she scanned the bookshelves. "Here's the book about women in Victorian England," she said. She selected a paperback and handed it to Enid Rollins. "That's on your list, isn't it?"

Enid's green eyes sparkled. "Yes, this is one of the Morgan Agency's books," she said, thumbing through it. "And look: The author thanks one of my new bosses in the acknowledgments!"

Maria Slater grabbed the book from her and looked down at her friends with a fake haughty expression. "Special thanks to my agent, Roberta Morgan, for her expert advice and invaluable assistance," she read aloud in a pretentious English accent that made Elizabeth and Enid giggle. Maria grinned and switched back to her normal voice.

1

"By the time your internship at the literary agency is over," she told Enid, "authors across the country will be writing notes like this about you!"

The three Sweet Valley High juniors were standing in the women's studies section of The Book Case, a store in the mall. It was Sunday afternoon, and their school's miniterm internships were starting the next morning.

Enid laughed at Maria's confidence. "I don't think so," she said. "I doubt I'll offer much 'expert advice and invaluable assistance' in a high-school internship that lasts only two weeks!" She shook her head. Her coppery brown hair, which had only recently fully grown out after she had dyed it black some time ago, swung against her neck. "But with an accent like that, Maria, you're a shoo-in for the role of Queen Victoria!"

"I don't think the Bridgewater Theatre Group will need someone to play Queen Victoria in the next two weeks," Maria pointed out, "even if they decided to be experimental enough to cast an African American in the role."

"With your experience?" Enid argued. "They'd cast you in a minute—in any role."

"Whatever," Maria said, rolling her dark brown eyes. "Anyhow, it takes a lot longer than two weeks to put together a production. And I'm just a little ol' student intern, not a leading lady. I'll probably be painting scenery and helping the real actors get into their costumes."

"Maybe," Elizabeth said. "But how often does a community theater get an intern with real Hollywood experience? You were the hottest child star in the country."

"I bet the actors will be asking for your autograph," Enid said confidently.

Maria frowned. "Stop! That was a long time ago," she reminded them. "And *hello!* I was the Softees toilet paper girl—I wasn't exactly performing in a play by Ibsen."

"You did movies and television too!" Elizabeth reminded her friend.

"Get over it!" Maria pleaded. "This is totally embarrassing. Besides, it's Liz's turn now! What do you think, Enid? Should we check out Elizabeth's magazine?"

"My magazine?" Elizabeth exclaimed as they walked toward the periodicals section. "It's a nice thought. But remember, I'll be a lowly editorial assistant at *Flair,* not the editor in chief!"

"Ha!" Enid said. "You're the most talented student writer in southern California. By the end of two weeks you'll be running the place!"

"That would send Todd screaming into the night," Elizabeth replied ruefully, thinking of her longtime boyfriend, Todd Wilkins. "He's already stressing about how this internship will take too much time away from him."

"He'll survive," Enid assured her.

"Todd has no right to give you attitude, Liz!"

3

Maria said. "He should be proud of you for hitting the big time. *Flair* is the hottest new magazine in the fashion world. It's been around less than two years. But even in New York City everyone's reading it." Maria had recently moved back to Sweet Valley after relocating with her family to New York for a few years. She and Elizabeth had been close in junior high. Now that she was back in town, she had renewed her friendship with Elizabeth. And Maria and Enid were quickly becoming friends too, although there had been some conflict between them at first.

"A magazine that popular wouldn't accept just anybody as an intern," Enid said.

Maria laughed. "They accepted Jessica, didn't they?"

"She probably impersonated Elizabeth in the interview," Enid suggested dryly. Elizabeth's identical twin sister, Jessica, had been known to borrow her sister's identity when it suited her goals.

"Jessica is such a trip," Elizabeth said, an amused grin highlighting a dimple in her left cheek. "Her internship position is photographer's assistant, but she plans to convince the photographer to make her a model and put her on the cover of the magazine. You know how much Jess loves being in the limelight."

"It's not all it's cracked up to be," Maria said seriously.

4

"Speaking of Liz's evil twin, *look*," Enid whispered urgently.

All three girls turned to see Jessica Wakefield entering the store, accompanied by her best friend, Lila Fowler.

"If it isn't Tweedledum and Tweedledummer!" Maria teased. "I never expected to see them putting in a cameo here. I'd have thought those two were allergic to bookstores."

"No, no—Jessica can do bookstores all right," Elizabeth joked, "as long as she stays in the magazine section. History gives her hives, and reference books make her sneeze."

To most customers in the store the sixteen-year-old Wakefield twins would have looked absolutely identical at first glance. Both had California tans, sun-streaked hair, and eyes the color of the Pacific Ocean. Both were five-foot six and had trim, athletic figures.

But Elizabeth, always the practical twin, had pulled her hair back in barrettes. For her trip to the mall she'd worn a denim skirt with a hemline just above her knees, a white T-shirt, and no makeup except a touch of lip gloss.

Jessica's hair was loose and as meticulously tousled as a movie star's. Her makeup was carefully applied, including a hint of violet eye shadow that was her latest cosmetic experiment. Her floral minidress left her shoulders bare, and her high-heeled sandals were the same shade as her eye shadow.

5

Even if they'd been dressed identically, the twins' classmates could have told them apart the instant either twin opened her mouth. Both were articulate. But Jessica's favorite topics of conversation included boys, clothes, parties, and cheerleading. Elizabeth was more likely to be heard advising a friend on a personal problem, conducting an interview for an article in the school newspaper, discussing a book with a classmate, or raising money for charity.

Despite their differences, each twin knew she could count on her sister when she was in trouble. But it was usually Jessica, the younger sister by four minutes, who got herself into ridiculous situations and needed her more sensible sister to bail her out. Elizabeth sighed as she continued walking toward the magazine racks. Sure enough, Jessica and Lila were standing in front of a brilliantly colored display of fashion and beauty magazines. Elizabeth hoped her twin wouldn't find a way to turn the internship into another one of her disasters.

"Yo, Lizzie!" Jessica called, holding up a magazine. Elizabeth winced at the hated nickname but let it slide. "Did you see the new issue of *Flair*?" Jessica asked.

"That's Simone on the cover," Maria said, sticking her nose up in the air as she emphasized the model's name. "I read that she moved to Los Angeles recently—just after Mode, the company

6

that publishes *Flair,* moved its headquarters here. Simone was totally big in New York last year."

Enid laughed as she took the magazine from Jessica. "Big? She looks like she wears about a size one! I've never seen anyone so emaciated in my life."

"You can never be too thin or too rich," Lila reminded them haughtily. "But especially rich."

"Please!" Jessica complained, grabbing the magazine back from Enid. "We can't all have multimillionaire parents like you, Lila." She stared thoughtfully at the sophisticated, black-haired model on the cover. "But maybe you *can* be too thin. Guys can't possibly think women like Simone are sexy. Can they?" Her voice sounded worried.

"A lot of them do," said Maria. She grinned evilly. "Especially after her plastic surgery."

"What plastic surgery?" Jessica demanded. "Tell me!"

"I don't know, really," Maria said. "But there have been rumors."

"Well, I can't believe a guy would find her sexier than someone like me," Jessica insisted. "I mean, she's attractive, I guess. But she looks more like a department store mannequin than a real person!"

Elizabeth shrugged. "Don't worry about it, Jess. The boys who really count—nice boys like Todd—care more about who you are than what you look like."

"*Nice* isn't at the top of my wish list for a guy, Lizzie," Jessica reminded her.

"You are so *naive*, Elizabeth," Lila told her, holding out her hand wordlessly until Jessica passed her the issue of *Flair*. "Guys are letches. The point is to get what you can out of them." She gestured with the magazine. "Obviously Simone has found the look that works for her. You'd be surprised at how many men would fall all over themselves trying to get close to somebody famous and glamorous. Not my darling Bo, of course," Lila amended, speaking of her boyfriend in Washington, D.C., Beauregard Creighton the Third. "He's hopelessly devoted to me. But most guys would."

"But Liz is totally right about wimpy old Todd," Jessica said with a sigh, shaking her head at the thought of her sister's long-term relationship. "I've told you over and over again, Liz. Todd may be a hunk. But you're too young to be tied down to somebody so boring!" She turned to Lila. "Todd Wilkins doesn't have the imagination to drool over supermodels like Simone."

"*Imagination?*" Maria asked with a hoot, swiping the magazine from Lila. "This bikini Simone is wearing doesn't leave much to a guy's imagination. But Todd doesn't need to drool over supermodels. He's in love with Elizabeth—" She smiled loyally at her friend. "And Liz is as gorgeous as any supermodel."

"I really may vomit—," Lila began.

"I guess I'm not up on my supermodels," Enid interrupted. "I know I've seen this girl's face—or should I say her *pout?* But exactly who is she? Simone who?"

"She's just *Simone*," Lila said, as if Enid should have known. "When you're that famous, who needs a last name?"

"This will be me someday," Jessica bragged. She took the magazine from Maria and stared at it as if trying to imagine her own face on the cover. "All over the world my adoring fans will know me only as *Jessica*. Or should I use *Jesse?* Does that sound more sophisticated?"

Lila shook her head. "Jessica Wakefield, you are the most conceited person I've ever met."

"And you are the expert," Jessica interjected.

Lila stared at Jessica coldly for a moment before turning to Elizabeth, Enid, and Maria. "You should have seen Jessica this afternoon, making a photo album of herself! Have you ever heard of anything so vain?"

"You can call it vain," Jessica said. "I call it enterprising. I need a proper portfolio ready when Quentin Berg discovers me."

Enid sighed. "Again I'm clueless. What's a *Quentin Berg?*"

Jessica's mouth dropped open in shock. "Quentin Berg is only the coolest photographer in the fashion business," she told Enid. "And he's under contract to *Flair* magazine."

"Jessica's about to become his assistant," Elizabeth explained, taking the magazine from her. "I feel sorry for the poor man."

"Ha, ha," Jessica said flatly. "You won't be making fun of me when he promotes me from camera carrier to cover girl."

Elizabeth tuned out her sister's prattling and thumbed through the cosmetics advertisements in the front of the magazine until she came to the staff listing. "This is it!" she cried excitedly. "This is the first issue of *Flair* with the new managing editor listed. Her name is Leona Peirson. All I know about her is that she's young to be in such a high-powered position and that everyone says she's got a brilliant career in publishing ahead of her."

"Is she your new boss?" Maria asked.

Elizabeth nodded. "I can't wait to meet her. This internship is what I've been dreaming of my entire life!"

A few hours later Todd sat with Elizabeth in the front seat of his BMW, gazing over the lights of Sweet Valley. They were parked at their favorite spot on Miller's Point, and Todd was kissing her passionately, but Elizabeth seemed preoccupied. Finally she pushed him away.

"What's the matter?" Todd asked, annoyed and mystified. "Did I do something wrong? Is it my breath?"

Elizabeth smiled. "No, you're still the world's

number-one kisser. I'm just distracted tonight."

"Let me guess," Todd said with a groan as his good mood evaporated. "You're thinking about that magazine."

"Sorry," she replied, smiling wanly at him. "I've been looking forward to the miniterm for so long that I can hardly believe it starts tomorrow. Todd, I'm going to be working on a national magazine! Do you know what that means?"

Todd slouched in his seat with his arms crossed in front of him. "It means we'll have to go for two whole weeks without being able to see each other at school," he said. "What's so awesome about that?"

"Think about what a great opportunity this is!" Elizabeth urged. "For both of us," she added quickly, running her fingers playfully through his wavy brown hair.

"Right," Todd replied grumpily. "I'll be an intern at my dad's company—big deal. I already know everyone at Varitronics. And I've spent the last few months listening to my father talk about everything that goes on there. This internship will be the thrill of my life."

"You could have applied for a position somewhere more interesting," Elizabeth reminded him.

Todd rolled his eyes. "You don't seem to realize that most of the kids in our class think this miniterm thing is a joke! So does the rest of the world, for that matter."

"That's not true!" Elizabeth protested.

"Why do you suppose so many of us are working for our parents' firms?" he asked. "Even Lila Fowler is working at Fowler Enterprises. I'll bet Jessica isn't letting her forget that!"

Elizabeth laughed. "My sister never passes up an opportunity to gloat—especially over Lila."

"When it comes to exciting internships, you and Jess are the exceptions," Todd said. He sighed miserably, but deep down he knew that his boring internship was his own fault. He'd been too busy with basketball finals to think about applying anywhere until it was much too late. Still, it hurt to admit that he'd screwed up. And plenty of kids had applied early and still ended up with boring prospects. "How many adults with really neat careers are willing to baby-sit high-school students for two weeks?" he asked.

Elizabeth's blue-green eyes were beginning to show annoyance. "It's not baby-sitting!" she insisted. "And it's not just me and Jess who are working at something we're interested in. Aaron Dallas managed to find a great internship!"

"Don't remind me," Todd said, hating himself for being so jealous of his friend Aaron. "While I'm photocopying invoices for my father, Aaron will be working for the L.A. Lakers! And you'll be throwing yourself into that magazine the same way you always do with new activities. Plus you'll be commuting all the way to Los Angeles. I'll be lucky if you have time to see a movie with me over the weekend."

Todd knew it wasn't like him to be so negative, but he couldn't help it. He felt like an idiot for the way he'd neglected to plan ahead for the miniterm. And the thought of not seeing Elizabeth every day for the next two weeks made every muscle in his body tense up. "Life isn't fair," he concluded.

"You aren't being fair either," Elizabeth said. "Todd, I'm *excited* about this internship! Can't you please be happy for me?"

He smiled weakly. "I guess I am," he admitted. "But you may be getting your hopes up for nothing. What if you spend the whole two weeks answering the phone? It's not like anyone's going to let a sixteen-year-old make real decisions."

Elizabeth bit her lip, and Todd knew he'd struck a nerve. But she recovered quickly. "Even if I'm only answering the phone, I'll be watching and learning from real professionals," she said philosophically.

"It's not like you've never worked on a professional publication before," Todd pointed out. "You've written articles for the *Sweet Valley News* and even the *Los Angeles Times*. And you and Jessica had internships at that newspaper in London last summer. Look what happened there—you forgot all about me, you started dating some wacky poet, and you nearly got yourself killed!"

Elizabeth winced. "Well, the newspaper part was good experience anyway. And I promise the other part will not happen this time!"

"How can you be so sure?" Todd demanded.

"I learned my lesson about dating guys at the office," Elizabeth assured him with a peck on the cheek. "I'm not interested in anyone but you. And *Flair* magazine doesn't even cover serial murders! The biggest danger on this internship is the risk of having my face break out from reviewing too many makeup samples."

"But will I see you at all in the next two weeks?"

"Absolutely," Elizabeth promised. "No matter how exciting life is in the world of high fashion, I'll always have time for you."

"I certainly hope so," Todd said, grudgingly accepting another kiss.

Chapter 2

Jessica felt her sister's tug on her backpack. It was Monday morning, and the twins were walking along a sidewalk in downtown Los Angeles. Just ahead was the front entrance of the high-rise that housed *Flair* and Mode's other publications.

"For someone wearing four-inch heels, you're moving as fast as an Olympic track star," Elizabeth complained. "Wait up!"

Jessica smiled and shrugged, but she forced her feet to match Elizabeth's slower pace. "I can't help it!" she said, admiring her new Italian platform shoes. She couldn't afford them, of course. But it would be weeks before her mother received the credit card bill. By then, Jessica was sure she'd be on her way to a lucrative career as a supermodel.

"I'm anxious to get there too," Elizabeth said, her voice quavering slightly. Jessica felt some

15

nervous energy about their first day on the job, but Elizabeth, she realized, was downright tense.

"I am so excited about *Flair* magazine, Liz. This is the most awesome job we've ever had!" Jessica exclaimed. "Anyhow, you're just jealous of my shoes. I mean, well . . ." Her mouth twisted with distaste as she pointed to Elizabeth's simple, low-heeled navy pumps.

"What's wrong with my shoes?" Elizabeth asked, her voice several tones higher than usual.

"Well, nothing's *wrong* with them, exactly," Jessica said, trying to be reassuring. "But they're so . . . middle management."

"What's that supposed to mean?" Elizabeth asked, mystified. "They're practical, and they're a classic design. Two years from now I'll still be wearing these shoes. In six months those stacked heels of yours will be out of style."

"So what's your point?" Jessica asked. "When platform shoes are out of style, I'll just buy something different. That's how fashion works!"

"Never mind," Elizabeth said miserably, gesturing for Jessica to precede her through the revolving door.

Jessica nudged Elizabeth as they stepped onto the shiny marble floor inside. "Look at the way they're all dressed!" she whispered, nodding across the huge lobby toward a group of sleek, well-groomed women waiting for the elevator, as well as a few men. Almost all the women wore long, body-hugging jackets with miniskirts.

"They don't look very businesslike," Elizabeth noted, whispering back to her sister as the twins stopped near the entrance to watch the stylish group. "Those short little skirts are so tight, they could have been painted on! How do they sit down? And why are they all wearing purple lipstick?"

"You are so *last season*, Liz," Jessica remarked. "That's not purple. Nobody wears purple lipstick anymore. That's *plum!* It's all the rage. And look at the metallic gold eye shadow. That is *so cool!*"

"I thought you were wearing nothing but violet eye shadow from now on," Elizabeth reminded her.

Jessica rolled her eyes. *"Please,"* she said, dismissing the fashion trend she'd been raving about for a week. "Honestly, Liz—do you really think I'd wear eye shadow that clashed with the new plum lipstick I'm going to buy?"

"Horrors!" Elizabeth said. "I can't keep up with crazy trends. They change too fast for me. Anyhow, I bet all those women are models. Nobody else could get away with clothes and makeup like that in the office."

"Look at the way most of them are wearing their hair—longer in the front," Jessica observed, pulling wings of hair straight on both sides of her face. "Tomorrow I'm going to find a way to make mine look that way. Maybe if I curl it some in back

17

and use a ton of mousse to get these pieces perfectly straight—"

"You're only working here for two weeks, Jessica," Elizabeth pointed out. "Does it really matter if your hair is just like everyone else's?"

"It won't be just like everyone else's," Jessica said impatiently. "Mine is naturally blond. And it's important to be in style when you're working in the fashion industry. C'mon, Liz. Your skirt is tons longer than those skirts. And do you think I'm OK in a pantsuit instead of a skirt?"

"My navy suit is classic. It should be fine for any office situation," Elizabeth said staunchly. "I wasn't sure about those pants of yours, to tell you the truth. They're awfully tight for the office—or so I thought. But if those women can get away with skirts the size of headbands, nobody can say *you're* inappropriate."

Jessica appraised her own outfit critically. "I'll wear a miniskirt tomorrow instead of pants," she decided. "But my jacket's tailored like their jackets. And my black pants are almost as close-fitting as those black tights those women are all wearing. I think my clothes will do. At least they make a statement."

"And what statement am I making?" Elizabeth asked, glancing down at her conservative suit with a new uncertainty in her blue-green eyes.

Jessica thought her sister's boringly correct suit made only one statement: *I am hopelessly dowdy*.

18

And Elizabeth's hair, pinned up with barrettes, looked high-schoolish. But Jessica smiled reassuringly. "Chill out, Liz," she said. "You're right. Those women probably *are* models. If I want Quentin Berg to make me a cover girl, I have to dress like them. But you're working in an office where a bunch of brainiac writer types will be sitting in front of computers. I doubt they'll be as trendy as those of us in the art department."

The first group had vanished into the sleek, shining elevator. But another group was gathering as Elizabeth and Jessica stepped toward the mirrored doors. Again almost every woman wore a miniskirt and a fitted blazer.

As the girls walked with them into the elevator Jessica noticed one woman gazing coldly at her. She was in her forties and ultraslim, with long tendrils of chestnut hair curled under so that they nearly touched her chin. The woman looked Jessica up and down. "Aggressive choice," she pronounced finally, her voice low and throaty.

Jessica wasn't sure if it was a compliment, but she decided to take it as one. She nodded slightly, allowing the faintest of disdainful smiles to tug at the corners of her mouth. Fashion models didn't grin.

Elizabeth gulped as the women in the elevator gazed coldly from the top of Jessica's tousled blond head to the rounded tips of her black-and-cranberry platform shoes. After a moment they looked away again, as if their curiosity was satisfied. Every set of gold-shadowed eyes pivoted back to the display of numbers above the elevator door. Nobody else said a word. And nobody even glanced at Elizabeth. She wasn't sure if that was a good sign or a bad one. When she'd left the house this morning, she'd felt stylish and professional in her blue suit. Now she felt invisible.

Elizabeth seldom sought out the limelight. But total invisibility was a new sensation, and it made her uneasy. Being an identical twin—and an attractive, blond identical twin—usually caught people's eye. She told herself that it didn't matter. Her writing and proofreading skills would be more important to Leona Peirson than the length of her blazer. But her elation about the internship had abruptly shifted to terror.

Elizabeth envied her sister's composure. Quietly humming to herself, Jessica looked as though she was born to ride in an elevator with these svelte, plum-lipped denizens of the fashion world. Elizabeth shifted her weight from one sensibly clad foot to the other, squeezing the leather handle of her briefcase with both hands as she stared at the greenish numbers above the elevator doors.

The crowded elevator stopped at the ninth floor, where *Flair*'s art department was located. Jessica squeezed her sister's shoulder. "Relax, Liz. You'll do fine," she whispered into

Elizabeth's ear. Then Jessica added in a louder voice, "See you at lunchtime!" as she bounced out of the elevator.

All the men and a few of the women Elizabeth had pegged as models also stepped out. But most of the fashionable women stayed, and Elizabeth had the depressing feeling that they were all headed for the editorial offices, on the eleventh floor. As the doors glided shut, separating her from Jessica's stylish pants and tousled hair, Elizabeth suddenly felt very much alone.

A few minutes later, on the eleventh floor, an administrative assistant pointed out Leona Peirson's office and told Elizabeth to walk right in. A tall woman stood with her back to the door, her dark blond hair slightly longer in the front. She wore a black pinstripe miniskirt with a matching tailored blazer the same length as the skirt.

"I'm Elizabeth Wakefield," Elizabeth said, glad that her voice was steadier than her trembling knees. "I'm the new student intern."

The woman turned around, and Elizabeth was horrified to see that she'd interrupted a phone call. But Leona Peirson smiled broadly, as if genuinely glad to see her new intern. Elizabeth began to back out of the office until the tall woman gestured toward a chair. Elizabeth sat down gratefully. For the first time since she'd entered the lobby of the building, she began to relax.

* * *

Jessica glided into the hallway leading to Quentin Berg's studio. Her backpack dangled from one hand, and she walked with her hips thrust forward like a model on a runway. A photographer had once told her she was too short, at five-foot six, to be a fashion model. But she was sure that a maverick like Quentin Berg could see beyond that tiny little deficiency and appreciate her unique spark. "And if he can't, well, that's what the four-inch heels are for," she whispered under her breath.

The studio was a cavernous room with a jumble of ladders, props, and lights near the far end and a couch in one corner. Open doors showed glimpses of offices, meeting spaces, smaller studios, and storage areas beyond the main room. Jessica could hear people bustling around in those rooms and at the far end of the main studio. But it wouldn't do for her to seek anyone out. Like the elevator women, she would be stylishly aloof.

She sauntered to the center of the room and pivoted there, as if inspecting her surroundings, with a vague look of boredom. Four youngish-looking men were climbing the ladders, assembling the props, and adjusting some bluish lights a few yards away. Jessica was careful not to look directly at them. But she made sure they had a good view of her.

She gave them a moment to admire her body-hugging outfit, her movie-star hair, and her flawless face. Nobody even glanced up. A moment later the four men finished their work and hurried out of the room.

Through several of the open doors Jessica watched the four men and various other people hurrying in and out of adjoining rooms. Most seemed intent on moving props and lights around. Jessica was beginning to get annoyed. Either she was losing her famous Wakefield charisma or these guys were too stupid to realize that admiring a sexy blonde was more interesting than draping muslin over a ladder.

Suddenly Jessica knew how Elizabeth had felt when the women in the elevator had ignored her. Well, nobody ignored Jessica Wakefield for long. *Ever*.

She cleared her throat loudly, and a guy's head popped into the room through one of the open doorways. He was almost young—no more than twenty-five. And he was wearing overalls with a safari-looking vest. His outfit was kind of grunge, Jessica decided. She figured he had to be some sort of assistant photographer. But he was good-looking, in a stylish kind of way, with thick reddish blond hair and nice broad shoulders. So she struck a casual pose and waited breathlessly while his eyes traveled up and down her body.

"Are you the intern?" he asked in a deep voice, standing in the doorway.

Jessica decided aloofness worked only on women. She flashed him her most dazzling smile. "Yes," she said. "I'm Jessica Wake—"

"Get me coffee!" he barked, cutting her off. He spun on the heel of his work boot and disappeared through the door.

Jessica followed him. "Who are you to be giving me orders?" she demanded.

"I'm Quentin Berg, your *boss*," he said. He pointed toward a coffee machine in the corner of the room. *"Now move!"*

Jessica gasped in fury. Then she whirled around and stomped off toward the coffee machine, her platform soles thumping loudly on the wood floor. Her internship wasn't starting off exactly the way she'd imagined.

So far, Todd's internship was even duller than he'd expected. He sat in his windowless cubicle at Varitronics, checking the sales numbers on a draft memo against a sea of tiny figures on a green-and-white-striped spreadsheet printout. In two hours on the job the most exciting task he'd handled was making lunch reservations for his father and one of the vice presidents. And when his father was too busy to assign him tasks, he was at the beck and call of Margaret Meeks, the tyrannical administrative assistant for the executive suite.

It was only ten o'clock on Monday morning.

But it already seemed as if the day had dragged on forever.

Todd rubbed his deep brown eyes. The tiny print was making him see double. He turned to his blank computer screen. THIS JOB REEKS! he typed in capital letters. Certainly it was time for his ten-minute coffee break.

With a guilty glance around him Todd deleted the line from his computer screen. Then he unfolded his cramped legs and rose slowly to his full height of six-foot three. The creaky chair had surely been designed for miniature office workers. Todd would never have guessed that his father could subject him to such torture, on top of the stupid spreadsheets. Bert Wilkins was usually such a kind, reasonable man.

Either Dad secretly morphs into Sadistic Psycho Boss whenever he walks into this building, Todd thought, *or he's gone overboard trying to show his staff that the president's son doesn't get special treatment.* Either way, Todd didn't think he could stand another nine days, five hours, and fifty-six minutes of slaving away at his father's firm.

To make matters worse, the Varitronics dress code required everyone to wear a suit—even the high-school intern. Margaret's hawklike eyes followed Todd as he walked across the room to the coffee counter. He wanted to yell, "What are you looking at? Haven't you ever seen somebody take a coffee break before?"

Instead he tugged impatiently at his too-tight tie, wondering if anyone had ever died from being strangled by paisleys. Thinking of his tie made Todd think of Elizabeth, who'd surprised him with the fashionable instrument of torture for his sixteenth birthday. In all honesty, he reminded himself, he'd always loved the paisley tie. But today nothing felt right. He realized that he missed Elizabeth terribly, even though he'd seen her only twelve hours earlier. He hoped she was having a more exciting morning at *Flair* than he was at Varitronics.

He stood near one of the room's few windows, gulping the bitter black coffee and wishing it were root beer. He felt the administrative assistant's glare on his back, but he decided to ignore it. If Meeks had more work for him to do, she would have to wait until his coffee break was over.

As he turned toward the coffeemaker to contemplate a second cup his eyes fell on the fax machine in the corner of the room. For the first time all morning Todd smiled a genuine smile. The internship meant he couldn't see Elizabeth during the day. And someone might overhear him if he called his girlfriend on the phone during company time. But that didn't mean he couldn't let her know he was thinking about her.

Elizabeth's eyes widened when Leona Peirson hung up the telephone and turned toward her. The managing editor of *Flair* magazine was even younger than Elizabeth had imagined—twenty-nine or thirty, Elizabeth guessed, looking at the woman's slender figure and unlined face.

The editor smiled again and grasped Elizabeth's hand in a firm handshake. "I'm Leona Peirson," she said unnecessarily. "I'm fairly new in this position myself, so don't feel intimidated about dropping by to ask questions. Sometimes we might just have to discover the answers together."

"Ms. Peirson," Elizabeth began. "I want you to know how grateful I am—"

"Please call me Leona," the editor interrupted, her brown eyes warm. "And no thanks are necessary. I consider us a team, Elizabeth. I know from your application that you're here because you truly want the experience of working on a professional magazine. I'll consider my time with you well spent if you work hard and learn a lot in the next few weeks. I expect you might even teach us a thing or two."

"I doubt that," Elizabeth said modestly. "I've never had any experience with magazines, only newspapers. But I promise you that I'll work hard at whatever you ask me to do."

Leona leaned back in her chair and looked thoughtfully at her new intern. "I have every confidence that you will," she said. "I can't promise that all the work will be glamorous. A lot of the tasks that go into putting a magazine together are what we call 'scum' work. You'll spend some of your time opening mail, proofreading articles, and fact checking product information."

"Oh, I don't mind at all," Elizabeth said, mesmerized by the aura of confidence Leona projected. "I want to get experience in all areas of publishing."

"I'm glad to hear that," Leona said. "Because it's the only way to get a realistic picture of what it's like to be a magazine professional. At the same time I think we might find some real writing or substantive editing for you to do now and then as well."

Elizabeth beamed.

"I want your input, Elizabeth," Leona continued, ticking off points on her fingers. "I welcome your ideas, so don't be shy about speaking out. I like to see creativity and hard work rewarded. My other ground rule is to tell me what's really on your mind—no hiding the truth if you have a problem. As long as we're both completely honest with each other we should get along wonderfully. Am I making myself clear?"

"Absolutely," Elizabeth said, feeling as if this internship really could be the start of a lifelong career. The insecurity she'd felt on the elevator was gone, banished by Leona's powerful presence. The editor was obviously an assertive, intelligent woman who knew how to get where she wanted to go. And she seemed truly interested in helping Elizabeth forge a career.

"Your office is just around the corner from mine," Leona said as she walked out from behind her desk and guided Elizabeth toward the door.

"My *office?*" Elizabeth asked, her eyes wide. "I assumed I'd sit in a cubicle somewhere."

Leona smiled. "One of our associate editors is out on family leave for several months, so we've given you his office," she said. "I want you to spend the next hour or two familiarizing yourself with the magazine. A stack of back issues is on the desk for you to look through."

"I'll get right to it," Elizabeth said with a nod.

"Oh, and Elizabeth . . . ," Leona began as Elizabeth left the room. "I don't mean to be critical. But you might want to pay a little more attention to your wardrobe," she suggested. "I'm sure the navy suit would be fine in most workplaces. But this is a *fashion* magazine."

Elizabeth nodded again, blushing. As she hurried out of Leona's office she wished, for once, that she had Jessica's sense of style—though not even Jessica was dressed in as sophisticated a manner as the goddesses of style who roamed the halls of *Flair*. But Elizabeth vowed that she would find a way to impress her new boss. Working for Leona Peirson was a dream come true. Elizabeth would do whatever she could to be worthy of her attention.

Chapter 3

"Hold the elevator!" Jessica called to Shelly Fabian, a makeup artist who prepared many of Quentin Berg's models. Shelly lunged for the keypad, and two long, skinny braids swung around her face with a bright tinkle of glass beads.

Jessica hobbled onto the elevator just as the doors slid shut. "Thanks, Shelly," she said with a groan. She let her backpack slide to the floor. Then she slipped off one Italian platform shoe and massaged her cramped toes, ignoring the cold glare of a sleek, burgundy-haired woman who stood in the corner of the elevator, dressed entirely in black. Jessica couldn't wait to get to the cafeteria and pour out her troubles into Elizabeth's sympathetic ear.

"Already among the walking wounded, Jessica?" Shelly asked, checking her ebony-skinned reflection in the mirrored elevator door. "It's only noon!"

Jessica caught sight of her own straggly hair in the door and quickly turned away. It was better not to think about how messy and sweaty she looked. "After this morning my feet are screaming four-letter words at me!" Jessica replied. "I broke two nails moving a three-ton lighting array back and forth across the room."

"Quentin's not the most decisive person in the world when it comes to where to put his props," Shelly said.

"I could tell him where to put a few," Jessica said mock threateningly. "Is it always so crazy in the art department?"

Shelly laughed knowingly. "It's going to get a lot crazier after lunch, when we actually do the big shoot!" she warned. Her voice dropped to a whisper, and she spoke close to Jessica's ear. "Just wait until the toothpick chicks show up! Get a few of those skinny prima donna models in the studio, and you'll be taking orders from a bevy of spoiled brats as well as Quentin."

"That settles it," Jessica replied. "I've got to find a way to become a leggy supermodel in the next hour. I wasn't cut out for manual labor."

"At least you can say things like that without being laughed at," said Shelly, smoothing her hands ruefully over her own ample hips under her requisite miniskirt. The makeup artist was about thirty-five, and Jessica had to admit that she was overweight, but her legs were as great as any model's. "As for the manual labor," Shelly continued, "all you can do is grin and bear it."

"I tried that once before," Jessica said with a grimace. "For about a week, when I was suffering from temporary insanity, I was a roadie for this totally gross rock band called Spontaneous Combustion. I didn't think life could get any worse than lugging amplifiers around. Today it did. At least I wasn't wearing four-inch heels for Spy and Wheels."

"You worked with people named Spy and Wheels?" Shelly asked. "I hope they were hunks at least."

Jessica shuddered. "I'd rather kiss a cockroach!" she said. "These guys made my skin crawl."

"That's one thing Quentin has over them," Shelly said. "He's definitely a hunk—until he opens his mouth," she added in a whisper.

The elevator stopped at the second floor. "Can you point me toward the company cafeteria?" Jessica asked.

"I can do better than that," Shelly said with a smile. "I can walk you there. I'm meeting a friend for lunch."

"I'm meeting my sister," Jessica said, hoisting her backpack again and wondering if someone had slipped a few bricks into it. As they entered the busy lunchroom she caught sight of a wall clock. "Liz is probably here somewhere, freaking out because I'm ten minutes late," she told Shelly with a sigh. "My sister has a terminal case of punctuality."

Shelly caught sight of her date and waved across the room. "Have a good lunch!" she told Jessica. She wiggled her eyebrows comically. "But whatever you do, don't eat the chicken potpie!"

Jessica collapsed into the nearest chair, surprised to realize that Elizabeth hadn't arrived yet. *When Liz shows up, I'll make her go through the cafeteria line for me,* she decided silently. *I'm too tired to move.*

A moment later Elizabeth rushed into the cafeteria. Jessica brightened up when she saw her sister. A little pampering was exactly what she needed, and Elizabeth was one of the most sensitive, helpful people she knew.

"Sorry I'm late, Jess!" Elizabeth exclaimed, her voice frantic but happy. "I am having the most exciting—"

"Man, am I glad you're here!" Jessica began. "You are so lucky to be sitting at a desk all day. My feet are going to sue me for assault. So while you're getting your own lunch, would you—"

"I can't stay!" Elizabeth said. "I'm going to grab a salad and eat at my desk. I'll talk to you tonight!" She whirled away, blond hair flying, before Jessica could say another word.

Elizabeth waited breathlessly for the letter she'd just drafted to come out of the printer. She skimmed it quickly and raced around the corner to her boss's office. Leona wasn't there, so Elizabeth dropped the letter in the in-box on her desk.

The letter informed a writer that her manuscript was unacceptable, but that Leona would reconsider it if she'd make certain changes. It wasn't a complicated letter, but it was Elizabeth's first tangible product as a member of a professional magazine staff, and she'd worked hard to get the tone just right. Now she just had to wait for Leona's opinion of her work. By her usual standards the letter was a good one. But was it good enough for *Flair*? She had no way of knowing except to wait for Leona's verdict. And that might be hours away. Elizabeth took a deep breath and forced herself to walk slowly back to her own office.

A few minutes later Elizabeth was sitting at her desk. As she finished up the salad she'd bought for lunch, she studied a back issue of *Flair* that she'd draped over the keyboard of her computer. She looked up to see a young Asian woman standing in the doorway.

"Hi! You must be Elizabeth, the new intern," the woman said, a smile lighting her features. She held out something wrapped in a napkin. "I'm Reggie Andrews. Would you like a cookie? They're chocolate chip."

Elizabeth grinned. "I'd love one. They're my favorite."

Reggie was several inches shorter than Elizabeth, with almond-shaped eyes and a flawless complexion. Her straight black hair was a little shorter than Elizabeth's. Like most of the other women at *Flair*, she wore it with long tendrils in the front. Her fine-knit sweater was of fuchsia silk, and her black leather miniskirt wasn't quite as short as most of the other skirts Elizabeth had seen at the office. Elizabeth was sure that a long, fitted blazer was draped over a chair in Reggie's office.

"I'm an assistant fashion editor here," Reggie said. "But I started out last year, after I graduated college, as an editorial assistant. So I have a pretty good idea what you're in for in the next few weeks. If you have any questions . . ."

Elizabeth flashed her another smile. "Thanks!" she said eagerly. "I'm sure I'll have a ton of questions. I feel like a little kid, running to Leona every time I need to know something. I've been trying to ask other people too. But I'm just not comfortable yet with most of the editors."

"Would you like to have lunch together tomorrow?" Reggie asked. "We can go somewhere besides the company cafeteria. I'll fill you in on all those Things the Managers Never Tell You."

"That sounds great," Elizabeth replied. "I'm psyched to get the lowdown on what really goes on in the world of high-fashion publishing."

"It's a date!" Reggie said. "I'll stop by here

about noon, if that's OK." She turned to leave. "What's that taped to the wall over your computer?" she asked suddenly. Reggie leaned over to inspect the fax Elizabeth had received from Todd that morning. It showed a crudely drawn cartoon of a guy and a girl, each in a different workplace setting. Above the boy's head a dialogue bubble read "Your office or mine?"

"The stick person with the bow in her hair is me," Elizabeth explained. "The one with the tie is my boyfriend, Todd." She pointed to a small framed photograph of Todd that she'd placed on the corner of her desk. "Believe me, he's a better boyfriend than he is an artist!"

"Ooh!" Reggie exclaimed. "He's a *major* hunk. Much better looking than the stick-person version."

Elizabeth laughed. "Yes, he is, isn't he?"

Reggie turned back to the fax and read aloud the note he'd scrawled beneath the cartoon: "Elizabeth, I'm sorry I've been a jerk. I guess I can share you with the fashion world for two weeks. You've got too much talent to waste. I hope your internship is everything you want it to be. Love, Todd." Reggie seemed genuinely touched. "Oh, Elizabeth. That's so sweet! That's a pretty special guy you've got. It sounds like you two have a wonderful relationship."

Elizabeth experienced the same warm glow she'd felt when she'd first seen the fax. "He is special," she agreed. "In fact, I'm meeting him for a soda tonight at nine. It's the only time we could work out. We won't see all that much of each other during our two-week internships. But nothing can really come between us."

"It's almost one-fifteen," Shelly said to Jessica that afternoon in the photography studio. For the moment the two women were alone in the main studio. "The models for the big photo shoot will be here in a half hour. If I were you, I'd be sure the set is ready. Quentin will pitch a fit if a single one of those fake rocks is out of place."

Jessica rolled her eyes. "Fake?" she asked, struggling to get her arms around a faux boulder the size of an ottoman. "Believe me, these things are just as heavy as the real thing. *Argh!*" she exclaimed suddenly, her voice rising. She dropped the fake rock.

"Are you all right?" Shelly asked, concerned.

"No!" Jessica wailed. "I broke another nail!"

"You'll break more before the day is through," Shelly predicted as she turned back to the makeup trays she was setting out in one corner of the room for touch-ups on the set.

"Why is Quentin using rocks in a fashion spread?" Jessica asked. "Who's modeling the new fall line? The Flintstones?"

"Close," Shelly replied. "An up-and-coming designer, Lina Lapin, has a whole line of stuff trimmed with leather and faux fur. I guess Quentin thinks the rocks will give it that natural look. He plans to pose Simone and another female model there, surrounded by admiring guys—all of them dressed in Lapin designs with fake leopard and tiger skins."

"It sounds majorly stupid," Jessica said, painfully hoisting the rock back up and eyeing the distance it had to be moved.

Shelly shrugged. "I'd say the same thing except I've seen him pull off weirder ideas than this. Quentin may be an arrogant louse—you didn't hear that from me, by the way—but he does have good instincts for what will look great in a fashion spread. Besides, he didn't design the clothes."

Jessica dropped the fake rock with a thud. She tried to nudge it into place with her foot but only succeeded in bursting one of her new blisters. She stifled a cry and sat down hard on the rock. "I bet he designed these stupid *rocks*—just to test me! I've *got* to find a way to become a model instead of bulldozer. This body was not made for heavy lifting."

Shelly laughed. "Your *shoes* certainly weren't," she said. "Jessica, I hate to disillusion you. But photography assistants don't get promoted to model. That's not the career path. It just doesn't happen."

"Well, I intend to *make* it happen," Jessica

vowed. "Doesn't the photographer get to choose the models? I mean, if he suddenly noticed a girl—"

Shelly shook her head. "It's a lot more complicated than that. The editors and the art director and the photographer all work with an agency to choose the models they want. The fashion designer gets involved too, if they're doing a spread on one designer's work. It's a group decision."

"But Quentin Berg is such hot stuff right now," Jessica said. "If he wanted to use one person in particular, they'd go with his choice, wouldn't they?"

"Well . . . yes," Shelly admitted. "To an extent. I mean, that's why we're using Simone so much these days. You know, she and Quentin have a thing going," she confided, raising her eyebrows suggestively. "Michael says they've been out to all the coolest nightspots in town."

"Michael who?" Jessica asked.

"Michael Rietz, the hair stylist," Shelly said. "I think you met him this morning." Jessica remembered an intense-looking guy with long dark hair who seemed to take his job very seriously. "He does the models' hair for photo shoots," Shelly explained. "Michael said Simone and Quentin were spotted together this weekend at that trendy new club, the Edge. I bet the tabloids this week will be full of pics of the Dastardly Duo, gazing adoringly at each other."

40

Jessica's mouth dropped open. "So *that's* the way to do it," she said, her eyes lighting up. *All I have to do is get Quentin Berg to fall in love with me.* With a top photographer at her side, gazing adoringly at her, she'd be a rich, famous super-model in no time—even at five-foot six. She could put up with dating a jerk if he was as useful—and handsome—as Quentin. "Of course," she mur-mured, half to herself. "It makes perfect sense."

"You said it," Shelly replied, misunderstanding her intent. "It makes sense for both of them. Simone gets the cover spot of *Flair* handed to her on a silver platter. And Quentin gets to be seen in public with the Fashion Witch."

"You don't think much of Simone?" Jessica asked. To carry out the plan that was forming in her mind, she would need to learn everything she could about the skinny, black-haired supermodel. "What's she like?"

Shelly glanced around to make sure they were still alone. "Simone has attitude, *big time*," Shelly said. "She's a total brat to other women, but she acts like she's heaven's gift to men. I don't think I've ever seen her smile. She goes around with this obnoxious scowl, like she's been sucking on a lime all day."

"Sounds charming," Jessica said sarcastically.

"I don't know if it's true, but I've heard she had silicone injections to make her lips fuller," Shelly whispered. "And maybe a nose job too."

"Yuck!" Jessica exclaimed. "That lip thing hurts even just to think about. What does Quentin see in this . . . goddess?"

"A ticket to the ritziest parties in L.A.," Shelly said. "And a way to show the paparazzi types that he's made it as a photographer. I doubt he even likes her that much. She's just convenient. Anyhow, he's obnoxious too. Quentin and Simone deserve each other."

"I don't know about that—," Jessica began.

"Shhh!" hissed Shelly. "Simone's here."

A girl of about nineteen sauntered into the studio, hips first. Jessica immediately recognized her signature pout and asymmetrical haircut from the magazine covers. Simone looked even skinnier in person than she did in her photographs.

"She's got to be six feet tall," Jessica whispered, rising to her aching feet. "I've never seen a toothpick with legs before."

Simone had skin so pale that Jessica doubted it had ever seen the sun. Her lips did seem impossibly full, and they were drawn into a sensuous pout. Her sleek, unevenly cut hair was unnaturally black. She gazed at Jessica with pale blue eyes that were cold and strangely blank. Jessica loathed her at first sight.

"You," Simone said, pointing as if Jessica were a piece of furniture. "You're the intern, right?" She went on without waiting for a reply. "Go downstairs and find me some mineral water. *Now*."

"If I were you, I'd demand a refund from that charm school," Jessica suggested under her breath. Shelly turned her face away from Simone, a hand clapped over her mouth to hide her laughter. But Jessica couldn't afford to make an enemy of Simone so soon.

"What did you say?" Simone asked, raising her skinny, highly arched eyebrows even higher. Apparently she was accustomed to having her orders carried out with no discussion.

Jessica's voice flowed like honey through her clenched jaw. "Would you prefer the mineral water that's bottled in the Rocky Mountains or the Swiss Alps?" she asked.

Simone sighed loudly. "France, of course," she announced in a pained voice. "Is there anywhere else?"

"Of course," Jessica said. *"Pardonnez-moi."* She bent again to give the fake rock one last shove into place.

"I said *now,*" Simone repeated. *"Run."*

Jessica took a deep breath, and her face froze into a smile that was as genuine as the color of Simone's hair. "Yes, of course," she replied stonily.

As she stalked down the hall toward the elevator Jessica slammed her right fist into her left palm. *Stealing Quentin away from Simone will be a good start,* she decided. *But that's not enough. Somehow or other I'll bring Simone down.* Hard.

A few hours later Elizabeth hesitated in the doorway of Leona's office. "You wanted to see me?" she asked.

Leona smiled. "Come on in, Elizabeth. Please, take a seat. I wanted to talk to you about that letter you drafted for me."

"I'd be happy to make whatever changes you suggest—," Elizabeth began.

"It's excellent exactly the way it is," Leona said. "You clearly conveyed to the author my suggestions for rewriting her manuscript. And you did it tactfully and succinctly. Besides that, your spelling and grammar were flawless. You'd be surprised at how many people we get in here—even professional editors—who are careless when it comes to routine correspondence."

"Thank you," Elizabeth said, thoroughly relieved. "I always proofread everything four times."

"As a matter of fact, I'm pleased with every aspect of your first day on the job," Leona told her. "I know I've been tied up in meetings for much of the day, but you've worked well on your own, without a lot of hand-holding. You did an excellent job of proofreading the fashion-show calendar. And the other editors tell me you've taken the initiative and asked intelligent, insightful questions about what you've seen in back issues of *Flair*. I'm very impressed."

Elizabeth beamed. "I'm relieved to hear you say that," she admitted. "I was afraid I might be bothering people."

"Not at all," Leona assured her. "A successful woman isn't afraid to go out and get the information she needs to do her job and get ahead." Leona paused, staring thoughtfully at Elizabeth.

"What is it?" Elizabeth asked.

"Speaking of getting ahead," Leona began, "I just wanted to let you know that if you keep up the good work, there is a strong possibility that this magazine could offer you a real summer job when school lets out in a few months."

Elizabeth almost gasped. She had never even allowed herself to dream of a real, paid job with *Flair*. She imagined how impressive such a credential would look on a college application and what a head start it might give her after college. "Do you really think so?" she asked.

"The potential is definitely there," Leona said. "Of course, such an opportunity would require a one hundred percent commitment from you in the next two weeks. That might mean a lot of extra hours."

"Oh, I'll give you and *Flair* one hundred fifty percent!" Elizabeth assured her. "I promise you'll see just how dedicated I can be to something I care about. I'll sacrifice everything else."

As Elizabeth walked back into her own office a minute later her eyes caught sight of Todd's fax hanging over her desk. Todd's note said he was willing to share her with the magazine for two weeks. But he'd been assuming she would be free at night and on the weekend. How understanding would he be about her one hundred fifty percent commitment?

"I'll sacrifice everything else," she had promised Leona. She stared at her framed photograph of Todd and wondered exactly what that sacrifice might include.

Jessica trudged toward the mail room behind the first-floor lobby of the Mode building. The day was drawing to a close, and she'd become so used to the pain in her feet that she barely noticed it anymore. *Or maybe,* she speculated, *the pain in the rest of my body has gotten so bad that it's drowning out the screams from my new blisters.* She vowed that she would never wear the four-inch heels again.

Back in Five Minutes, read a sign on the mail-room door. Jessica pushed open the door and stared around her in surprise. Unlike the building's snazzy, sumptuous lobby and the modern, efficient art department, the mail area was a cluttered warren of storage nooks, sorting rooms, and loading docks. The place was kind of grungy, and the furnishings were decidedly run-down. But when she saw a shabby, soft-looking couch sitting empty, Jessica felt as if she'd come home. She fell onto the couch, kicked the expensive Italian torture chambers off her feet, and lay across the cushions to wait for the mail-room staff to return so she could pick up the package of prints Quentin had asked her to retrieve.

After an afternoon of running errands for both Quentin and Simone, lugging around camera equipment and fake boulders, and watching Simone preen for the lens, Jessica wished she'd never heard of *Flair* magazine. For the moment the tattered sofa felt as comfortable as her own bed—no, as comfortable as Lila's bed, with its satin sheets and mountains of pillows. *I'll just rest my eyes for a minute while I wait,* she decided, allowing her eyelids to gently fall shut.

Suddenly something brushed against her lips. Startled, Jessica popped open her eyes, and she realized she'd been asleep. A very cute guy was standing in front of her, grinning. He was tall and well built, with curly brown hair and big brown eyes that crinkled at the corners when he smiled. She guessed he was about twenty years old.

But he just kissed *me!* she thought as her brain came fully awake. Jessica sat up straight. She gulped, not sure whether to feel flattered or horrified.

"Sorry," he said with a sheepish grin. "I couldn't help it. You looked just like Sleeping Beauty, lying there with your golden hair spread out across the cushions. . . ."

"Well, I feel more like Cinderella," Jessica replied truthfully. "*Before* the fairy godmother."

He laughed. "Speaking of fairy-tale heroines,

what did Snow White say when the mail-room guy announced that her photographs hadn't arrived yet?"

Jessica raised her eyebrows. "I don't know. What?"

The guy sang in a warbling voice, "Someday my prints will come!"

"I get it." Jessica groaned. "*P-r-i-n-t-s* instead of *p-r-i-n-c-e!* That's bad. I mean, that's *really* bad!" But she couldn't help laughing.

"Good, I'm glad to see you can laugh," the guy said. "Now tell me what's wrong. What's got you feeling like you need a fairy godmother?"

"Quentin Berg," she answered testily. "Or Simone I'm-Too-Important-to-Need-a-Last-Name, queen of La-La Land. Take your pick."

"No, thank you," he said. "I don't pick either one of them. What have they done now?"

"I'm Quentin's new intern—that translates as *slave*, by the way," Jessica added. "I've always thought of myself as a slave to fashion, but this isn't what I had in mind."

"So Quentin's got you doing his heavy work?" the guy asked.

"I thought it was bad enough when it was just him ordering me around. Then Simone showed up and started playing control freak—as if I had nothing better to do than to fetch and carry for that stuck-up witch! Nobody told me that being a photography assistant included waiting on spoiled-brat models."

"If you ask me, you're worth ten of Simone," he said, leafing through a stack of bulging overnight envelopes. "She ought to be waiting on you—not the other way around."

Jessica gave the cute guy one of her most brilliant smiles. "You're obviously an extremely good judge of character," she told him.

He pulled an envelope from the stack and handed it to her. Jessica looked down in surprise. It was an overnight package addressed to Quentin. It was from the lab, and it was marked Photographs. "How did you know that this is what I came down here for?" she asked. "Are you a mind reader?"

"Absolutely," he said. "But it was Quentin's mind I read. It was very easy to do. Especially after he called down here a few minutes ago to find out—and I quote—'where in blazes that ditzy intern ran off to.' You've got to admit: The man has a way with words."

"He's channeling William Shakespeare," Jessica agreed.

"Well, he did sound a trifle vexed," the mailroom guy said in a bad British accent. "So if I were you, I'd get back up there lickety-split. Quentin can be a bear when he's irritated."

"I haven't seen him yet when he's *not* irritated!" Jessica complained. She tucked the envelope under her arm. "But you want to know the most irritating thing of all?" she called back to him as she hobbled toward the door as fast as her platform shoes allowed.

"What's that?" he asked, his voice amused.

"The prints in this envelope are all of *Simone!*" Jessica said, wrinkling her nose. "This innocent-looking envelope contains dozens of copies of that smug, pouting, surgery-enhanced face!"

"Don't look at those photographs," he warned. "You'll turn to stone!"

Jessica was laughing as she waited for the elevator. It was the first time in hours that she'd felt good about something. Talking with the cute guy in the mail room had given her the energy to survive the last half hour of the day. It was only as she stepped onto the elevator that she realized she didn't even know his name.

Chapter 4

Maria looked at her watch again. "It's nearly seven o'clock," she said to Enid, who sat across from her in a booth at the Dairi Burger Monday night. "It's not like Liz to be so late."

Enid shrugged. "She had to battle rush-hour traffic out of Los Angeles," she pointed out. "I'm sure she'll be here any minute, as soon as she drops off Jessica."

"I hope Liz doesn't mind that we ordered without her," Maria said as a waiter slid plates full of burgers and fries onto the table.

"Tell me more about the set you're designing for *Evita*," Enid urged.

"I'm not really designing it," Maria said. "Remember, I'm only the student intern. I'm just helping the real set designer. Tell me more about your literary agency."

"My day was fantastic!" Enid replied. "But you tell me about your day first. Doesn't the set for *Evita* call for high-tech stuff like audiovisual screens?"

Maria nodded and sipped her milk shake. "It's going to be so cool—"

Suddenly Enid stood up and waved toward the door. "Elizabeth, over here!" she called. "Maria was just about to tell me about the set she's helping to design for a musical," she continued as Elizabeth approached the booth. Unlike Maria and Enid, Elizabeth was still wearing her work clothes. She slid onto the bench beside Maria.

"Are you ready to order?" the waiter asked. Maria saw Elizabeth glance at the cheeseburgers in front of her friends.

"The chef's salad," Elizabeth decided. "And a diet soda."

Enid raised her eyebrows. "That's not your usual order," she pointed out.

"I know," Elizabeth replied. "But I've been working all day around women who look like they live on celery and rice cakes. I have to watch my calories if I'm going to make it in the fashion industry."

Maria laughed. "Girl, get *over* it! It's only a two-week internship."

"Maybe not," Elizabeth said. "My new boss says I could wrangle a summer job out of this—if I play my cards right."

"That's wonderful, Liz!" Enid said. "You'll have to tell us all about it. But first I want to hear about *Evita*. Go on with what you were saying, Maria."

"For the palace scenes we'll have the palace—the Casa Rosada—on stage left, with the balcony where the actors will stand," Maria explained. "I'll be painting the wall of the building to look like pink marble. Then there will be a huge movie screen . . ." Maria's voice trailed off. "Elizabeth?" she asked. Her friend was staring at a spot on the wall over Enid's shoulder. "Are you OK?"

Elizabeth seemed surprised, as if she'd just been awakened. "Sure, I'm fine," she said, blinking. "Do you think this navy suit is too old-fashioned?"

"Of course not," Enid said. "You only bought it last season." She winked at Maria. "I know—now that you're in the fashion industry, you can't be seen in public wearing last year's suit! Gee, Maria. After one day she's turned into Lila Fowler."

"A fate worse than death!" Maria intoned dramatically.

Elizabeth smiled weakly. "I'm not worried that the suit's from last season. It's the style. I feel frumpy."

"You're not frumpy," Enid assured her. "You're professional-looking."

"You could borrow Jessica's leopard-print bikini

to wear to work tomorrow," Maria suggested. "Nobody would call you frumpy then."

"You two are no help," Elizabeth said with a distracted laugh.

"Go on, Maria!" Enid urged. "Tell us more about *Evita*. Speaking of fashion, what are the costumes like?"

"The Rainbow Tour sequence has the most fabulous gowns!" Maria said. "There's this scarlet one with a tight bodice and a full skirt that is totally to die for. Listen to this, Liz. . . . Liz? Oh, *E-liz-a-beth!*" Elizabeth's eyes again were fixed, unblinking, on a spot on the wall. Maria waved her hand in front of her friend's face until Elizabeth emerged from her reverie and shook her head. "What planet are you visiting this evening?" Maria asked, beginning to get annoyed.

"Are you sure there's nothing wrong?" Enid asked, her eyes showing concern.

"I need an emergency shopping trip!" Elizabeth announced, rising to her feet.

"I was right!" Enid said. "She's been Lila-fied!"

"Bummer," replied Maria. "Do you think it's contagious?"

"I'm not kidding, you two!" Elizabeth argued. "My clothes were all wrong today. You should have seen all those women at *Flair*. They looked so stylish and sophisticated. And I looked like a nineteen fifties schoolgirl."

"That's so untrue, Liz," Maria said. "Nobody at

Flair expects you to run out and buy a whole new wardrobe for a two-week internship."

"Besides, what would you buy it *with?*" Enid asked. "You may be developing a Lila attitude, but I doubt her credit cards come with it."

"I'll use some of my savings," Elizabeth replied.

"That," Maria objected, "is the lamest idea you've ever had. I thought you were saving for a new computer."

"I was," Elizabeth said with a shrug. "But I've got this terrific opportunity to jump-start my future career. I can't let a dowdy wardrobe stand in my way."

"Maybe you should give this some more thought," Enid suggested evenly.

"There's no time for that!" Elizabeth protested. "And there's no time for hanging around here arguing about it. I only have two weeks to make a good impression. I can't blow it. I'm going to the mall tonight. *Now!*"

"I thought you were meeting Todd after we finish dinner," Maria reminded her.

"Not until later," Elizabeth said. "I've got time for a shopping spree first if I hurry." She stopped and looked at both her friends. "You two can sit here getting fat—or you can come with me to Valley Mall."

Maria, perplexed, looked at Enid, who shrugged. They threw some money on the table to pay for their meals, and they followed Elizabeth out of the Dairi Burger.

* * *

Elizabeth sat at Cheveux, a hair salon at Valley Mall, scrutinizing her reflection in the mirror as she described what she wanted to Fifi, the styling specialist.

"*Oui*," Fifi replied. "You want the style *du jour*."

"The style of the day?" Elizabeth asked.

"Every couple of months the beautiful people in L.A. discover a new one," Fifi explained with a shrug. "Right now it's cut long in the front. Next month it might be layered, or snipped short all around, or swept off the face, or teased on top."

In the mirror Elizabeth noticed Enid and Maria exchanging glances. They were sitting in the waiting area, a few steps away, with shopping bags full of Elizabeth's new outfits clustered around them. Obviously her friends thought she was out of her mind to pay a small fortune for a trendy haircut and clothes. But if she needed to revamp her appearance in order to impress Leona Peirson—and get a summer job at *Flair*—then that's exactly what she would do.

She watched in the mirror as Fifi began snipping away at her hair. As the blond tresses fell to the linoleum around her Elizabeth's eyes widened. A new, more sophisticated version of herself was gradually appearing in the mirror.

Fifi pulled out a blow dryer and a bottle of spritzer and began shaping Elizabeth's new style. And the sophisticated Elizabeth in the mirror replaced the old Elizabeth completely.

"That's perfect!" Elizabeth whispered, hardly recognizing herself. "You didn't cut that much off, but what a difference!" With her new hairstyle and her new clothes, she'd be as sophisticated as any of the sleek women who'd ignored her in the elevator that morning. She imagined herself walking into a high-level editorial meeting at *Flair*, as sure of herself as Leona was. Suddenly it wasn't that hard to picture. She turned to her friends. "What do you guys think?"

"Très chic!" Maria said with a whistle.

"You look great, Liz—very stylish," Enid said. She bit her lip. "But have you seen the time? You were supposed to meet Todd fifteen minutes ago."

"Oops," Elizabeth said with a shrug. "I guess he's just going to have to wait."

At ten-thirty that night Jessica sat on a stool in the bathroom that separated her room from Elizabeth's. Her hair was wrapped in a towel, and her blistered feet were submerged in a pan of steamy water. She leaned forward, her face almost against the mirror, to examine her left eyebrow once more. In her hand a pair of tweezers gleamed.

"I'm getting close, Prince Albert!" she announced to the family's golden retriever. Prince Albert lay with his face on his front paws, gazing quizzically at her from the open doorway to her bedroom. "I only have a few more hairs to tweeze

57

away, and my eyebrows will look just like Simone's!"

Prince Albert whined his play-with-me whine.

"Not now, Albert," Jessica told the dog. "This is serious business!"

Jessica was usually the retriever's first choice for a playmate. But that night she was the only choice. The twins' parents were at a party for the partners in Mr. Wakefield's law firm. Their older brother was a student at Sweet Valley University and only came home for an occasional weekend. And Elizabeth was out with Enid and Maria. Or Todd. Jessica couldn't remember which. As for Jessica herself, she'd been too tired after work to do anything except stagger home and vegetate in front of the television until it was time to begin her before-bed beauty routine.

Now she stared at the one offending eyebrow hair that was still out of place. She reached up to pluck it away. Then the doorbell rang downstairs and she jumped, tweezing the wrong hair. "Rats!" she cried. "What mentally challenged bonehead is at the front door at this hour?"

Prince Albert slowly rose to his feet and barked once, his tail wagging.

"Some watchdog you are!" Jessica said. "Couldn't you have barked to warn me—before the doorbell rang?"

She sighed, reluctantly pulled her feet from the soothing water, and hobbled downstairs to answer the door.

"Elizabeth?" she asked, her newly thinned eyebrows arching up her forehead as she opened the door for her twin.

"Sorry," Elizabeth said, noting Jessica's fuzzy pink bathrobe and the towel around her hair. "My hands were too full to reach my keys." She stepped over the threshold and deposited a half-dozen shopping bags on the carpet.

"Wow!" Jessica exclaimed. "You hardly look like us anymore! Your hair is totally awesome!"

"Do you really think so?" Elizabeth asked. "Is it stylish enough for *Flair*?"

"Absolutely," Jessica breathed. "You'll be the talk of the elevator tomorrow. Why didn't you tell me? I'd have gone with you. After work tomorrow I'm going to get mine cut just like it!"

Elizabeth rolled her eyes. "I don't think so," she said, sounding a little snooty. "Do you have any idea what Cheveux charges for a cut like this? There's no way you can afford it—unless you've saved a lot more of your allowance for the past six months than you've let on."

Jessica narrowed her eyes. "You know, Liz," she said. "It's bad enough that I have to deal with a stuck-up brat at *work* for two weeks—"

"*Relax*, Jess," Elizabeth interrupted. "You're just jealous because you still look like a high-school student. I'm sorry. I'm not trying to upstage you. But it's more important for *me* to look stylish."

Jessica crossed her arms menacingly. "And why is that?" she asked in a cold, steady voice.

"I have a chance to turn this internship into a career!" Elizabeth answered. "I'm not talking about a fantasy, like becoming a supermodel. I'm talking about a real summer job as an editorial assistant at *Flair*. But I can't get it if I don't make the right impression."

"You know, Elizabeth," Jessica said icily, "I like your new haircut a whole lot better than I like your new attitude."

With those words, Jessica spun around and stomped back upstairs, her feet stinging with every step.

Chapter 5

Elizabeth felt the other women staring behind her as she stepped out of the elevator on the eleventh floor Tuesday morning. No one had actually complimented her new clothes and hairstyle, but at least she didn't feel invisible.

After the doors closed, she checked her appearance in their mirrored surface. She pursed her plum-colored lips and tried to inspect herself objectively. Her new periwinkle blue ensemble wasn't quite as elegant as some of the ones she'd seen on the elevator that morning. But it was more stylish than anything else she owned, with a short skirt, a fitted vest, and a long, tailored blazer. She knew it suited her.

"Elizabeth, is that you?" exclaimed a voice behind her. She whirled to see Leona appraising her new look. "I'm overwhelmed by the change,"

Leona raved. "Your hair is absolutely fabulous! And the outfit is perfect. That pink blouse really brings out your complexion."

Elizabeth felt as if she'd just passed some secret initiation ritual. "Thanks, Leona," she said as they walked together down the corridor. "I was nervous about trying something so different from my usual chinos and oxford shirts."

"There's nothing wrong with the preppie look for hanging out at home, if that's what you're comfortable in," Leona said. Elizabeth tried, but she couldn't imagine sophisticated Leona in baggy khaki trousers and a button-down shirt—not at home or anywhere. "But a career in fashion publishing requires an up-to-date look," Leona continued, ushering Elizabeth into her office. She motioned to a chair, and Elizabeth sat down.

"I'm glad I went out and bought some new things," Elizabeth began tentatively. "I know I fit in around here much better, dressed this way. But it also bothers me a little—" She stopped, wondering if she was out of line.

"Go on, Elizabeth, please," Leona urged as she poured coffee for both of them. "I told you to be completely honest with me, and I meant it."

Elizabeth plunged ahead. "It's just that I hate to think people will judge me on my appearance instead of on my work," she concluded.

"Every businesswoman dreams of a day

when we're judged solely by the quality of the work we do," the managing editor said thoughtfully. "But the reality is that appearances do count—and much more so for women than for men."

"But that's not fair!" Elizabeth exclaimed.

"No, it's not," Leona agreed. "But to make it in any industry, you have to be a pragmatist. And this industry is extraordinarily competitive. Of course, if you can't do the work, you don't stand a chance. But a lot of women are skilled. Qualifications are a given, and they aren't the deciding factor in success."

"Then what is?" Elizabeth asked, thrilled to be discussing issues of feminism and business with someone as successful as Leona. "You can't mean to tell me that clothes and hair are the only difference between women who get ahead and those who don't."

"Of course not," Leona replied. She took a long sip from her coffee mug. "Image is important. But drive, ambition, and that extra spark of creativity are the things that really count. You have to be willing to take risks, to go out on a limb when necessary."

Elizabeth grimaced. "I'm not sure I'm enough of a risk taker," she confessed. "My twin sister, Jessica, is the one who goes out on limbs—and most of the time they get cut out from under her!"

"I'm talking about *calculated* risks," Leona clarified. "And I think you're wrong about not being a risk taker. You took a big risk today, changing your entire image just because of a comment I made. That took courage."

"Not really—," Elizabeth objected. "It would have taken more courage to keep showing up looking like a schoolgirl."

"Well, it does take courage to be different," Leona admitted. "But in this case being different served no purpose. I'm impressed that you have so much desire to succeed at *Flair* that you would make such a big change, even though you're only guaranteed a two-week run."

Elizabeth smiled shyly. "I do have one confession to make," she said. "I didn't have enough courage to try the gold eye shadow I bought!"

Leona laughed. "Give it two weeks," she joked. "We'll have your eyelids sparkling before you know it. But as long as we're talking about fashion, I'd love your opinion on a new dress I bought last night."

"You have it here?" Elizabeth asked. She felt flattered that Leona was taking the time to talk to her about something personal rather than business related.

"I'm dropping it off for alterations at lunchtime," Leona said, pulling a shopping bag from under her desk. She unfurled a short black dress with a plunging neckline, a body-skimming shape, and suede trim. "It's a Lina Lapin," she explained.

A week earlier Elizabeth would have rolled her eyes if Jessica had raved about such a trendy dress. But one day at *Flair* had left her more open-minded about fashion. Besides, the dress would look terrific on Leona's tall, slim frame. "Very chic," Elizabeth said truthfully.

"You don't think the hemline is too high for me, do you?" Leona asked. "My legs aren't what they were when I was your age."

"Nonsense," Elizabeth replied. "Your legs are perfect. What color hose will you wear with it?" Then she nearly laughed out loud at herself. It was exactly the kind of question Jessica would have asked.

Leona raised her eyebrows. "Black lace," she said dramatically.

Elizabeth remembered the evening fashion spreads she'd seen the day before in recent issues of *Flair*. "Lace is totally in," she told Leona. Elizabeth had noticed some Lina Lapin designs in those magazines; the new dress must have cost Leona a fortune. "But what's the occasion? Are you going somewhere special?"

"I think so," Leona answered, her voice tinged with nervous excitement. "My boyfriend's been hinting that he has something big to discuss with me. I'm almost positive he's going to ask me to marry him. I wanted to be wearing a real knockout dress when he pops the question."

"Congratulations—prematurely, I guess," Elizabeth said, giving her boss a warm grin. "That's fantastic!"

"Apparently I'm not the only one with a love life," Leona said, leaning forward conspiratorially across her desk. "I noticed a photograph of a very handsome young man on your desk yesterday."

"That's my boyfriend, Todd," Elizabeth explained, blushing slightly.

"Is he doing an internship this week as well?" Leona asked.

Elizabeth nodded. "He's working in the executive offices of a software company just this side of Sweet Valley," she replied. "To tell you the truth, he's not too excited about it. But I bet he'll learn a lot anyhow."

"I'd love to meet him," Leona said. "Let me know if he can manage a couple of hours away from the office sometime. Maybe the two of us and our significant others can do lunch."

Elizabeth beamed. She'd been excited yesterday that Leona was taking an interest in her as an employee and protégée. Now it seemed that they were becoming friends too.

Jessica sidled into one of the rooms off the main studio in the photography department. "Oh, hello, Michael," she said to Michael Rietz, the hairstylist, pretending to be surprised to see him. "I didn't realize you were in. It's awfully quiet around here this morning."

"You're not complaining, are you?" Michael asked with an amused grin as he set a row of bottled styling gels and mousses on the counter. "If you like, I could call Quentin out of his meeting with the art director and tell him you need some work to do."

"I wouldn't want to interrupt him," Jessica said with mock seriousness. "He's a very important man."

"If you can hang on for a few hours, Simone will be in around lunchtime," Michael said. "I noticed yesterday how much you enjoy helping her out."

"I enjoy helping her, all right," Jessica replied darkly. "I'd really enjoy helping her out the door!" She had experienced enough of Michael's personality to know he wouldn't be shocked by her lack of reverence for the leggy model. Michael focused his attention on a bottle of setting lotion, but Jessica thought she saw a grin curl the corners of his lips. She stared at herself in the mirror. "You know, Michael," she began tentatively, "I've been thinking about making a change in my own hairstyle. Nothing too drastic—just an update. How do you think my hair would look if I wore it shorter in the back?"

Michael squinted at her thoughtfully before

reaching out and running his hand in a professional manner through the long blond waves that framed her face. "Your hair has enough body to hold the look," he finally decided. "Yes, I think it could be a good style for you."

Jessica grinned. "*You* seem to have some time now," she said. "I mean, it would be good practice for you—"

"And heaven knows I need that," Michael added sarcastically. Jessica silently cursed her choice of words. But Michael didn't seem to mind. He shrugged. "All right. I never could say no to a pretty girl. You can be my first customer of the day."

"You won't regret this, Michael. When I'm a famous model, I'll tell everyone that you helped me get started," Jessica vowed as she hopped into the chair. "You'll be so popular, you can open your own fancy salon and charge two hundred dollars for a haircut!"

"Right," he said. "And how do you plan to become a famous model?"

Jessica reached into her backpack and pulled out the scrapbook she'd made with all the best photos of herself. "With *this*," she said. "Here, let me show you how photogenic I am." She handed him the album, opened to a spread of photographs of herself in her Sweet Valley High cheerleading uniform. After giving him enough time to admire the snapshots, she flipped the page to a photograph of her standing on the beach in an aqua bathing suit with a daring neckline and high-cut legs. Then she turned to see how impressed he was. Instead Michael snickered.

Jessica felt rage boiling up inside her. "What's wrong?" she asked hotly as the stylist laid the album on the counter, pulled out a smock, and tied it around her neck. "I think I look great in those pictures. So does everyone else who's seen them!"

Michael shook his head, grinning broadly. "You're a beautiful girl," he said. "But the photographs look as if someone took them with a disposable camera. The exposures are all wrong, you've got shadows on your face, and the colors are murky." He turned her chair and reclined it so he could wet down her hair in the sink. "Sorry to break the news, Jessica. But that album would get you laughed out of any modeling agency in California."

"But *why*?" Jessica demanded as he wrapped a towel around her head. "I want to be a *model*—not a photographer!"

"Modeling's very competitive," Michael replied with a shrug. "There are a lot of pretty girls around. Nobody wants to waste time on one who doesn't present herself as a professional."

"You think I'm too unprofessional to be a model?" Jessica asked, stricken.

"It has nothing to do with what you are. It's all *image*," the stylist answered as he whirled her chair to face the mirror again. "A professional-looking portfolio is everything," he continued. "Get yourself a state-of-the-art camera, find somebody who knows how to use it, and put together a portfolio that looks like you mean business."

"But I can't *afford* a state-of-the-art camera until I start making money as a model!" Jessica wailed.

Michael selected a pair of scissors and began snipping away at Jessica's hair. "The only people who make it in this business are the ones who take risks," he said. "If you're not willing to go all out to achieve your goals . . . well, you'd better get used to running downstairs every half hour to fetch Simone's fancy Swiss mineral water."

"*French* mineral water," Jessica put in. But her mind was working feverishly to come up with a plan for getting her hands on an expensive camera. She was a risk taker. And she was determined to become a model before the internship was over. It shouldn't be too difficult to figure out how.

"So how many of the editors came here from New York when the magazine moved a few months ago?" Elizabeth asked during lunchtime on Tuesday, leaning eagerly across

70

the table at the Mission Café, next door to the Mode building.

"About half," Reggie confided. "Me included. I'm sure the turnover helped get me my promotion to assistant fashion editor. The others didn't want to relocate."

"Beyond the move, what kind of a record does the magazine have for promoting people from within?" Elizabeth asked, twirling a few strands of pasta with her fork.

Reggie shrugged. "I don't pay much attention to things like that, but it seems pretty good. Warren, the guy whose office you're borrowing, was promoted from features assistant to features associate last year."

"I'm still a little hazy on the difference in responsibilities between assistant editor and associate editor," Elizabeth said. "And for that matter, between editorial assistant and assistant editor. What—"

"You are just too much!" Reggie broke in, laughing. "All these questions! It's like you're planning a whole career, not just a two-week internship."

Elizabeth shrugged, but she forced a smile. "I guess I *am* planning a career—or at least exploring the possibilities for one. I mean, isn't that what an internship is for?"

"I wouldn't know," Reggie said. "I never had the guts to apply for this kind of internship when I was sixteen. It's a cutthroat field. But you've sure got the ambition to succeed. I bet the dragon lady loves that!"

"Dragon lady?" Elizabeth asked. "Who are you talking about?"

"Leona Peirson, of course," Reggie replied.

"Leona?" Elizabeth repeated, amazed. "You can't mean that. I think she's terrific! Have you had a problem with her?"

"She really knows her stuff," Reggie admitted. "And no, I haven't exactly had a problem with her. I think it's just that our styles are different. Leona is about the most focused person I've ever met. And she's so aggressive. She intimidates me."

"That's the way a woman has to be if she wants to get ahead," Elizabeth told her new friend.

"I guess you're right," Reggie said. "And I'm not at all like that. I could never be like Leona."

"What are your ambitions, Reggie?" Elizabeth asked. She'd learned enough about Reggie's work to know that the young woman was a top-notch proofreader. Elizabeth knew it was too early to worry, but she couldn't help thinking that Reggie could be tough competition if Elizabeth were ever a full-time employee at *Flair*.

Reggie shook her head slowly and took a sip of her diet soda before replying. "I used to think I wanted a job like Leona's," she said. "But I've been at *Flair* long enough to realize I'm not cut out for it."

"I've heard you're the best proofreader on the staff," Elizabeth said.

"Thanks," Reggie said with a grateful smile. "It's nice to know some people think so. I like my job, and I take pride in my work. But I'm a detail-oriented person, not a big-picture type like Leona."

"You could learn to be," Elizabeth pointed out.

"Maybe," Reggie agreed. "But it's more than that. Getting to the top takes a lot of commitment and sacrifice. I've seen how hard the top editors work, and I can't see myself putting everything else on hold."

Elizabeth grinned. "You mean you want to have a *life* too?"

"Exactly," Reggie replied. "I'd like to get married someday, have a couple of kids, and maybe work part-time while they're babies. Publishing's a pretty good business for that—but only if you're not worried about getting ahead."

"You want to stay in your current job for your whole career?" Elizabeth asked. "Wouldn't you get bored?"

"Maybe not my *current* job," Reggie admitted. "I'd like to move up to associate editor, like Warren. But I'm not ambitious enough to set my sights any higher than that."

"That sounds very sensible," Elizabeth said,

trying to keep the relief out of her voice. She mentally crossed Reggie's name off her mental list of the competition for future jobs at *Flair*.

Jessica glided into the cafeteria of the Mode building during lunchtime on Tuesday, hips thrust forward in her best imitation of Simone's walk. It was easy to feel sophisticated with her stylish new haircut and her fitted purple blazer that was longer than her black leather miniskirt.

"Great hair!" Shelly called, breezing by on her way out of the room. "Quite modern."

Jessica grinned a very un-Simone-like grin. "Thanks," she said. "Michael whipped it up for me this morning. Aren't you going in the wrong direction?"

"I ate early," the makeup artist said. "I have to pick up some cosmetics for this afternoon's shoot so I can make Simone look properly disgusted with life. I wonder when we all decided that models should be snarly."

"Probably when somebody noticed their personalities," Jessica said. "Not that I wouldn't like a chance to abuse the people who've been rotten to me over the years."

"Wouldn't we all?" Shelly replied with a smile.

"Have you seen my sister in here?" Jessica asked.

Shelly shook her head, and the beads in her braids jingled. "I wouldn't know if I had," she pointed out. "Remember, I haven't the faintest idea what your sister looks like."

"Actually you know *exactly* what she looks like," Jessica explained with amusement. "She looks like a clone of me, only more boring. We even have the same hairdo now. Except that hers cost a fortune, and mine was free!"

"Identical twins?" Shelly asked. "That's wild! But nope, I haven't seen anyone who looks like you." She checked the clock on the wall. "Sorry," she said. "Gotta run. You know how the fashion goddess gets if you keep her waiting!"

Jessica proceeded toward the cafeteria line, digging in her backpack for her wallet. It wasn't there.

"Rats!" she cried, blushing when she noticed several sophisticated, carefully groomed women turning to stare at her. She silently chastised herself. Fashion models didn't say things like "rats." Suddenly she had a perfectly clear vision of her wallet, sitting on the kitchen counter at home, where she'd set it down that morning. Without it she was flat broke.

She scrambled to the telephone in the lobby, completely forgetting to walk like Simone, and dialed Elizabeth's department.

"Come on, Liz," she said aloud. "Answer your phone. You always have a few extra dollars to lend me." When Elizabeth didn't answer, the call was switched to the department's administrative assistant, who said Elizabeth had left for lunch a half hour earlier.

"Rats!" Jessica yelled again, turning the stylishly coiffed heads of several women who were waiting near the elevator.

Oh, well, Jessica told herself. If people were going to stare at her, at least they would see her chic new hairstyle. She was hungry, but she couldn't do much about that with no money. She'd noticed a courtyard between the Mode building and the high-rise next door. It seemed like the perfect place to give people a chance to compliment her on her new hairstyle as she worked on her suntan.

A few minutes later she was lounging on a concrete bench, with her sunglasses on and her eyes closed. The sun felt deliciously warm on her face and arms, and her hair slid lightly and stylishly against her shoulders. She tried to concentrate on the sun and on the fabulous photo opportunity she was providing for any passing shutterbugs. But it was no use. Her stomach was growling so loudly, she didn't know how she would survive until dinnertime.

"Uh-oh," said a sexy voice nearby. "It's Sleeping Beauty again. Do I dare kiss you in front of all these people?"

Jessica opened her eyes and raised the sunglasses to her forehead. The mail-room hunk from the day before was standing over her. "Would that cause a big enough scandal to get my photograph in *Flair* magazine?" she asked him.

"Would you settle for the *National Inquisitor*?" he replied, looking even more sexy than he had yesterday. The sunlight brought out a golden twinkle in his deep brown eyes that Jessica found mesmerizing.

Jessica shaded her eyes with one hand as she pretended to consider his question. "Nah," she decided. "I've been in trashy tabloids before. There's no future in it."

"Then I guess I'll have to restrain myself," the guy said, sitting on the edge of the bench. "It'll take all the willpower I've got, though. Do you have any idea how great you look in that short skirt, with your hair shining in the sun?"

"Yes," Jessica replied truthfully, bending one knee in order to show off her toned, tanned leg. "But I wouldn't mind hearing it again."

"You look gorgeous—much better than any slinky fashion model Quentin Berg has ever photographed," he told her. "But at the same time you seem kind of sad. Are you trying to imitate the famous Simone I'm-so-bored-with-life frown? Or is something wrong?"

Jessica swung her legs around so that she was sitting beside him. "I'll say!" she replied. "I was a total space cadet this morning and left my wallet with all my money at home. My sister seems to be off power-lunching with some publishing tycoon, so I'm stuck with nothing to eat."

"Bummer," the guy sympathized. "But that's easy enough to fix." He pulled a paper bag from his backpack. "You can power-lunch with me! How does half a tuna sandwich sound?"

"Terrific," Jessica replied gratefully.

"Also on the menu today at Chez Bench we have a lovely half bag of potato chips, sliced thin and cooked to order with a delicate sheen of grease," the guy said as he unpacked the rest of his lunch. "The house wine is a diet cherry cola, aged to perfection. And on the dessert menu the specialty of the day is Oreo cookies."

"This is terribly, terribly embarrassing," Jessica said, picking up on his fake-posh accent. "But with whom do I have the pleasure of eating?"

"Your charming luncheon companion is Mr. Cameron Smith," the guy replied with a slight bow.

"And I'm Jessica Wakefield," she introduced herself after swallowing her first bite of sandwich.

"Oh, but your fame has preceded you," Cameron said, gesturing with a potato chip. "I know your name, and I know you're the photography intern—or *slave,* as you put it yesterday. I even know that you live in Sweet Valley and have a twin sister who's in editorial."

"How do you know so much about me?" Jessica demanded.

Cameron smiled mysteriously. "We mail-room

guys know everything about everyone," he said with a vaguely European accent.

Did you have to remind me about your job? Jessica almost asked aloud. For a few minutes Cameron's thoughtfulness, good looks, and obvious admiration for her had made Jessica forget that he was a lowly mail-room worker. Now, looking into his laughing brown eyes as he began telling funny stories about *Flair* staff members, she forced herself to remember that she wasn't interested in him. Cameron was smart without being nerdy and nice without being boring. He was funny and warm and full of life—and an undeniable hunk. But he was a nobody.

She had to keep her sights set on Quentin. Of course, the photographer was a jerk and a control freak. But he was a jerk and a control freak who could make her career.

"So when are you going to give me the chance to regale you with more of my scintillating stories?" Cameron asked, breaking into her thoughts.

Jessica smiled. "Oh, I'm sure we'll see each other around," she said evasively, reminding herself again, more sternly this time, that she wasn't interested in Cameron.

"I get it," Cameron said. "I'm talking too much. But next time I'll show you what a great listener I can be. Just try me. You know, I'm dying to hear the story behind that remark you made earlier about being in the trashy tabloids." He paused and looked away momentarily. When he glanced back at Jessica, a faint blush colored his cheeks, and his deep brown eyes looked nervous. "How about if you let me take you to dinner tomorrow night and you can tell me all about it?" he asked in a rush.

Even though his adorable shyness sent a warm tingle right up Jessica's arms, she lied, "I'm, uh, *busy* tomorrow night."

"I know, you're worried about the menu," Cameron pressed on. "I promise you can have a whole sandwich to yourself next time. Maybe even french fries!"

"That's tempting," Jessica said. "But I really can't. You know, I'm so tired by the time I get home from work. And I have a long commute in the morning—"

"Friday night it is!" Cameron exclaimed. "You can play Sleeping Beauty again all Saturday morning."

"Thanks, Cameron," Jessica said, "but I really can't."

Cameron examined her carefully, obviously disappointed. "Does this have anything to do with the fact that I work in the mail room?" he asked, unable to keep a hurt tone from creeping into his voice.

"Of course not!" Jessica replied quickly. "I just—"

"Don't make excuses," Cameron said quietly. "I

get it. And I'm really sorry you feel that way. I was beginning to like you a lot."

"Me too," Jessica whispered under her breath as Cameron abruptly stood up and walked away. But she was sure she had done the right thing. To succeed in the fashion industry, she had to stay focused. She had to create careful alliances and make hard sacrifices.

Still, she felt curiously deflated as Cameron disappeared into the Mode building.

Elizabeth pulled out her wallet to pay her half of the bill at the Mission Café. Then she froze. One of the most handsome men she'd ever seen was walking across the pink-and-gray dining room, wearing an expensively cut suit and a narrow, multicolored tie. He was tall, at least six-foot four, with longish brown hair, bright blue eyes, and chiseled features.

Across the table Reggie sighed audibly, her black eyes following him across the room. "Isn't he beautiful?" Reggie asked in a breathless whisper.

"Who is he?" Elizabeth asked. "Do you know him?"

Reggie shrugged, still watching the man. The waiter was seating him at a table near the window, where a distinguished, silver-haired man was already sipping a glass of wine. "I wouldn't say that I know him exactly," Reggie confessed, more flustered than Elizabeth had seen her before. "I mean, I've had a big, big crush on him ever since I was introduced to him at an office party. But I'm sure he doesn't have the slightest recollection of me."

"An office party?" Elizabeth asked. "He works for *Flair*?"

"He is *Flair*," Reggie replied dreamily. "Don't you recognize him? That's Gordon Lewis, the hotshot new publisher."

"That's Gordon Lewis?" Elizabeth asked. "The Gordon Lewis who brought *Flair* to Los Angeles?"

"The one and only," Reggie said. "All the New York publishing snobs said it couldn't be done, but he was determined to start a new center for fashion publishing on the West Coast."

"I was expecting him to be older," Elizabeth marveled. "He can't be more than twenty-eight!"

"Something like that," Reggie said, her eyes still glued to the tall, handsome publisher.

"Who's the man with him?" Elizabeth said. "Should I recognize him?"

Reggie shook her head. "I don't know. Probably a big-time advertiser—president of a cosmetics firm or something. Who cares? Gordon Lewis is much more interesting."

Elizabeth agreed, but for different reasons. Reggie was right: Gordon Lewis was astonishingly good-looking. But Elizabeth's interest in the publisher was mostly professional. She memorized every detail of his face and tried to remember everything she'd ever read about him. Here was a man who could help her go places. Elizabeth vowed that before her internship was through, Gordon Lewis would know her name.

Chapter 6

Jessica hurried into the photo studio, hoping nobody would notice she was ten minutes late returning from lunch. Quentin was busy harassing two carpenters who were building something that looked like a giant sandbox on one end of the room. On the couch in the corner reclined Simone, chomping on a stalk of celery. As Jessica walked by she spoke.

"It must be difficult, having such a terrible weight problem," Simone observed, looking Jessica up and down.

Jessica trembled with rage. But she clamped her mouth shut before a barrage of insults spilled out. Quentin was nearby; she couldn't risk having him listen in while she broke the Toothpick into kindling. *But someday—soon—I'll put that twig in her place,* she swore to herself. Taking over

Simone's modeling job was no longer a desire. It was a *necessity*.

Todd aligned his hundredth document of the day against the inch marks on the glass surface of the photocopying machine. For the hundredth time of the day he cursed himself for being stuck at Varitronics while Aaron was assisting the manager of the L.A. Lakers. To make matters worse, he'd spent the whole day doing routine office work for Margaret Meeks, who reminded him more of a drill sergeant than an administrative assistant. He jabbed the green copy button on the top of the machine and waited for the all-too-familiar whirring sound that meant the invoice was being copied. Instead the machine beeped twice. Then silence.

The greenish electronic display line on the front of the machine announced Out of Paper. Todd gritted his teeth. He pounded one fist on the top of the machine—but not nearly as hard as he wanted to hit it. Then he sighed and dropped to his knees to open the front panel.

"What do you mean, out of paper?" he asked the machine, grateful that nobody was near enough to hear him talking to a pile of metal. "There's a whole *stack* of paper in there!"

He slammed the panel closed, pressed the clear button, and hit the copy button again.

Close Panel Door, the machine's display demanded.

"I closed it!" he hissed back. "The door is closed. You've got paper. What more do you want?" Sighing again, he wrenched the door open and slammed it, harder.

Out of Paper, the machine complained.

"Try switching it off," called a junior staff member who was walking by, trying to hide a grin. "Turn it back on after thirty seconds, and it might decide to cooperate."

Todd punched the off button with his thumb. Then he waited thirty seconds, staring at his watch and wishing it were later than two-thirty in the afternoon. He switched the machine back on, waited for it to warm up, and then pressed the copy button again.

The machine whirred obediently and then stopped. Out of Toner, the display announced.

"You are *not* out of toner," Todd said to the machine through clenched lips. "I fed you a new cartridge just this morning."

Out of Toner, the machine blinked.

Todd wrenched open the door on the front panel, exposed the toner cartridge, and slammed it with the heel of his hand to make sure it was in place. A cloud of black powder erupted from the cartridge and quickly settled all over his suit, his white shirt, and the elegant dove gray carpeting.

"That's *it!*" he announced. "I can't take another second of this place." His father and most of the managers were tied up in a meeting that was expected to last until dinnertime. And Meeks was in the accounting department, arguing about some invoices. If he was lucky, nobody would even notice if he cut out early. He would drive into the city and surprise Elizabeth by picking her up at the magazine.

Todd shut the front panel of the photocopying machine. Then he sauntered back to his own cubicle, ceremoniously loosening his tie and tossing it onto his workstation. As he passed Meeks's empty desk and made for the door he shrugged out of his blazer and unfastened the top button of his shirt. *Free at last*, he thought happily.

Jessica slipped into a small photo studio that was empty except for a few camera bags and some photographic equipment lying on a desk. She picked up the telephone and punched in the number for Fowler Enterprises.

"Fowler Enterprises," growled Lila. "May I help you?"

"You sound like you're transmitting death rays through the telephone with your voice," Jessica observed. "You make about as good a receptionist as I do a common laborer."

"Well, greetings to you too," Lila seethed. "Honestly, Jess, I'd love to transmit death rays to the dweeb who dreamed up these internships. Lila Fowler—millionaire, world traveler, best-dressed girl in southern California, and *telephone lackey?*

Do you know that they expect me to be *nice* to everyone who calls here? They've absolutely *got* to be kidding."

"Nobody cares if I'm nice," Jessica said. "I could be a robot. I'm just supposed to keep my mouth shut and take orders."

"I am *not* an *answering machine!*" Lila declared. "This whole thing is just too surreal."

"Yeah, well, I'm learning all about surreal," Jessica said, eyeing Quentin and Simone through the open door to the main studio. "Right now Simone is refusing to pose—it seems that her mineral water is from the wrong country! And Quentin, who's Mr. Control Freak when it comes to ordering me around, is telling the poor girl how brave she is to continue in the face of such disaster. Lila, I swear I'm going to be sick!"

"Spare me the whining, Jessica," Lila said. "At least you're somewhere glamorous. I mean, I knew my father made computer chips for a living, but nobody here can talk about anything else! Can you imagine anything so boring?"

"Don't mention chips," Jessica begged. "I only had half a lunch today. I'm dying of starvation!"

"And I just broke a fingernail on this idiotic switchboard," Lila said. "My father is definitely going to hear about this!"

"Li, listen to me," Jessica said. "This is an emergency. I need you to meet me at the beach after work today."

"The beach?" Lila asked. "What kind of emergency is this?"

Jessica glanced through the door toward Quentin and the Toothpick. "I can't talk about it now. Just meet me at the beach."

"But why—?"

"Don't ask questions," Jessica ordered. "Just do it. Oh, and bring those new sunglasses you bought at the mall Sunday—the retro ones with the rhinestones. And your purple headband. And your makeup kit."

"Jessica—"

"Please, Lila!" Jessica begged. "I'll explain everything when I see you tonight."

After she hung up the phone, Jessica glanced back into the main studio, where Simone was finally stepping into the enormous sandbox that was supposed to make the photographs look as if they'd been shot on a stylized beach. She waited until all eyes were upon her. Then she slowly unwrapped her silk robe to expose one of the tiniest bikinis Jessica had ever seen.

"Spectacular, honey!" Quentin called as he snapped photograph after photograph. "Now take a step to the left. I want to get the beach umbrella in the shot . . . and let the robe fall behind you so I can see every bit of that bathing suit . . . perfect!"

Jessica slitted her eyes and clenched her jaw. As far as she was concerned, Simone looked as appealing as a praying mantis—she was certainly as skinny as one. *Come to think of it,* Jessica remembered, *don't female praying mantises eat the heads off their mates? It would serve Quentin right, the way he's carrying on over that six-foot toothpick.*

But Jessica needed Quentin. He was her ticket to fame and fortune. First, though, she needed a professional portfolio. And for that she needed professional equipment. She eyed one of Quentin's spare cameras, lying out on the desk. Did she dare borrow it for the night?

Suddenly Michael Rietz's voice echoed in her head. *The only people who make it in this business are the ones who take risks.* If she wasn't willing to go all out to achieve her goals, the stylist had said, then she'd better get used to fetching Simone's mineral water.

"That's not going to happen," Jessica said aloud with determination. She glanced through the doorway again. Nobody was paying her the slightest bit of attention. There were advantages to being invisible. *Quentin has more cameras than Lila has bathing suits,* Jessica rationalized. He'd never miss this one. Would he? Besides, it was only for one night.

She stuffed the camera in her backpack and zipped it up.

Elizabeth clicked the mouse button to maneuver through cyberspace to the Library of Congress database. As a subject heading she punched in the name of a chemical found in certain sunscreens. Leona was writing an article on studies that had shown the chemical to cause breathing difficulties, and Elizabeth was glad to help research a topic more important than how to color-coordinate accessories.

"You're beautiful when you're surfing the Net," said a voice from her doorway. Elizabeth looked up, startled. Todd was lounging against the door of her office, smiling at her. He wore a distinctly unprofessional outfit: a Sweet Valley University T-shirt and a pair of cutoff shorts.

"What are you doing here?" she asked.

"Bringing you coffee," he replied, setting a steaming cup beside her keyboard.

"You came an awfully long way to bring me a cup of coffee," Elizabeth noted, turning back to the screen to narrow her search parameters.

"That's OK. It's really awful coffee," he explained. "But I know you professional journalists drink it black and bitter."

Elizabeth gulped a mouthful. "You're right on both counts," she said. "It's awful, and everyone around here does drink it black. But it's just what I needed. Thanks." She tilted her face up to accept a kiss.

"So how about you knock off a little early here and let me take you home?" Todd asked, rubbing her aching shoulders.

"Mmmm," Elizabeth murmured. "That sounds great. And it feels great. But I can't. I have to compile a bibliography for Leona before I leave here tonight." She looked down at her watch. "Todd, it's only four o'clock! You're supposed to be at Varitronics! Wearing a suit!"

Todd shrugged. "I got sick of fighting with the copying machine, so I gave myself the rest of the afternoon off," he admitted. "I changed into the most un-Varitronics outfit I could find, and here I am. It's about time I saw your office."

"What do you think?" Elizabeth asked, peering at her monitor to check on the progress of her search.

"Pretty classy digs you've got here at *Flair*," Todd said, nodding. "Your own office! With a door and everything. At Varitronics I have to fold myself into a cubicle about the size of my gym locker."

"So much for being the boss's son," Elizabeth noted. "Didn't anyone care that you decided to bag the rest of the day?"

"I wouldn't know," Todd replied. "I didn't tell anyone. I bet you could do the same thing—just slip out of here with me without anyone knowing."

Elizabeth shook her head. "Maybe I *could*, but I won't," she said. "I promised Leona I'd finish this tonight."

"Come on, Liz!" Todd urged. "Just this once. She'll understand."

"I've got too much to do," Elizabeth told him

firmly. "It's not just this bibliography. I could stay all night and not finish everything."

"Well, *sorry*," Todd said, his voice sounding hurt. "I thought you'd be happy to see me."

Elizabeth smiled apologetically. "I *am* happy to see you," she said soothingly. "And I know you drove all the way from Sweet Valley to pick me up. But I can't just blow off the rest of this work. You know it's important for me to make a good impression in this internship. My future career may depend on it!"

"OK," Todd said, massaging her shoulders again. "I understand. And I did agree to share you with the publishing world for two weeks. So I'll just sit here and watch you. Maybe I can even help you finish sooner."

"That won't work," Elizabeth objected. "There's only one computer. And I can't concentrate with you right behind me." She thought for a moment. "I have an idea. Why don't you go down to the photo studio and visit Jessica? I'm sure she'd love a distraction."

Todd's mouth twisted as if he'd eaten something sour. "Visit *Jessica?*" he asked. "You said this internship might require some sacrifices, but isn't that a little extreme? When was the last time I voluntarily hung out with your psycho twin?"

"I know she's not your favorite person," Elizabeth said, smiling up at her boyfriend. "But watching somebody type must be even more frustrating than wrestling with a photocopying machine. Jessica's working in a photography studio. There must be props and colorful sets and clothes down there, with photographers running all around. It's got to be more exciting than this." She gestured with her hand at the piles of paper on her desk.

Todd sighed. "If I go down to see Jessica for twenty minutes, do you promise you'll let me take you away from all this afterward?"

"Make it thirty minutes, and you've got a deal," Elizabeth told him, relenting. "I think I can finish this bibliography in a half hour."

"Thirty minutes it is," Todd agreed. "Do you promise you won't change your mind and beg to stay longer when I come back up here for you?"

"Scout's honor!" Elizabeth promised. "I came in early this morning, so Leona won't mind if I leave a little early—if I take the 'Fashion Flops' section home with me to proofread tonight."

"You're a total grind," he said fondly.

"It's not being a grind," Elizabeth corrected. "It's *career planning!*"

"Whatever it is, I'm not sure I like it," Todd admitted. "But I guess I'll live." He leaned in to kiss the tip of her nose, but Elizabeth ducked.

"Go, Todd!" she ordered, already staring back at the screen. "The art department is on the ninth floor."

"I don't even get another kiss?" Todd asked.

"In a half hour," Elizabeth promised, fingers already clicking again on the keyboard.

Todd muttered something as he trudged out the door, but Elizabeth was too intent on her work to pay attention.

Chapter 7

Jessica wiped a strand of sweaty, sand-streaked hair out of her eyes. She was grateful that she couldn't see what her stylish new hairdo looked like after a half hour of hard labor under Quentin's white-hot lights.

"*No*, Jessica!" he barked. "I want the sand dune on the *left* to be higher than the one on the *right*."

Jessica motioned to the left with her push broom. "It *is* higher!" she insisted, facing him defiantly.

"Not *your* left!" Quentin chastised her. "*My* left!"

"You could have said so before I swept all that sand around!" she pointed out, trying not to lose her temper with the one person who could make or break her career.

"Just do it like I said and stop arguing,"

Quentin ordered. He turned to consult with the set decorator about the painted backdrop. As soon as he wasn't looking, Jessica turned her back on him long enough to make a bug-eyed face at Shelly, who was touching up Simone's makeup.

"Jessica!" Simone called sharply. "When you're through playing in the sand, I expect you to fetch me that mineral water I asked for ten minutes ago. You have no idea how dehydrating it is, posing under those bright lights." In her white macramé bikini Simone looked as cool as an icicle.

Jessica bit her lip to keep from shrieking. "You're right," she muttered under her breath. "I have no idea what it's like posing under the bright lights. All I know is what it's like *pushing three tons of sand* under the bright lights. I've never been so sweaty and sandy and gross in my entire *life*."

"Did you say something?" Quentin asked sharply.

"Not a thing," Jessica replied sweetly. She had sand in her shoes, sand in her clothes, and sand in her eyes and hair. She could even taste sand in her mouth, crunching between her teeth. *It's a good thing nobody I know can see me like this,* she thought, wondering if the sand was making her eyes bloodshot.

Suddenly Jessica noticed through her gritty eyes that a guy was standing in the doorway, staring at her. And he appeared to be a real hunk. She rubbed furiously at her eyes until she could see clearly.

"Todd?" she exclaimed weakly. She wasn't sure if she should be glad he wasn't a cute guy she cared about impressing or horrified that he was someone who could tell all her friends just how glamorous her internship really was.

"Jessica?" he asked, his eyes widening. "You look, uh . . . *different*."

Quentin was also staring at Todd, Jessica noticed. And the photographer had a strange look on his face, as if he had never seen a teenage guy before.

Uh-oh, Jessica thought. *Todd's about to get thrown out of Quentin's studio!*

For a moment Todd couldn't tear his eyes away from Jessica's forlorn figure. She stood in the middle of some sort of sandbox that took up nearly a quarter of the huge studio, pushing sand around with a broom. She wore a long purple blazer and a short black skirt, but both were spotted with sand. Her eyes were red, she had sand in her hair, and sweaty trails of makeup ran down her face. Her expression was furious in stark contrast to the bright, cheerful beach scene painted in bold strokes of blue and gold on the backdrop behind her.

Todd couldn't decide which was more amazing—the sight of Jessica looking terrible or the sight of Jessica pushing a broom.

He didn't wonder for long. Standing beside the sandbox was one of the best-looking girls he had ever seen. And she was wearing a tantalizingly small bikini made of some sort of white knotted string. As soon as the tall, black-haired beauty turned toward him Todd forgot that Jessica was in the room. With a start he realized that he'd seen the leggy goddess before, on the cover of magazines in the grocery store. She giggled, and Todd blushed. He hadn't meant to stare, especially at that slim, perfectly formed body.

A man's laugh interrupted Todd's stunned daze. Painfully he shifted his gaze away from the breathtaking model. For the first time he noticed the man who was obviously in charge. He was in his midtwenties, with scruffy blond hair, and he stood behind a camera that had as many buttons as a flight simulator, mounted on a tripod. Another camera hung around his neck.

"I'm Quentin Berg, the photographer," the man barked, as if he expected Todd to have heard of him. He didn't sound unkind, but he did sound as if he was used to immediate respect. "And this," he said, gesturing toward the model, "is Simone, wearing the latest Rafael Bartucci design."

"Um, I'm—uh—Todd Wilkins," Todd stammered. "I'm sorry if I interrupted. I can leave if—"

"Have you ever done any modeling?" the photographer asked, studying his face and body in a way that made Todd want to run and hide.

Todd shook his head. "No," he choked out.

"There's no time like the present," Quentin decided. "You've got a look—classic, but hip. Clean-cut, but full of life. I can make it work."

"Do you want me to make him up?" asked an African American woman who stood near Simone at a table covered with tubes and jars of cosmetics.

"Not now, Shelly," Quentin decided. "We've got a male model coming tomorrow to pose on this set with Simone. For now we'll just use Todd as a stand-in for some test shots. But take a look at his features under the lights and decide what you'd do with his coloring. Nothing heavy; keep it natural. If this session works out, I might want to use him on the second Bartucci shoot."

"Are you finished with those sand dunes, Jessica?" Simone asked impatiently. "I'm still waiting for my mineral water."

"Yes, ma'am," Jessica replied, saluting. Simone grunted acknowledgment, but Todd knew Jessica well enough to recognize the wrath in her bloodshot eyes. Jessica stomped into an adjoining room and appeared a moment later with a bottle. She handed it to the taller girl. "Here you are," she said with syrupy, un-Jessica-like sweetness. "French mineral water. I brought a whole stash up here so I don't have to make you wait every time."

Todd didn't understand the surprise he saw on Simone's face or the triumph on Jessica's. But he didn't have long to ponder it.

"Take off your shoes and step onto the sand," Quentin instructed him. "Simone, I'll want you next to Todd, on his right. Todd, put your arm around her waist."

Todd gulped, his mind racing. If Simone hadn't been standing there in that tiny little bikini, he'd have scoffed at the whole idea. He'd always thought modeling was for vain airheads. But one look at Simone left him practically speechless. He allowed himself to be moved into position beside her. When Simone, smiling, lifted his hand and placed it on her right hip, Todd let it rest there. Her skin felt cool and silky smooth under his hand. A curtain of black hair rustled against his shoulder, as soft as a caress.

Todd's heart was pounding in his chest. He was terrified. He was embarrassed. And he couldn't believe his good luck.

"Earth to Liz!" called a voice.

Elizabeth looked up from her computer after sending the results of her latest database search to the printer. She blinked, realizing she'd been staring at the screen for a long, long time. Reggie was standing in the doorway.

"You're working too hard," Reggie told her. "I just wanted to say good night. It's five-thirty, and I'm *outta* here!"

"Five-thirty!" Elizabeth exclaimed. "How did it get to be five-thirty?"

"I couldn't say," Reggie joked. "I hear it happens every night at around this time."

"*Todd,*" Elizabeth said, suddenly remembering the deal she'd made with him.

"No, it's Reggie," Reggie corrected. "Am I missing something here? Or are you suffering from the dreaded Computer Daze Disease?"

"I guess I am," Elizabeth admitted. "My boyfriend, Todd, came by to pick me up a while ago. I made him go down to the photography studio to visit my sister so I could finish this research. But I expected him back here an hour ago."

"Maybe he's having fun down there and lost track of the time," Reggie suggested. "Hanging out around photo shoots is a much more exciting spectator sport than watching us edit."

"That's what I told him," Elizabeth agreed, switching off her computer and scouting around the office for a file she needed to take home. "But Todd has a very low tolerance for hanging out with my 'psycho twin,' as he calls her."

"He'll survive," Reggie assured her.

Elizabeth threw the "Fashion Flops" file into her leather briefcase and headed into the hallway with Reggie. "I feel bad about abandoning him with Jessica," she confided as they stepped onto the elevator. "The poor guy must be out of his mind with boredom."

To his surprise, Todd was loving every minute of having his photo taken. It didn't hurt that Simone was gorgeous and was wearing practically nothing. And it especially didn't hurt to have her wrap her arms around him and hold her body close against his. Underfoot, the sand was as soft and warm beneath the bright lights as if he really was at the beach.

"Now turn to the other side!" Quentin called. "Let me see that profile. . . . Todd, you're a natural! I've never seen anyone take to modeling so quickly!" Todd grinned. He'd never understood Jessica's fascination with modeling. But maybe she was right, for once in her life. Maybe there really was something to this modeling gig. For some reason she was staring at him with venom in her bloodshot eyes. Todd couldn't think of anything he'd done to annoy her. But with Jessica, you never knew. He decided not to worry about it. Whatever his offense was, she'd have forgotten it herself in an hour.

"Take a step forward, Todd," Quentin instructed. "Put both arms around Simone. . . . Yes, just like that! Hold it for a second. This is going to be fantastic! You've got a real future in this business."

Todd dreamed of walking into Varitronics the next morning, throwing his tie on his father's desk—no, scratch that. He dreamed of using his tie to throttle the psychotic photocopying machine. Then he would announce to his dad and the rest of the staff that he'd found a new internship. And by the way, they could see his work on the cover of next month's issue of *Flair*.

Even Aaron would be jealous.

Jessica pursed her lips as she watched Todd strut and preen in front of the camera. "He looks like an overgrown peacock with mousy brown hair," she whispered to Shelly.

Shelly shrugged. "I don't know," she said. "I think he's a hunk."

"Believe me, I've known Todd for years," Jessica said. "He may look like a hunk, but he's got the least hunky personality you can imagine. When he has any personality at all. I can't believe he's making a total fool of himself the first time anyone with a camera shows interest."

"Quentin's not the only one showing interest," Shelly whispered back.

"That's for sure," Jessica said. "Look at the way Simone the Stick is drooling over him. It's positively sickening."

Shelly rolled her eyes. "She probably thinks he's your boyfriend," she remarked, packing up her tote bag. "That would put him on her radar screen for sure."

"I didn't know witches' brooms came equipped with radar."

"You know Simone—always on the cutting edge," Shelly said.

"I'd like to sharpen it for her," Jessica muttered.

"I hate to abandon you here, Jess, but I was supposed to be off ten minutes ago," Shelly said. "I've got to catch my bus. I'll see you tomorrow!"

Shelly strolled out of the studio, swinging her bag. As the door shut behind her Jessica realized she was fresh out of allies. Todd had obviously gone over to the enemy camp. He stood in the sand with Simone, grinning stupidly at her skinny, sulky face. Life wasn't fair. Todd wasn't interested in modeling. He'd always told her it was a dumb ambition. But now there he was, posing in front of the camera. And Jessica wasn't.

Jessica dropped her broom with a clatter, hoping it would break Quentin's concentration. Or Simone's. Or Todd's. But nobody even flinched. She ticked off everything she was miserable about. She despised Simone. She hated the way Simone looked in the five-hundred-dollar Bartucci bikini. She was sick of doing everybody's dirty work. Todd was stealing her modeling career. Her entire body itched from the tiny particles of sand that had worked their way into every article of clothing she wore. Her hair was a mess. And she was furious with Quentin for making Todd a model while he ignored her own much more obvious charms.

Suddenly the door opened. For the first time in hours Jessica perked up. Elizabeth took a few purposeful steps into the room and then froze, her eyes widening at the sight of Simone locking Todd in a tight embrace in front of the garish beach-scene backdrop.

If I have to be miserable, then it's only fair that somebody else should be miserable too, Jessica told herself. Besides, Elizabeth's reaction to Simone and Todd's modeling session would at the very least add some excitement to a long, tedious day.

"And if we're really lucky," Jessica whispered, balling both hands into fists, "Liz will do us all a favor and punch Simone right in her perfect little nose job!"

Elizabeth blinked, fully expecting the hallucination to dissipate like fog. It didn't. Todd was standing in a sandbox, caught in the tight embrace of a tall, gorgeous, and impossibly slim young woman. A woman wearing nothing but a skimpy macramé bikini. Suddenly Elizabeth knew exactly who the siren was. It was Simone, the *Flair* cover girl to whom Jessica had taken such an instant and intense dislike. *The Fashion Witch,* Jessica had called her. For once Elizabeth agreed completely with her sister's assessment.

Elizabeth realized her own mouth was hanging open. She snapped it shut, grateful that nobody except Jessica—a bedraggled, furious-looking Jessica—had even noticed she was in the room. Elizabeth marched up to the set, strengthened by the approval she saw in her sister's eyes.

"Get your hands off my boyfriend!" she demanded.

Todd blushed bright red and jumped off the set as if the sand had caught fire. "L-Liz!" he stammered. "We were just, uh, passing the time waiting for you. Quentin, um, asked me to be a stand-in for his lighting check."

Simone didn't even have the grace to look guilty. "It's been a lot of fun, Todd," she cooed, thrusting one hip forward. "I hope we'll do it again sometime soon."

Todd kept his eyes on Elizabeth's face. "Are you ready to go?" he asked, steering her back toward the door before Simone had a chance to say anything else.

"Todd, don't run out of here so quickly," Quentin called. "I meant what I said about using you as a model. I have a feeling you're going to turn out to be incredibly photogenic."

"Oh, yes, Todd!" Simone echoed. "I just know you are."

"I'll give you a call after I've had a chance to print the shots we took today," Quentin promised Todd. He totally ignored Elizabeth. "If they show what I think they will, I believe you have a promising career ahead of you as a model."

Elizabeth noticed that Jessica's face was turning positively purple.

"We have to go now," Elizabeth said, pulling Todd toward the door. She stopped and fumbled in her purse for a moment. She fished out her car keys and tossed them to Jessica. "I'm riding with Todd. You take the Jeep."

"Can you *believe* it, Liz?" Todd asked as soon as the elevator doors shut behind them. "That photographer, Quentin, really thinks I've got talent as a model. I mean, I can't believe I'm saying this. I never thought models had any talent. But it's a lot harder than it looks, and he says I'm a natural!"

"Um, Todd, if I were you, I wouldn't get my hopes up," Elizabeth said carefully. "Modeling is a very competitive field; most people who are successful at it started out as kids. I wouldn't want you to be disappointed."

"Don't worry about me," Todd replied. "I'm not thinking too much about the future. All I want is to do this now and have some fun—and maybe get out of my boring internship. If something else develops out of these two weeks—well, I'll take it as it comes."

But Elizabeth was worried. And she knew exactly what was developing. She'd seen the way Todd was gazing at Simone—like an adoring puppy. And she'd noticed the way Simone was eyeing Todd—like a bird of prey. Of course Quentin would decide to make Todd a model. In Elizabeth's opinion, Todd was the best-looking guy around. Once he and Simone were working together every day, it was inevitable that he'd fall under the Fashion

Witch's spell. Especially if all Simone's work clothes were as revealing as the macramé bikini.

As they walked to Todd's car he chatted excitedly about the possibility of modeling for Quentin—studiously avoiding any mention of Simone, Elizabeth noticed. She had never seen Todd look so happy and so alive. And she had never felt so rotten.

Chapter 8

Jessica raised her face to the breeze and let the wind toss back her hair. She breathed in the salt air appreciatively. *The real Pacific Ocean makes a much better photo background than Quentin's garishly painted one,* she decided.

"So when do we get started?" Lila asked. "We don't have all night. The sun will set in another hour, and I can't take decent pictures after dark without high-speed film—even if this is the world's most expensive camera."

"I just need a minute to feel clean again," Jessica insisted, reveling in the knowledge that the only sand-covered part of her was the soles of her feet. "You would never believe how disgustingly sweaty and sandy I was this afternoon from creating dunes in Quentin's sandbox."

"And that was supposed to be *work?*" Lila

asked. "Fowler Enterprises doesn't even have a sandbox for its employees. How unenlightened. I should file a complaint with the Labor Department."

"Ha, ha," Jessica said, smoothing down the floral miniskirt that wrapped over the briefs of her pink-and-lavender halter-top bikini. It wasn't a five-hundred-dollar Bartucci bathing suit, but she knew she looked terrific in it.

"What do you do at work *tomorrow?*" Lila asked. "Build sand castles?"

"I don't know about castles, but tomorrow is the day for convincing Prince Charming to ask me out on a date," Jessica planned aloud.

"Charming?" Lila scoffed. "Are you kidding? This Quentin character sounds like an obnoxious control freak."

"OK, so he's not charming," Jessica conceded, checking her face in her mirrored compact. "But he's great looking, and he's totally necessary if I'm going to become a model within the next ten days."

"That's what I like about you, Jess," Lila said. "You don't expect instant gratification of your every wish. You're willing to work for the long-term—"

"Shut up and take pictures," Jessica ordered with a laugh.

"Move a little farther up the beach," Lila instructed. "Your face will be in shadow if the sun is right behind you. That's better. Hold it there. . . . Good. . . . You know, Jess, you are so lucky to have

112

a best friend who's used a superexpensive camera before. You'd be totally stuck if you were expecting anyone else to figure this thing out."

"It would have been easier if you could have brought me your father's camera," Jessica pointed out, throwing one arm behind her head dramatically. "I hated having to borrow this one from Quentin."

"My father took his camera with him on his business trip to Washington, D.C.," Lila said. "But I'm surprised Quentin let you take this one. This thing is worth hundreds of dollars."

Jessica shrugged. She practiced her Simone pout for the camera, stepped forward with one foot, and placed her hands on her hips. "He didn't exactly let me take it," she admitted. "I sort of gave myself permission."

"*What?*" Lila shrieked. "Are you out of what's left of your puny little mind? I'm taking pictures with a stolen camera?"

"*Borrowed,*" Jessica corrected. "A *borrowed* camera. Hold on a minute; let me pull off this wrap skirt so you can get my bikini in all its skimpy glory. You should have seen this piece of string Silicone Simone was calling a bathing suit this afternoon. It made her look even more like a toothpick than usual."

"Don't change the subject!" Lila protested. "We were talking about a *felony*. And now I'm an accessory!"

"Speaking of accessories, let me have your rhinestone sunglasses," Jessica said. She slid them on and then pushed the lenses up onto her forehead. "How do I look?"

"Like a felon with good taste," Lila said. "Maybe I should take your mug shot as long as I'm at it. Save the FBI some work."

"Chill out, Li," Jessica urged. "I'll return the camera first thing in the morning, and Quentin will never know the difference. He's got about a million cameras lying around the studios. I bet he can't even tell one from the other. Now let's move into the water so you can take some of me with the waves crashing against my knees."

"Not yet. I'm going to have to put in a new roll of film in a couple of minutes," Lila said. "But are you sure you want me to take this hot camera into the water? Remember, if anything goes wrong with your stolen property, I wasn't here. I never saw this camera. It's totally your responsibility."

"What could go wrong?" Jessica assured her. "Borrowing this camera is the most brilliant idea I ever had!"

"A few days ago the most brilliant idea you ever had was putting together that first scrapbook of photos of yourself. Obviously one monument to your monumental vanity wasn't enough."

Jessica shrugged. "Now it's three days later, and I'm three days more brilliant," she explained.

"You'd better give me back my sunglasses,"

Lila mocked. "Your brilliance is blinding me."

"Now that I'm in the real world of fashion photography, I know that my little scrapbook was too amateurish," Jessica said. "No professional photographer can take you seriously as a supermodel when you're posing in a cheerleading uniform. And the photos could have been taken by my brother. The ones you're doing now will be part of my professional portfolio."

"Do you really think it will make a difference?" Lila asked.

"With these photos I'll knock Simone out of the spotlight in no time," Jessica boasted. "And I hope she lands flat on her smug little face. Come on, let's go in the water now! Do you think I should put my hair up?"

"Ooh, good idea. But leave a few tendrils hanging down in front," Lila advised. "Just give me a minute to load new film." She crouched beside Jessica's backpack and fished out a roll. "You know, it doesn't sound as if Todd needed a professional portfolio to get into the real world of fashion photography," she pointed out as she popped open the back of the camera. "From what you said, Quentin took one look, and he was in the picture."

"Can you *believe* it?" Jessica fumed. Bile rose in her throat every time she thought of Todd, hamming it up with Simone in front of the camera. "How can he see Todd, of all people, as a potential cover boy?"

"I hate to break it to you, Jessica, but your sister's boyfriend is a hunk. And he's got money too. If he had any taste in women, he'd be the perfect guy."

"Todd's OK if *boring* turns you on," Jessica said as they walked into the rolling waves. "But he doesn't have that *jello-say-kwah*."

"I think you mean *je ne sais quoi*," Lila corrected. "It means roughly, 'that certain something.'"

"Well, sorry, Ms. French Scholar. But Todd is a certain *nothing!* He doesn't have that extra spark of personality that I have. He has *zero* charisma!"

Lila rolled her eyes. "If anyone should be a fashion model, it's me," she said. "I have more experience trying on expensive clothes than anyone."

Jessica remembered a time when a modeling agency representative had told Lila she wasn't photogenic enough to be a model. But she forced herself not to bring it up. Being turned down as a cover girl for *Ingenue* magazine was a sore spot with Lila. And Jessica needed Lila's help now, not her wrath. She put her arm around her friend's shoulders. "I promise that as soon as I'm famous, I'll bring you along for the ride."

"Gee, *thanks*," Lila said cynically. "As long as we're getting soaked you might as well do some more posing. Why don't you splash around a little?"

116

"OK, but keep your distance," Jessica said. "We can't afford to get that camera wet."

"The camera? I was more worried about my hair," Lila replied. "These waves are getting higher. I'm glad I wore shorts."

"Just keep that thing on the strap around your neck," Jessica cautioned as she splashed water on her upper body. "Take some of me wet, like those bathing-suit models in the sports magazines. Here, get this!" She allowed a wave to gently lift her off the ocean floor as she tilted her face into the setting sun.

"You just jump and splash around. Keep your face dry, and let me worry about when to click the shutter," Lila instructed. "I know what I'm doing."

"Ooh! Look at that big wave coming our way!" Jessica called. "I'm going to bodysurf this one. Make sure you get a good angle. The left side of my face is my best side."

"Big wave?" Lila cried, turning in horror to see it bearing down on her. *"Jessica!"* She ran for the shore—too late. The wave crashed over her, tumbling Lila's slender body over and over in the sand. A moment later she was sitting in a few inches of water with a dazed expression on her face, her long, light brown hair plastered to her shoulders. Water streamed from her hair, her face, and her silk T-shirt. And it streamed from the camera that still hung around her neck.

"Oh, no!" Jessica screamed. "Lila, is the camera all right?"

"I'm touched by your concern," Lila spluttered. "I could have been *drowned*. And my hair is *ruined!*"

Jessica unlooped the camera from around her friend's neck. "It's full of water! Do you think it will dry?"

"Face it, Jess," Lila seethed. "It's ruined. You should have stolen a waterproof camera."

"This can't be happening!" Jessica wailed, inspecting the camera from every angle. "Lila, lend me the money to buy Quentin a new one!"

"Obviously your brain is waterlogged," Lila told her. "I will *not* lend you the money. You already owe me for this silk top. I thought you were taking complete responsibility for your actions this time?"

Jessica closed her eyes and dropped to her knees, clutching the soggy camera. "I'm *toast*," she said glumly.

"The set designer, Kevin, is teaching me all about how to paint scenery so that it looks real," Maria told Elizabeth that evening as they sat on the edge of the pool at the Wakefields' house. She was only two days into her internship at the Bridgewater Theatre Group, but she had already learned more about backstage work than she'd thought possible. "The set we're working on is made of plywood and Styrofoam," she said. "But it looks exactly like marble!"

"I saw the set in the photography studio today," Elizabeth said. Her eyes were fixed on the sparkling water of the pool, but the expression in them was far away. "Quentin set up kind of a stylized beach—not that anyone would notice the scenery, with that tiny scrap of a bikini Simone was wearing."

"Get your mind off it," Maria urged, kicking at the water with her foot. "Concentrate on how much you're learning in your own department. You know, until this internship I never knew how much I could enjoy this side of theatrical work. Actors are so caught up in what they're doing that they don't realize how much work goes into the rest of the production."

"Todd tried to tell me how much work it is to model," Elizabeth said. "As if he was some sort of expert after being a stand-in at a lighting check for an hour."

Maria sighed. "Let me tell you more about Kevin," she said. "I'm learning so much from him. He—"

"I'm learning a lot from Leona too," Elizabeth interrupted. "I really admire her. I've never met a woman who's so sure of herself. She knows exactly where she wants to go. And she'll do whatever it takes to get there."

"Sounds a little too single-minded to me," Maria cautioned. "I met a lot of people like that in

Hollywood. They act like your best friend as long as they think you can help them. But as soon as you turn around, they'll stab you in the back."

Elizabeth turned on her with an intensity that made Maria sit up straight. "You don't even *know* her!" she cried. "Leona's not like that. She genuinely wants to help young women just entering the field. She wants to help *me!*"

"Sorry," Maria said, surprised. "I didn't mean to diss Leona specifically. Some people really do want to help. Kevin, for example. He knows everything there is to know about backstage work. And I don't think I mentioned that he is unbelievably cute—"

"Cute isn't everything," Elizabeth said, interrupting her again. "Todd is cute. But today he was a real jerk. That bimbo had her hands all over him. Not only did he let her do it, but he *liked* it!"

"Have you heard even a single word I've said?" Maria asked, annoyed. "We've talked about nothing but *Flair* magazine for the last two days! Every time I try to tell you what I'm doing, you change the subject back."

"I'm sorry," Elizabeth apologized. "I guess I'm preoccupied. You were telling me about the set painter?"

"He's the set *designer*," Maria corrected. "Kevin's a university student, working at the theater for college credit. And I've been saving the best for last—he asked me out!" She smiled the dazzling smile that had sold millions of rolls of Softee toilet paper. But Elizabeth didn't notice; she was intent on picking at the hem of her shorts. "It's only lunch," Maria continued, glaring pointedly at her friend. "But you've got to start somewhere."

"Quentin is supposed to know what he's talking about," Elizabeth said glumly. "And he says Todd has a future as a model. I just can't see it."

"Why not?" Maria asked, losing patience. She jumped up from the edge of the pool and sat in a folding chair nearby, crossing her arms in front of her. "That man of yours is just as good-looking as any of the actors I worked with in films. If he wants to try modeling, why shouldn't he?"

"But he's not a model!" Elizabeth argued. "He's just a normal guy. He always said models were brainless and conceited."

"So, he changed his mind."

"What if he changes his mind about me too?"

Maria rolled her eyes. "Liz, you're not making any sense. Todd loves you. So what if he likes it when a supermodel runs her hands all over him? What guy wouldn't? It's not like anything happened. They were in a roomful of people!"

"You're right," Elizabeth agreed quietly. "Nothing happened. But what if it does?"

"What if we have an earthquake tomorrow and

121

the whole state slides into the Pacific Ocean?" Maria countered. "You can't deal in what-ifs!"

Elizabeth sighed. "I know."

"Personally, I'm not thinking any further ahead than my lunch with Kevin tomorrow. We're going to an artsy little bistro a block down from the theater." Maria clenched her jaw when she noticed that Elizabeth's eyes had a faraway look again. "After a lunch of snake gizzards and poison toadstools," she continued, "I thought we'd hijack the space shuttle and fly to Jupiter for dessert."

"That's nice," Elizabeth murmured. "The scary thing is that deep down, I'm afraid Todd is seriously attracted to Simone. She's drop-dead gorgeous, and she's famous—"

"That's it!" Maria yelled, jumping to her feet. "I am so *fed up* with your attitude. You know, Liz," she scolded, shaking her finger, "if you weren't so caught up in yourself lately, maybe Todd wouldn't be enjoying another girl's attention so much!"

"What do you know about it?" Elizabeth screamed back, tears of frustration in her eyes. "You don't understand the pressures of the *real* world. Interning at a rinky-dink community theater isn't like working somewhere *important*, like *Flair!*"

Maria slitted her eyes. "Important?" she asked in a low, controlled voice. "You've lost all sense of what's *really* important." She spun on her heel and stomped away.

"Quentin is crazy if he thinks he can make Todd into a model," Elizabeth muttered on Wednesday morning as she merged the Jeep into a rush-hour traffic jam on the Santa Monica Freeway. "Todd doesn't know the first thing about modeling."

"I'll say!" Jessica agreed. "He looked like a total dweeb, posing with Silicone Simone yesterday. How am I ever going to get Quentin to notice me if he's too busy trying to put Todd's boring face all over the newsstands?"

"Boring?" Elizabeth protested, a twinge of loyalty rising in her chest. "This *is* my boyfriend we're talking about."

Jessica rolled her eyes. "So? You said you're mad at him. I thought we were in agreement here."

"We are, I guess." Elizabeth relented. "But we're the only ones who are. Even before he lost his mind over Simone and this modeling idea, Todd was a pain in the neck. He doesn't understand the kind of pressure I'm under, trying to make a good impression on Leona."

"Lila is clueless about working in the real world too," Jessica complained. She leaned over to honk the horn at a slow truck driver in front of the Jeep, but Elizabeth pushed her hand away. "Lila doesn't see why it's so important for me to get on Quentin's good side," Jessica concluded.

"Maria came over yesterday afternoon, and she was no help at all," Elizabeth added. "You're the only person around who has any idea what it's like in the real world."

"Enid's at a real literary agency," Jessica said. "It's part of the real publishing world—even if it is a boring part. Didn't she call last night for one of those long, dull gab sessions that put me to sleep when I listen in on the extension?"

"Jessica!" Elizabeth protested.

"I didn't listen last night!" Jessica assured her.

"There was nothing to listen to," Elizabeth said with a sigh. "I thought Enid might understand what we're up against at *Flair*."

"Does she?" Jessica asked.

"She called to tell me about some dumb manuscript, but she knows nothing about deadline pressure," Elizabeth replied. "I could tell she was ticked off when I said I couldn't talk. Maybe I was rude to her, but I had *Flair*'s 'Fashion Flops' section to proofread. I didn't have time for trivial conversations."

"Lila knows nothing about *any* kind of pressure," Jessica said. "She really ought to help me make things right with Quentin. It's not like she can't afford it."

"Make what things right with Quentin?" Elizabeth asked, steering the Jeep into an open spot in the next lane.

"I sort of borrowed a camera from him," Jessica

explained. "And Lila sort of dropped it in the ocean."

Elizabeth's eyes grew larger. "You ruined his camera?"

"Sort of," Jessica admitted. "Look, Liz. My entire career hangs in the balance here. I have to replace Quentin's camera, or he'll never give me my big break!"

"If you don't replace it fast, he may break some bones," Elizabeth pointed out.

"Lend me the money," Jessica pleaded. "You've got a ton saved up for that new computer."

"Not anymore," Elizabeth said, gesturing toward her stylishly long blazer and short skirt.

"Rats." Jessica sighed. "I'm doomed."

"Lila's got more money than the Federal Reserve," Elizabeth reminded her. "And you said she was the one who wrecked the camera. Can't you get it from her?"

"Lila doesn't understand the seriousness of the situation," Jessica said huffily. "And she claims the camera was my responsibility. Some loyal friend!"

"I know what you mean," Elizabeth replied, nodding. "These internships are teaching me a lot about friendship and loyalty that I was in no hurry to learn."

"Me too," Jessica agreed. "It's been an eye-opening experience, that's for sure."

Chapter 9

Jessica knew she was in trouble before she even reached the photography studio Wednesday morning. From the hallway she could hear Quentin's voice. Long before she could make out his words, she could tell he was haranguing an employee.

She slipped inside the studio, willing herself to be invisible. Quentin's back was to her as he yelled at an assistant. "Photographic equipment doesn't walk away on its own!" he shouted at a cowering man nearly twice his age. "Somebody misplaced that camera or walked out of here with it. And I intend to find out who!"

Jessica cringed. She'd hoped it would take him a few days to realize that the camera was missing. She didn't even know how he could tell them all apart. Now other employees were skirting around the edges of the room, trying to do their jobs while keeping out of Quentin's path. Jessica decided that was an excellent idea. Certainly this would not be a good time to try to seduce Quentin into asking her out.

Simone was the only person in the room who didn't seem concerned about Quentin's tirade. She was languishing on the couch, chomping on her celery and sipping from a bottle of mineral water. Her expression held nothing but pure boredom; she didn't seem the least bit interested in Quentin's problem. *No doubt*, Jessica figured, *she knows she's above suspicion*.

"Has anyone seen those proofs of me in Lina Lapin's latest?" Simone drawled. "They should be up from the mail room by now."

Her expression darkened when nobody responded. Jessica could see that Simone hated it when anybody else was the center of attention. Jessica rolled her eyes. Surely even a supermodel could lift a telephone receiver to call the mail room without overburdening her skinny little body too much. *Maybe it's too complicated a task for her skinny little brain*, Jessica thought.

Quentin's eye fell on Shelly. The unhappy photography assistant who'd been bearing the brunt of his anger scampered away. "Shelly!" the head photographer shouted, storming across the room. The African American girl stood in her usual corner, setting up her makeup table. "Have you touched my Minolta? The big one, with the telephoto?"

"Sorry, Quentin," said the makeup assistant in a low voice, keeping her eyes on her jars and tubes. "I haven't seen it. I don't touch anything that doesn't remove with cold cream."

Quentin hardly listened to her answer but launched into an angry explanation of where he'd last seen the camera and demanding to know if Shelly had noticed anyone in that room.

Jessica was getting nervous. Sooner or later—probably sooner—Quentin would pounce on her. And even her well-practiced skill at concealing the truth might falter under his furious gaze.

"Isn't anybody going to see what's keeping the mail room from delivering those proofs?" Simone called out again in a louder voice.

Jessica jumped. She hated complying with one of Simone's prima donna requests. But it would be a good way to remove herself from Quentin's reach. *And I wouldn't mind seeing Cameron again,* she mused. *But only because he was fun to talk to. As a friend,* she reminded herself. She wasn't the least bit interested in any mail-room clerk as anything more than a friend.

"I'll go down there right now, Simone," she offered, keeping her voice low so as not to attract Quentin's attention.

"It's about time you started paying attention when I give an order," Simone said smugly. "Interns are supposed to be here so that the important people don't have to waste our time on trivia."

"Of course," Jessica said sweetly. "We wouldn't want to tax you with any real work." She slipped back toward the door before Simone could reply, taking care to keep out of Quentin's line of sight. On her way out she grabbed a photography catalog from a rack in the corner. She needed to know exactly how much the ruined camera was worth in case she found a way to get her hands on the money.

Jessica pressed every button in the elevator to drag out the trip for as long as possible. If Quentin was already busy with his morning meeting before she returned, then he wouldn't be able to question her about the camera until later. Besides, she could use the time to find the right camera in the catalog. If Simone questioned her about her lateness in returning, she could always exclaim truthfully, "I'm so sorry! I swear that elevator stopped on every single floor on the way down."

Once on the first floor Jessica walked as slowly as she could to the mail area. Then she scouted the cluttered main room, peering through doorways into some of the adjoining rooms. She didn't see Cameron anywhere. But she reminded herself sternly that it didn't matter. She wasn't interested in Cameron. He was probably delivering a package somewhere in the building.

"Oh, well," she said under her breath, "I'll just find Simone's proofs myself." From Monday afternoon she remembered where Cameron kept the newly arrived overnight packages. She searched through the pile until she came to a thick envelope marked Photographs, addressed to Quentin's department. She imagined dozens of copies of Simone's surgically enhanced pout inside and shuddered. But at least Simone's face was giving her a reason to stay away from the photo studio. Now all she needed was an excuse to stay away awhile longer—until she could be sure that Quentin was in his meeting.

Out of the corner of her eye she spotted a telephone behind the main counter. If she couldn't talk to a cute mail-room worker, she could at least call Lila and beg her, one last time, to lend her the money to replace Quentin's waterlogged camera.

Cameron hunched in front of a computer screen, tracking an overnight package that should have arrived at *Flair* first thing Wednesday morning and had not. The software was new, and it took all his concentration to figure out which keys to push. Out in the main part of the mail room somebody was shuffling around. Cameron gave a silent thanks for his secluded computer alcove, tucked behind some shelves and nearly invisible from most of the main room. If he stopped his search now, he would have to start all over again. Whoever was in the mail room could wait.

After a few minutes he had what he needed. The first two digits in the zip code had been transposed; the package had gone to Delaware instead of California. He punched in a few more commands to have the box rerouted. Then he stood up, stretched, and stepped around the cluttered shelves to see whoever was waiting for him.

A woman stood near the counter, cradling the telephone against her shoulder. Her back was turned to him, but Cameron knew of only one person with such beautiful golden hair.

"Lila, it's me," Jessica said into the receiver.

"*Yes*, I'm going to ask you about the camera again," she said after a pause.

"But you're my *best friend!*" she wailed. "Besides, *you* were the one who dropped Quentin's camera and ruined it."

"I know it wasn't *exactly* your fault—," Jessica began, but her friend obviously interrupted her. She twirled a lock of hair around one finger while she waited.

"OK, OK, it wasn't your fault at all," Jessica admitted finally. "I *know!* I'm the one who borrowed it without asking. How many times do you have to remind me of that?"

"Come on, Lila! I swear I'll pay you back, even if it takes the rest of my life!" she promised. "But it won't take that long. I'll have plenty of money soon."

"What do you mean, *how?*" Jessica responded a

moment later. "We must've gotten at least one good roll of photos last night, right? With you taking the pictures, I'm sure they'll be awesome. They'll be delivered here tomorrow, and then I'll put together a professional portfolio. I'll be rolling in modeling contracts in no time!"

"*Yes,*" she said with a loud sigh, answering a query from her friend. "I know about my rotten credit history. *Everyone* knows about my rotten credit history! But credit histories shouldn't matter between friends! Especially when it's such a teensy-weensy amount of money—to *you* anyway. You know you could afford to buy every one of Quentin's cameras and *still* have cash left over for film!"

As Lila replied, Jessica pulled a dog-eared booklet from her pocket.

"Yes, as a matter of fact I *do* know what it costs," Jessica replied, opening the booklet to a page with a turned-down corner. "I've got a sales catalog right here, with the exact model and price of the Minolta you—*we* ruined."

She paused, and Cameron knew from the slump of her shoulders that she didn't like her friend's response.

"Aw, Lila!" Jessica said, her voice rising. "When Quentin finds out it was me, he'll strangle me with a camera strap. And probably fire me. But if I can replace that camera today, he won't have to know."

"Yeah, *right*. Thanks a bunch." She dropped the

receiver back onto its hook and rested her head forlornly on her arms. "What am I supposed to do now?" she wailed. She looked so sad that Cameron wanted to run over and hold her. Before he could move, she straightened up and gave a loud, long sigh. Then she ripped the catalog in two and tossed it in the trash can.

Cameron ducked back behind the shelves and watched thoughtfully as Jessica trudged out of the room. She walked as if she were heading to a firing squad.

At noon that day Elizabeth studied the newsstand of a drugstore a block away from the Mode building. She had already read as many issues of *Flair* as she could get her hands on at the office. *Now*, she decided, *it's time to see what the competition's doing*. Maybe she could find out what worked well for other magazines and build on those ideas to help Leona make *Flair* even better. If she could come up with just one great suggestion, she was sure Leona would seriously consider hiring her for a summer job.

She reached for a copy of *Dazzle* and thumbed through it. The "Letters to the Editor" section was longer than Flair's, with more readers' responses to articles they'd seen in the magazine. But the photography throughout the magazine was weak, and the articles weren't as well written as the ones in *Flair*. Elizabeth could see why *Flair* had outpaced *Dazzle*'s sales so quickly.

Fashion Forward, she saw, was advertising its own interactive Web page. Readers could call it up on their computers, see footage from the most recent fashion shows, and vote on the clothes they liked best. *Flair* was already available on the Internet, but there was no forum for readers to register their own views.

Next she paged through a copy of *Bella*, one of the hottest-selling magazines in the business. She stopped at a page titled "Woman on the Street." Each month a reporter chose one question to ask a variety of ordinary women from all walks of life. This month, Elizabeth saw, the question was about hemlines and just how high they should be.

"Now that's not a bad idea," she said in a low voice. Then she looked up, embarrassed that she'd spoken out loud. A salesclerk glared at her from the counter. He wasn't near enough to have heard her words, but he was watching her with narrow eyes and obviously had been for some time.

"Pick a magazine and buy it!" the sour-faced man instructed. "I'm not running a lending library here."

Elizabeth smiled and nodded. "Sorry," she said. "I've almost decided."

In Elizabeth's opinion the length of a skirt wasn't a scintillating topic of discussion. And a one-line response wasn't enough space for exploring an issue and expressing a viewpoint. But she liked *Bella's* concept of asking the opinion of real people—not the usual models and designers whose faces were already all over the pages of the fashion press. How could she adapt that idea to use in *Flair*?

Suddenly Elizabeth remembered a discussion Mr. Collins had led with some of the staff of the *Oracle*, Sweet Valley High's student newspaper. Mr. Collins, her favorite teacher and the newspaper adviser, had told them about community journalism, a new trend in newspapers that got readers involved with their local newspaper and pushed the newspaper into a higher level of involvement with the community. Elizabeth hadn't been sure how she felt about a newspaper being involved in community events rather than remaining an objective observer. But she'd liked the part about getting more readers' viewpoints into the newspaper.

Now she realized that all the elements that had impressed her in the competing fashion magazines did just that. They gave the readers a forum for sharing opinions and hearing what other people— regular people, not experts or celebrities—were thinking. And an idea began to take shape in her mind.

"Could I get you a cappuccino and an easy chair so you can be comfortable while you read that?" asked the sarcastic salesclerk.

"Uh, sorry," Elizabeth apologized weakly, holding out the copy of *Bella*. "I'll take this one."

*   *   *

Todd stood at a bank of file cabinets in the executive suite of Varitronics. He opened a folder of expense reports from a recent trip several of the vice presidents had made to Singapore. "One copy to accounting; one to each VP's file," he chanted aloud, repeating the instructions he'd received from Meeks.

The first expense report was from Harriet Roy, the firm's vice president of manufacturing. "*R*," he said aloud, scanning the file cabinets for the correct drawer. "Where are the *Rs*?"

This is ridiculous, Todd reflected. How could any adult with half a brain put up with such a boring job? Even as a junior in high school he was overqualified for alphabetizing files. *Any seven-year-old could do this job*, he told himself. *A trained chimpanzee could do this job. Even Jessica and Lila could do this job!*

"I have to get out of here!" he said under his breath. Suddenly he understood what was behind the reports he'd heard about mild-mannered office workers in various parts of the country suffering breakdowns and showing up at work with machine guns. "Todd was such a quiet boy," he could imagine his friends and neighbors telling reporters. "He always seemed so normal."

If he didn't find a way to cut short this internship soon, they would have to drag him away from Varitronics in a straitjacket.

A phone rang—or rather *beeped*. Even the

telephones in this office were abnormal. From across the room he recognized the sound as the phone in his own cubicle. He dropped the file and sprinted toward the cubicle, remembering Meeks's rule that phones had to be answered in two rings. On the way there he stubbed his toe against the thin wall of a neighboring cubicle and stumbled, nearly hurling himself to the carpet. He caught himself just in time. As he hopped into his cubicle on his unhurt foot he grabbed the phone as it rang a third time. So much for Meeks's rules. Then he fell into the creaky office chair, holding his foot in one hand and the telephone receiver in another.

He ignored a giggle coming from the woman in the next cubicle.

"Hello!" he barked into the phone. "Um, I mean, Varitronics. May I help you?"

"This is Quentin Berg, calling for Mr. Todd Wilkins," said the voice of the photographer he'd met the day before.

"Yes, Mr. Berg!" Todd said, suddenly psyched. He forgot about the pain in his toe. "What can I do for you?"

"For starters, call me Quentin," answered the photographer. "After that, well, it looks like I've got a modeling job for you if you're interested."

Todd took a deep breath. He'd sweep sand into dunes for Quentin if it would get him out of Varitronics. As for posing with a gorgeous young woman in a bikini while a roomful of people told him how handsome he was—well, he thought he could handle that. "Yes, sir!" he replied eagerly. "I'm very interested."

"Good," Quentin said. "But the shoot's this afternoon. I'll need you at my studio right away so we can get your hair and makeup done. Can you make it?"

"I'm leaving now!" Todd answered with a grin.

He was already pulling off his tie when he called his father's voice mail a minute later.

"Sorry to break this to you, Dad," he said in response to the recorded message. "But I'm quitting my Varitronics internship. Another job has come up, and I'm sure I can sell the teachers on it back at school. There might be a real future in this. I'll tell you all about it tonight."

Elizabeth took a deep breath and marched up to Leona's door. She'd rushed back to the office from the newsstand and had spent the last half hour mapping out her new idea for *Flair*. Deep down, Elizabeth thought it was a wonderful suggestion. On the other hand, she was only a high-school student. What did she know about running a professional fashion magazine? What if her idea was stupid?

"What if Leona hates it?" she asked under her breath. *Well*, she decided, *there's only one way to find out*. She knocked on the door, and Leona told her to come in.

The managing editor gestured to a chair. "Sit down, Elizabeth," she said. "Would you like a cup of coffee?"

"No, thanks," Elizabeth said. She was jittery enough already. "I'm sorry to bother you. I can come back later if this isn't a good time—"

Leona smiled reassuringly. "Of course this is a good time. What can I do for you?"

"I . . . um . . . had an idea for the magazine," Elizabeth stammered. "And I wanted to run it by you."

"That's wonderful, Elizabeth," Leona said. "I meant it when I said I welcome suggestions. Tell me what's on your mind."

"I thought it would be great if we allowed one reader each month to write a column in *Flair*," she blurted. As she spoke she warmed to her subject and felt herself growing more confident and articulate. "We already show our audience how the models and clothing designers interpret style. But we don't have any way for women to see how other people—people just like them—view fashion. Each month a different reader would write about fashion and how it affects her life."

Leona had a thoughtful look on her face. "Do you have a name for this column?" she asked.

"My working title is 'Free Style,'" Elizabeth replied. "But of course, you could call it anything you want."

"Why do you think our readers and advertisers

would like to see something like this in *Flair*?" Leona probed.

"We're not as interactive as many other publications," Elizabeth explained. "This monthly column would be a forum for making readers feel more involved in the magazine. Yesterday I read in *Publishing Age* that readers are more likely to continue buying the magazine if they feel that they're a part of it. And that will help us hold on to advertisers."

"Have you thought about the costs of starting up a new column?" Leona asked. She sounded like Mr. Collins in English class, making sure his students had thought through their views. And like Mr. Collins, her voice was so nonjudgmental that Elizabeth couldn't tell if the editor liked her idea.

"The art director would have to come up with a design—a new look for 'Free Style,'" Elizabeth said. "But it would fit the same general format as the other columns, so the design wouldn't be a major outlay of time."

"And the manuscripts themselves?" Leona asked in that same tone of noncommittal questioning.

"I've been looking into what other magazines pay, and I believe we can get good-quality writing for much less than what professional fashion writers normally charge," Elizabeth said quickly. She held out the notes in her hand. "I've recommended some amounts if you'd like to see—"

"Later," Leona said with an encouraging smile. "Right now tell me more about the general idea. How would we ensure the quality of the writing?"

"Of course, the writers wouldn't be professionals," Elizabeth said. "The manuscripts might require a little more editing than usual. But if we restrict the column to one page in the magazine, that wouldn't take a lot of time."

"At least you've done your homework," Leona said diplomatically. "I'm proud of the way you anticipated my questions and had answers ready."

"But?" Elizabeth asked, sensing that the editor wasn't saying everything that was on her mind.

Leona took a deep breath. "I don't want to discourage your creativity, Elizabeth," she began. "But it's not really up to me. I'll run your idea by the editor in chief. But my instincts tell me that it isn't going to fly. The editor feels very strongly about maintaining the high quality of writing in *Flair*. It's one of the things that distinguishes us from our competitors."

Elizabeth felt as if she'd been kicked in the stomach. "Oh," she said in a small voice. Leona was too polite to say it was a rotten idea, but Elizabeth got the message. She concentrated very hard on not crying.

"May I have the notes on the research you've done?" Leona asked. "They might help when I meet with the editor. But don't get your hopes up, Elizabeth. And please feel free to come back with any other suggestions that occur to you."

Elizabeth trudged back to her office, staring at the floor. Leona had been as kind and encouraging as always. But she'd made it clear that Elizabeth's idea would never find its way into the pages of *Flair*. Elizabeth sank into her desk chair. "My first idea is a failure," she whispered, still fighting tears. A half hour earlier she'd been so excited about "Free Style." Now she felt utterly defeated. For the first time she seriously wondered if she had any real talent.

Her eyes fell on Todd's fax, still taped to the wall over her computer. "You've got too much talent to waste," he'd written, as if in answer to her unspoken question. "I hope your internship is everything you want it to be."

She wiped the tears from her eyes and resolved to keep trying. She still had seven days left in her internship. She would just have to try harder to come up with an idea that was truly exceptional.

In the meantime she was glad that she and Todd had a date planned for that night. The fax reminded her of how much she loved him. She knew she needed to get away from the office and relax a little. Even more than that, she needed to make things up to Todd. *Maria's right,* Elizabeth decided. *I have been too hard on him about the modeling.* And the tension between them now hung over her head like a storm cloud. Tonight was her chance to clear the air. She and Todd would spend a nice evening together and she would apologize for overreacting. He would give her one of his superdeluxe kisses. And then everything would be fine.

Chapter 10

Jessica checked the clock on the wall of the photography studio. It was nearly two o'clock. She'd managed to keep out of Quentin's way so far. Sooner or later he would realize she was the only person on his staff who hadn't been questioned about his missing camera. And when he finally did, she wasn't sure she could keep the truth from showing on her face.

She decided that her best strategy was to keep avoiding him. In the meantime she still hoped she'd come up with a lot of money—or a brilliant plan—before Quentin confronted her. The best way to avoid Quentin, she'd realized in the past two days, was to anticipate his every wish. The only time he seemed to notice her was when he needed her to do something.

Photo shoot this afternoon, she reminded

herself under her breath. *So what needs to be done?* Today's shoot would use the same set as yesterday, she remembered, but with Todd as a real model instead of a stand-in. Quentin had been so impressed with the pictures from Tuesday afternoon that he'd canceled his professional model for today. At the moment Todd was in Michael's salon, having his hair styled.

Suddenly Jessica knew what she could be working on to keep Quentin from having a reason to yell at her. The sandbox from yesterday was still set up. But Jessica's sand dunes seemed to have eroded slightly overnight. She knew the photographer would want them to be perfect. She sighed loudly and headed for the broom in the corner, trying to console herself with thoughts of what a wonderful "how-I-got-my-start" anecdote this would make when she was a supermodel being interviewed on a late-night talk show. They didn't help.

She picked up the broom and trudged to the sandbox to sweep the dunes back into shape.

"You're not planning to fly out of here on that thing, are you?" Simone asked, gesturing toward the broom.

Jessica cursed her luck. She hadn't noticed the model come in. "You made a joke, Simone," she replied. "That's very good. I guess you finally found two brain cells to rub together."

Jessica was sure that for just an instant, she saw

146

a hint of fury in Simone's cold eyes. *Score one for the Wakefield twin!* Jessica thought with glee. With Quentin out of sight, she couldn't think of a single reason to be nice to the Fashion Fink.

"Simone, I've been waiting for you!" Shelly called from the makeup room. "Quentin wants to start shooting in half an hour. You'd better hurry."

Simone's usual mask of disdain fell back over her face. The model didn't reply to either Jessica or Shelly. She cast a cold, superior glance in Jessica's direction. Then she turned and sauntered to the makeup artist, hips leading the way. Jessica realized that she'd just made a serious enemy of Simone. But she really didn't care. Quentin would probably murder her within the next half hour. Or at least fire her. Either way, she wouldn't have to worry about the wrath of the supermodel.

"The Wrath of the Supermodel," she said under her breath, repeating the thought as she stepped gingerly into the sandbox and began brushing sand toward her drooping dunes. "That's a great name for a horror movie." Simone would be the supermodel returned from the dead, sentenced to saunter through eternity, casting cold-eyed pouts on innocent young teens. They would run in terror, screaming into the night—

"Jessica!" called Quentin's voice behind her.

Jessica jumped, her feet sliding in the sand.

"I'm fixing up these sand dunes right now, Quentin," she responded, pretending to be intent on her work. She crossed her fingers on the broom handle, praying that he wouldn't have time before the shoot to ask her about his Minolta. "These dunes will be absolutely perfect before you're ready to begin," she assured him.

From behind her Quentin placed a hand on Jessica's shoulder. She nearly jumped out of the sandbox. There was no telling what he might do to her if he'd discovered she took his missing camera.

"Don't worry about the sand dunes," Quentin said. Jessica froze. His voice sounded almost . . . *nice.* "You did such a terrific job on them yesterday that they still look fine," he continued. She whirled, expecting to see a Quentin clone or another staff member yelling, "April fool!" But the real Quentin Berg was standing there. And around his neck hung the fancy Minolta camera she'd borrowed the night before. The camera she'd ruined. Except that it looked perfect. In fact, it looked new. Her eyes widened.

"Your camera—," she began, pointing to it.

"I wanted to thank you for what you did with it, Jessica," Quentin said, a grin lighting his face as he stroked the camera. Even in her current state of shock Jessica noticed that he was even cuter when he smiled. She couldn't remember seeing him smile before. She'd never noticed his eyes before either. They were a deep, mysterious gray. "I somehow missed you when I asked everyone about the camera this morning," he continued. "If I'd talked to you, I could have saved myself a lot of frustration."

Jessica was beginning to wonder if she'd dreamed the whole incident with Lila at the beach. Now she had a terrible urge to hum the theme song from *The Twilight Zone*.

"But that's all right," Quentin said. "I found the camera on the desk where you left it, and I got your note about how you saw that it needed a thorough cleaning and overhaul." He held up the camera. "You did a terrific job on this! If I didn't know better, I'd swear it was a brand-new camera."

"I . . . uh . . . knew how meticulous you are about your equipment," Jessica said weakly, her mind racing for an explanation. Maybe her fantasy about the undead wasn't far off. But even in zombie form Simone wouldn't lift a finger to solve a problem for Jessica. Maybe the camera was still ruined, and what she was experiencing now was a hallucination.

"I have never had an intern who was astute enough to notice that my equipment needed work and to take the initiative like this," Quentin said, gesturing with the note she had supposedly written him. "If you'd asked me, I would have told you not to touch my cameras. But you really knew what you were doing! This is in perfect working condition."

Suddenly Jessica had visions of being asked to take apart and clean every one of Quentin's cameras. "Actually I didn't do the work myself," she admitted. Suddenly a vague theory began forming in her mind about the source of the new camera. "I . . . uh . . . asked a friend who knows about things like that."

"Well, your friend did a really professional job!" Quentin exclaimed. "And now I see that you've been doing one too. I'm afraid I've been remiss in not taking more interest in your work here."

"Quentin!" Shelly called from a doorway. "Do you want anything special on Simone's eye makeup?"

"Gotta go, Jessica," Quentin said with a wink. Then he turned and practically skipped off to the makeup room.

Jessica stared after him, flabbergasted. After a moment she realized her mouth was hanging open. She snapped it shut, glad that nobody had noticed. Then she saw something on the floor and stooped to pick it up. It was the note she had supposedly left for Quentin when she returned his camera. It was signed with her name, but she'd never seen the note before.

Todd stood in the sand, feeling awkward. He was wearing a pair of black-and-red Bartucci swim trunks that luckily were less revealing than the bathing suit Simone had modeled the day before. At the moment Simone was nowhere in sight. Quentin was loading film into a camera, his assistants were adjusting lights, and Jessica was helping Shelly set out makeup on a table for touch-ups. Todd was the only person in the room with nothing to do. And he was the only one wearing nothing but a bathing suit.

Screens had been set up in two corners for costume changes. Suddenly Simone stepped out from behind hers. And without meaning to, Todd whistled.

Simone's eyes were outlined in something dark and sultry looking. Her full, sensuous lips were the same shade of red as her bathing suit. And her hair swung enchantingly around her bare white shoulders. But Todd was having trouble keeping his eyes on her face. The tall, slender model looked incredible in a bright red one-piece bathing suit that had huge geometric shapes cut out of it, as if someone at the clothing factory had gone crazy with a pair of scissors. He didn't know how practical it would be for swimming. But he sure didn't mind the extra glimpses it allowed of Simone's flawless ivory skin.

The makeup on his own skin felt odd, as if he were wearing a mask over his face. But Shelly had assured him it would look perfectly natural under the bright lights. *And she must be right,* he decided. Since he'd stepped out from behind his own dressing screen, so many people had complimented Todd on his appearance that he realized he must be better looking than he'd thought.

These people worked with professional models every day. If they said he had great hair, a great face, and a great body—well, who was he to argue? Of course, Elizabeth had always said those things. But she was his girlfriend. She had to say nice things about him. He wondered how he'd managed to go all these years without knowing he was a very handsome guy.

"Jessica, there's no bathrobe in there for me to wear between takes!" Simone barked.

Jessica rolled her eyes. "I'll get one from the wardrobe room," she said in a controlled voice. She scurried off.

The model's features and voice smoothed into silk as she sauntered toward Todd. She stepped onto the sand and linked her arm around his. "Hi, good-looking," she greeted him. He'd never been so close to a woman who was nearly as tall as he was. It was strangely exciting to see her eyes so close to his and to feel her breath on his cheek. "Are you ready to play in the sandbox with me?" she purred into his ear. "Later we can see what develops in the darkroom."

Todd gulped. This had to be a dream.

And he was in no hurry to wake up.

*   *   *

"Can you believe the way he's acting?" Jessica whispered to Shelly as they watched Todd and Simone cavort in the sand in front of Quentin's camera. "I've never seen him so gaga over anyone—not even my sister!"

"He's not the only one," Shelly whispered back. "I've never seen the Silicone Queen hang all over a male model like that."

"Great chemistry, you two!" Quentin called out to his models as he dropped to one knee to shoot from a lower angle. "Keep it coming!"

"Jessica," Simone called from the set, "you picked out the wrong sunglasses. Run to the wardrobe room and get me another pair! These don't fit; they pinch my ears."

"Sorry about that, Simone," Jessica replied. "I guess your head is even bigger than I thought."

Simone glared.

"Good emotion, Simone!" Quentin called. "It's real. It's intense. Lots of energy!"

"I'd like to give her some good emotions," Jessica whispered to Shelly as she headed for the wardrobe room to find another pair of sunglasses. Shelly covered her mouth to hide a giggle.

"I haven't seen Quentin in such a good mood since he got our last art director fired," Shelly confided after Jessica returned with a different pair of sunglasses. "You should steal his camera every day." Jessica had filled Shelly in on the incident, including the mysterious appearance of what

153

seemed to be a brand-new camera to replace the ruined one.

"No, thanks!" Jessica whispered back. "I've learned my lesson this time. I'm never taking anything without permission again for as long as I live . . . or at least until a very good reason comes along."

"You said you had a theory about the mysterious replacement camera," Shelly said. "Did you recognize the handwriting on the note?"

"No, it was block-printed," Jessica replied. "But I think I know who must have done it. The note is on really heavy, textured stationery. The classy, expensive kind. I know only one person who can afford stuff like that."

"Your friend Lila?" Shelly whispered.

Jessica shrugged. "It's *got* to be Lila," she said. "She must have taken pity on me at the last minute and bought a new camera just like the old one. Or she's planning to charge me outrageous interest on the loan—once I'm a rich, famous model."

"I thought she absolutely refused to lend you the money."

"She did," Jessica admitted. "But you have to understand Lila. She hates it when people think she's a pushover. She's afraid they'll ask her for money all the time if they hear she's a soft touch."

"So she did it in secret to save her reputation for being selfish and unbending?" Shelly asked, eyebrows raised in a skeptical frown.

"Exactly," Jessica agreed.

"Isn't that a little weird?"

"Like I said, you have to understand Lila."

"Jessica, if you're finished socializing over there, I want to try this with sandals on," Simone interrupted from beneath the lights. "There's a scarlet pair of Bartuccis in the wardrobe room, with high heels."

"Nobody wears high-heeled sandals with a bathing suit!" Jessica protested.

"That shows how much you know about fashion," Simone said, tilting up her nose. "Get me those sandals. *Now!*"

After shifting her position so that Shelly's back hid her from Simone, Jessica stuck out her tongue at the model.

"While Jessica gets those sandals, Shelly, give Todd a touch-up. I'm getting some shine on his face."

"Probably from Simone rubbing up against him," Jessica whispered to Shelly as she walked by on her way to the wardrobe room. She refused to run this time. She wasn't going to act as if chasing down Simone's every whim was important to her. Once inside the cluttered room she rooted around until she found a pair of red Bartucci sandals. Then she sauntered back to Simone and deposited them at her feet.

"I said *scarlet!*" Simone complained. "Those are *crimson*. Can't you do anything right?"

"Well, sor-*ry,*" Jessica told Simone. Quentin was out of the room, looking for a different lens. So Jessica allowed just the right amount of cold condescension to creep into her voice and expression. *Perfect,* she thought. *Lila would be proud of me.* For an instant Simone had looked genuinely flustered.

"The scarlet sandals are behind your dressing screen," an assistant art director told Simone. From the expression on Simone's face Jessica realized the model had known it all the time. Simone fixed a bored, expectant gaze on Jessica's face. Jessica sighed and sauntered to the corner to get the scarlet sandals.

"You're going to put them on for me, aren't you?" Simone asked when Jessica dropped them at her feet.

"Oh, I forgot," Jessica said. "You haven't learned buckles yet. That's one of those advanced motor skills."

Simone began sputtering like a broken fountain. Before she could formulate a reply, Jessica felt a tug on her shoulder and whirled to see Todd standing there, his face full of dismay. "Can I talk to you a minute, Jess?" he asked, pulling her aside. Jessica was glad to leave Simone's company.

She had to admit that she'd never seen Todd looking better. His bronze shoulders, muscular arms, and lean, basketball player's build were set off to perfection by the designer swim trunks. And Michael had used a huge handful of mousse to make his hair look windblown and natural. *Too bad he's still the same old clueless Todd,* she thought.

"If you're going to start giving me orders too now that you're a hotshot fashion model," Jessica threatened, "I will personally tell Simone about the time in sixth grade when you cooked a southern meal for social studies and put in too much hot sauce and used salt instead of sugar and the whole class got sick!"

"I swear I won't give you any orders!" Todd said quickly. "But why are you being so mean to Simone?"

"In case you haven't noticed, she's the one who's treating me like dirt," Jessica pointed out.

"You're an intern. It's your job to run and get things for her."

"Jessica Wakefield is *nobody's* slave!" Jessica declared, arms folded across her chest. "But I bet you'd jump if the Fashion Witch gave *you* an order. It's really disgusting, the way you two are hanging all over each other. In case you've forgotten, you have a girlfriend!"

"Simone and I are not hanging all over each other!" Todd insisted. "It's called modeling, Jessica. I wouldn't expect you to understand, since you're only a photographer's assistant."

"What about Elizabeth? Remember her? Do you think my sister would understand?"

Todd bit his lip. "You're not going to tell her some exaggerated version of what's going on here, are you?"

"*Exaggerated?*" Jessica asked. "Why would I have to exaggerate? You're wearing a bathing suit and playing contact sports in the sand with a half-naked supermodel. In front of a roomful of witnesses! I couldn't *invent* anything better than this."

"All right, people!" Quentin called, striding back into the room. "Places, everyone! Simone and Todd, I'll want a few more shots in these suits. Then get into your second change of clothes."

Todd stepped off the set a while later so that Shelly could touch up his makeup. But he couldn't keep his eyes off Simone, posing again in the skimpy white bikini from the day before. He'd always thought he was attracted to wholesome, all-American types, like Elizabeth. But one look at Simone made his temperature shoot up, even without the bright lights.

"It's past three-thirty, but we've got several hours of work to finish here tonight," Quentin said when he stopped to switch cameras. "Can everyone stay late?"

The staff agreed immediately—even Jessica, though she rolled her eyes at Shelly as she told Quentin yes. Todd hesitated. He and Elizabeth had a date to go to Guido's after work. Jessica glared at him expectantly, but Todd avoided looking at her.

"Todd, is that OK with you?" Quentin asked. "Is there a problem?"

For a moment Todd wondered if it *would* be a problem. When he'd called Elizabeth to tell her he'd quit Varitronics and was on his way to the studio, she had seemed surprised but no longer angry. He thought she'd adjusted to the idea of him becoming a model. But she'd also said she was looking forward to their date.

"There's no problem, Quentin," Todd said. "I . . . uh . . . had some plans. But it's nothing I can't cancel."

Jessica cast him one of those witheringly cold stares she must have learned from Lila. But Todd told himself that Elizabeth would understand his decision. Elizabeth was the one who'd lectured him on the importance of making a good impression in an internship. She'd been talking all week about making sacrifices in order to build a career. Now he knew she'd been right all along.

"The brim on this hat is too wide," Simone complained during the next break from shooting. She snatched a white canvas hat from her head and threw it in Jessica's face. "Get me the other white one."

"*Flair*'s fashion experts say wide brims are chic," Jessica objected. "Besides, this is a Bartucci design. Isn't that what we're supposed to be show-casing?"

"It's casting shadows on my face," Simone explained, pronouncing every syllable distinctly, as if she were speaking to a five-year-old. "Nobody can see what I look like."

"So?" Jessica whispered. "You wouldn't want the plastic surgery scars to show, would you?" She pitched her voice loud enough for Simone to hear but too low to reach Quentin's ears. Luckily he was far across the room.

Jessica heard gasps from both Shelly and Todd when they realized what she'd said. But she kept her eyes on Simone, challenging the tall, skinny girl to respond. The stony look on the model's face made Jessica wonder if this time she'd gone too far. She dismissed the thought almost immediately. The fashion business was no place for wimps. Besides, a thrill raced through her entire body every time she saw the Toothpick at a loss for words, as she was now.

Jessica smiled sweetly. "I'll go find you that other hat," she promised.

Jessica saw the hat in the wardrobe room almost immediately. But she decided Simone could wait while she tried on a few others in front of the mirror, practicing for her own career as a model. She was sure she'd be more successful than Simone. She had more sex appeal than Simone, easily. The only thing she didn't have was Simone's height, but she knew she could overcome a tiny little obstacle like that.

"Now that Quentin doesn't hate me," she whispered to her reflection as she tied a scarf loosely around her neck, "I'll convince him to fall in love with me in no time. And my professional-looking photos are due here tomorrow." She tossed the ends of the scarf over her shoulder. "After that the sky's the limit!"

"Jessica!" called Simone's voice, managing to sound bored and exasperated at the same time. "Where is my hat?"

"I see it!" Jessica called back, hastily untying the scarf. "There's so much stuff in here, it's hard to find anything."

She tossed the hat on her head and sauntered out of the wardrobe room, hips first, in a close impersonation of Simone's sultry walk. Simone was standing near Shelly's makeup table while Quentin and Michael fussed with Todd's hair on the other side of the set. Jessica approached the tall, leggy girl and was about to whip off the hat and hand it to her.

Suddenly the tile floor slammed up to meet her. Quentin, Michael, and Todd spun around just in time to see her sprawl forward on her stomach, desperately trying to break her fall with her hands. She was sure she heard laughter coming from that side of the room.

Jessica was the only one who noticed the

movement of Simone's long, skinny foot as the model wrenched it out of the way. The Toothpick had *tripped* her!

Jessica ignored the crushing pain in her chest. She rose from the floor with all the dignity she could muster, her eyes fixed on Simone's face. *This is war,* she promised the model silently. *And Jessica Wakefield always wins.*

Chapter 11

Wednesday afternoon Elizabeth waited for the elevator on the eighth floor. She'd just come from the advertising department, where she'd been running an errand for Leona. Normally she would be thrilled to handle any detail for the managing editor. Now she just wanted the day to be over. But her watch said it was only four o'clock.

The rational part of her brain told her not to be discouraged about one rejected idea. Writers had to learn to live with rejection. But her creative mind could still visualize her "Free Style" column as a page in the magazine, with a trendy logo and a snapshot of the reader who'd submitted that month's manuscript. She could see it so clearly. Why couldn't Leona?

She stepped into the elevator and reached up to press the button for the editorial offices. On the spur of the moment she decided to visit the photo studio instead. Todd was there, working on his first real shoot. Maybe seeing him and thinking about their date that night would cheer her up. She needed something to dispel the feeling of impending doom that seemed to have settled in around her, making the elevator seem much smaller than usual.

"I have to get a grip on myself!" She said it aloud, without meaning to, and was grateful to be alone in the elevator. One failed idea didn't translate into a doomed career. It didn't mean she had no talent and would never be successful. Leona certainly hadn't treated her any differently since rejecting her idea.

She pushed open the door of the studio and was immediately sorry she'd stopped by. Todd was lying on a beach chair on the same sand-covered set Quentin had posed him on last time. But now he was wearing a swimsuit—a tight, tiny, green one that in Elizabeth's mind gave new meaning to the word *brief*. Elizabeth recognized it as an Italian design. But if one of their friends had shown up on the beach in something like that, Todd would have been the first one to make fun of it. She had to admit that he looked terrific—in an obvious sort of way. But it made her uncomfortable to see her boyfriend in such a skimpy bathing suit. And she was surprised that Todd seemed so much at ease.

Maybe I don't know Todd as well as I thought I did, she mused, hoping her face wasn't as pink as it felt.

Even worse was Simone. She was standing by Todd's beach chair, leaning over him so that her swimsuit top was practically in his face. She wore a yellow polka-dotted bikini that was nearly as skimpy as the white macramé one she'd worn the day before. And Todd was watching her so closely that he didn't even look up when Elizabeth walked into the room.

"Great, kids!" Quentin called. He sounded much happier than he had the day before. "Now I want you both standing. . . . Jess, would you move the beach chair out of the way?" Jessica complied, with a smile for Quentin and an icy gaze for Simone and Todd. "Todd, you face me, straight on," Quentin instructed. "And Simone, I want you in profile. Put your hands on Todd's shoulder and lean in to give him a kiss on the cheek, kicking up one leg behind you. . . . Perfect!"

"How about one with me kissing him on the lips?" Simone asked. "Just like this . . ." She demonstrated, and Quentin obligingly kept clicking off shots while Elizabeth felt a volcano of fury rising inside her, threatening to explode.

"Fantastic!" Quentin shouted. "Let's break now. Shelly, I think Simone's face needs a little work."

Elizabeth almost offered to work it over for her, but she fought the urge. "Todd, can I talk to

165

you a minute?" she asked, forcing herself to stride purposefully across the room, as if to stake her claim.

"Hi, Liz!" Todd called, seeing her there for the first time. Suddenly his face colored. "Uh, um, let me get a robe." He ducked behind a screen in the corner and came out tying a terry-cloth robe around his waist. Elizabeth was sure she saw a triumphant little smile playing around the corners of Simone's usually sulky mouth.

Elizabeth leaned toward Todd for her usual peck on the lips, but he didn't seem to notice. "Elizabeth, you wouldn't believe what a great time I'm having," he said. Elizabeth tried to steer him out of Simone's earshot, but he didn't take the hint. "I mean, modeling is a lot of work too. But Quentin says I'm a natural."

Elizabeth had been hoping Todd would hate his first afternoon as a real model. She swallowed her disappointment and gave him a weak smile. "That's great, Todd. I'm glad you found something more fun than filing and photocopying."

"There is *no* comparison!" Todd raved. "I think I might have just found myself a whole new career!"

Elizabeth's now familiar sensation of impending doom pressed down harder from all sides. "But Todd," she began carefully, "the internships end a week from Friday. After that it's back to school as usual."

"I've been thinking about that," Todd said. "And if Quentin's right and I really have a future as a model, then there's no use waiting. You've been telling me all week about making sacrifices and taking risks in order to jump-start a career. I've decided that you're right."

"What are you saying?" Elizabeth asked, her eyes growing wide.

"If Quentin thinks I can make a go of it, I just might find myself an agency and start modeling right now. I'm sure I can fit in school around the edges somewhere. Simone said she could give me some tips on that. And college can wait a few years."

"Are you *crazy?*" she asked, her voice rising. She tried not to think about when he might have had time to talk with Simone about careers and education. "Your parents will never go for that!"

"I think they might, as long as I can get my high-school diploma on time," Todd countered. He glanced around at Jessica, Shelly, and Simone, who were all pretending to go about their own business while they listened to every word. "But we can talk about this later, Liz."

Elizabeth nodded, shaken. "We really do need to talk," she said. "I can't tell you how much I'm looking forward to our date tonight—"

"About that date," Todd began. "Can I get a rain check? Quentin needs me to stay late to finish this shoot."

"You're canceling our date?" Elizabeth asked in a small, desolate voice. She was terrified she would burst into tears in front of everyone. Again a smug smile tilted the corners of Simone's bloodred lips.

"You know how it is," Todd said with the dazzling grin he always used when he wanted something. "When the boss asks you to stay late, you've got to make a good impression. If I don't show that I'm willing to go the extra mile, Quentin might decide I'm not dedicated enough to want to help me get started." Suddenly his face was dead serious. "It's kind of like what you were saying about Leona the other night."

Leona didn't lure me into her office with a half-naked member of the opposite sex, Elizabeth wanted to point out. *When I'm working late, I don't have a gorgeous model kissing me.* But she wasn't about to let Simone see that she was angry at Todd—and terrified of losing him to her. "Of course," Elizabeth said in a controlled voice. "I wouldn't want to stand in your way."

She spun around and stomped out of the room. Jessica caught up with her near the elevators.

"Liz, I'm really sorry about that man-eating toothpick," Jessica said. "I promise you, I'm going to find a way to put her in her place before I'm through here."

"I hope you do," Elizabeth seethed, clenching

her hands into fists. "Did you hear the way she suggested kissing him on the lips? She knew exactly what she was doing. And she knew exactly who was watching her do it."

"Look, I've got to stay late tonight too," Jessica said. "If you're not riding with Todd, how will we both get home? Are you working late?"

"No, I'm leaving just as soon as I can," Elizabeth replied.

"You're not going home to mope in your room because you don't have a date, are you?" Jessica asked.

"No!" Elizabeth answered hotly. "I'm going home to mope in my room because Leona didn't like my brilliant idea today, and because Todd wants to destroy his life to become a model, and because you-know-who is a total witch!" She took a deep breath. "And because I don't have a date."

Jessica shook her head. "You're going about this all wrong," she said. "If a guy is treating you rotten, the best defense is a strong offense. Find somebody else to go out with here in the big city. Have a blast without Todd."

"You're absolutely right!" Elizabeth exclaimed. Suddenly she knew just what she would do with her evening.

Jessica's mouth dropped open. "I am?" she asked.

"I *refuse* to go home and feel sorry for myself,"

Elizabeth said. "I'm going right upstairs to call Enid and Maria."

"That's not precisely what I had in mind," Jessica said.

"I know, but I've been a jerk to both of them this week. This is my chance to make it up to them," Elizabeth explained. "I'll ask them to meet me here in the city. We'll go out somewhere nearby, and then I can swing back around in the Jeep and pick you up after your shoot. When will you be finished? Is eight o'clock late enough?"

"This is it!" Maria exclaimed to Enid as the two girls reached the entrance of the Mode building that evening.

"Finally!" Enid said. "After two buses and three traffic jams to get here, Liz owes us some spectacular cappuccinos. No, *double* cappuccinos. This outing would've been a lot easier if one of us had access to a car today."

"You know it, girl," Maria agreed. "If it were for anyone but Liz . . ."

"I am really glad she called tonight," Enid said. "She's been so preoccupied this week. The three of us will have a nice long chat, and we'll all feel a lot better. Besides, it feels so elegant and sophisticated, meeting in the city for coffee. Though I guess it's the kind of thing you're used to, being a former movie star."

Maria laughed as she pushed the button outside the gleaming elevator doors. "I was just a kid. I was more into cookies than cappuccino," she said. She licked her lips. "*Mmmm,* cookies. Do you think the coffee bar Liz has in mind will sell cookies too?"

"If I know Liz, the place will be flowing with chocolate chips," Enid replied.

"And she's offered to drive us home afterward in the Twinmobile," Maria said.

Enid laughed. "Thank goodness for that Jeep!" she agreed. "I couldn't face two bus rides back to Sweet Valley tonight."

The elevator opened. The girls stepped inside into the midst of a group of blatantly fashionable women. They wore stylishly long blazers and stylishly short skirts in various colors and fabrics. And almost every one of them had some variation on Elizabeth's new haircut. *It's exactly like a uniform,* Maria decided. Like everyone else, she stood facing the mirrored doors. The women stood behind her, but Maria could watch them in the mirror. And their identical, condescending expressions made them seem like clones.

"Oops, we're going to the parking garage!" Maria sang out as she felt the elevator moving downward. "We must have zoned out. We should have checked to see if the arrow was pointing up."

The women studiously avoided glancing at her and Enid, but Maria felt a wave of disapproval. Apparently talking glibly in an elevator filled with stylish snobs was a *Flair* faux pas. Maria grinned mischievously at Enid. Enid looked embarrassed.

The elevator stopped at the parking garage, and the women glided out. *Like identical suitcases on a conveyor belt,* Maria thought. As soon as the doors closed again the girls glanced at each other, and both burst into giggles.

"Send in the clones!" Maria sang.

"Did you see the one with the maroon hair?" Enid asked when she stopped laughing. "Nobody's hair is naturally that color."

"She acted like we weren't even there," Maria replied. "So did all her stuck-up friends. I bet they were holding their breath so they wouldn't breathe air that was contaminated by us, the Great Unfashionables."

"You're not unfashionable!" Enid protested. She tugged playfully on Maria's antique lace vest. "That vintage look is terrific on you. I wish I was tall enough to wear it without feeling like a kid playing dress-up."

"But you have a real sense of style," Maria argued. "I adore that scarf, by the way. At least you look professional, coming straight from work at the literary agency."

"*Professional,* maybe," Enid said. "*Stylish,* no. I

can see why Liz was afraid of looking frumpy."

"Me too," Maria agreed. "But I still think she went overboard on the new clothes."

The elevator stopped on the eleventh floor, and the girls followed Elizabeth's directions to her office. As they rounded the corner Elizabeth herself was standing in the hallway.

"Hi, guys!" Elizabeth exclaimed. Her forehead was creased, and her eyes were tired. But she seemed genuinely happy to see them. "We can get going right away. Come see my office, and I'll grab my purse."

As the girls walked back toward the elevator a few minutes later a tall woman in her late twenties hurried out of an office. "Elizabeth!" she called. "I know it's time for you to get out of here, but I was hoping you wouldn't mind staying a couple hours late. I have some ideas for upcoming articles I wanted to bounce off you."

"Leona, there's a call for you on line three!" said a receptionist who sat nearby.

"Excuse me a minute, Elizabeth," Leona said, already rushing back to her office. "This won't take long."

"So that's the famous Leona," Maria said.

"Isn't she impressive?" Elizabeth asked, pulling them into a quiet corner. "I'm sorry about tonight, you two, but—"

"What?" Enid asked. "You can't mean you're staying with her!"

173

Elizabeth seemed surprised. "I was looking forward to our evening too! But you heard Leona. She needs me here."

"Tell her you've got plans," Maria suggested. "What's the big deal?"

"I guess she would understand," Elizabeth said. "But I need to show her I'm a loyal, dedicated employee."

"You're an intern," Enid reminded her. "You don't even get *paid* for this. Besides, we both left work early and sat on two gross, smelly buses—just to spend the evening with you! What about loyalty and dedication to your friends?"

"I'm sorry," Elizabeth replied. "But I can't afford to miss this opportunity. I promise I'll make it up to you sometime soon."

"Elizabeth, I'm ready for you now!" came Leona's voice from her office.

Elizabeth shrugged and scurried to the door. After she closed it behind her, Maria turned to Enid with a sigh. "So that's life in the real world," she said sarcastically. "Looks like it's just you and me for double cappuccino."

"And a double bus ride home," Enid added. "I can't believe she stood us up."

"I hope Liz is scoring big points as a worker bee this week," Maria said as they trudged back to the elevator. "Because she sure isn't scoring any as a friend."

•   •   •

That night Jessica waited in the wardrobe room, drinking one of Simone's bottled mineral waters and pretending to be busy. Supposedly she was organizing the Bartucci swimwear and accessories that Simone and Todd had used in the shoot. But what she was really doing was waiting for Simone and Todd to leave. She could hear the two of them in the studio, talking and laughing as they pulled on their shoes and collected their things. Todd apparently had overcome his initial awkwardness around the leggy model. She could hear him out there, dropping casual mentions of his BMW and parties at the country club.

Jessica rolled her eyes. Guys were disgusting. They'd do or say anything to impress a pretty girl.

She was glad when she heard their voices trail off as they walked out of the studio. To give them time to get out of the building, she stopped to check her appearance in the mirror, brushed her hair, and freshened her lipstick. Then she took a deep breath and sauntered to the darkroom, where Quentin was making some prints.

She opened the outer door of the darkroom and stepped into the closetlike space. The small entryway ensured complete darkness in Quentin's sanctuary. Letting any light in would destroy the pictures he was developing, and Jessica couldn't afford to have him mad at her again. She closed the outer door behind her and waited a few seconds for her eyes to adjust to the dark.

Jessica gently opened the interior door and slid soundlessly into the darkroom. The air smelled strongly of chemicals. Cutting-edge rock music spilled from a radio in the corner, filling it with sound. A dim, red safelight enabled Quentin to work but protected the prints he was making. By its eerie glow Jessica could see him standing at a long table. His back was to her, and he faced a row of tubs filled with mysterious chemicals. As Jessica watched, Quentin used tongs to carefully lift a print from the last tub. He shook it gently, spraying drops of liquid on the table. Then he hung it on some sort of clothesline that was stretched over the table.

Jessica stepped up behind him and reached around his arm to flick off the dim red light. The room was in total blackness.

Before Quentin had time to react, she wrapped her arms around him and brushed his lips with hers. "I thought you'd left," he murmured. He pulled her closer and began to kiss her, first tentatively and then with passion. Suddenly he pulled away. "You're not Simone!" he whispered, startled. Jessica leaned against his strong, broad chest and shook her head just enough for him to feel it. Then she raised her face to his once more in the dark. And he kissed her again.

Well, he's not the best kisser in the world, Jessica decided. But he wasn't bad either. In fact, she was beginning to feel herself swept away by a familiar rush of emotion. But she pulled her mind back to her goal. She had a plan to follow. And it depended on leaving Quentin wanting more. The next day she would show him the pictures Lila had taken of her on the beach. She wanted Quentin primed to give them—and her—a good, long look.

Without a word she pulled away from Quentin and hurried from the darkroom.

Unfortunately she ran into Simone as she passed through the studio on her way out.

"I thought you'd left," Jessica said, realizing as she spoke that it was the same thing Quentin had said in the darkroom.

"I did," Simone said in a smug voice. She held up a ring of keys. "But I forgot the keys to my Porsche."

Naturally Simone would drive a Porsche, Jessica thought. *Typical.*

"I saw you go into the darkroom a few minutes ago," Simone said, raising her eyebrows. "And I think I know why."

Jessica shrugged. "I just wanted to see what might develop!"

"I can guess exactly how it ended," Simone said. "If Quentin had shown the least bit of interest, you would have been in there a lot longer."

"Oh, you think so, do you?" Jessica asked mysteriously, trying not to give anything away.

"What a pathetic attempt to get Quentin's attention!" Simone said. "You can just forget it, Jessica. Quentin is *mine*. Besides, do you honestly think he'd waste his time on a *high-school* girl?"

"You seem to be taking some interest in a high-school *boy*," Jessica retorted. "And he happens to be my sister's boyfriend."

"It really *is* a shame," Simone said. "When I first saw Todd, I was hoping he was *your* boyfriend. It would have been such a pleasure to watch you squirm while I made him forget you ever existed. But obviously Todd has better taste than that."

"He *used* to," Jessica said. "I guess he's made an exception in your case. Do you think Quentin's too stupid to see that you're after Todd? And sooner or later Todd is going to hear that you're dating Quentin."

"Who ever said one guy was enough?" Simone asked with a designer shrug. "I guess that's hard for you to understand since you can't *get* even one. Anytime you need some tips on how to attract a man, just stop by, Jessica. I'd be happy to give you some expert advice."

"I'll keep that in mind," Jessica said with an innocent smile. As she watched Simone saunter out of the studio Jessica's smile turned victorious. Her mind replayed the scene in the darkroom. Simone would have a fit if she knew what was probably going on in Quentin's mind right now. By the end of the week Quentin and Jessica would be an item.

"I've got her!" Jessica said under her breath. Simone was about to be struck by Hurricane Jessica. And she was too stupid even to hear the storm warnings.

Chapter 12

Jessica raced to the mail room late Thursday morning to see if her photographs had arrived. She'd sent to the lab the film Lila had taken of her on the beach Tuesday night. And the prints were being delivered to her at *Flair* by courier. She couldn't wait to see how gorgeous and professional she looked.

As she ran into the room Cameron was poring over something at a desk in the corner.

"*Cameron!*" she yelled, louder than she meant to.

Cameron jumped. "Jessica!" he reacted, blushing furiously. He scrambled to put away whatever he was looking at.

"You don't have to drop everything else," Jessica said quickly. "I can help myself if you tell me where to look. I'm expecting a courier package this morning from a photo lab in Pasadena. It's for me, not Quentin."

"Right," Cameron said, still flustered. "From the lab in Pasadena."

"Is it here?" Jessica demanded excitedly. "Which pile should I look in?"

Cameron's shoulders slumped. "I . . . uh . . . have it right here," he confessed, gesturing at the papers he'd been poring over. "The lab only addressed the package to *Flair*, without your name. I kind of . . . um . . . had to open it up to see who to deliver it to."

"That's OK," Jessica said, jumping to his side. "I'm just dying to see those pictures. How do they look?"

"I guess I got a little carried away," Cameron said. "I didn't really have to go through every single photograph just to figure out who to route the package to. But you're so darn pretty in these. . . ."

Jessica grinned, feeling a blush spreading across her own face, though she wasn't sure why. Guys complimented her on her looks all the time. Cameron was no different than any other guy who'd been attracted to her. She grabbed a handful of prints from him. "Ooh," she exclaimed as she leafed through them. "These *are* great shots! Thank goodness for that camera I sto—" She stopped.

"What camera?"

"Uh, just a fancy camera I borrowed from a friend," Jessica lied.

182

Cameron pulled out a photograph that showed Jessica dancing in the sand, one arm reaching gracefully over her head. "You've got talent," he said in a wistful voice. "You're beautiful, and you have a special kind of charisma that jumps off the page."

"Really?" Jessica asked, hoping he'd say more.

Cameron blushed again. He dropped the photo as if it were on fire. Then he stared at the desk. "Too bad your insides aren't as attractive as your outsides," he said, his voice suddenly bitter.

"What's *that* supposed to mean?" she asked.

"I don't know why I thought you'd be any different," he said. "But I did. I thought you were special."

"You don't think so anymore?" Jessica asked, wondering why the mail-room clerk's opinion was suddenly so important to her.

"From the first time I met you, I told myself you weren't just another Simone," Cameron explained. "But you fooled me. You're no better than she is."

"*What?*" Jessica yelled, furious at being compared with her arch rival. "How can you say that?"

"You're interested only in people with classy titles or flashy cars or tons of money!"

"Where do you get off talking to me like that?" Jessica demanded, hands on her hips. "We've had a total of two conversations. You don't know enough about me to pass judgment!"

"It doesn't take long to figure out whether someone's genuine," Cameron countered, jumping from his chair to face her. "And you're not!"

"And you're a sanctimonious jerk!" Jessica yelled back, jabbing a finger at his chest. "You're stuck in a dead-end job, so you're jealous of people who have the potential to go higher than that!"

"You've got the potential to make it as a model, all right!" Cameron replied. Jessica could practically see sparks shooting through the air between them. "Every model I've ever met was vain, superficial, and hung up on appearances. You'll fit right in!"

Suddenly Jessica was aware of how close Cameron was standing. If they hadn't been screaming at each other, they could have been slow dancing. Without thinking about it, Jessica tilted her head back to kiss him. For a second Cameron seemed to be leaning forward. Then he scowled and turned away.

"And isn't that just like a model," he observed bitterly. "You all assume that every guy is dying to kiss you, anytime you're ready. Well, this guy isn't! I kiss when I choose to. And *only* when I choose to!"

Jessica felt her face grow prickly hot. She glared at him, humiliated and furious, as she gathered up her photographs. And she stalked out of the room, vowing never to speak to Cameron again.

Elizabeth swallowed as she stopped outside Leona's office door after lunch on Thursday. She wasn't sure why the managing editor wanted to see her. But after having her "Free Style" column idea rejected the day before, she was nervous—even though the brainstorming session Wednesday evening had been pleasant and productive.

"You wanted to see me?" Elizabeth asked, hesitating in the doorway. "Was there a problem with the research I did for you?"

Leona smiled. "No, there's been no problem with any of your assigned work, Liz. You've been consistently impressive. I just wanted to let you know about an upcoming event. Have a seat."

Elizabeth sat down, relieved. "What kind of event?" she asked. "Is there a meeting you'd like me to help you with?"

"No, nothing like that," Leona said. "This is an unofficial event—a party, really. Most of the key editors will be there. I hope you will be too."

"It sounds great," Elizabeth said. "I'd love the chance to get to know the other editors outside of work. When is it?"

"I thought you'd say that," Leona replied. "The party is tomorrow night. It's after hours, and it's not an actual *Flair*-sponsored gathering. So of course attendance is not mandatory."

Elizabeth leaned back in her chair, disappointed. "I'm glad to hear it's not mandatory," she said. "Normally I'd be excited about something like this. But I can't make it. I already have plans for tomorrow."

Leona raised her eyebrows. Then realization dawned in her eyes, and she nodded. "I understand," she said. "It's Friday night. You and Todd probably have a date planned. You don't have to cancel it. Just change the venue. In fact, most staff members bring their significant others to this kind of party. Todd is welcome to join us. I'd love to meet him."

"It's—it's not Todd!" Elizabeth stammered, surprised at Leona's persistence. "I have these two best friends I've been neglecting all week. After I got home last night, I called them and made plans to go out together tomorrow."

"I can't *order* you to go to this party, Elizabeth," Leona said, her voice suddenly cold and hard. "But I strongly recommend that you call your friends back and suggest another night for your outing."

"Leona, I really can't," Elizabeth said, wondering why she felt compelled to explain. "They're already mad at me for standing them up earlier this week. I owe this to them." She didn't explain that she and Todd were barely on speaking terms.

"Maybe I'm not making myself clear," Leona said. "You asked me earlier this week how women get ahead in this field. This is what it takes. The social side of things is just as important as the quality of work you do."

"I thought you said attendance was optional," Elizabeth ventured.

"It's optional for the average employee," Leona said. "But for people who expect to move up—both at *Flair* and in the industry at large—attendance is an absolute must. It's up to you, Liz. You have to decide if you're a fast-tracker or a middle-of-the-roader."

"Do you mean that missing one party—not even a meeting, but a *party*—could hurt my career?" Elizabeth asked.

"I don't want to make this sound like a threat," Leona said. "But I strongly suggest that attending this party and similar events is in your best interests—if you're still interested in having a future with *Flair*. If you know what's good for your career, Liz, you'll cancel out on your friends and come along."

Leona seemed like a different person. Her warmth and friendliness had evaporated. A chill skated up Elizabeth's spine. For the first time she saw a glimpse of what it would be like to have Leona angry with her. It was not a pleasant thought.

"All right," Elizabeth said weakly as she walked toward the door, anxious to get away from this new, scarier Leona. "I'll see what I can do about changing my plans," she promised. "But I might have to come alone. I don't know if Todd's busy tomorrow."

She reached the door and turned back to Leona with a new idea. "Wait a minute—is this the kind of thing I could bring Maria and Enid to?"

Leona shook her head. "I'm sorry, Liz," she said. "There's no actual rule against bringing your best chums to this sort of function. But it just isn't done. Everybody brings a date. A *real* date."

Elizabeth nodded, feeling doomed. Somehow she had to find a way to make up with Todd and to put up with his new ego. And she had to find it fast. She sighed as she plodded back to her own office.

Life in the real world was a lot more complicated than she'd imagined.

By four o'clock that afternoon Jessica had managed to force Cameron out of her mind. At least she kept telling herself she wasn't still thinking about what had happened in the mail room that morning. She couldn't believe that a guy who had seemed so nice would say such awful things about her—and then humiliate her by pulling away right before they kissed. She could have sworn he wanted that kiss as much as she had.

"But I *didn't* want it," she repeated under her breath. "I'm not interested in a guy who works in the mail room!" But why wasn't he interested in *her?*

She shoved Cameron's image out of her mind and concentrated on Quentin instead. It was time to make her next move. Finally the photographer was alone. She had seen him walk into the wardrobe room a few minutes earlier.

Jessica ducked into Michael's salon to check her reflection in the mirror. She'd persuaded him to style her hair that afternoon, and it was perfect. The longer part in front was swirled around her face in dramatic waves of gold. She wore a long white blazer over a low-cut white minidress. Both pieces were trimmed in gleaming silver. And both were still spotless since she hadn't set up any photo shoots all day. With her suntan she decided she looked much better in white than pale-skinned Simone could ever hope to look.

Jessica winked at herself in mirror. Quentin wouldn't be able to resist her. Then she strolled into the wardrobe room and stood in the doorway for a moment, watching while the photographer rummaged through colorful articles of clothing.

"Hi, Quentin," she said in her brightest, most helpful photography-intern voice. "Can I help you find something?"

Quentin opened his mouth to answer, but then he stopped, staring at her as if he'd never seen her before. He took a step closer and rested his hands on her shoulders. "Jessica!" he whispered. "It was you, wasn't it?" he asked, gazing at her with those smoky gray eyes. "You're the girl who kissed me in the darkroom last night, when I was making prints."

Jessica batted her eyelashes and smiled enigmatically. She could tell from his wide eyes and ragged breathing that Quentin was intrigued. But she couldn't make it too easy for him.

"Speaking of prints," she began after a moment, "I have a few here that I wanted to show you. I never really thought about being a model before. But a friend took one look at these and told me I had a lot of potential. What do you think?"

She handed him a half dozen of her favorite shots. While she waited for Quentin to examine them, Jessica casually began folding a pile of wrinkled scarves to show that she didn't really care about his verdict. She'd originally planned to put the photographs together into a professional portfolio, but she could do that later. Today she had Quentin's attention. She couldn't risk losing it.

Quentin stopped on the photograph of her dancing on the beach—the one Cameron had liked best. He whistled. "Jessica, I am really impressed," Quentin said at last. "You're not quite tall enough for runway modeling, but we might be able to play around that for photo work. I could help you if you're interested in taking a shot at it."

"That would be awesome!" Jessica exclaimed. She modulated her voice. "I mean, I've been watching Simone and Todd all week, and I think this is something I'd really like to try. If you think I might have the talent."

"No question about it," Quentin said. "You've got talent. You're photogenic. You have a great look—wholesome but sexy. In fact, I'd love to talk to you more about this, but I'm out of time right now. Can we discuss it over dinner tomorrow night?"

Jessica was ecstatic. "That would be great!" she replied.

"I almost forgot what I came in here for," he said, gazing around the room. "There it is," he said, pointing to two scraps in her pile of scarves. "Would you hand me those pieces of gold lamé?"

Jessica picked up the shiny bits of fabric and realized she was holding a bikini. "A bathing suit?" she asked as she handed it to him.

"We're planning a fashion spread to illustrate an article on the Return of Metallics," Quentin explained, standing in the doorway. "Simone needs to try this on ahead of time."

"Oh," Jessica said softly. Quentin left, whistling, and she plopped herself down in a chair. It was too bad that he could still remember Simone's name. But another day or two would make all the difference. Jessica almost had him exactly where she wanted him. She couldn't believe how easy it had been to manipulate him.

Quentin may be a famous photographer, she told herself, *but when it comes down to it, he's just another guy. And he's just as dumb as the rest of them.*

Thursday had been an easy but interesting day

for Todd. He hadn't been in any photo shoots. Instead he'd spent the day talking to various members of Quentin's staff, learning about lights, sets, and props. In between the lessons his thoughts had been drifting back and forth all day between Elizabeth and Simone.

He knew Elizabeth was ticked off at him. And that made him ticked off at her. For some reason it was OK for her to be too wrapped up in a career to spend time with him. But it didn't seem to work both ways.

Things were much simpler with Simone. Simone understood the pressures of a career as a model. She was a professional; she knew that touching and kissing were no big deal. They were part of the job. They were nothing for Elizabeth to have a fit about—even when the person who happened to be touching and kissing him was a sexy, six-foot-tall model with a flawless body that was frequently on display for everyone to see.

The image had just begun to flow through his mind as slowly and sweetly as molasses. And suddenly Simone stepped into the room—in the flesh, so to speak. She wore another skimpy bikini, this time in some shiny gold stuff. As always she looked like a fantasy. For a moment Todd thought he'd conjured her up, like a genie from a lamp.

"Hi, Todd," she said in that throaty voice of hers. "I was just trying this bathing suit on for an upcoming shoot. What do you think? Is it too tight?"

Todd shook his head. "It looks good," he said, keeping his eyes on her face.

"You hardly looked at it," Simone chided him, giggling. She walked over and stood very near. "Come on, Todd. I'm asking you as one professional model to another. Take a good, close look at my bikini. And tell me what you think."

Jessica sat in the wardrobe room, hoping nobody would find her there. It was late in the day, and she didn't feel like working. In another twenty minutes she could go home. Until then she was content to sit in a room that contained more beautiful outfits than even Lila's closet and to pat herself on the back for her success with Quentin fifteen minutes earlier. Suddenly she stiffened. Cameron was hesitating in the doorway, holding an overnight express package. Jessica rose from her chair.

"This just arrived for your department," he said, holding out the package. "A couple of models are in the studio, but I'm supposed to give it to Quentin or one of his assistants. You're the only other person I could find."

Jessica nodded. "I can take it," she said, feeling her cheeks turning pink again. She reached out to take the package from him, and their hands touched. Electricity crackled between them, and Cameron took her hand in his. He pulled her close and wrapped his arms around her as if he never intended to let her go. Then his lips were on hers, and he was kissing her in a way that sent fountains of sparks cascading through her body.

After a long, exquisite minute he pulled his lips from hers. Jessica stared into his deep brown eyes, sure that her heart had stopped. She could barely catch her breath.

"There's more where that came from," Cameron said simply. "We're having dinner together tomorrow night." Jessica nodded mutely, still overwhelmed from the kiss. Cameron dropped the package on the chair and disappeared through the door.

Jessica stood in the center of the cluttered room. Her head was reeling. She felt too stunned to move or even think. Suddenly she looked up. The lights in the main studio had just blinked off. Cameron said the only people left in the department were two models—Simone and Todd, she guessed. They must have closed up shop and gone home, flicking off the studio lights on their way out. That left Jessica alone, but she didn't care. Cameron had just given her one of the most incredible kisses of her life.

There's more where that came from, he had said. She closed her eyes and imagined a second kiss, even better than the first. Her eyes flew open when she remembered exactly where the first kiss had come from. *The mail room.* She was falling for a cute, sexy guy who could do absolutely nothing to help her career.

Meanwhile the jerk who could help her seemed to be falling for her. But Quentin just didn't make her heart pound the way Cameron did. What was the solution? Would she really have to choose between a great guy and a fabulous career? *And now,* she realized with a start, *I've got a date with both of them for the same night!*

"What am I going to do?" she whispered to the empty room.

Elizabeth stepped out of the elevator on the ninth floor Thursday evening, hoping Todd was still in the photography studio. She had to resolve things with him. She wanted to apologize. It was more than the unofficially mandatory office party. She'd finally admitted the truth about spending so much time away from Todd in the past week: She *missed* him. It was true that he was getting a swelled head from being told all day long how handsome he was. But that was understandable. She had to trust Todd enough to assume he'd be reasonable again as soon as the novelty of the situation had worn off.

For now she just wanted to kiss and make up. She wanted her boyfriend back.

She pushed open the door to the photo studio and realized she was too late. The room was almost completely dark. Todd and everybody else must have left for the day. Of course, she remembered, there were some smaller rooms in back, off the main studio. Maybe some of them still had lights and people in them. It was worth checking out. But first she had to light her way across the big studio.

Elizabeth groped along the wall for the overhead switch. She flicked it on. The room flooded with light, and Elizabeth blinked. She gasped. Todd and Simone stood in one corner of the room—locked in a passionate embrace. And the leggy model was wearing nothing but a shiny gold bikini.

Elizabeth couldn't breathe. Todd looked stunned, like a deer caught in the Jeep's headlights. But Simone had a triumphant smirk on her face.

That's it, Elizabeth thought, her mind spinning. She'd found the source of the suffocating certainty that something terrible was waiting to pounce. Elizabeth's world crashed around her and splintered into jagged bits. She'd been afraid of choosing between her personal life and her work life. Now she no longer had any choice. She'd lost Todd. And she'd lost her chance at a career at *Flair*.

Elizabeth fled the studio, sobbing.

Will Jessica choose Cameron or Quentin? Will Elizabeth ever manage to impress Leona? And how will the twins defeat the evil supermodel? Turn the page for a sneak peek at Sweet Valley High #130, Model Flirt, the second book in this very fashionable three-part mini-series. Don't miss it!

It was only nine P.M., but Elizabeth was in bed, tossing and turning. The memory of Todd and Simone together kept dancing before her eyes, tormenting her. Elizabeth flipped on her side and wrapped the covers around her, trying to shake the image from her mind. Outside, rain was pouring down steadily. Usually the sound of rain soothed her, but tonight it just added to her anxiety.

Think of the ocean, she told herself. She concentrated deeply, imagining the picturesque view at Ocean Bay. She saw hot, white sand and the foamy blue-green sea. White-capped breakers crashed onto the shore, and seagulls cut arcing patterns above the waves. Then she saw Todd and Simone walking hand in hand along the shore. Simone was barefoot and carrying her sandals in one hand, but her storklike legs were so long that she was almost as tall as Todd. *I can't believe you took her to the beach,* Elizabeth irrationally told Todd in her mind. *Our beach. . . .* Pain stabbed at her heart.

Elizabeth shook her head and threw off the covers, sitting up in bed. It was no use. She couldn't sleep. She couldn't stop thinking about Todd and Simone. Sighing deeply, she reached over and turned on the lamp next to her bed. The first thing she saw was a copy of *Flair* on her nightstand. Leona had given her a stack of back issues so she could familiarize herself with the magazine, and this one featured a barely bikini-clad Simone. Elizabeth sucked in her breath, feeling assaulted by the photograph.

She picked up the magazine and examined the cover. Usually pictures of models in bathing suits offended her feminist sensibility, but this one was particularly artistic. It had clearly been shot by Quentin Berg. The photo was in black and white, with a grainy quality that gave it a dated look. Elizabeth had to admit that Simone looked good. She was perched on a white boulder, her long legs folded gracefully underneath her. Her sleek, asymmetrically-cut jet black hair provided a sharp contrast to her flawless ivory skin. Her full lips were pursed together in a pout and her eyes stared directly at the camera, pale and strangely blank. She was obviously beautiful, but she seemed empty—and cold. And she was so skinny that she looked like a starvation victim. But obviously, that's what Todd wanted. He didn't want someone with life. He wanted someone with status. Supermodel status.

Elizabeth scowled, feeling like a nobody, a nothing. She felt like her entire self had been made worthless. She could change her interests, but she couldn't change her looks. She'd never be six feet tall. She'd never look like a supermodel. Elizabeth balled her hands into fists, seething with frustration. Then she tore off the cover of the magazine, ripping it into tiny pieces. She threw the pieces on the floor, watching in satisfaction as they scattered over her cream-colored carpet.

Sliding out of bed, Elizabeth kicked at the torn-up pieces on the floor, grinding Simone into the carpet with her heel. She paced from one side of her bedroom to the other, gnashing her teeth. She stopped at the door and surveyed her room, itching with dissatisfaction. It was so impeccably neat and orderly. She looked in disgust at her perfectly clean desk with her reference books and computer, at her armoire with her shoes all perfectly lined up, at the immaculate bookshelves. . . . Her room used to give her a sense of peace and a desire to work. Now she felt caged in. Elizabeth yanked open a window, letting in a gust of cold, windy air. Then she grabbed her clothes from the bed and threw them on the floor in a heap.

Maybe it's all my fault, Elizabeth thought, kicking her clothes out of the way as she crossed the room again. After all, she *had* been neglecting Todd. Ever since she had found out about her internship, the job had been the only thing on her mind. Todd had called her—and faxed her—and had even driven all the way to L.A. to see him. But she hadn't given him a second of her time.

Then Elizabeth dismissed the thought as ridiculous. When Todd had trained like a madman for the basketball finals last season, she had barely seen him at all. And she had understood. Besides, this internship was just two weeks long. Just because Todd hadn't bothered looking for an interesting position was no reason Elizabeth shouldn't try to make a future for herself.

Elizabeth grabbed a woolen blanket from her bed and flopped onto her pale velvet divan dejectedly. If a little bit of neglect would make Todd turn to other girls, then he wasn't worth her time—and their relationship wasn't worth her time either. Tears came to her eyes. To think that all these years could be erased in a second—in a kiss. Todd was her constant companion, her other half. It seemed like they'd always been together. And Elizabeth had thought they'd *always* be together.

A jumble of random memories flooded into her

mind, causing her chest to constrict in pain. She saw Todd at basketball practice the week before, wearing blue cutoff sweatpants and a canary yellow T-shirt. She'd stopped by to see him after school, and he'd turned and sent her a kiss, mouthing 'I love you' in the air. She saw his brown eyes staring at her intensely at Miller's Point, a popular parking spot high above Sweet Valley. And then she saw herself and Todd together one afternoon years ago, when they had shared their first tentative kiss. . . .

Elizabeth curled her legs underneath her and wrapped her blanket around her shoulders. She didn't know how she was going to make it through the school year. Sweet Valley was full of too many memories. She reached over and picked up the framed picture of Todd on her bookshelf. He was smiling at her, and his deep brown eyes were warm and trusting. She quickly put it back, laying it face down on the shelf. *How could you throw it all away, Todd?* she thought, hot tears coming to her eyes. *How could you betray me like this? How could you betray us like this?*

The tears trickled down her cheeks and she jumped up, brushing them angrily away. She couldn't let herself go to pieces. After all, she still had her pride. It was bad enough that Todd had fallen in love with someone else, but he had cheated on her—at her own workplace. Elizabeth shook her head in disgust. She had thought that

Todd was different from other guys. She had thought he cared about things that really mattered. But no, as soon as a supermodel walked into the vicinity, he was history.

A flash of lightning illuminated the sky and a blast of rain shot through the open window. Shivering, Elizabeth pulled the window shut. Then she prowled across the room, feeling restless. She didn't know what to do with herself. She wanted to talk to someone. Jessica was wonderful, but she needed a friend who would truly understand her situation—like Enid. Enid always managed to make her feel better. She was levelheaded and could always give Elizabeth a sense of perspective about things.

Picking the phone up off her nightstand, she carried it to the floor and plopped down on the carpet, bringing her knees up to her chest. She punched in Enid's number and waited as the phone rang. But no one answered.

Elizabeth blinked back tears, feeling a little desperate for support. She stared at the number pad, wondering if she should call Maria. She had been giving her friends the brush-off lately, and they were probably mad at her. But then again, they were her best friends. They would understand. They would be there for her.

Without thinking about it any further, Elizabeth quickly dialed Maria's number. She twisted the phone cord around her finger as the phone rang. *Maria, please be there,* she thought.

Finally Maria picked up. "Yes?" she asked, her voice giddy. Elizabeth breathed a sigh of relief.

"Maria, it's Elizabeth," she said.

"Oh, hi, Elizabeth," Maria responded, her voice turning distinctly cold. Elizabeth winced. Then she heard giggling in the background.

"Is this a bad time?" Elizabeth asked. "Is somebody over?" She twisted the phone cord harder in her hand, cutting off the circulation in her fingers.

"Enid is staying over tonight," Maria explained, her voice distant. "We're helping each other out with stuff for our internships."

"Oh," Elizabeth said softly, hit with a pang of jealousy. Enid and Maria never used to hang out without her. "Why didn't you invite me?" she asked, trying to keep the hurt out of her voice.

"Hmm," Maria said. "Just a minute." Elizabeth could tell she had covered the receiver with her hand, but her muffled voice came through anyway. "Enid, Elizabeth wants to know why we didn't invite her over." Elizabeth heard the girls giggle. Tears welled up in her eyes again. What was going on? Was the whole world turning on her?

Enid got on the phone a moment later. "Hi, Elizabeth, it's Enid," she said.

"Hi," Elizabeth responded tentatively.

Enid's voice was cold and clipped. "In answer

to your question, we weren't aware that you'd have time to hang out with two peons like us. You've been so busy with the power players that we didn't want to disturb you."

Elizabeth didn't even have the energy to respond. She said good-bye and hung up the phone.

Elizabeth wrapped her arms around her body, feeling worse than she had before. She was completely alone in the world. First she'd lost Todd. Now she'd lost her two best friends.

The rain pelted down around her, enveloping her in her solitude.

Todd took Simone's hand and spun her around the center of the dance floor. It was almost midnight, and they were at the Edge, a hip new nightclub in downtown L.A. This was the latest he'd ever been out on a school night. The dance floor was packed with a chichi L.A. crowd, and loud techno music blasted from the speakers. Todd felt his head whirling with the pulsing beat of the electric music.

"This is what it's like living on the edge, Todd," Simone whispered in a husky voice in his ear. "How do you like it?"

Todd shrugged. "No big deal," he said, trying to sound cool. But his voice came out as a squeak and he blushed.

Simone grinned. "You are so *cute*, Todd," she

squealed. Todd's blush deepened, but Simone was already turning her attention to the other side of the room. "Look," she said, pointing an elegant finger at the bar. "That's Sven Sorensen, the editor in chief of *Ingenue* magazine."

Todd followed her gaze. A Swedish-looking man with a blond beard was sitting at the bar with a group of tall models crowded around him.

Todd nodded, searching in vain for something intelligent to say. Then he realized that Simone wasn't paying attention anyway. She was too busy posing for Sven. She steered herself and Todd around so he could get a view of her profile. "Spin me, Todd," she commanded in an intense voice. Todd swung her around obediently, and she twirled wildly, trying to get Sven's attention.

Todd blushed, feeling more self-conscious than ever. He could see every guy in the place looking at him with total envy. He was wearing jeans and a t-shirt, and he wished he'd worn something a little more hip. The crowd was made up of chic actors and models, and they were all dressed almost entirely in black. The women were all wearing short skirts and tight dresses, and most of the guys had on black jeans and funky retro jackets.

Sven stood up from the bar, and Simone stopped midspin. "Oh, I'll be right back," she said, her voice breathless. Then she rushed off.

Todd stood in the middle of the dance floor. He

tried to make out Simone through the crowd, but gyrating bodies blocked his view. There were a few couples on the dance floor, but most of the people were dancing alone, swaying to the music as if they were in a trance.

"Hey, you wanna join the Love Parade?" a sultry voice whispered in his ear.

"Huh?" Todd said, blinking. He turned to see a woman with short, scarlet hair standing by his side. She had an earring in her nose and an earring in her lip. A trail of dancers followed her in a line, bobbing rhythmically in an almost hypnotic state.

"It's a communion with Being," she said. "You close your eyes and let the music fill your body."

"C'mon, get in line," urged a blond woman with a purple streak in her hair. "You'll see. It's a natural high."

"Uh, no thanks," Todd said quickly. "I was just going to get a drink."

He waved and walked away, the eerie sound of the women's laughter echoing in his ears. Weaving through the grinding bodies, he made his way quickly to the bar.

"What'll you have?" the bartender barked. He was a bulky man with a huge grizzly beard.

Todd gulped. He was tempted to order a drink, but he was underage. If he got carded, he would get kicked out of the club and would be totally humiliated.

"Just a mineral water," he said quickly.

The bartender nodded and picked up a bottle of seltzer. He poured the bubbling water into a tall glass.

Todd picked up his drink and leaned against the bar, taking in the surroundings. The club was done in ultramodern decor, with stark white tables and shiny black floors. A flashing neon red strip surrounded the wall, and a shimmering disco ball hung over the middle of the dance floor. The stylish crowd looked as electric as the club itself.

Todd took a sip of his drink, feeling entirely out of place. He wondered if anybody knew he was underage. He was trying to play it cool, but he felt as if he was wearing a huge sign on his back that screamed "*Sixteen!*"

"Oh, Todd, there you are!" Simone breathed by his side. "C'mon, let's go back to the dance floor," she said, taking his hand.

"Sure," Todd agreed, downing his drink and following her. He definitely preferred the dance floor to the bar. Dancing was one thing he could legitimately do. At the bar, he felt like a total fraud.

Simone wrapped her arms around his waist and pressed her body to his.

Todd coughed uncomfortably, shifting back up a few inches. "So, did you have any luck with the editor in chief of *Ingenue?*" he asked.

Simone nodded in pleasure. "He's going to call

me," she said. "He wants to use me for the cover of the next issue." She giggled gleefully. "That means I'll be replacing Justine Laroche. She's going to be *green*."

"Hey, that's great," Todd said, trying to sound happy for her. *But I just can't think of a modeling job as important*, he realized. Then he swallowed hard, suddenly struck by how hypocritical he was being. *He* was a model too. This was his crowd now.

As he danced with Simone, Todd looked at the beautiful people around him and tried to convince himself that he was having a great time—and that the nagging feeling in the pit of his stomach had nothing to do with Elizabeth. He decided that he must be allergic to the shrimp cocktail he and Simone had eaten earlier.

Then, out of the corner of his eye, he glimpsed a blond girl across the dance floor. For a split second his heart leaped. *Elizabeth!* he thought, the blood pounding in his temples. Maybe she had come here to find him—to reconcile with him. But then the girl turned. It wasn't Elizabeth. Simone pulled him closer in his arms.

A wave of disappointment washed over him, and suddenly Elizabeth's bitter words came back to him. *You're not the person I thought you were.* Todd felt a sharp pang in his heart.

He shook off his negative feelings. Obviously

Elizabeth was right: he wasn't just a normal teenager. He was *model* material. He was meant for fame and fortune. It was going to be difficult to leave his old life behind, but he'd have to get used to it. He'd have to rise to the challenge.

I'm happy to be in Simone's arms, he told himself. *Very, very happy*.

Jessica paused on the top rung of a six-foot ladder in the main photography studio, surveying her work. For the past hour, she had been setting up for the morning's shoot. Nick Nolan, the set director, had come in early to prep her. It was a Greek isles scene with a bright blue backdrop, huge fake rocks, and a cascading waterfall.

Jessica gazed at the set in satisfaction. She had transformed the cool, airy studio into a hot Mediterranean paradise. The fake rocks cluttered together really looked like dusty white boulders, and they glinted against the backdrop as if against a blinding blue sky. Jessica had propped up the waterfall on the far left, but she wasn't quite sure how to hook up the mechanism.

She climbed all the way to the top of the ladder and carefully positioned the lights above the backdrop, trying to set them up just like Quentin did. Then she stepped down carefully and took a seat on the highest rung. She rubbed her shoulders and stretched out her neck. It was only ten A.M., and

Jessica's back and shoulders were already aching from moving the fake rocks around and transporting huge buckets of water.

Where is everybody? Jessica wondered. Usually Quentin was there at the crack of dawn, barking out orders. And Simone normally didn't give Jessica a moment's peace, keeping her occupied with the most mundane tasks imaginable. *Maybe she won't show up,* Jessica thought hopefully. *Maybe one of her high heels got caught in a sewage drain and she twisted her ankle. Or maybe she slipped down the drain entirely.* Then Quentin would have no choice but to use Jessica in her place. With Simone out of the way, Jessica was sure she could get through to Quentin.

The door swung open and Quentin breezed through, a camera slung over his shoulder. Jessica's tongue went dry. What if Quentin had forgotten all about the day before in the darkroom? What if he forgot about their date entirely? After all, you could never tell with artists. And Quentin was a particularly temperamental one.

But Quentin whistled under his breath as he took in the set. "Hey, looks good," he said, smiling up at her. "A Greek paradise and a Greek goddess on her modern Mount Olympus." He sauntered over to her. "Want some help getting down from there?"

"Sure," Jessica said softly, standing up and turning around.

Jessica took a few steps down the ladder. Then Quentin put strong arms around her waist and lifted her to the floor. His hands lingered on her waist as he turned her around to face him. "Looking forward to our dinner tonight?" he asked in a low voice.

"Of course," Jessica said coyly.

"You should be, because I'm taking you to the most exclusive restaurant in all of L.A.," he whispered in her ear. "It's called Chez Paul's and it's on Hollywood Boulevard. I'll meet you there at eight."

"Am I interrupting something?" came a saucy voice from behind them. Jessica and Quentin whirled around. It was Simone, a lazy catlike look of contentment on her cold features. Jessica bit her lip. It was a well-known fact at *Flair* that Simone and Quentin had been involved for some time. Jessica was thrilled to flaunt her flirtation with Quentin, but she wasn't sure he'd feel the same way.

Quentin looked disturbed. "Simone, you're late," he said flatly.

Simone shrugged. "I needed my beauty sleep."

Quentin headed for the darkroom, suddenly all business. "Simone, go to wardrobe. Jessica, set up the lights. We'll be shooting in an hour."

Jessica pounced on Simone as soon as Quentin had disappeared into his cave of chemicals. "So, did you have fun with my sister's boyfriend last night?"

Simone was totally unperturbed by Jessica's attitude. "Todd's okay for a high school boy," she responded. "He'll be good for a few photo ops, at least.

"Photo ops?" Jessica demanded. "Like what?"

Simone whipped out a copy of *Los Angeles Living* and held it up for to Jessica see. On the front page was a huge, tacky color photo of Todd in Simone's arms.

Jessica was speechless. This girl was too much. She was just glad that Elizabeth would never read a paper of such low quality. If she saw the photo, she'd really flip out.

"Now, if you'll excuse me," Simone purred, waltzing past her, "I've got to get dressed." She turned back before she entered the dressing room. "Oh, I'd like to try out a few pairs of shoes. Would you mind bringing me a half-dozen pairs of Italian sandals from wardrobe?"

Jessica's eyes narrowed as she walked away to do the Toothpick's bidding. She was going to find a way to get Simone, if it was the last thing she did.

MODEL
FLIRT

Written by
Kate William

Created by
FRANCINE PASCAL

BANTAM BOOKS
NEW YORK · TORONTO · LONDON · SYDNEY · AUCKLAND

To Hilary Bloom

Chapter 1

Sixteen-year-old Elizabeth Wakefield ducked into the darkroom of the art department at *Flair* magazine on Thursday afternoon, her whole body trembling in shock. She leaned against the heavy door of the outer chamber and wrapped her arms around her sides, squeezing her eyes shut. But there was no escaping the horrendous image that reappeared in her mind, clear as a summer day. The image was of her longtime boyfriend, Todd Wilkins, locked in a passionate embrace with Simone, a striking supermodel.

In the cool darkness of the closetlike space, Elizabeth replayed the scene she'd just witnessed like a movie in slow motion.

Opening credits. Elizabeth Wakefield is searching for her boyfriend, Todd Wilkins, to tell him that she misses him and that she is sorry they have spent so little time together this week. She pushes open the door of the main photography studio on the ninth floor. The room is shrouded in darkness. Todd, are you still here? she wonders. She flicks on the overhead light.

Tight close-up. Elizabeth stares in horror at the sight before her.

Simone's long arms are entwined around Todd's neck, her barely clothed body inches from his. Todd's hands are resting lightly on Simone's narrow hips. And his lips are closed on hers. Focus on Simone's smooth profile. And the angular cut of her sleek black hair. And the shiny gleam of her gold bikini.

Elizabeth gasps and stumbles backward, grabbing on to a table edge for support. Todd and Simone both turn at the sound. The blood rushes from Todd's face. Simone looks on coolly, triumphant sparks shooting from her ice blue eyes. A small smile curls on her artificially full red lips.

Elizabeth turns and flees. The End.

Elizabeth slid down the wall to the floor, her heart constricting in pain. *That's not the way it would have happened in a film,* she thought. In the movies, there were always happy endings. But not in real life. Real life was just betrayal and deception. A hot tear rolled down her cheek.

When Elizabeth and her twin sister, Jessica, had landed their positions as interns at *Flair* magazine, Elizabeth had thought a whole new world was opening up to her. But now she felt as though she were trapped on a uncharted desert island—*all alone*. Elizabeth leaned her head back against the door and closed her eyes, tasting the bittersweet saltiness of her tears.

She jolted at the sound of a door slamming shut.

"Elizabeth, where are you?" Todd called down the hallway.

Elizabeth stood up quickly and opened the interior door. She never wanted to see Todd again. And she particularly didn't think she could face him now. She crept into the developing room. A dim, red safelight cast an eerie glow in the otherwise dark room, and tall tubes that smelled of chemicals lined a long table. A row of prints hung from what looked like a clothesline, and Elizabeth stooped underneath it, looking for a way out.

Elizabeth caught sight of a side entrance and silently pushed it open. She looked around quickly, blinking in the light as she tried to orient herself. She was in some kind of prop room. A jumble of ladders and lights crowded the small space.

After weaving through the ladders, Elizabeth pulled open a door and found herself in a small photo studio. She breathed a sigh of relief, feeling safe in the hidden space.

But then she heard the sound of approaching footsteps.

"Elizabeth, wait!" Todd exclaimed, opening the door behind her.

At the sound of his voice, Elizabeth rushed across the room, hurrying through the swinging doors back into the main studio. She dodged some props and sprinted across the cavernous room. But Todd caught up with her at the door, grabbing her arm roughly.

Elizabeth shook off his hand. *"Don't touch me,"* she hissed through clenched teeth. "Don't *ever* touch me again."

"Fine!" Todd responded defensively, pulling his arm back.

"Sharing isn't my style," Elizabeth bit out angrily. "What's wrong? Isn't Simone woman enough for you?"

Todd's coffee brown eyes clouded over in pain. "Please, Elizabeth, let me explain," he pleaded.

For a moment Elizabeth softened. Todd's handsome face was so woeful that she had a sudden urge to hug him.

But then she remembered the horrible picture of Todd and Simone together, and a frozen calm fell over her. *It's too late,* she realized. Nothing that Todd said could take back what he had done. Nothing could erase the painful image engraved in her mind. "There's nothing to explain," Elizabeth said softly. "It's simple. You're not the person I thought you were." Then she shrugged. "I can do better."

Sparks of anger replaced the pain in Todd's eyes. He looked at her coldly, his face an implacable

4

mask. "I guess I already have," he retorted.

Elizabeth winced at his cruel words. "I guess so," she responded sadly. "Good-bye, Todd," she said. With that, she opened the door of the main studio and stepped into the hall. Without a backward glance, she hurried down the corridor to the lobby.

Elizabeth took a deep breath and punched the button at the elevator bank. The mirrored doors opened almost immediately, revealing a full elevator of tall models wearing short skirts and long blazers, all gazing coolly ahead. Elizabeth gasped. All the models looked like carbon copies of Simone. She gritted her teeth and stepped inside. Her head throbbing, she leaned against the wall and closed her eyes. The elevator ride seemed to take forever.

When the elevator finally reached the ground floor, Elizabeth pushed her way out first.

"Well, *excuse* me," a pointed voice said.

"Interns," said another disgusted model.

But Elizabeth ignored the haughty voices of the fashion clones. She flew across the shiny marble floor of the huge, elegant lobby and pushed through the swinging doors to the sidewalk. She just wanted to get far away from *Flair* magazine and Todd and Simone as quickly as possible. Once outside, she took big gulps of fresh air. She yanked off her high-heeled pumps and held them by their straps in one hand, hurrying across the sidewalk in her stockings.

Elizabeth jumped into her Jeep and revved the engine. Then she tore out of the parking lot.

As she sped down the Santa Monica Freeway, Elizabeth unrolled the window and took long, haggard breaths, trying to calm herself. Normally she was a careful driver, but now she felt like throwing caution to the wind. She cut across the four-lane highway and darted into the left lane. The ground rushed underneath the wheels of the Jeep, echoing a strange rushing in her head. All week she'd had an eerie premonition, and finally it had come to pass. And it was worse than she'd ever imagined.

Elizabeth couldn't understand how everything had changed so quickly. In just a few days, Todd had gone from being a Sweet Valley High basketball star to a fashion model—and from her loyal boyfriend to a swinging playboy.

This week certainly hasn't turned out like I expected, Elizabeth thought dejectedly. As part of a new career program, Sweet Valley High juniors were taking part in a two-week-long internship program. Most of the students weren't taking it seriously. Todd hadn't bothered looking for an interesting position and had ended up as an assistant at his dad's software company, Varitronics. His job had consisted mostly of making copies and filing invoices. Jessica's best friend, Lila Fowler, hadn't done much better, filling in as a receptionist at Fowler Electronics, one of her father's computer chip companies.

Some of the students had been more entrepreneurial, though. Aaron Dallas had found a spot working for the general manager of the Lakers, and Winston Egbert was assisting the head chef of an exclusive gourmet Italian restaurant in Beverly Hills. Elizabeth's best friends Enid Rollins and Maria Slater had found perfect positions as well: Enid, who had a passion for literature, was acting as an intern at Morgan Literary Agency, and Maria, a former child actress, was serving as an assistant at the Bridgewater Theater Group in downtown Sweet Valley.

But Elizabeth and Jessica had landed the most exciting positions of all. They were interning at *Flair*, a hot new fashion magazine. *Flair* was less than two years old, but it was already the most popular publication of the Mode Magazine Group. Elizabeth was working in the editorial department of *Flair* as an assistant to Leona Peirson, the managing editor, and Jessica was working in the art department for the head photographer, Quentin Berg.

When she and Jessica had first heard about their internships, Elizabeth had been ecstatic. Even though Elizabeth wasn't exactly a fashion buff, she was thrilled to be learning the inner workings of a real magazine. And the job had surpassed her wildest dreams. Elizabeth had expected to do mostly grunt work—or "scum work," as Leona had called it. And while she had a fair amount of tedious chores to do—opening mail, making copies, and fact checking articles—Leona had entrusted her with some serious assignments. In the few days she'd been at *Flair*, Elizabeth had already drafted a letter, proofread sections of the magazine, and used the Library of Congress database to do research for an upcoming article. Not only that, but Elizabeth had her own plush office complete with a state-of-the-art computer and printer. She had thrown herself into her duties, and Leona had been so impressed with the results that she had mentioned the possibility of a summer job.

But then everything had changed. Fueled by her success, Elizabeth had done research on her own and had come up with a great idea for the magazine: an interactive reader-written article. Her idea was that the magazine would feature a one-page column called "Free Style" in which a reader of the month would write her personal opinions about fashion. Armed with a write-up of her research and notes, Elizabeth had presented the idea to Leona. Leona had flatly rejected it, explaining that it would bring down the quality of writing in the magazine. But she had promised to run the idea by the editor in chief. Elizabeth cringed at the memory. It was bad enough that Leona had rejected her idea, but it was even worse that she had condescended to her.

It began to drizzle, and wind whistled through the car. Elizabeth shivered and rolled up the window.

Then she caught sight of the familiar Sweet Valley exit sign on the far right. *Darn,* she muttered under her breath. Without bothering to put on her turn signal, she flew across the four lanes of the highway. A blue Toyota blared its horn and swerved out of her way, causing another car to screech on its brakes.

Elizabeth skidded onto the exit ramp and slowed down, shaking slightly. *Elizabeth Wakefield,* she reprimanded herself. *Get a hold of yourself.* The rain was coming down steadily now, and Elizabeth turned on the windshield wipers. Her life was falling apart but that was no reason to get in an accident.

Elizabeth stared gloomily ahead as she drove down the familiar winding roads of Sweet Valley. First her job turned out to be a failure, then her relationship. Elizabeth shook her head, feeling her cheeks burn again as the sight of Todd and the Fashion Witch, as Jessica called Simone, came back to her. Her life had gotten so bad so quickly. One moment Todd was sending her love-faxes from his internship at Varitronics, the next he was wrapped up in Simone's black widow spider arms.

Last Tuesday afternoon, Todd had stopped by unexpectedly to pick up Elizabeth, but she had been mired in work. So she had sent him down to the art department to entertain himself. *And entertain himself he did,* she thought bitterly.

Todd had walked in on a photo shoot with Simone that Quentin was directing. According to

9

Jessica, Quentin knew immediately that he wanted to photograph Todd's youthful face. And apparently Todd fell in love with Simone's *overexposed* face at the same moment. Quentin had taken a few test shots of Todd, and the next day he called to hire him as a model. Todd quit his internship at Varitronics to be the next big thing, and the rest was history.

Hot tears rolled down Elizabeth's cheeks as she pulled into the driveway of the Wakefield house on Calico Drive, and she wiped them away. It was just so humiliating. It didn't matter how interesting you were, it didn't matter how much character you had. What all guys really wanted were supermodels.

Jessica Wakefield stormed into the house after work, furious at Elizabeth. Her twin was supposed to give her a ride home, but when Jessica got to the parking lot, the Jeep was gone. So Jessica had to suffer rush hour traffic on two buses to get back to Sweet Valley. Plus, it was raining, and she had gotten soaked to the skin. It was one thing to be stranded at Sweet Valley High, but it was another to be stranded in downtown L.A.!

Jessica headed to the kitchen and threw her black leather bag on the counter. She was angry, she was hungry, and she was drenched. Jessica peeled off her wet blazer and shook out her damp hair. *It figures*, she thought. The weather had been clear and beautiful all week. Of course it had started to rain the one evening that Elizabeth decided to abandon her. Jessica didn't wear a watch, and she never carried an umbrella. That's what her twin was for. But apparently, her sister wasn't there for her anymore. A bolt of thunder rocked the house as if it were emphasizing Jessica's angry thoughts.

Swinging open the refrigerator door, Jessica uncapped a container of orange juice and drank directly from the bottle. Then she foraged hungrily through the fridge, grabbing a carton of yogurt, a bowl of cut vegetables, and a wedge of cheddar cheese. Balancing the food in one hand, she pulled a box of crackers from the cabinet and then dropped everything in a heap on the counter.

Jessica jumped up on a stool and munched aggressively on a baby carrot. She didn't know what had gotten into her sister. Normally Elizabeth was the responsible twin, and Jessica was the unpredictable one. Elizabeth was a straight A student with high ambitions to be a professional writer someday. A staff writer for the school newspaper, the *Oracle,* Elizabeth spent much of her time in the *Oracle* office working on her "Personal Profiles" column or writing feature articles. In her spare time, she preferred quiet pursuits, such as taking walks with her boyfriend, Todd, or going to the movies with her best friends, Enid and Maria. Fashion had never been a big priority for Elizabeth, and her looks tended toward the conservative. Elizabeth's signature attire was beige pants and a polo shirt or jeans and a cotton blouse.

11

Jessica, on the other hand, lived to make fashion statements. She was always at the forefront of new fads, and her taste bordered on the outrageous. Mini-miniskirts and wild colors suited her best. Jessica's personality matched her clothes. The co-captain of the cheerleading squad and an active member of Pi Beta Alpha, the most exclusive sorority at Sweet Valley High, Jessica was always at the center of the crowd. When she wasn't at cheerleading practice, she could usually be found in one of three places: the mall, the ocean, or the dance floor of the beach disco.

But ever since we've started our internships, Jessica thought, *Liz has become a totally different person.* Suddenly Elizabeth was only interested in fashion and success. She had entirely revamped her look with a chic new haircut and a brand-new professional wardrobe. After one day at work, Elizabeth took all the money she had been saving for a new computer and blew it on a shopping spree at the mall.

Jessica sighed. Elizabeth hadn't just undergone a physical transformation, but a personality transformation as well. Ever since she had started at *Flair,* she hadn't had a moment for Todd, or for Enid and Maria. Jessica cut off a wedge a cheese and sandwiched it between two crackers, biting into the concoction thoughtfully. It seemed as though considerate, polite Elizabeth Wakefield had turned into a power-hungry shark with an eye only for her own success.

Jessica's eyes narrowed. Her sister was definitely changing, and Jessica didn't like it one bit. *In fact,* Jessica thought worriedly, *Elizabeth is becoming more and more like me!* Jessica took a gulp of juice, shuddering at the thought. Despite their physical resemblance, from their silky golden blond hair to their blue-green eyes to their slim athletic figures, the two girls were so different on the inside that their friends could always tell them apart. Instead of competing for attention, they'd always complimented one other. And Jessica liked it that way. One Jessica was enough! After all, if Elizabeth started acting like her, then who was going to act like Elizabeth? Who was going to cover for Jessica when she needed it?

Jessica hopped off the stool and wiped crumbs from her skirt. It was time to give Elizabeth a piece of her mind. She had to straighten her out before it was too late.

With determination, Jessica marched up the stairs and down the hall. She burst into Elizabeth's room. "I can't believe you left me stranded in downtown L.A.!" she yelled. "It's one thing to blow off your friends, but I'm your *sister!* This is going too far! If you think—"

Jessica stopped midsentence. Elizabeth was lying facedown in her bed, sobbing her heart out. A big box of blue tissues sat next to her on the bed, with a mountain of crumbled tissues surrounding it.

Jessica's anger immediately turned to concern.

"Hey, what happened?" she asked, picking up the box and taking a seat next to Elizabeth on the bed.

Jessica's question only provoked a fresh outpouring of tears. "Shh . . . it's OK, it's OK," she said soothingly, rubbing her sister's back.

Finally, Elizabeth hiccuped and pulled herself up to a sitting position. Her face was red and blotchy, and her hair was in disarray. "It's Todd," Elizabeth choked out between tears. "He and—I saw—art department—*Simone*." She burst into tears again and grabbed a tissue, blowing her nose loudly.

Jessica's eyes widened. "You caught Todd with Simone?" she asked.

Elizabeth nodded, a rivulet of tears streaming down her cheeks.

"That is so *despicable*," Jessica declared. She brushed back a long lock of hair from Elizabeth's cheek and tucked it behind her ear.

Elizabeth nodded and sniffed, wiping at her eyes. "I'm not surprised about the Stick," she said. "But T-Todd—" She waved a hand in the air.

Jessica nodded. "I think this modeling thing has gone to his head." She was about to say that it was all for the best, since boring-as-butter Todd Wilkins was a total drip, but she bit back her words. Now was clearly not the time.

Elizabeth brought her knees up to her chest and wrapped her arms around them. "Jess, I'm sorry," she said. "I went to the art department to find Todd, and when I saw him with Simone, I just freaked out and ran. I was so upset that I forgot about giving you a ride." Fresh tears came to her eyes.

"Hey, you're going to drown if you keep this up!" Jessica said, scooting back across the bed and leaning against the wall next to Elizabeth. "Now don't worry about it," she said, propping a throw pillow behind her sister's back and placing a comforting arm around her shoulders. "There's nothing I'd rather do on a Thursday night than take public transportation in the rain."

Elizabeth smiled through her tears. "You're the best, Jess," she said. Then she closed her eyes and rested her head back on the pillow.

Jessica narrowed her eyes, her anger displaced from Elizabeth to Simone. Ever since Jessica had met the superskinny, supersnobby supermodel, she had known there would be trouble. Simone was a spoiled prima donna who thought she was the center of the universe. And as the photographer's assistant, Jessica was at Simone's beck and call—which meant fetching mineral water and celery sticks and supplying her with a constant supply of outfits and props.

It was bad enough that Simone had been treating Jessica like dirt, ordering her around and making ridiculous demands. Messing with *her* was one thing. Jessica could defend herself. But moving in on her twin's boyfriend was something else altogether. Simone was going to pay.

Chapter 2

It was only nine P.M., but Elizabeth lay in bed, tossing and turning. The picture of Todd together with Simone kept dancing before her eyes, tormenting her. Elizabeth flipped on her side and wrapped the covers around herself, trying to shake the image from her mind. Outside, rain was pouring steadily down. Usually the sounds of rain soothed her, but tonight it just added to her anxiety.

Think of the ocean, she told herself. She concentrated deeply, imagining the picturesque view at Ocean Bay. She saw hot, white sand and the foamy blue-green sea. White-capped breakers crashed onto the shore, and seagulls cut arcing patterns above the waves. Then she saw Todd and Simone walking hand in hand along the shore. Simone was barefoot and carrying her sandals in one hand, but her storklike legs were so long that she was almost as tall as Todd. *I can't believe you took her to the beach,* Elizabeth irrationally told Todd in her mind. *Our beach.* . . . Pain stabbed at her heart.

Elizabeth shook her head and threw off the covers, sitting up in bed. It was no use. She couldn't sleep. She couldn't stop thinking about Todd and Simone. Sighing deeply, she reached over and turned on the lamp next to her bed. The first thing she saw was a copy of *Flair* on her nightstand. Leona had given her a stack of back issues so she could familiarize herself with the magazine, and this one featured a barely bikini-clad Simone. Elizabeth sucked in her breath, feeling assaulted by the photograph.

She picked up the magazine and examined the cover. Usually pictures of models in bathing suits offended her feminist sensibility, but this one was particularly artistic. It had clearly been shot by Quentin Berg. The photo was in black and white, with a grainy quality that gave it a dated look. Elizabeth had to admit that Simone looked good. She was perched on a white boulder, her long legs folded gracefully underneath her. Her sleek asymmetrically-cut jet black hair provided a sharp contrast to her flawless ivory skin. Her full lips were pursed together in a pout, and her pale and strangely blank eyes stared directly at the camera. She was obviously beautiful, but she seemed empty—and cold. And she was so skinny that she looked like a starvation victim. But obviously, that's what Todd wanted. He didn't want someone with life. He wanted someone with status. Supermodel status.

Elizabeth scowled, feeling like a nobody, a nothing. She felt like her entire self had been made worthless. She could change her interests, but she couldn't change her looks. She'd never be six feet tall. She'd never look like a supermodel. Elizabeth balled her hands into fists, seething with frustration. Then she tore off the cover of the magazine, ripping it into tiny pieces. She threw the pieces on the floor, watching in satisfaction as they scattered over her cream-colored carpet.

Elizabeth slid out of bed and kicked at the torn pieces on the floor, crushing Simone's lips into the carpet with her heel. She paced from one side of her bedroom to the other, grinding her teeth. She stopped at the door and surveyed her room, itching with dissatisfaction. It was so impeccably neat and orderly. She looked in disgust at her perfectly clean desk with her reference books and computer, at her armoire with her shoes all lined up, at the tidy bookshelves. . . . Her room used to give her a sense of peace and a desire to work. Now she felt caged in. Elizabeth yanked open a window, letting in a gust of cold, windy air. Then she grabbed her clothes from the bed and threw them on the floor in a heap.

Maybe it's all my fault, Elizabeth thought, pushing her clothes out of the way with her foot as she crossed the room again. After all, she *had* been neglecting Todd. Ever since she had found out about her internship, the job had been the only thing on her mind. Todd had called her—and faxed her—and had even driven all the way to L.A. to see her. But she hadn't given him a second of her time.

Then Elizabeth dismissed the thought as ridiculous. When Todd had trained like a madman for the basketball finals last season, she had barely seen him at all. And she had understood. Besides, this internship was just two weeks long. Just because Todd hadn't bothered looking for an interesting position was no reason Elizabeth shouldn't try to make a future for herself.

Elizabeth grabbed a woolen blanket from her bed and flopped dejectedly onto her pale velvet divan. She couldn't believe that all these years could be erased in a second—in a kiss. Todd was her constant companion, her other half. It seemed like they'd always been together. And Elizabeth had thought they'd *always* be together.

A jumble of random memories flooded into her mind, causing her chest to constrict in pain. She remembered seeing Todd at basketball practice the week before, wearing cutoff blue sweatpants and a canary yellow T-shirt. She'd stopped by to see him after school, and he'd turned and sent her a kiss, mouthing "I love you" in the air. She saw his brown eyes staring at her intensely at Miller's Point, a popular parking spot high above Sweet

Valley. And then she saw herself and Todd together in the park one afternoon years ago, when they had shared their first, tentative kiss. . . .

Elizabeth curled her legs underneath her and wrapped her blanket around her shoulders. She didn't know how she was going to make it through the school year. Sweet Valley was full of too many memories. She reached over and picked up the framed picture of Todd from her bookshelf. He was smiling at her, and his deep brown eyes were warm and trusting. She quickly put it back, laying it face down on the shelf. *How could you throw it all away, Todd?* she thought in pain, hot tears coming to her eyes. *How could you betray me like this? How could you betray us like this?*

Tears trickled down her cheeks, and she jumped up, brushing them angrily away. She couldn't let herself go to pieces. After all, she still had her pride. It was bad enough that Todd had fallen in love with someone else, but he had cheated on her—at her own workplace. Elizabeth shook her head in disgust. She had thought that Todd was different from other guys. She had thought he cared about things that really mattered. But no, as soon as a supermodel walked into the vicinity, he was history.

A flash of lightning illuminated the sky and a blast of rain shot through the open window. Shivering, Elizabeth pulled the window shut. Then she prowled across the room, feeling restless. She didn't know what to do with herself. She wanted to talk to someone. Jessica was wonderful, but she needed a friend who would truly understand her situation—like Enid. Enid always managed to make her feel better. She was levelheaded and could always give Elizabeth a sense of perspective about things.

Picking the phone up from her nightstand, she carried it to the floor and plopped down on the carpet, bringing her knees up to her chest. She punched in Enid's number, waiting as the phone rang. But no one answered, and she hung up when Mrs. Rollins's answering machine picked up.

Elizabeth blinked back tears, feeling a little desperate for support. She stared at the number pad, wondering if she should call Maria. She had been giving her friends the brush-off lately, and they were probably mad at her. But then again, they were her best friends. They would understand. They would be there for her.

Without thinking about it any further, Elizabeth quickly dialed Maria's number. She twisted the phone cord around her finger as the phone rang. *Maria, please be there,* she thought.

Finally Maria picked up. "Yes?" she asked, her voice giddy. Elizabeth breathed a sigh of relief.

"Maria, it's Elizabeth," she said.

"Oh, hi, Elizabeth," Maria responded, her voice turning distinctly cold. Elizabeth winced. Then she heard giggling in the background.

"Is this a bad time?" Elizabeth asked. "Is somebody over?" She twisted the phone cord tighter in her hand, nearly cutting off the circulation in her fingers.

"Enid is staying over tonight," Maria explained, her voice clipped and distant. "We're helping each other out with stuff for our internships."

"Oh," Elizabeth said softly, hit with a pang of jealousy. Enid and Maria never used to hang out without her. "Why didn't you invite me?" she asked, trying to keep the hurt out of her voice.

"Hmm," Maria said. "Just a minute." Elizabeth could tell she had covered the receiver with her hand, but her muffled voice came through anyway. "Enid, Elizabeth wants to know why we didn't invite her over." Elizabeth heard the girls giggle, and tears welled up in her eyes again. What was going on? Was the whole world turning on her?

Enid got on the phone a moment later. "Hi, Elizabeth, it's Enid," she said.

"Hi," Elizabeth replied tentatively.

Enid's voice was cold. "In answer to your question, we weren't aware that you'd have time to hang out with two peons like us. You've been so busy with the power players that we didn't want to disturb you."

Elizabeth didn't even have the energy to respond. She said good-bye quietly and hung up the phone.

Elizabeth wrapped her arms around her body, feeling worse than she had before. She was completely alone in the world. First she lost Todd. Now she'd lost her two best friends.

The rain pelted down around her, enveloping her in her solitude.

"What horrible weather!" Enid exclaimed later that evening as she and Maria ducked out of the beating rain into the Dairi Burger, Sweet Valley's most popular teenage hangout. Enid shivered as she took off her raincoat and hung it up on a peg.

Maria closed her dilapidated umbrella with difficulty and then dropped it into the bucket by the door. "I don't know why I bothered bringing that," Maria said, looking down at the umbrella in dismay. It was so windy that the umbrella had turned inside out, and the girls had gotten soaked during the short walk from the parking lot to the restaurant. A bolt of thunder rocked the sky, and a gust of cool wind shot through the door.

Enid pushed the door shut and wrapped her olive green cardigan sweater tightly around herself. "Let's take a booth in the back," she suggested. "It'll be warmer farther away from the door."

Despite the bad weather, the restaurant was hopping. The booths were jammed with students talking and laughing in groups. *Pings* and *bleeps* sounded from the game room.

Enid headed for a booth in back, Maria a step behind her. A series of whistles and catcalls followed in their wake.

"Lookin' good!" Bruce Patman, the richest and most arrogant student at Sweet Valley High, called out.

"Foxy mama!" yelled out Paul Jeffries.

Enid turned to see the commotion. A bunch of senior guys at a corner table were staring at Maria, practically drooling.

Enid shook her head. "Looks like you're creating a stir, as usual," she said with a grin. "You've still got that movie star aura."

Maria rolled her eyes. "Oh, come on," she scoffed, taking Enid's arm and hurrying her to the back. "Toilet paper commercials do not a movie star make."

Even though Maria looked like a movie star, Enid knew she didn't want to be treated like one. Maria had been a successful film and commercial actress as a child. But when she hit puberty, the roles had stopped coming. Her family had recently moved back to Sweet Valley from New York, and now she wanted more than anything to be a normal teenager.

"Well, you *do* look pretty chic," Enid said, glancing at her friend admiringly. With her funky retro look, Maria had a style all her own. Tonight she was wearing a pale blue forties dress with huge square buttons and thick army boots on her feet. An exotic green silk scarf was tied over her head, hiding her hair completely. "Maybe *you* should be interning at *Flair* magazine."

"Ugh," Maria groaned, sliding into the booth

24

opposite Enid. She pulled off her scarf and ran a finger through her short-cropped dark curly hair. "Don't even *mention* that name." She shivered and wrapped the scarf around her neck, tying it adeptly at the back.

Enid shook her head. "I don't know what's gotten into Elizabeth lately."

A waiter appeared at their table, and the girls quickly placed their orders—fries and shakes for both of them.

Maria spoke in a low voice after the waiter had left. "You know, I'm worried about Elizabeth—she isn't acting like herself."

"You can say that again," Enid agreed. "She's acting like some self-centered fashion plate. I would say that she's turned into Jessica—but in this case, that's being kind."

Maria frowned. "I don't know, Enid. Maybe something's going on that we don't know about. I've known Elizabeth forever, and I've never seen her act like this. She's not usually inconsiderate— or egotistical. And she's *never* been interested in fashion."

It's true, Enid thought. Usually Elizabeth was a totally loyal friend, and Enid could always count on her. But ever since she'd gotten her internship, Elizabeth had become an entirely different person. She was preoccupied, and all she talked about was herself. She had completely ignored Enid and Maria all week, and Wednesday night had been the last straw. In order to make up for neglecting them, Elizabeth had invited them to meet her in L.A. to go to a cappuccino bar after work. Enid and Maria had endured two bus rides and three traffic jams to meet Elizabeth downtown, only to find that Elizabeth couldn't make it because her boss wanted her to stay late. Elizabeth hadn't even been the slightest bit apologetic. Enid and Maria had been furious.

The waiter set down strawberry shakes and two plates of fries in front of them. Enid squeezed out a mound of ketchup on her plate and grabbed a few fries hungrily.

Maria bit her lip. "Maybe we should invite her to meet us tonight," she said thoughtfully. "She sounded upset on the phone." She pulled the wrapper off her straw and took a long draw on her shake.

Enid looked at her friend in shock. "Maria, are you crazy? Did you forget about Wednesday night already?"

Maria shrugged, dragging a fry through Enid's ketchup. "Well, we had fun anyway."

After Elizabeth ditched them, Enid and Maria decided to make the best of being in L.A. They had strolled down Rodeo Drive and peeked in all the shops. Then they had gotten their pictures taken in a color photo booth and had gone dancing at an underage club. The teenage crowd had been a bit too superficial for their tastes, but they'd had a fantastic evening anyway.

"Hey, that reminds me," Enid said, her eyes lighting up. "There's a guy at my literary agency who saw the pictures we took in the booth the other day. His name is Shane Maddox, he's an editorial assistant, and he's dying to meet you."

Maria shook her head, waggling a fry at Enid. "Forget it. After my disastrous date with Kevin yesterday, I'm swearing off all guys. At least guys I don't know."

Kevin Anderson was the set manager at the theater, and they'd gone out for lunch to an artsy little bistro. Maria had been talking about her date for days, but it turned out they had nothing in common. She'd said they spent an hour talking about California weather.

Enid shrugged. "Oh, well, too bad. Because Shane's pret-ty cu-ute."

"What does he look like?" Maria asked. "Just out of curiosity," she added quickly.

Enid crossed her legs and leaned back in the booth. "Well, let's see. He's about six feet tall, broad-shouldered, and handsome. *Plus,* he has beautiful ebony skin." Enid knew that the last detail would get Maria. Even though her friend didn't prefer any single type, she had a soft spot for really dark-skinned guys.

Maria's eyes widened, but Enid waved a dismissive hand in the air. "Oh, well . . . too bad. I'll just tell him you're not interested."

Maria refused to rise to the bait. "OK," she said with a smug smile.

"Hmmph," Enid pouted, drumming her fingers on the wooden table.

Maria laughed and leaned in closer to Enid. "But, on the other hand, I think I might have a guy for you."

"Oh yeah, who?" Enid asked, dipping a spoon into her strawberry shake. She was trying to sound nonchalant, but actually, she was thrilled. Ever since her obsession with Jonathan Cain, a deranged transfer student who had been at Sweet Valley for a month, her life had been entirely guyless.

"Kevin, the set manager."

"What?" Enid sputtered. "The guy you went out with yesterday?"

Maria grinned. "What's wrong? You don't like to share?"

"Forget it, Maria," Enid said firmly. "If Kevin's interested in you, then he won't be interested in me. There's no way I'm going out with him. Absolutely *no way*."

"Enid, I'm telling you, it didn't click between us," Maria insisted. "We had *nothing* in common. Zero. Zilch. There was no spark at all."

Enid's eyes narrowed. "Well, maybe not for you."

Maria laughed. "Honestly, he wasn't interested either." Then she turned her sly almond-shaped eyes to Enid. "Actually, I told him a little bit about you. He said you sounded really interesting and that he'd like to get to know you better."

Enid shook her head. "Well, I'm not interested. I do not compete with Maria Slater, former child actress. *Period*." She dipped a spoon into her shake and brought a spoonful of ice cream to her mouth.

Maria frowned. "Hmm. There's just one little problem. I sort of told him you were free Friday night."

Enid choked on her ice cream. "You—*what?*"

"Well, aren't you?" Maria pressed.

Enid shook her head. "Maria Slater, you are totally outrageous. I am going on that date on one condition and one condition only."

"And what is that?" Maria asked with a grin.

"That you come along—with Shane Maddox."

Maria grimaced. "A double blind date?"

Enid shrugged. "It's that or nothing."

"OK, you're on," Maria agreed with a laugh.

Jessica sat cross-legged in bed late Thursday night, turning the pages of the latest issue of *Ingenue*. She stopped at a spread covering upcoming spring fashions and studied the chic models featured in it. They were all blondes, with hazel eyes and fair complexions, and they were all wearing short dresses in shades of green and orange. Even though the women had similar coloring, each of them seemed to have a unique, individual look. *Some day, that will be me*, Jessica thought happily. *Some day soon. . . .*

Jessica hugged her arms around her body,

thinking excitedly about her future as a super-model. In just one day, her entire life had turned around. And it was all because of Quentin Berg, the hotshot photographer she was working for at *Flair*.

Quentin, who was under contract to *Flair*, was one of the biggest names in the fashion business. He was in his early twenties, with shaggy blond hair, broad shoulders, and deep, mysterious gray eyes. He was good-looking in a rumpled, artistic kind of way, but he wasn't really Jessica's type. Jessica liked a tougher, more masculine look. But Jessica was determined to charm him, because Quentin could help her advance her career as a model.

At first, Quentin had treated her like dirt. For the most part, he had acted like she wasn't on the set at all. And when he did notice her, it was just to snarl at her. He had basically been a total jerk, ordering her to get him coffee and pick up his prints at the mail room.

But then everything had changed. Driven to extreme measures, Jessica had stolen one of Quentin's cameras, a state-of-the-art Minolta with a telephoto lens, and had coerced Lila into taking pictures of her at the beach. Lila had shot two roles of film with Jessica cavorting on the water's edge, but unfortunately the camera had ended up in the ocean as well.

When Quentin discovered that his camera was

missing, he had been livid, and Jessica had done her best to avoid him. But out of nowhere a brand new camera had mysteriously appeared in its spot, with a note from Jessica saying she had given it a thorough overhaul and cleaning. At first, Jessica had been baffled. But then she realized that Lila must have secretly replaced the camera for her.

After that, Quentin had warmed up. He had even begun to notice her work and had complimented her efforts with the sets. And then Jessica had made her move. Wednesday night after work, she had snuck into the darkroom and approached Quentin from behind, giving him a mysterious kiss and then disappearing into the night. When he saw her at work the next day, he was clearly intrigued, but Jessica just smiled enigmatically. Then she had shown him her photos. He had been impressed and had invited her to dinner—to discuss her potential as a fashion model.

Jessica's stomach tightened in excitement. Tomorrow could be the start of her career as the newest supermodel on the fashion scene.

Not only had Quentin made a 360-degree turnaround at work, but so had Cameron Smith, a cute guy who worked in the mailroom. Jessica propped up her pillow and sat back against the wall, thinking dreamily of her encounters with Cameron. The first time she had met him, she had been dozing on a couch in the mailroom. He had kissed her awake like the prince in *Sleeping Beauty*. His gallantry had continued after that, and he had made his interest in her clear.

But, bent on advancing her career through Quentin, Jessica had steadily avoided Cameron, and eventually he had figured that out. "You're only interested in people with classy titles or flashy cars or tons of money!" he had spat at her this morning. Jessica had finally convinced him he was wrong. And this afternoon, he had found her alone in the wardrobe room and kissed her in a way that she'd never been kissed. Then he'd asked her out for Friday night.

Jessica leaned back against her pillow, reliving his passionate kiss. She could feel his strong arms wrapped around her and smell his deep, masculine scent. She shivered again as she remembered the fountain of sparks that had cascaded over her entire body. Jessica closed her eyes contentedly. She didn't know how she'd make it to Friday night.

That she bolted upright. *Friday night!* That's when she was supposed to go out with Quentin. *I knew it was too good to be true,* she thought dejectedly. *I knew my life couldn't completely change in one day.* Now she had to make a choice—between a dream guy and a dream career.

Jessica sighed and climbed into bed. It was an impossible dilemma. She couldn't give up Cameron or her chance to become a model. Jessica pulled the covers tightly around her. *How can I possibly choose?*

* * *

Todd took Simone's hand and spun her around at the center of the dance floor. It was almost midnight, and he and Simone were at the Edge, a hip new nightclub in downtown L.A. This was the latest he'd ever been out on a school night. The dance floor was packed with a chichi L.A. crowd, and loud techno music blasted from the speakers. Todd felt his head whirling with the pulsing beat of the electronic music.

"This is what it's like living on the edge, Todd," Simone whispered in a husky voice in his ear. "How do you like it?"

Todd shrugged. "No big deal," he said, trying to sound cool. But his voice came out as a squeak, and he blushed.

Simone grinned. "You are so *cute*, Todd," she squealed. Todd's blush deepened, but Simone was already turning her attention to the other side of the room. "Look," she said, pointing an elegant finger at the bar. "That's Sven Sorensen, the editor in chief of *Ingenue* magazine."

Todd followed her gaze. A lanky, Swedish-looking man with a blond beard was sitting at the bar with a group of tall models crowded around him.

Todd nodded, searching in vain for something intelligent to say. Then he realized that Simone wasn't paying attention anyway. She was too busy posing for Sven. She steered herself and Todd around so Sven could get a view of her profile. "Spin me, Todd," she commanded in an intense voice. Todd swung her around obediently, and she twirled wildly, trying to get Sven's attention.

Todd blushed, feeling more self-conscious than ever. He could see every guy in the place looking at him with total envy because he was with Simone. He was wearing jeans and a T-shirt, and he wished he'd worn something a little more hip. The crowd was made up of chic actors and models, and they were all dressed almost entirely in black. The women were wearing short skirts or tight dresses, and most of the guys had on black jeans and funky retro jackets.

Sven stood up from the bar, and Simone stopped midspin. "Oh, I'll be right back," she said, her voice breathless. Then she rushed off.

Todd stood in the middle of the dance floor. He tried to make out Simone through the crowd, but gyrating bodies blocked his view. There were a few couples on the dance floor, but most of the people were dancing alone, swaying to the music as if they were in a trance.

"Hey, you wanna join the love parade?" a sultry voice whispered in his ear.

"Huh?" Todd said, blinking. He turned to see a woman with short scarlet hair standing by his side. She had a nosering and a lipring. A trail of dancers followed her in a line, bobbing rhythmically in an almost hypnotic state.

"It's a communion with Being," she said. "You close your eyes and let the music fill your body."

"C'mon, get in line," urged a blond woman with a silver streak in her hair. "You'll see. It's a natural high."

"Uh, no thanks," Todd said quickly. "I was just going to get a drink."

He waved and walked away, the eerie sound of the women's laughter echoing in his ears. Weaving through the grinding bodies, he quickly made his way to the bar.

"What'll you have?" the bartender barked. He was a bulky man with a huge grizzly beard.

Todd gulped. He was tempted to order a drink, but he was underage. If he got carded, he would get kicked out of the club and would be totally humiliated.

"Just a mineral water," he said quickly.

The bartender nodded and picked up a bottle of seltzer. He poured the bubbling water into a tall glass.

Todd picked up his drink and leaned against the bar, taking in the surroundings. The club was done in ultramodern decor, with stark white tables and shiny black floors. A red, flashing neon band surrounded the wall, and a shimmering disco ball hung over the middle of the dance floor. The hip L.A. crowd looked as electric as the club itself.

Todd took a sip of his drink, feeling entirely out of place. He wondered if anybody knew he was underage. He was trying to play it cool, but he felt as if he were wearing a huge sign on his back that screamed Sixteen!

"Oh, Todd, there you are!" Simone breathed by his side. "C'mon, let's go back to the dance floor," she said, taking his hand.

"Sure," Todd agreed, downing his drink and following her back to the floor. He definitely preferred the dance floor to the bar. Dancing was one thing he could legitimately do. At the bar, he felt like a total fraud.

Simone wrapped her arms around his waist and pressed her body to his.

Todd coughed uncomfortably, shifting back a few inches. "So, did you have any luck with the editor in chief of *Ingenue*?" he asked.

Simone nodded in pleasure. "He's going to call me," she said. "He wants to use me for the cover of the next issue." She giggled gleefully. "That means I'll be replacing Justine Laroche. She's going to be *green*."

"Hey, that's great," Todd said, trying to sound happy for her. *I just can't think of a modeling job as important*, he thought. Then he swallowed hard, suddenly struck by how hypocritical he was being. This was his crowd now. *He* was a model too.

Todd looked at the beautiful people around him and tried to convince himself that he was having a great time—and that the nagging feeling in the pit of his stomach had nothing to do with Elizabeth. He decided that he must be allergic to the shrimp cocktail he and Simone had eaten earlier.

Then, out of the corner of his eye, he glimpsed

a blond girl across the dance floor. For a split second his heart leapt. *Elizabeth!* he thought. Maybe she had come here to find him—to reconcile with him. But then the girl turned. It wasn't Elizabeth. Simone pulled him closer in her arms.

A wave of disappointment washed over him, and suddenly Elizabeth's bitter words came back to him. *You're not the person I thought you were.* Todd felt a sharp pang in his heart.

Then he shook off his negative feelings. Obviously Elizabeth was right: He wasn't just a normal teenager. He was *model* material. He was meant for fame and fortune. It was going to be difficult to leave his old life behind, but he'd have to get used to it. He'd have to rise to the challenge.

I'm happy to be in Simone's arms, he told himself. *Very, very happy.*

Chapter 3

Todd was alone at a nightclub with supermodels, and techno music was pounding in his brain. Rap rap rap, the pulsing musical beat throbbed. Rap rap rap. The girls were getting thinner and thinner and taller and taller and the music was getting louder and louder. "Wanna join the love parade?" a husky voice on his left asked. "Wanna join the love parade?" a voice on his right echoed. Suddenly Todd felt like he was going to go mad. He looked around for a way out of the club, but all he saw were grotesquely smooth and angular made-up faces looming in on him.

Todd moaned and opened his eyes, trying to orient himself. Then the sound repeated itself. *Rap rap rap.*

Todd's head was aching, and the beats of music merged with the pounding in his temples. He held his head, trying to place the sound. Then the evening came back to him. *Simone. The Edge.* He squinted at the digital clock on the nightstand. *Eight o'clock.* He had slept through his alarm.

Todd groaned, realizing he felt lousy. His head was throbbing, and his whole body ached. *This must be what it feels like to have a hangover,* he thought, punching the blankets around him and burrowing deeper into his covers. He felt like staying inside all day. The prospect of getting out of his warm bed seemed overwhelming—and nearly impossible.

I shouldn't have stayed out so late with Simone, he thought with regret. He hadn't even had a good time. He had felt completely out of place.

Then the rapping sound came again, and Todd realized it was coming from the door. "C'mon in," he croaked out in a groggy voice.

His father stuck his head into Todd's room. "Be downstairs in two minutes," Mr. Wilkins ordered in an authoritative tone. Then he turned and marched away. Todd groaned. His dad did *not* sound happy.

Todd slid out of bed, rubbing his eyes wearily as he headed for the shower. This day was not starting out well. And he had a sinking feeling that it was only going to get worse.

When Todd turned down the hall to the kitchen, he saw his mom and dad waiting for him at the table. They were both dressed for work, and they

39

were sitting perfectly still, like two wax figures. Emily Wilkins, a management consultant, had on a forest green wool suit that complimented her short glossy auburn hair and deep green eyes. In his plaid blue shirt, wine-colored tie, and blue suspenders, Bert Wilkins looked every bit the executive. The round wooden kitchen table was covered with a bright yellow tablecloth, and a platter of scrambled eggs stood in the middle. Todd's seat was empty and waiting for him, a bowl of cereal and a glass of orange juice set out on a place mat in front of it.

Todd hesitated at the doorway. Everything looked too ordinary. Something was definitely up. What was going on? Did his parents know he went out last night? He had gotten home around two in the morning and had snuck in the back door. But nobody had stirred. He had even peeked his head into his parents' room, and they had both been fast asleep.

His mother caught sight of him at the door. "Good morning, Todd," she said with a tight smile.

"Uh, morning," Todd mumbled, heading for the table. He sat down at his seat and stared at the tablecloth. Then he grabbed a piece of toast from the plate in the middle of the table and took a bite. The sounds of his chewing reverberated oddly in the silent room.

Bert Wilkins took a sip of black coffee. "You mother went grocery shopping this morning," he said.

Todd glanced at his father warily. He had definitely entered an alternate universe.

"And I picked up this copy of *Los Angeles Living*," Mrs. Wilkins put in, holding up a newspaper for Todd to see. *Los Angeles Living* was a tabloid paper that came out daily. Todd glanced at the paper in confusion. His mother never read junk like that.

"Uh-huh," Todd said warily, feeling as if he was being lead into a trap. Usually his parents were relaxed and casual at breakfast. Normally, his dad would be making jokes, and his mother would be asking Todd questions about school and his love life. Today they were acting so civilized that it was weird. It was like the calm before the storm.

Then Todd focused in on the picture on the cover and almost choked on his toast. It was a large color photo of himself and Simone on the dance floor at the Edge. Todd's mouth dropped open. Underneath the photo, a caption read, "Supermodel Simone and playboy Todd Wilkins danced till dawn."

"Are you aware that you have a curfew?" Mr. Wilkins asked in an ominous voice.

Todd gulped. He was in *big* trouble.

Elizabeth dragged herself into the *Flair* office on Friday morning after a sleepless night. For the first time since her internship had started, she didn't feel excited about the day ahead of her.

41

After tossing and turning for hours the night before, she'd finally managed to fall asleep. And then visions of Todd and Simone had haunted her dreams.

Elizabeth stared at the computer, wondering how she was going to get any work done. Then her eyes lit on the fax that Todd had sent her a few days ago. It was a cartoon of a guy and a girl in their respective offices. Above the boy's head was a dialogue bubble that read, "Your office or mine?" *Mine*, Elizabeth whispered aloud. *Right office, wrong girl*. Elizabeth ripped the fax off the wall and crumpled it in a ball, tossing it into the waste basket in disgust.

She cupped her fingers around her steaming mug of coffee, sighing deeply. It was bad enough that Todd was cheating on her with Simone. But they were both working at *Flair* as well. Elizabeth rubbed a weary eye. She didn't know how she was going to make it through the next week.

Elizabeth lifted her coffee mug to her lips, hoping to send a jolt of caffeine to the energy centers in her brain. But before she could take a sip, a head popped through her doorway. It was Reggie Andrews, an assistant fashion editor of the magazine.

"Good morning!" Reggie said, a smile lighting up her delicate features. A young Asian woman with fine black hair and a flawless complexion, Reggie was Elizabeth's closest friend at *Flair*. She had just started working at *Flair* after graduating college the year before and had filled in Elizabeth on all the ins and outs of the publishing world.

"Morning," Elizabeth responded in a lackluster tone.

"Uh-oh," Reggie said, her dark brown, almond-shaped eyes filled with concern. "You look like you just lost your best friend."

Elizabeth set down her coffee cup. "That too."

"Hey, what happened?" Reggie asked. She quickly took a seat in the chair opposite the desk.

But Elizabeth just shook her head. "I can't talk about it in the office," she said, her voice coming out as a whisper.

"Why don't we take a quick trip to the cappuccino bar for a cup of coffee?" Reggie suggested.

"I've already got coffee," Elizabeth said, pointing to her mug.

"Not anymore," Reggie responded. She stood up and picked up Elizabeth's mug off the desk. Then she flung the contents into the potted plant in the corner.

Elizabeth couldn't help smiling at Reggie's behavior.

"Ah! There we go! Got a smile out of her," Reggie said, clapping her hands lightly. "Now come on." She waved a hand in the air. "Get up."

Elizabeth stood up reluctantly. "OK," she agreed.

Reggie linked arms with her and lead her down the hall to the elevator, chatting all the way. "I have the feeling I never left this office," she said with a moan. "I was here until nine P.M. last night proof-reading the fashion features for this month's issue. And then I had to fact check all the info for the Milan runway show."

"Wow," Elizabeth said in appreciation as they stepped into the elevator. "That's a lot of work for one day." Elizabeth knew that Reggie was a top-notch editor. That's why she had gotten promoted to assistant editor after one year of working at *Flair*.

"You're telling me," Reggie said. "Sometimes I think I live here."

They got out at the first floor and crossed the elegant lobby. Then they hurried around the corner to Café Costa, a hip, new cappuccino bar. The coffee bar was almost deserted, and Reggie and Elizabeth walked right up to the counter.

"Double mocha cappuccinos for both of us," Reggie ordered. Then she turned to Elizabeth with a smile. "My treat."

Elizabeth returned her smile gratefully. Reggie was really a wonderful friend. After losing Todd, Enid, and Maria all in one night, it was nice to have a sympathetic ear.

"Here you go," Reggie said, handing her a steaming tall cup of coffee. "Why don't we sit down for a minute?"

Elizabeth hesitated. She knew she shouldn't take a break at the beginning of the day, but she was anxious to share her troubles with somebody.

"What if Leona needs me?" she asked worriedly.

"The dragon lady will have to wait," Reggie declared.

Reggie didn't share Elizabeth's high opinion of Leona Peirson. For some reason, Reggie didn't trust the managing editor at all. But Reggie couldn't really come up with a reason for her suspicions. "Women's intuition," she had said.

They took their seats on stools at a high round table in the corner by the window. "So what happened?" Reggie asked. She ripped open a package of brown sugar and poured it in her coffee.

Elizabeth took a deep breath. "It's Todd," she said. Her heart constricted, and she felt tears spring to her eyes. "He's—he's going out with Simone."

Reggie looked shocked. "With *Simone?* The Fashion Fink?"

"Shh!" Elizabeth cautioned, looking around wildly. But nobody was within earshot.

Reggie leaned in closer. "Elizabeth, are you sure? Maybe it's just a rumor. From what you've told me about Todd, he doesn't seem to be the type to go for flaky supermodels."

"Positive," Elizabeth said with a sigh. "I saw them with my own eyes. Yesterday after work—in the photography studio." She took a sip of her mocha coffee.

Reggie's eyes widened. "But what's gotten into him? Is he mad at you for something?"

Elizabeth nodded. "Yeah. He thinks I've been ignoring him." She picked up her napkin and shredded it. "It's all my fault," she said sadly, scattering the pieces on the table. "I shouldn't have given him the brush-off. I practically pushed him into Simone's arms."

But Reggie shook her head firmly. "It is absolutely *not* your fault," she countered. "Todd is his own person. He must not have much strength of character if he can be seduced so easily by a stupid model."

Elizabeth nodded. She knew Reggie was right. If a little bit of neglect could make Todd turn to other girls, then he wasn't worth her time—and then this relationship wasn't worth her time either.

"Look on the bright side," Reggie went on. "It's good that you found out what Todd's like now—before it's too late. Now you can find someone who *really* appreciates you."

Elizabeth nodded, but Reggie's words fell flat. There wasn't a bright side.

Elizabeth shut her office door and locked it, feeling dangerously close to tears. Somehow Reggie's sympathy had only made her feel worse. She wasn't ready to give up Todd. It wasn't a relief to find out that he wasn't the person she had always thought he was. It was a shock—a horrible shock.

Suddenly the phone jangled.

Elizabeth groaned, blinking back her tears. She took a deep breath to compose herself. Then she picked up the receiver. "Elizabeth Wakefield," she said.

Leona Peirson's voice came through the phone. "Could you come see me for a moment in my office?" she asked.

"Sure, Leona," Elizabeth said, trying to infuse her voice with some enthusiasm. "I'll be right there."

After redirecting her calls to the reception desk, Elizabeth grabbed a pen and tucked a yellow memo pad underneath her arm. She sighed as she crossed the plush gray carpet leading to Leona's spacious office. Unfortunately, she was going to have to tell Leona about Todd. She and Leona had made plans to go on a double date that evening. She bit her lip, wondering if Leona already knew that Elizabeth had been replaced by a supermodel. After all, news traveled fast on the *Flair* grapevine. Elizabeth's tongue went dry at the thought. She didn't think she could handle public humiliation on top of her broken heart.

Leona's voice carried down the hall, and Elizabeth hesitated at the door of the managing editor's office. Leona was sitting behind her sleek black desk, talking on the phone and gesticulating wildly. Elizabeth knocked quietly on the open door.

Leona looked up and smiled, holding up an index finger as a sign meaning, *Just one minute*. Then she waved Elizabeth in.

Elizabeth took a seat in the leather armchair across from Leona's desk, watching the managing editor in admiration. Leona was clearly agitated, but her voice was controlled and quietly authoritative. A tall, stylish woman with an aggressive management style and clear charisma, she was everything Elizabeth wanted to be someday.

Elizabeth had liked Leona from the start. From day one, her boss had been straightforward with her. She'd made it clear that she expected a lot of hard work from Elizabeth, including meeting tight deadlines and putting in long hours. But she'd made her feel at home as well. She'd told Elizabeth she considered them a team, and as a team, she wanted diligence, input, and honesty. "As long as we're both completely honest with each other, we should get along wonderfully," she had said. She had all the qualities Elizabeth admired—independence, drive, and integrity.

Leona drummed her pearl-colored French-cut nails on the desk top. "The deadline is this afternoon at two o'clock," she was saying. "I want the article here *then*, on my desk. Is that clear?" She listened for a minute, then smiled. "Of course, I know. Creativity can't be forced." Leona ran a finger through her dark blond hair. "Don't force it, dear. Just *push* it a little, OK?"

Leona hung up the phone and exhaled deeply, blowing a long blond lock out of her face. "Writers!" she said with a sigh. "They're quite a temperamental group." Leona shook her head. "Sometimes I think they're worse than models."

Then Leona clapped her hands brusquely and turned her attention to Elizabeth. "So, how are you?"

"I'm OK," Elizabeth said slowly. "But I'm afraid we won't be able to do our double date tonight, after all," she said. "It's all over between me and Todd." She blinked, willing herself not to cry in front of her boss. Elizabeth clenched her fingers together in her lap, praying that Leona wouldn't ask for details.

But Leona was all business. "Oh, it's just as well," she said, waving a dismissive hand. "Your career should come first anyway. You're too young to be tied down. Believe me, Elizabeth, if you want to succeed, you have to throw yourself body, mind, and soul into your work. Romance just gets in the way."

Elizabeth let out her breath, relieved at Leona's matter-of-fact tone. If she had been sympathetic, Elizabeth was sure she would have burst into tears.

Leona leaned back and crossed one long, lean leg over the other, bobbing a low-heeled black pump in the air. "Actually, I was going to have to cancel our date anyway," she said. "I have a feeling that Sam—my boyfriend—is going to pop the question tonight." She gave Elizabeth an intimate smile. "Obviously, we'd want to be alone for that."

Elizabeth looked at her in surprise. "But what about career first?" she asked.

Leona shrugged. "Some of us can do it all," she responded lightly.

Elizabeth looked down, feeling like a total failure. She wished she were more like her boss.

"Now, enough woman talk," Leona said, sitting up straight and brushing her hands together. "Let's talk business. I want to give you the rundown of the upcoming special edition. We worked out the details last night in a brainstorming session." Leona's hazel eyes gleamed. "Elizabeth, you're going to love this idea."

Elizabeth forced a smile, but she felt completely lethargic inside. At the moment, she couldn't care less about *Flair* magazine or fashion or professional success.

Leona held up a mock pasteup of the cover. It featured a model in front of some kind of ancient ruins, with the title *Antiquity Today*. "It's a Greek and Roman antiquity edition," Leona explained. "We're going to play with the idea of past and present—with special fashion exclusives on modern styles in ancient settings, the fashions of antiquity, and the past in the present."

Despite herself, Elizabeth's ears perked up. "Like the retro look," she said. "Only *really* retro."

"Exactly," Leona said with a smile. She picked up a note pad and scanned it. "The travel section will contain a layout on Mediterranean holidays," she continued, "and the issue will contain feature articles on ancient mythology and on the lives of

Greek and Roman women in ancient times, with an emphasis on social structures, women's issues, sexism, and so forth."

As Leona continued to explain the concept, Elizabeth began to get some of her enthusiasm back. A million ideas popped into her head for the new issue. She pictured an article entitled "The Goddess in You" covering the ancient mythological figures. She wondered what the quality of life was for women in ancient times and what their social roles had been. Her fingers itched to do a search on the Lexis/Nexis machine in the office. Lexis/Nexis was a dream source of information for journalists, providing access to articles from every major newspaper and magazine in the United States.

Leona snapped her notebook shut. "So what do you think?"

"Leona, it's a fabulous idea," Elizabeth breathed.

Leona smiled in satisfaction. "I knew you'd like it." She leaned in closer. "But this means a lot of work during the next week—fact checking, proofreading, and some major research. And remember, the idea is highly confidential. We don't want anyone to know what the issue is about until it hits the newsstand."

Leona stood up, and Elizabeth took that as her cue to stand up too.

"I've written up a list of some of the things for

you to take care of today," Leona said, handing her a typed memo. "The most important task is research. I want you to search the Library of Congress and do a Lexis/Nexis run. By the end of the day, I want to know everything that's been printed on Greek and Roman antiquity in the last fifty years. And I mean *everything*."

"No problem," Elizabeth said, her chest tight with excitement. She headed back to her desk, filled with a new sense of determination. Leona was right. Relationships just got in the way. She was going to emulate Leona and throw herself into her work. After all, if she wanted to be successful in business, she couldn't let her personal life get her down.

Elizabeth sat down at her desk and flicked on her computer, ready to get to work.

Jessica paused on the top rung of a six-foot ladder in the main photography studio, surveying her work. For the past hour, she had been setting up for the morning's shoot. Nick Nolan, the set director, had come in early to prep her. It was a Greek Isles scene with a bright blue backdrop, huge white boulders, and a cascading waterfall.

Jessica gazed at the set in satisfaction. She had transformed the cool, airy studio into a hot Mediterranean paradise. The fake rocks cluttered together really looked like dusty white boulders, and they glinted against the backdrop as if against a blinding blue sky. Jessica had propped up the waterfall on the far left, but she wasn't quite sure how to hook up the mechanism.

She climbed all the way to the top of the ladder and carefully positioned the lights above the backdrop, trying to set them up just like Quentin wanted. Then she stepped down carefully and took a seat on the highest rung. She rubbed her shoulders and stretched out her neck. It was only ten A.M., and Jessica's back and shoulders were already aching from moving the fake rocks around and transporting huge buckets of water.

Where is everybody? Jessica wondered. Usually Quentin was there at the crack of dawn, barking out orders. And Simone normally didn't give Jessica a moment's peace, keeping her occupied with the most mundane tasks imaginable. *Maybe she won't show up,* Jessica thought hopefully. *Maybe one of her high heels got caught in a sewage drain and she twisted her ankle. Or maybe she slipped down the drain entirely.* Then Quentin would have no choice but to use Jessica in her place. With Simone out of the way, Jessica was sure she could get through to Quentin.

Suddenly the door swung open and Quentin breezed through, a camera slung over his shoulder. Jessica's tongue went dry. What if Quentin had forgotten all about the other day in the darkroom? What if he forgot about their date entirely? After all, you could never tell with artists. And

Quentin was a particularly temperamental one.

But Quentin whistled under his breath as he took in the set. "Hey, looks good," he said, smiling up at her. "A Greek paradise and a Greek goddess on her modern Mount Olympus." He sauntered over to her. "Want some help getting down from there?"

"Sure," Jessica said softly, standing up and turning around.

Jessica took a few steps down the ladder. Then Quentin put his strong arms around her waist and lifted her to the floor. His hands lingered on her waist as he turned her around to face him. "Looking forward to our dinner tonight?" he asked in a low voice.

"Of course," Jessica said coyly.

"You should be, because I'm taking you to the most exclusive restaurant in all of L.A.," he whispered in her ear. "It's called Chez Paul, and it's on Hollywood Boulevard. I'll meet you there at eight."

"Am I interrupting something?" came a saucy voice from behind them. Jessica and Quentin whirled around. It was Simone, a lazy catlike look of contentment on her cold features. Jessica bit her lip. It was a well-known fact at *Flair* that Simone and Quentin had been involved for some time. Jessica was thrilled to flaunt her flirtation with Quentin, but she wasn't sure he'd feel the same way.

But Quentin wasn't disturbed by Simone's arrival. "Simone, you're late," he said flatly.

Simone shrugged. "I needed my beauty sleep."

Quentin headed for the darkroom, suddenly all business. "Simone, go to wardrobe. Jessica, set up the lights. We'll be shooting in an hour."

Jessica pounced on Simone as soon as Quentin had disappeared into his cave of chemicals. "So, did you have fun with my sister's boyfriend last night?"

Simone was totally unperturbed by Jessica's attitude. "Todd's OK for a high-school boy," she responded. "He'll be good for a few photo ops, at least."

"Photo ops?" Jessica demanded. "Like what?"

Simone whipped out a copy of *Los Angeles Living* and held it up for Jessica to see. On the front page was a huge, tacky color photo of Todd in Simone's arms.

Jessica was speechless. This girl was too much. She was just glad that Elizabeth would never read a paper of such low quality. If she saw the photo, she'd really flip out.

"Now, if you'll excuse me," Simone purred, waltzing past her, "I've got to get dressed." She turned back before she entered the dressing room. "Oh, I'd like to try out a few pairs of shoes. Would you mind bringing me a half dozen pairs of Italian sandals from wardrobe?"

Jessica's eyes narrowed as she walked away to do the Twig's bidding. She was going to find a way to get Simone. If it was the last thing she did.

Chapter 4

Leona stopped in Elizabeth's office before lunch, a smooth black leather briefcase in her hand. "Elizabeth, I'll be in a brainstorming meeting for a few hours," she said. "That means I'll be indisposed. OK?"

"Sure, Leona," Elizabeth responded. "I'll field all your calls."

Leona turned back before she walked out the door. "I'm going to be pitching a few new ideas. Wish me luck." Then she winked and headed toward the elevator.

Elizabeth's heart began to pound. What did that wink mean? Did that mean that Leona was going to pitch *her* idea? When Elizabeth had first come up with the idea for an interactive monthly column, she was sure she had hit on something. She had done some research into other fashion magazines and found reader involvement to be both a popular trend and a good selling point for fashion magazines. She had been sure her idea would fly because it was interactive, but simple to implement. But when she approached Leona with the idea on Wednesday, the managing editor had been very discouraging, and Elizabeth had deflated like a popped balloon.

Elizabeth had been very disappointed at the time. But now she tapped the eraser end of a pencil on her Lexis/Nexis printout, deep in thought. Maybe Leona was taking her idea more seriously than she had realized.

Well, even if she weren't, Elizabeth resolved to push the idea. After all, journalists had to be aggressive. They had to pitch their ideas—and not take no for an answer. Her boss's pep talk this morning had done its job. Elizabeth was determined to make a name for herself, even if that meant putting herself on the line. She could already picture the column in the next issue—the theme would be women's advances from ancient times to the present and how fashion reflected that change.

Elizabeth turned back to the computer screen and typed in the last line on her report. Then she pressed "save" and "print." The document rolled out of the printer, and Elizabeth pulled it out with a flourish, looking at it with satisfaction. It was only noon, and she had already completed her research.

Not only had she printed out a list of all the articles published in the United States on the topic of women in antiquity in the last fifty years, but she had written up a small report with article titles and summaries as well. Elizabeth was sure Leona was going to be impressed. Slinging her blazer over her arm, Elizabeth tucked the collection of articles into a file folder. Then she stopped in Leona's office and dropped her work on the desk.

On her way to the elevator, Elizabeth peeked into Reggie's office. Reggie was sitting behind her desk, almost hidden behind an enormous pile of papers, photographs and magazine layouts.

"Feel like getting some lunch?" Elizabeth asked.

Reggie shook her head ruefully, pointing to a half-eaten sandwich laying on a blueprint. "It's going to be another long day," she said with a sigh.

"Well, let me know if you need any help," Elizabeth offered.

"Thanks, Liz," Reggie said. Then she cocked her head and studied Elizabeth. "Hey, you look much better. Did something happen that I should know about?"

Elizabeth shrugged. "No, nothing at all." Then she smiled. "Who needs men, anyway?" she asked.

Reggie grinned, giving her a thumbs-up signal.

Elizabeth hummed as she headed for the elevator bank, feeling pleased with herself. She checked out her appearance in the mirrored elevator doors as she waited. Her hair was a bit wild, and she combed it into place with her fingers, admiring the snazzy, shoulder-length cut with longer pieces in front. She looked every bit the young professional. She was wearing a short, light green dress and black pumps with green-colored toes. Though the color was somewhat daring, it suited her, bringing out her rosy-colored complexion and the golden highlights in her hair. Elizabeth smoothed down her skirt and put on her long blazer, shifting from one foot to the other as she waited.

Finally, the doors opened and Elizabeth stepped in gracefully.

"Hey, great color," said a woman in the elevator with burnt amber–colored hair. "Is that a Bartucci design?"

Elizabeth smiled. "Actually, it's one of Bibi's latest—she's an unknown designer," she said. She chuckled inwardly at her own words. Bibi's wasn't exactly a designer, but rather a store at the Sweet Valley Mall.

The woman nodded. "Up-and-coming fashions are really the way to go. Unknowns are often one step ahead of the rest."

As she headed down the hall to the cafeteria, Elizabeth felt halfway decent for the first time since she had seen Todd kissing Simone. She had thrown herself into her work that morning and was proud of herself for being able to concentrate. Not only had she had a productive, professional morning, but she looked the part of a young executive as well. Leona was right—she didn't need a boyfriend. She could make it all on her own.

Elizabeth held her head high as she walked by the newsstand in the lobby. Then she gasped out loud and did a double take. A copy of *Los Angeles Living* was displayed right in the middle of the newsstand, with a horrendously garish photo of Todd in Simone's arms.

"Supermodel Simone and playboy Todd Wilkins danced till dawn," the bold caption read.

Elizabeth's throat constricted, and she took a few steps back. She felt as though she had been whacked in the chest with a ten-ton stack of magazines. Tears of anger and frustration sprang to her eyes. Breaking her heart wasn't enough. Now Todd had to *humiliate* her as well.

"Wow, nice job, Jessica," Shelly Fabian said to Jessica in the photography studio at lunchtime. Shelly was the makeup artist and had become Jessica's friend. She was a warm woman with smooth ebony skin and ample hips. She cocked her head to the left, the colorful glass beads at the end of her long, skinny braids tinkling lightly. "You've really captured the look of the Mediterranean."

Jessica rubbed her dirty hands on her tangerine-colored miniskirt, eyeing the set wearily. "I should hope so," she said. "Because I've spent about four hours putting this together."

The set was all ready for the Greek Isles shoot. One of the set designers had helped Jessica connect the mechanism for the waterfall, and it was set up to drip down the rocks. Now Simone the Stick just had to jut her bony hips into the scene.

Jessica swiped her hair out of her eyes and smacked her hands together, sending bits of blue chalk into the air. She blinked, looking in dismay as bits of the blue backdrop landed all over her new pale orange skirt. She didn't know why she bothered getting dressed up for work anymore. By the time she got home, she looked like a rag. Her cream-colored blouse was already stained and wrinkled, and her skirt was smudged with dirt.

Jessica took a seat on one of the extra fake rocks on the corner, slipping off her high-heeled pumps and massaging her toes. Then she closed her eyes and leaned her head against the wall, wishing for two basic things: food and sleep. She was dirty and exhausted from spending the morning at the Stick's beck and call. Plus, she hadn't eaten anything at all that day, and sharp hunger pains were shooting through her stomach.

Just then Simone emerged from the dressing room. "What's wrong?" she asked Jessica in a haughty voice. "Can't handle the pace of the fashion world?"

"No, I can't handle the *face* of the fashion world," Jessica retorted.

"Very cute. You made a pun," Simone said

tightly, strutting across the room. She was wearing a body-hugging, floor-length blue silk halter dress with an oval hole cut out over the midriff. Her blue eyes were piercing, and her skin was paler than ever in the dress. She was supposed to be a Greek goddess, but she looked more like an ice princess. Or an ice *witch*.

Simone struck a pose, jutting one hip forward. "What in the world is Quentin doing?" she complained, rubbing her forehead with her right hand.

"Hey, watch it honey," Shelly said quickly. "This face of the fashion world is mine. I spent an hour on your makeup this morning, and I don't want you ruining my creation."

"Sorry," Simone scowled, dropping her hand quickly. She crossed her long legs, waiting impatiently. Then she stood back and studied the scene, her cold blue eyes squinting.

"Jessica, I think that rock is off," Simone said, pointing to the large white boulder in the center. "It should be further to the left."

Jessica rolled her eyes. Simone had no idea where anything belonged on the set. But she slipped her pumps back on and stood up. She hobbled onto the set and kneeled down to pick up the fake rock.

Suddenly the waterfall rushed on. "*Wha—?*" Jessica sputtered as water crashed over her, drenching her hair and clothes.

"Oh, *sorry* about that," Simone said. She had

stepped on the lever controlling the water supply. "I didn't realize you were in the way."

Jessica flung her wet hair back, splattering droplets of water all over Simone's silk dress. Shelly tried not to grin as she handed Jessica a white towel.

Simone gasped and took in the splattered dress in alarm. "Look what you've done! You've ruined my outfit!"

"Oh, *sorry* about that," Jessica said, echoing Simone. "I didn't realize you were in the way." She rubbed the towel briskly through her hair.

"Well, you're going to have to go to wardrobe and fetch me another one," Simone demanded, gazing at the stains on the dress in dismay. "This is an original Rafael Bartucci design. I don't think Quentin is going to be too happy when he sees what you've done." She sent Jessica a withering glance. "In fact, he'll probably fire you on the spot."

Jessica shrugged. "I'll just explain to him that it was all a mistake—that you didn't mean to turn on the waterfall." She stepped out of a low-heeled pump and turned it upside down, dumping water on the ground.

Simone sputtered angrily. "How dare you accuse me—"

"Hey, what's going on here?" Quentin suddenly asked in his deep voice.

Simone and Jessica both turned and started speaking at once.

"Jessica ruined my dress!" Simone shrieked.

"Simone turned on the water!" Jessica exclaimed at the same time.

"Simone needs to change," Shelly explained.

Quentin raised a hand in the air. "OK, everybody take a break and get cleaned up. We'll do the shoot after lunch." He turned back to the darkroom shaking his head. "Women," he muttered.

Shelly leaned in close to Jessica. "Models," she said.

Jessica giggled, giving Simone a sugary sweet smile. "See you after lunch!" she said, then she waltzed toward the elevator. She didn't even care about the fact that her hair was plastered to her head and her outfit was damp. It was worth it just to see Simone sputter.

The elevator bank opened and a cute young delivery boy with straight brown hair came out. Jessica smiled at him and stepped in.

"Are you Jessica Wakefield?" he asked.

"The same," Jessica nodded.

"I've got a delivery for you," he said. Jessica stepped back out quickly, and the guy handed her a package. "This was sent to you anonymously." Then he winked and got back in the elevator.

Jessica looked at the brown package curiously, holding it up to her ear and shaking it. It didn't move, but it smelled delicious. Smiling, Jessica quickly ripped open the envelope and pulled out a plastic dish. Then she lifted the cover off the platter.

It was an elaborate plate of colorful sushi. Jessica's stomach growled hungrily, and she smiled. Quentin had really outdone himself. She was impressed. And she was looking forward to their date tonight.

But as she sat down on the rock in the corner, a disturbing thought struck her. She had almost forgotten about her date with Cameron tonight, a date that she was looking forward to as well—maybe even more so. Jessica dipped a piece of sushi into teriyaki sauce, pondering what she'd do about the fact that she had to be in two places at once. . . .

"Life as Humiliation," Elizabeth said out loud to the computer screen, typing in titles for her teenage autobiography in her office after lunch. "I Was Ditched for a Supermodel." "From Bad to Worse." She lifted a forkful of salad to her mouth and forced herself to chew and swallow.

After having seen the incriminating photo of Todd and Simone, Elizabeth had been too upset to show her face in public. She had bought a salad from the salad bar and had taken it up to her office to eat. But the food was just making her nauseated. Elizabeth pushed away her half eaten plate, staring dejectedly at the titles on the screen.

Elizabeth heard Leona return to her office and sunk lower in her seat. *Time to face the music,* she thought, preparing herself for the worst. She braced herself mentally and pulled herself out of the chair. After seeing Todd's picture, Elizabeth felt immune to other pain. Even if Leona told her the entire editorial board hated her idea, Elizabeth wouldn't feel worse than she already did.

Still, her heart pounded as she knocked on Leona's door.

"Yes," Leona called out.

Elizabeth popped her head in. "Hi—I," she said, stuttering slightly. She took a deep breath and tried to sound casual. "I just wanted to know if you by any chance ran my idea by the editorial board."

"Oh, yes, your little idea," Leona said. "As a matter of fact, I did." She gestured to the chair across from her desk. "Why don't you come in?"

Little idea? Elizabeth felt her face flush as she slid into the leather chair.

"Well, I'm sorry to tell you this, Elizabeth, but the board rejected the idea."

Elizabeth swallowed and nodded. *From Bad to Worse,* she thought. *Definitely.*

"Now, don't take it badly, dear," Leona said. "The material was very well written, but unfortunately, the idea wasn't terribly original. The reader-writer concept has been tossed around editorial for years. We've discovered that kind of thing just isn't viable."

"Not—not viable," Elizabeth stuttered, flushing as she heard herself repeating Leona's words like an idiot.

"Yes, you see, when readers write our material,

the quality of writing goes way down. And quality of writing is what makes *Flair* stand out from other fashion magazines."

"I see," Elizabeth said, nodding and blinking back tears. She was wrong when she thought she couldn't feel worse. Because she could—and she did. One rejection on top of another was just too much. Even worse than her words was the look in Leona's eyes—it was a mixture of pity and disappointment.

Leona gave Elizabeth a condescending smile. "Keep trying, Elizabeth," she said. "You've got potential. I'm sure you'll come up with something one of these days."

Elizabeth was crushed. She scraped back her chair and stood up quickly.

"Oh, and can you proof these notes?" Leona asked, handing her a huge stack of yellow memo paper.

Elizabeth bit her lip. "Sure," she said, slinking out of the office.

Chapter 5

"Stupid," Todd muttered, glancing at his reflection critically in the rearview mirror as he switched lanes on the highway. "Stupid, stupid, stupid." Todd was on his way to *Flair* for a late afternoon photo shoot. It was only one P.M., but he wanted to get to the office early to try to make up with Elizabeth. He was hoping to get to her before she heard about the photo on the cover of *Los Angeles Living*.

As he sped along the Santa Monica Freeway in his black BMW, Todd berated himself for having been so thoughtless the day before. He really had let this modeling thing get to his head. He was just so flattered by Simone's attention that he hadn't resisted her kiss—or her invitation to go to one of the hottest nightclubs in L.A.

But Todd knew that Elizabeth was the one he

really loved. To be honest, even when he had been with Simone, all he could think about was Elizabeth.

Todd screeched into the parking lot of the Mode building, a modern high-rise that housed *Flair* and the other magazines in the Mode group. He jumped out of his car quickly, anxious to talk to his girlfriend. He really hoped she'd understand. And forgive him. Of course, even if she accepted his apology, he wouldn't be able to go out with her anyway. He was grounded. For a month.

A whole month, Todd thought, scowling as he crossed the marble floor of the glamorous lobby. He couldn't believe how unfair his parents were being. So he went out to a nightclub and stayed out late. Big deal. He was almost an adult. There was no reason his life should be completely limited by his parents' dumb rules.

But at the moment, being grounded wasn't the problem. Elizabeth was. Todd bit his lip. He knew how stubborn Elizabeth could be when she was hurt. Or when her pride was wounded. Todd leaned against the wall in the lobby, wondering how he could get her back.

Then he was struck with an idea—*flowers*. Elizabeth loved flowers. He would buy her a beautiful bouquet, and when she caught sight of his repenting face and his flower-laden arms, she wouldn't be able to resist him. Todd quickly headed for the florist on the ground floor.

A few minutes later, Todd stood in front of the elevator, a dozen long-stemmed red roses in his arms. Whistling to himself, he punched the button. The elevator door wheezed open, and the cloying scent of perfume greeted him as he stepped in. All around him stood nearly identical leggy women in short skirts and long blazers.

"Looks like some lucky girl is going to be pretty happy," a sophisticated-looking brunette next to him said.

Todd gave her a half smile, hoping she was right. The elevator stopped at every floor, and Todd impatiently shifted his weight from one foot to the other. He pulled a pen out of his pocket and scribbled a quick note on the card stuck in the bouquet. "Please forgive me, Liz. I love you forever—Todd."

He tucked the card back into the flowers and looked up at the lighted numbers at the top of the elevator. He blinked as he realized they were already on the eleventh floor and the doors were about to close. Sticking an arm out, he caught the door and pushed it open. A few impatient sighs came from the women. Todd grimaced apologetically and pushed his way out.

Without glancing at the receptionist, he hurried down the hall to the editorial department. Taking a deep breath, he knocked sharply on the door to Elizabeth's office. But there was no response. Feeling nervous, he rapped again. Nothing. Todd pushed the door open slowly and peeked his head in. "Liz?" he asked. But her chair was empty.

Todd sighed and headed back to the main desk. "Excuse me," he said to the receptionist, a young woman with glossy auburn hair and horn-rimmed black glasses. "Do you know where Elizabeth Wakefield is?"

The receptionist pushed up her glasses, glancing down at a list in front of her. "I believe she's in Leona Peirson's office at the moment."

A wave of disappointment washed over him. Todd hesitated, wondering what to do. He could leave the flowers with the receptionist, but he didn't want to leave without seeing Elizabeth. He needed to work things out with her—*immediately*. There was no way he'd get through his photo shoot with Simone if he didn't resolve things with Elizabeth.

Todd cleared his throat nervously. "Could you please buzz the office and tell her I'm here?"

The receptionist lifted a sharply arched eyebrow. "Is she expecting you?" she asked.

Todd nodded, his face flushing.

"And who shall I say is calling?" she asked sharply.

"Todd," he said, trying to sound authoritative. "Todd Wilkins."

"Next category: feature articles," Leona said, pacing across the wine-colored carpet that lined

71

the floor of her sleek office. "'Greek Island Getaways,' 'Roman Empires,' 'Empresses,' and 'Sexism in Athens.'"

Elizabeth quickly scratched down Leona's words on a yellow legal pad, trying desperately to keep up with her boss.

Leona paused. "Did you get all that?"

Elizabeth nodded and repeated her words back to her. Dropping her pen on the pad, she stretched out her aching fingers. She was taking dictation from Leona for the layout of the upcoming Greek and Roman antiquity edition. Leona had been dictating nonstop for about an hour, and her words came faster than Elizabeth could record them.

Leona put a hand on a slender hip, her eyes narrowed in thought. "OK, great. Now, where were we?"

Elizabeth scanned her notes. "We're up to fashion exclusives."

Leona nodded. "Right, right. Fashion. Let's see. Make these bullets, OK?"

Elizabeth frowned. "Bullets?" she inquired.

"Put it in outline form," Leona explained quickly, a hint of irritation in her voice.

Elizabeth nodded and hunched over her pad, readying herself for the next barrage of words.

"First fashion spread—'Back to the Future'—the return of metallics in Rafael Bartucci designs, modern cuts, and fabrics. Second spread—'Retro-active'—that's with a hyphen—the retro look in forties and seventies designs. Third spread—'Lingering Luxuries'—the Lina Lapin faux-fur fall line and—"

The intercom crackled, and Leona stopped midsentence. Sighing, she pressed the button for the intercom. "Yes?" she asked, tapping a low heel impatiently.

"A Mr. Todd Wilkins is here to see Elizabeth Wakefield," Anne, the receptionist, announced.

Elizabeth's eyes almost popped out of her head. She couldn't believe Todd's gall. How *dare* he interrupt her in the managing editor's office! Elizabeth's face flamed in anger and embarrassment. Todd's ego was obviously getting way too big for his boy toy's body.

Leona pursed her lips together and gave Elizabeth a sharp look.

Elizabeth swallowed hard. "Sorry, Leona," she said softly. "This will just take a second." Then she leaned over the intercom on the desk and pressed the button.

Todd paced back and forth in the crowded receptionist area, his stomach twisting in anticipation. Since he had been waiting, the room had filled up with people. It seemed as though half of the editors in the department had after-lunch meetings scheduled. Chic, well-dressed models and suave literary types with manuscripts in their hands spoke in hushed voices in the waiting area, and a number of distinguished-looking men in suits were conversing in the corner.

Todd fluffed out his flowers and sat down in a chair, drumming his fingers on the arm of the chair.

Suddenly the intercom crackled and Todd stood up, waiting to be called into the office. He breathed a sigh of relief as he recognized Elizabeth's voice over the intercom. Her voice came through strong and clear, and everybody quieted down to listen. "This is Elizabeth Wakefield," she said. "Please inform Mr. Wilkins that I never want to see him again."

Mortified, Todd grabbed onto the arm of the chair for support.

The receptionist looked straight at him, barely suppressing a smile. "Uh, Mr. Wilkins, did you get that?"

Todd nodded quickly, his face flushing with embarrassment as everybody in the office turned to look at him. He swallowed hard, feeling his face grow prickly hot. For a moment, Todd stood paralyzed, wishing only that the floor would open up and he would fall through to the first floor. Then he became aware of the stares and whispers. A few people even giggled and pointed.

Feeling more humiliated than he had in his whole life, Todd grabbed his flowers and slouched out of the office. Trying to retain some dignity, he controlled his speed as he beat a path down the hall.

But as he punched the button at the elevator

bank, his embarrassment turned to anger. He couldn't believe Elizabeth wouldn't even hear him out. And he couldn't believe she would publicly humiliate him like that. He angrily bent the roses in half and threw them in a trash can, pricking his fingers as he did so. Then he tore up the card he had written, smearing it with blood. Oblivious to the pain in his fingers, he threw the blood-stained pieces into the trash and stepped into the elevator.

Fine, he thought, hitting the button for the art department on the ninth floor. *Elizabeth can have it her way. I'll never speak to her again!*

"Jessica, do you think you could run down to the mail room to pick up a package for me?" Quentin asked, blinking in the light as he came out of the darkroom after lunch. "I'd like to take a look at the proofs before we start this afternoon's shoot." His shaggy blond hair was more disheveled than usual, and he had a distracted air about him.

"Sure," Jessica agreed. She was just finishing up her lunch. She popped the last bit of sushi into her mouth and stuffed the empty container back into the brown envelope. She stood up and threw the bag into a nearby trash receptacle. "Thanks for lunch," she said, flashing the famous photographer a winning Wakefield smile.

"No problem," Quentin responded. "All of *Flair's* employees get a full hour."

Jessica frowned, trying to work out his puzzling

response. Then she shrugged. *Oh well,* she thought. *He's an artist. Artists are eccentric.*

As she headed to the mail room, though, her thoughts turned from Quentin to Cameron. Jessica had decided over lunch that she was going to have to cancel her date with Cameron, and she wasn't looking forward to it.

Jessica bit her lip as she headed for the mail room behind the first floor lobby. Now Cameron was never going to trust her. If he found out she was canceling their date to go out with Quentin, he'd never speak to her again. It would only confirm his worst thoughts.

Jessica sighed as she walked through the cluttered storage nooks and sorting areas of the mail room. Cameron was wrong about her. She *didn't* care at all about people with money or success. She did care about her *own* success, however, and Quentin was the only one who could help her with that. But Cameron would never understand.

Jessica caught sight of Cameron packing boxes in the back. Her heart skipped a beat at the sight of him, and she hid behind a loading dock to watch him for a moment. Cameron was about nineteen or twenty years old, with a strong build, curly brown hair, and big brown eyes. Today he looked particularly cute in faded jeans and a button-down denim shirt with the sleeves rolled up. He was lifting boxes and throwing them in piles, his biceps bulging with each movement. Jessica sucked in her breath. It was like watching a coiled animal in motion.

Not for the first time, she wished *he* were the guy who could help her further her career as a model—and not Quentin. Taking a deep breath, she stepped around the dock and cleared her throat.

Cameron turned and smiled. The sight of his deep brown eyes crinkling at the corners sent sparks down her spine.

"Doing some housecleaning?" Jessica asked with a smile.

Cameron nodded. "Exactly," he said. He heaved a few more boxes onto the loading dock, arm muscles rippling. Jessica felt a bit mesmerized. "I was feeling a little boxed in," he added with a grin.

Then his eyes widened as he took in her damp clothes and hair. "What happened?" he teased. "Was there a thunderstorm in the art department this morning?"

"Something like that," Jessica admitted, jumping up on a rickety old wooden desk in the corner. "I had an encounter with the Fashion Witch." Jessica had already given Cameron the full details of her difficult work situation. Now she quickly recounted the morning's events to him.

Cameron laughed and shook his head when she finished. "The famous Simone shows her claws again." He came up close to Jessica and wrapped his arms around her, rubbing her back briskly. "Am I warming you up?'" he whispered in her ear.

Heating me up is more like it, Jessica thought. Her whole body felt as if it were on fire. Unable to resist, she leaned back and lifted her face for a kiss. At the feel of Cameron's warm lips on hers, electricity cascaded down her whole body.

Then she pulled back abruptly, remembering that she had come down to cancel her date with Cameron, not to kiss him. "Uh, I'd better get back," she said. "Quentin sent me down for a package."

Cameron threw a box aside and reached for a package on the desk marked Photographs. "I know," he said, handing her the big brown envelope. "I've been expecting you." Then he glanced at his watch. "You're only a half hour late."

"Punctuality is not one of my best qualities," Jessica said. She took the package from him and laid it on the desk next to her.

"Oh? What are your best qualities?" Cameron asked, a sparkle in his beautiful brown eyes.

"Hmm, let's see," Jessica said, ticking them off on her fingers. "Beauty, talent, joie de vivre—"

"And modesty," Cameron interrupted.

Jessica lowered her head and batted her eyebrows, making Cameron laugh.

"So, are you excited about our date tonight?" he asked.

Jessica opened her mouth to say no, but found herself saying yes.

Then she hopped off the desk and picked up the package, wondering what she was getting herself into. "You might be surprised by what a date with me is like," she warned. "Some people have even told me that I have enough personality for two people. . . ."

Cameron winked. "I think I can handle it," he said. "What time should I pick you up?"

"Oh, you don't have to drive all the way out to Sweet Valley," Jessica said quickly. "Why don't we just meet at the restaurant?"

Cameron shrugged. "As you like. What did you have in mind?"

Jessica swallowed hard. "Um, I've always wanted to try out that French restaurant on Hollywood Boulevard—Chez Paul."

Cameron whistled softly, looking surprised. "Chez Paul," he repeated. "That's quite a choice."

"Is that OK with you?" Jessica asked worriedly.

"Of course," Cameron responded. "I love French food."

Jessica grimaced, concerned about Quentin's exotic choice. Maybe the famous photographer could eat out in style every night, but Cameron couldn't possibly afford a chic French restaurant. Jessica sighed inwardly. In any case, it was too late now. "How about eight-thirty?" she asked.

"Sounds perfect," Cameron agreed. Then he waggled a teasing finger at her. "Try to be on time tonight."

"I'll try," Jessica responded. "But I never wear a watch."

Cameron pulled her close for a last kiss. "You're worth waiting for," he said, his voice low and husky. Jessica shivered in pleasure as the heat of his body enveloped her. She found herself wishing for the thousandth time since they'd met that he wasn't merely a mail-room worker, that he was the one who could help her career instead of Quentin. . . . And then she forgot her wishes, lost in the hot passion of his kiss.

Chapter 6

"Lean your head way back, Todd," Michael Rietz, the stylist, directed on Friday afternoon.

Todd slid down obediently in the chair and hung his head backward, shifting impatiently as Michael teased a comb through his wavy brown hair. Todd had spent an hour in wardrobe and now he was in Michael's salon having his hair done for the upcoming Roman Empire shoot. He was outfitted in a white toga with gold trim around the neckline, and his feet were bare. Todd was supposed to look like Roman royalty, but instead he felt like some kind of fashion slave.

Michael eyed the array of styling gels and mousses on the counter, selecting a few bottles and setting them aside. Then he picked up a pair of scissors and began snipping expertly at the ends of Todd's hair.

"You're not going to cut it all off, are you?" Todd asked worriedly.

"Shh," Michael rebuked him lightly. "The artist is at work."

The well-known hair stylist took a step back and cocked his head, studying his creation through narrowed eyes. Then he nodded and picked up a bottle of gel. A young man with long, straight dark hair, Michael had a wry sense of humor. Even though he didn't seem to take anyone in the department seriously, he certainly took his *job* seriously.

Michael squeezed some gel onto his palm and massaged it deftly through Todd's hair. Then he slicked Todd's hair back and tucked the ends under, securing them firmly with bobby pins in the back.

"Close your eyes, Todd," Michael warned, lifting an ominous aerosol can in the air.

Todd squeezed his eyes shut, scrunching his nose as Michael spritzed his hair with the artificial-smelling fumes.

"OK, you can look now," Michael said.

Todd opened his eyes warily.

"Voilà!" Michael exclaimed with a wave of his hand.

Todd stared at his image in the mirror in horror. Michael had transformed his hair into a tiny cap on his head. Todd patted his head quickly. It felt hard and crusty. He turned his head quickly from left to right. Not a hair moved. "But—but it's a *hat!*" Todd sputtered, patting his head again.

Michael grinned. "Exactly! Now you look the part of Mark Anthony." He whipped off the towel from Todd's shoulders and whisked his neck with a brush.

"You're done?" Todd gasped in alarm.

Michael shook his head, a small smile on his face. "Don't worry, Todd. It'll look fantastic in the shoot. You'll see. You just need the proper lights and the proper camera."

Todd exhaled sharply. "OK, I hope you're right."

Todd stood up and wrapped his toga tightly around him. He took a deep breath as he headed out the door, feeling particularly naked with his flat hair and nothing but a sheet around him.

When Todd returned to the main studio, the place was bustling with activity. Quentin was conferring with the set director in the corner. A number of lighting specialists were scattered about the room, adjusting tall bluish lights in the corners. Shelly was setting up a makeup table covered with a vast array of tubes and jars of cosmetics. And a few assistants were carrying props and ladders across the room.

Even though everybody was running around, the set looked as though it was finished. A sparkling Roman Empire had been constructed, with a rich, gold palace flanked by two tall, pink marble columns. Todd had to admit that Jessica had done a good job. In fact, she even seemed to have a talent for set design. Todd blinked as Jessica materialized before him. She was kneeling on the ground, unrolling a long red carpet along the floor. He hadn't even noticed her. With her golden-blond hair and her pale paint-splattered outfit, she blended right in with the set.

"OK, everybody, I'm ready," Simone announced in a breathy voice, waltzing out of the dressing room. Todd sucked in his breath at the sight of her. Simone was dressed up as Cleopatra, and she looked stunningly beautiful. She was draped in a long shimmering dress of gold lamé that was slit all the way up the leg. Her black hair hung straight at her chin, with false bangs cut across her forehead. Her china blue eyes slanted upward and her lips glowed a deep ruby red, offsetting the luminescent pearl of her face.

Simone felt Todd's eyes on her and struck a pose for him, resting a hand on her hip. "I like the outfit, Todd," she said appreciatively, gazing up and down his barely dressed body. Todd could feel his cheeks burning, and he clenched his jaw, resisting the impulse to flee back into the dressing room.

"I like it too," Jessica said with a snort from the set, where she had been listening to the exchange. She stood up and wiped her hands on her dress, adding flecks of red carpet to her yellow paint stains. "You look *great* in a dress, Todd." Disgust was plain in her voice.

"A lot better than *you*, I must say," Simone shot back, looking down at Jessica over her imperial nose.

"Some of us don't just have to *stand* for a living," Jessica retorted.

"Well, some of us—" Simone began.

Quentin clapped his hands together. "Places everybody!"

"Humph," Simone pouted, annoyed at being cut off. "Let's go, Todd," she said, taking his hand and leading him up the majestic red carpet onto the set. Todd pulled his hand out of her grasp, beginning to feel like kept property. It seemed as though Simone was bent on using him to make Quentin jealous and Jessica mad.

Quentin approached an elaborate camera mounted on a tripod and adjusted the lens. "OK, I want both of you in front of the column on the right," he instructed, joining them on the set. He positioned Simone with her hip jutting out and Todd standing right behind her, his hand on her hip.

Quentin took his place behind the camera and peered through the lens.

Todd stood perfectly still, holding the pose. But his whole body felt uncomfortable under the white-hot lights. His face was tight and heavy from the caked-on makeup, his cheek was twitching, and his hair-cap itched.

"Shelly, can you do a touch up on Todd?" Quentin asked. "I'm getting a glare on his face."

"I think that's coming from me," Jessica muttered under her breath.

Todd winced, but he didn't bother responding. The Wakefield twins were highly protective of each other, and he knew Jessica was furious at him for hurting Elizabeth. Todd sighed. He really couldn't blame her.

Shelly ran onto the set with a cosmetic brush in hand and quickly dusted Todd's face. Todd closed his eyes as she powdered, unsure of how much more of this he could endure. Now he could see why Elizabeth didn't wear much makeup. He didn't know how girls could stand spending so much time fussing with their face and hair.

Quentin peered through the lens again. "Great!" he breathed. "Don't move!" He quickly took the shot.

"Todd, shift behind Simone and put both your arms around her waist," Quentin directed. The camera clicked again.

"OK, Simone, I want a sultry look. Todd, give me that all-American smile," Quentin said, snapping the camera all the while as he spoke. "Simone, turn your eyes left, to the distance; Todd, follow suit." *Click* went the camera. "Terrific, Todd, you're a natural!" Quentin exclaimed. "You've really got talent!"

Too bad Elizabeth doesn't realize that, Todd

thought. *She doesn't know what she's losing.* Simone moved her body closer to his, and Quentin zoomed in for a close-up. Todd looked straight at the camera, defiance in his eyes. *She's probably just jealous. She just can't handle me being in the limelight for a change.*

With each click of the camera, Todd got angrier and angrier, thinking of how unfair Elizabeth was being. Sure, Elizabeth had a right to be mad at him, but this was between the two of them. He couldn't believe she had embarrassed him publicly. The more steamed he got, the closer he moved to Simone.

"Turn and face each other," Quentin directed. "Simone, look up into Todd's eyes. Give me your profile, honey."

Simone gazed up at him with laser blue eyes, the intensity of her stare causing him to catch his breath. Suddenly she leaned in close and kissed him. *Click* went the camera. "Fabulous!" Quentin exclaimed. "Hold that pose!"

Simone increased the pressure of his lips, and Todd stood perfectly still, horrified. He forced himself to respond to the kiss, wishing the moment would end.

Out of the corner of his eye, Todd saw Jessica storm out of the room. He pulled back from Simone, wincing. Jessica was sure to report everything to Elizabeth—from his outfit to his actions. Now Elizabeth would *really* never forgive him.

Then Todd shrugged. What was he worried about? He and Elizabeth weren't speaking anyway.

"Great! That's a wrap!" Quentin said excitedly, rewinding the film. "This roll is going to sizzle!"

Simone stretched out her long body lazily, causing the body-hugging fabric to reveal every contour of her body. Todd looked quickly at the ground, but not before Simone caught his eyes on her.

"So, would you like to go to another club tonight?" Simone asked in a husky voice. "There's a great place on Rodeo Drive called Inside Out. It's very in."

Todd scuffed his bare feet on the ground. "Well, actually, I'm grounded."

Simone lifted a thin, imperial eyebrow. "Grounded?" she asked, as if the word were distasteful to her.

Todd felt a flush heat up his cheeks. "Yeah, my parents saw the photo of us in that tabloid—and well—" He shrugged, feeling like an idiot.

Simone scoffed. "So blow them off," she said. "You're an adult, aren't you?"

"Well, uh —" Todd stuttered.

"Oh, come on, Todd," Simone sneered. "What are you, a man or a mouse?"

Simone's remarks hit home. *She's right,* Todd decided. He was earning big bucks now. He deserved to live his own life. He swallowed hard and tried to sound more self-assured than he felt. "I didn't say I was going to listen to them. What time should I pick you up?"

"Eleven-thirty sharp," Simone responded, pivoting on a high Rafael Bartucci heel.

Todd watched her long frame glide away, and he bit his lip worriedly. How had he gotten himself talked into this? *Well*, he decided, *I'm not entirely crazy*. He'd sneak out after his parents went to bed.

"You should have *seen* Todd and Simone at the photo shoot this afternoon," an outraged Jessica told Elizabeth as she steered the Jeep down the Santa Monica freeway after work. "It was *so-oo* disgusting."

Elizabeth closed her eyes and leaned back against the headrest. She didn't think she could bear to hear any more bad news.

"Todd was wearing—get this—a sheet—or a *dress* rather, and Simone was in a glued-on gold lamé number," Jessica reported.

A searing white-hot flash of jealousy shot through Elizabeth.

"And her dress wasn't the only thing glued onto her," Jessica continued. "The heat coming from Todd and Simone was hotter than Quentin's lights. They got closer and closer, and then they starting kissing. Can you believe it? And Quentin didn't even ask them to. They were practically making out on the set. I'm telling you—it was totally gross. If you ask me —"

But Elizabeth held up a hand. "Jessica, I didn't ask you."

"What?" Jessica asked, looking at her sister quickly.

"Look, I've heard enough, OK?" Elizabeth said sharply.

Jessica looked wounded. "I was just trying to protect you," she told her twin, a defensive note in her voice.

Elizabeth's voice softened. "Sorry, I didn't mean to jump on you like that. It's just that I've had it up to here with this Todd and Simone story." She held up a hand forehead high.

Jessica nodded and flipped on the radio, turning the knob to her favorite rock station. "OK," she said, "let's talk about something cheerier—like our weekend plans."

Elizabeth sighed. "I don't have any plans."

"You don't?" Jessica asked brightly. "So . . . what are you doing tonight?"

Elizabeth looked at her sister quickly, wondering what kind of plan she was hatching. But Jessica kept her eyes glued on the road, and so Elizabeth shrugged. "I'm planning to crawl under my covers and stay there until it's time to go to work on Monday. Or maybe I'll stay under there for the rest of my life."

"You know, Elizabeth, you should really go out and have fun," Jessica said, cutting her speed and turning off onto the exit ramp. "Staying home and moping isn't going to help at all. Besides, boring-as-butter Todd Wilkins isn't worth it."

Elizabeth looked at her twin suspiciously. Her

face looked innocent enough, but Elizabeth recognized a gleam in her twin's eyes.

"Do you have something in mind?" Elizabeth asked in an ironic tone.

"As a matter of fact, I do," Jessica replied. She turned her suddenly anguished face to her sister. "Elizabeth, you won't *believe* the situation I'm in!" she wailed.

"Try me," Elizabeth said dryly.

Jessica explained her sticky date situation in vivid detail, from Cameron's first kiss to his last one, and from Quentin's initial brush-off to his recent interest in her.

"So what's the problem?" Elizabeth asked when Jessica had finished. "You've got to cancel one of your dates, since you can't possibly be in two places at once."

Jessica pulled to a stop at an intersection and bit her lip. "But, Liz, I can't cancel *either* of them!" she whimpered. She stared straight ahead, blinking rapidly—and obviously trying to make her eyes fill with tears.

Elizabeth rolled her eyes at Jessica's pathetic attempt to get sympathy.

The light turned green, and Jessica stepped on the gas. "This is my big chance with Quentin," she explained. "We're going to discuss my future as a model. It's now or never."

Elizabeth nodded her head. "Yep, you can't cancel that one."

"And if I blow Cameron off, he'll never speak to me again! He's sure to find out about my date with Quentin." Jessica held her hands dramatically to her heart. "Elizabeth, Cameron could be the *one*."

Elizabeth groaned at her twin's overly dramatic performance. "Jess, keep your hands on the wheel."

Jessica grabbed the wheel with her right hand and turned her imploring big blue-green eyes to her sister. "Elizabeth, please, *please*, can't you do a twin switch with me? Just this one time?"

"Absolutely, categorically *no*," Elizabeth responded. Usually Jessica could talk her into just about anything, but today Elizabeth felt majorly fed up. She was in no mood for her twin's cajoling.

"Please, just this one time?" Jessica begged. "I promise, Liz, I'll *never* ask you to do anything like this again."

Elizabeth shook her head, wondering how many times she had heard that before. "Jessica, you got yourself into this situation," she said firmly. "You've got to get yourself out of it."

"Fine," Jessica huffed, turning up the radio and putting her foot on the accelerator. She drove in stony silence all the way to Calico Drive.

But as she pulled into the driveway, Jessica turned to her one last time. "So do you think you can do just this one little, *tiny* thing for me?" she asked hopefully.

"Jessica, the answer is no," Elizabeth said firmly. "Read my lips. N-O." She pulled open the door and breezed out of the Jeep.

Elizabeth heard Jessica slam the car door behind her. *Fine*, Elizabeth thought, *let her be angry. There's no way I'm going to fall for another of her crazy schemes!*

Chapter 7

How in the world did I get talked into this?
Elizabeth wondered for the hundredth time that
evening as she and Cameron walked into Chez
Paul, a ritzy French restaurant in downtown L.A.
She was wearing the same dress as her twin, and
she had done her hair and makeup just like
Jessica's.

Elizabeth heaved a sigh. It was bad enough that
she had to waste her evening parading around as
her twin, but she had to be *dressed* like Jessica as
well—which meant she was wearing a tiny black
halter dress barely bigger than a cloth napkin. Not
only that, her face also felt like it was going to
crack off under the weight of all her makeup. The
only thing she felt comfortable with was her hairstyle. Her golden-blond hair was swept up high on
her head, a few curled tendrils hanging loose.

94

"After you, mademoiselle," Cameron said gallantly, holding the door open for her. Elizabeth gave him a gracious smile, walking ahead of him into the elegant room. As they headed for the maître d's stand, Elizabeth yanked at the material of her dress, trying to cover her upper thighs. She felt as though everybody in the restaurant was staring at her.

Elizabeth shook her head. She couldn't believe Jessica had managed to talk her into this. Even though she had come into Elizabeth's room and whined about her dilemma for two hours straight, Elizabeth hadn't broken down. But then Jessica had laid a thick guilt trip on Elizabeth, explaining how she'd been sticking up for her sister during Todd and Simone's modeling sessions. "I told the Stick straight to her face that I thought she was despicable for going out with my sister's boyfriend," Jessica had said. "And I'm not even *talking* to Todd. How can you refuse to help me, your *twin*, when I've been doing nothing but standing up for you?" Guilt always got Elizabeth, and Jessica knew it. She sighed. Her sister was certainly the master of manipulation.

As Cameron conferred with the maître d', Elizabeth took in the plush surroundings. Fortunately for Jessica, Chez Paul was a large two-story restaurant, and Cameron and Quentin had reservations on different floors. Painted grape vines trailed across the mint green walls, and the tables were covered with elegant white tablecloths.

Each table was adorned with a crystal bud vase holding a single red rose. The elegantly-dressed clientele spoke in hushed voices, and only the clink of wine glasses could be heard above the low din of the crowd.

"This way, please," said a waiter in a black tuxedo.

Cameron took her arm and led her through the crowded dining room. "Better than Chez Bench, huh?" he whispered in her ear.

"Uh-huh," Elizabeth said, forcing a laugh. Unfortunately, she had no idea what he was talking about.

The waiter directed them to an intimate candlelit table in the corner, and Cameron held Elizabeth's chair for her. She slid into her seat, relieved to hide her bare thighs under the tablecloth.

Elizabeth scanned her menu, feeling a little intimidated by the refined selection. All of the entrees were in French, but fortunately there were English translations as well. Elizabeth's eyes widened as she took in the extravagant prices. She couldn't believe Jessica would have the gall to invite Cameron to come to such an expensive restaurant. After all, he worked in the mail room for a living. The guy couldn't exactly be made of money. But Cameron didn't seem fazed by the menu at all.

"I've heard the foie gras is very good here," Cameron said. Then he winked at her. "Too bad they don't serve hamburgers and fries."

Elizabeth relaxed, giving Cameron a genuine smile. "I know what you mean," she said. "I wouldn't mind having a burger and a shake from the Dairi Burger, a popular hangout in Sweet Valley."

"Tell you what, Jess," Cameron said. "Next time we go out, I'll let you treat me to a deluxe strawberry milkshake."

Elizabeth laughed. "You got it."

She ran an index finger down the elaborate entrees on the menu, trying to make up her mind. Then a devious thought occurred to her. Calamari was one of Elizabeth's favorite dishes and one which Jessica happened to despise. A small smile played on her lips. She would order it to punish Jessica for putting her in such an awkward situation. Elizabeth looked at the appetizers, searching for a few things Jessica hated as well. With a smile, she snapped her menu shut.

"So what are you going to have, Jessica?" Cameron asked.

"I thought I'd have the frog legs first." She smiled devilishly. "I love French delicacies."

Cameron nodded approvingly. "Ah, a woman with taste," he said. But despite his words, his eyes were dancing with laughter, as if he didn't take any of it seriously.

An elegant waiter appeared at their table. "*Bonsoir,*" he said with a slight bow. "Have you made your selections?"

97

Cameron nodded, placing their orders in perfect French. Elizabeth looked at him oddly. For someone who worked in the mail room, this guy was pretty cultured. He seemed perfectly at ease in the elegant surroundings, as if he'd been frequenting posh French restaurants for years.

"Very good, sir," the waiter said, whisking the menus away.

Cameron winked. "Zee vaitor eez gone," he said in an exaggerated French accent. "Now vee can be ourselves."

Elizabeth laughed. Despite her initial reluctance, she was actually beginning to enjoy herself. Cameron was obviously a great guy. Jessica was crazy to risk him for Quentin the Jerk.

Cameron looked at her with a glint in his deep brown eyes. "I have to say, besides the fact that I know you're a beautiful girl who wants to be a model, I don't really know anything about you." He smiled, the tiny lines around his eyes crinkling.

Elizabeth swallowed hard, trying to think how Jessica would respond. She would smile coquettishly and say something funny and flirty. But what? Elizabeth stared at him blankly.

Fortunately Cameron kept talking. "So, what do you do when you're not looking and acting like a supermodel?"

Elizabeth exhaled slowly, realizing she had been holding her breath. "Well, I'm a pretty active member of Pi Beta Alpha, one of the sororities at

Sweet Valley High," she said. Elizabeth was a member as well, having been talked into joining the sorority by Jessica. But she never attended the meetings, and she had no idea what the girls' current activities were. "We . . . we're doing a fundraiser on Saturday," Elizabeth improvised quickly. "It's a car wash to raise money for charity."

Cameron grinned. "Maybe I'll come by Sweet Valley to have my car cleaned this weekend."

Elizabeth changed the subject, hoping he would forget about the car wash by the time dinner was over. "And I'm also the cocaptain of the cheerleading squad."

Cameron whistled underneath his breath. "You're the cocaptain of the squad?" he asked. He leaned in closer. "You know, I used to play soccer in high school, and the cheerleaders really helped to psych me up. I noticed that the moves are a lot more complicated than one might think."

"Yeah, they are," Elizabeth said brightly. "We even went to Nationals last season. We came in second."

"What are some of your most difficult moves?" Cameron asked, looking sincerely interested. He picked up the carafe of water and filled both his and Elizabeth's glasses.

Elizabeth gulped. When Jessica had quit the cheerleading squad because of Heather Mallone, her sworn enemy and cocaptain, she had formed her own squad to take to Nationals. She had talked

Elizabeth into joining her team, and Elizabeth had trained with the rest of the girls. Elizabeth racked her brains, trying to remember a move. She pictured leaps and splits, but she couldn't recollect any of the names. "Uh, pyramids are always hard," she replied lamely.

"What kind of pyramids?" Cameron asked.

Elizabeth's eyes widened. She couldn't believe that she was sitting across from the one guy in the history of the world who took an interest in cheerleading. "Um, well, two-two-two pyramids are pretty tough," she said, making up the move.

Cameron's brow furrowed. "Two-two-two? What does that mean?"

"Uh, two girls on each tier," Elizabeth explained, swallowing hard.

"That must be tough," Cameron said. "There's no balance on the bottom." He picked up his glass of water and took a drink.

Elizabeth nodded, glancing surreptitiously at her watch. She breathed a sigh of relief when she saw it was nine P.M.—time to meet Jessica in the bathroom so they could switch dates. "If you'll excuse me," she said, scraping her chair back and jumping up.

"Yeah, it was tough at the beginning," Quentin said, leaning back and crossing his long legs. He took a sip of his aperitif and shook his shaggy blond waves over his shoulder. "Calvin's the one who really gave me my first break. I did some test shots for him, and after that, well—" he gave her a smug smile, "I guess you could say the rest is history."

Calvin, Jessica thought in disgust. She stared out the window, phasing out as Quentin continued to go on and on about himself. She and Quentin were seated on the second floor at an elegant table overlooking Hollywood Boulevard. For the last half hour, he'd given her a complete bio of himself—all the great designers he'd worked with, all the beautiful models he'd photographed, and all the famous people he knew.

"Yes, I've worked with about every big name in the fashion industry," Quentin continued. "Chanel, St. Laurent, Givenchy." He ticked off the names on his fingers as he spoke. "And I've shot about every famous model there is."

Somebody should shoot you, Jessica thought.

"Tatiana, Marisa, Izzy," Quentin said, listing the supermodels he'd photographed.

Jessica shifted in her seat, growing more and more irritated by the moment. She was sick of hearing about Quentin's success, and she was sick of hearing about beautiful models who were too important to have last names.

"And of course, Simone," Quentin continued. "The first time we worked together was on a Chanel shoot."

Jessica sighed. She hadn't eaten anything since lunch, and sharp hunger pains were shooting through her stomach. The waiter was hovering politely in the corner, ready to take their order at the snap of a finger. But they hadn't even opened their menus yet.

The waiter caught her eye and hurried to the table, almost bowing as he greeted them. "May I take your order, Monsieur Berg?"

Quentin looked irritated and shook his head quickly, waving the waiter away.

Jessica rolled her eyes as the waiter hurried back to his spot in the corner. Obviously Monsieur Berg was used to making people wait for him.

"Now where was I?" he asked.

"You were talking about your Chanel shoot," Jessica said with a sigh.

"Ah yes, that was one of my most difficult shoots," Quentin said.

Jessica tuned him out and stared out the window at the elegant figures hurrying by on the street. She had known that Quentin was a bit of a jerk and a control freak, but she hadn't realized just how pretentious he was. When she and Elizabeth switched, Jessica decided, she'd tell her sister to spend the rest of the evening with Quentin. Otherwise, Jessica would die of boredom. Or starvation.

As the thought materialized, Jessica looked up at the antique brass clock on the wall. It was after nine o'clock. She was already five minutes late to meet Elizabeth in the bathroom.

"Uh, could you excuse me for a moment?" Jessica asked, pushing back her chair.

"Yes, of course," Quentin said, looking preoccupied.

What a relief, Jessica thought as she picked up her black pearl bag and headed for the stairs. She didn't know if she could stand one more moment of his insufferable company.

But then she heard Quentin's voice behind her. "Jessica, can you come back here for a moment?"

Jessica sighed, turning reluctantly back to the table.

"I was watching you walk away," Quentin said. "You've definitely got a model's carriage—good posture, long stride." He rubbed his chin thoughtfully. "You don't have the height for runway modeling, but I'm sure we could take some fantastic prints."

Jessica's spirits brightened. "Really?" she breathed.

"But we don't want to talk business over our meal," Quentin said. "Why don't we discuss your future as a model over dessert?"

Jessica flashed him a covergirl smile, deciding on the spot that she *did* want to return to this date after all. Quentin was the one who could help her. Cameron was just an amusing diversion.

"Man, I've never seen such a close game!" Kevin Anderson said on Friday night, referring to the Southern California state championship high-school football game the night before.

"Me neither!" Shane Maddox agreed. "That was an *awesome* last pass. I thought the fans were going to bring down the stadium."

Enid sighed and took a bite of her cheeseburger. She and Maria were on their blind double date at Bobo's Burger Barn, a low-key restaurant in downtown Sweet Valley where you could draw on the paper tablecloths with crayons.

Kevin was certainly cute, with longish sandy blond hair and hazel eyes, but he was more interested in Shane's guy talk than in anything Enid had to say. And even though Shane and Maria made a stunning couple, Shane didn't seem to realize that Maria was there at all. It turned out the two boys were both former football players who had just graduated from rival high schools, and they had spent the last hour in a heated discussion about sports.

"Yeah, the Panthers took a beating last season," Kevin was saying. "It's because they had a weak defense—they gave away too much yardage."

"I thought Derek Mallone was going to be able to pull them through," Shane responded. "But I guess a quarterback can't carry the whole team."

Enid turned in the boys' direction, trying to look interested. "Aren't the Panthers the team from Palisades?" she asked. The guys didn't even notice she had spoken.

Maria cleared her throat. "Enid asked you a question. She wanted to know if that's the team from Allboysarejerks High."

"Huh?" Shane asked, looking at Maria as if he just realized she was sitting next to him. "Yeah, that's right."

Enid and Maria snickered, but the boys were already engrossed in their conversation again.

Enid yawned and stuffed the last of her fries into her mouth. Then she took a long draw on her soda and pushed her plate away. Maria picked out a crayon from the jar and drew a fuschia-colored curly-haired Enid on the tablecloth. In the cartoon Enid's right hand was held up to her open mouth.

Enid picked out a blue crayon, and then leaned over and added a dialogue balloon to the cartoon figure. She wrote "yawn" inside the bubble. Enid heard Maria giggle and refused to look at her for fear of laughing.

Forcing herself to keep a straight face, Enid turned back to the boys' conversation. Shane was designing a football move on the table with a green crayon, detailing a particularly difficult maneuver.

Then she felt Maria nudge her. She glanced over and looked at the tablecloth. Maria had drawn two stupid-looking football players holding clubs like cavemen, with a dialogue bubble over one caveman's head. "Like, cool, man," the bubble said.

Enid burst out laughing and jumped up. "Excuse me, I've got to use the powder room," she said over the din of Kevin and Shane's conversation. Maria quickly followed. The boys nodded without looking at them.

In the bathroom, the girls doubled over with laughter. "Hey, don't you guys go to Allguysarestupid High?" Enid asked, imitating Shane's voice.

"Duh, huh?" Maria answered.

Enid shook her head. "I thought you said Kevin was quiet. He hasn't stopped talking since we got here." She pulled a tube of mauve lipstick out of her black minibackpack and pursed her lips in the mirror.

"I didn't say he was quiet," Maria said, retying the blue bandanna in her hair. "I said we had nothing in common."

"That's an understatement," Enid agreed, smacking her lips on a tissue. "The only thing he and I have in common is that we both know you."

Maria sighed and leaned back against a sink. "It's too bad they both turned out to be such total duds," she said, shaking her head. "They *are* pretty cute."

"I can't understand how seemingly intelligent guys can care more about hockey fights and football tackles than they do about holding interesting conversation with two totally hot babes," Enid said.

"Well, it's their loss," Maria declared.

Enid made a face of distaste. "I can't stand the thought of going back in there. If I hear the word *football* one more time, I think I might explode."

"Who said anything about going back in there?" Maria asked, a devilish smile on her face.

Enid smiled back. "Are you thinking what I think you're thinking?"

"Definitely," Maria affirmed. "Girl, we are outta here."

Enid giggled as she and Maria hurried out of the bathroom and snuck out the back entrance. "I wonder when the boys will notice we're gone," she said.

Maria shrugged. "Probably tomorrow morning."

Chapter 8

Elizabeth paced the length of the spacious powder room, wondering where her sister was. The women's room was just as elegant as the fancy restaurant. Pink marble sinks lined the wall, with a long beige leather couch opposite them. A full-length antique mirror stood in the corner, and Elizabeth cringed every time she caught sight of her dolled-up reflection in it.

Elizabeth heard the door open and wheeled around. It was Jessica, her face pink with excitement. "Jessica Wakefield, you're ten minutes late!" she exclaimed. "What in the world am I supposed to say I was doing in here?"

Jessica winced. "Liz, I'm sorry. Quentin started talking about my modeling career, and I couldn't get away," she explained. "Just say you were freshening up. Remember, you *are* me after all."

Elizabeth sighed, glancing at her skimpy dress in the standing mirror. "How can I forget?"

Jessica set her handbag on the counter and pulled out a cosmetic bag. Then she opened it and turned it upside down, dumping an array of jars and tubes on the counter. Closing one eye, she carefully applied plum eye shadow to an eyelid. "I almost perished of boredom out there. Quentin hasn't stopped talking about himself for a minute. We haven't even had time to order."

Elizabeth smiled to herself, anticipating Jessica's reaction when she saw her dish of frogs legs and calamari. "Don't worry, I'll order for you," she said.

"Thanks, Liz," Jessica said, outlining her lips with a pink lip pencil.

Elizabeth sunk down in the couch. "What in the world is Chez Bench, by the way?" she asked.

Jessica's brow furrowed. "Huh?" she asked, forming an O with her lips and painting them with crimson lipstick.

"A restaurant you went to with Cameron?" Elizabeth prompted.

"Oh," Jessica said, throwing her lipstick back into her cosmetic bag. "That's just a joke. Cameron and I ate on the bench outside the *Mode* building one day, and he called it Chez Bench."

Elizabeth laughed. "That's actually pretty funny," she said. "Jessica, Cameron's a terrific guy. I think you should just bag Quentin and stay with him."

"I wish I could," Jessica said, pulling out a few wispy strands to frame her face. "But Quentin said he wants to discuss my future after dinner."

Elizabeth tapped a foot on the ground, looking at her watch nervously. "Jess, don't you think we should get back to our dates? The guys might send an emergency squad in here."

Jessica waved a dismissive hand. "Oh, Lizzie, you don't know the first thing about dating etiquette. Guys are *supposed* to be kept waiting. In fact, that's what they do best. They wait."

Elizabeth shook her head. "Well, I don't," she said firmly, hopping up. "I'm going upstairs."

Jessica grabbed her arm. "OK, but just prep me on your conversation with Cameron first. Is there anything I should know about it?"

Elizabeth fell back down on the couch. "Not really," she said. "We mostly talked about French philosophers—you know, Sartre, Camus, and Descartes."

Jessica's mouth dropped open. "You didn't!"

Elizabeth rolled her eyes. "Of course not, you goof," she said. "Don't worry. We just talked about normal stuff—Pi Beta Alpha and cheerleading."

Jessica looked worried. "What about them?" she asked cautiously.

"Well, I told Cameron that Pi Beta Alpha was having a car wash for charity this weekend."

"A charity drive?" Jessica asked. "But there's no way the sorority would do that."

Elizabeth shrugged. "Well, he doesn't know that." Then she looked down at the ground. "The only thing is—he might drive to Sweet Valley to get his car washed on Saturday."

"Oh, boy," Jessica sighed. "Anything else I should know about?"

Elizabeth shook her head. "Otherwise, we just talked about cheerleading moves. I told him the most difficult maneuver was a two-by-two-by-two pyramid."

"A *what*?" Jessica asked, aghast.

Elizabeth glared at her sister, getting annoyed. "Look, Jessica, you're lucky I'm here at all. If you aren't happy with my conversational skills, maybe you should go on your own dates next time."

"OK, OK," Jessica grumbled. "But a two-by-two-by-two pyramid?" She shook her head. "It isn't possible."

"Don't worry," Elizabeth reassured her. "He's a guy. He doesn't know anything about cheerleading."

Jessica sighed. "Fine. But watch what you say to Quentin, OK?"

"So what's it like having a twin sister?" Cameron asked as soon as Jessica sat down.

Jessica was thrown off kilter, but recovered quickly. "Oh, it's OK," she said, avoiding his eyes and taking a bite out of her appetizer. She grimaced and almost spat it out. Her eyes widened as she recognized the rubbery dish—frogs legs—

111

gross! Jessica's eyes narrowed suspiciously. Elizabeth obviously ordered this on purpose.

Cameron looked concerned. "What's wrong? I thought frogs legs were one of your favorite dishes." He looked at her carefully. "Didn't you say you loved French delicacies?"

Jessica swallowed hard. "Uh, yeah, yeah, definitely," she said. "Just went down the wrong pipe." She forced a smile on her face and took another bite, trying hard not to gag at the foreign taste.

"Must be weird to have a twin," Cameron went on. "Like when you go into the bathroom and look in the mirror, it's almost like you're looking at someone else."

Jessica almost choked on her food this time. She grabbed a glass of water.

"Do you ever have an identity crisis?" Cameron asked, cutting into his fried mushrooms.

Jessica looked straight into his eyes, wondering if he knew what was going on. But he just stared back at her, his deep brown eyes not giving anything anyway. Then she dismissed the possibility. He couldn't possibly know. Her plan was going smoothly.

Cameron waved a hand in front of her face. "Jess? Did somebody steal your mind while you were in the bathroom?"

Jessica laughed. "Oh, sorry," she said. "I'm just a bit distracted tonight."

"I was asking you if you ever have an identity

crisis," Cameron repeated, taking a bite of his appetizer. Jessica looked at it enviously, but Cameron didn't offer her any. "Umm, delicious," he said, mopping up the plate with a piece of French bread.

"Actually, no," Jessica said, forcing her mind off the food. "Even though Elizabeth and I look identical, we're entirely different. Elizabeth's more serious—and studious—than I am. I like to be in the center of the action, and she's more of a behind-the-scenes kind of person."

"So that's why she's in editorial and you're in the art department—where the cameras are?"

Jessica nodded. "Elizabeth wants to be a writer someday."

"And you want to be a model," Cameron said.

Jessica shrugged. "Or an actress."

Just then their food arrived, and Jessica heaved a sigh of relief to have the conversation cut off.

"*Pour le monsieur, un steak frites,*" said the waiter, setting down a red steak and french fries before Cameron. Jessica's mouth watered at the tantalizing dish.

"*Et pour vous, Mademoiselle, le calamari,*" the waiter said with a flourish, lifting the lid off a steaming dish and setting it before her.

Jessica stared at the platter in alarm, trying to figure out what it was. It was viscous and white with a faintly purple tinge, and the whole thing was covered in some kind of lemon butter sauce. Then she realized what it was. *Squid!* Elizabeth had struck again.

113

"Bon appetit!" Cameron said, lifting a glass in the air. He picked up his knife and fork and cut off a piece of steak, biting into it heartily.

"Bon appetit!" Jessica echoed despondently. She slowly broke up her food in little pieces, wondering how she could get out of eating it.

"How is it?" Cameron asked.

Jessica took a tiny bit and forced herself to chew it. It was worse than she had expected. It had a salty sea taste and a horrible slimy texture. Jessica swallowed hard and took a gulp of water. "Um, delicious, thank you," she coughed.

"Mine too," Cameron said, spooning some Dijon mustard on his plate. He stabbed a pile of fries with his fork, dipping them into the mustard. Jessica stared hungrily, wishing he would offer her a bite. While Cameron devoured his steak, Jessica pushed the pieces of shredded squid around her plate, trying to make it look like she had eaten some of it.

Jessica heaved a sigh of relief when the waiter took their dishes away. Fortunately, she'd managed to eat only a few bites of the revolting dish.

Cameron smiled at her, taking her hand in his. "Jessica, I'm so glad you came out with me tonight. It's good to see you in the real world."

His hand was warm over hers. His brown eyes gazed deep into her eyes, and she felt her stomach flutter. As Cameron leaned forward to kiss her, she glanced down at the watch on his wrist. Ten o'clock. Time for a twin switch.

Jessica kissed Cameron quickly, then pulled away. "Better save something for dessert," she said lightly, pushing back her chair.

She sighed as she walked away from the table, feeling like Cinderella at the ball. Things were just beginning to heat up between her and Cameron, and now Elizabeth got to have him.

Elizabeth sat down and flashed Cameron a sincere smile, grateful to be back at his table. Quentin was one of the most tedious, unbearable, egotistical bores she had ever encountered. Elizabeth especially hated the way he kept raving about Simone, her least favorite person in the world—aside from Todd. Not only did Quentin keep talking about what a prima model Simone was, but about her exceptional beauty as well. Elizabeth had just felt sick during the entire conversation.

Just then the waiter arrived with a luscious-looking dessert tray in his hand. He set down two plates of chocolate mousse on the table and two cups of espresso.

"I took the liberty of ordering dessert," Cameron explained. "Is that OK?"

"Of course," Elizabeth said, her mouth watering. "It looks fantastic."

The waiter bowed slightly and turned away.

"*Mmm*," Elizabeth murmured, taking a bite of the rich chocolate cake. "This is delicious." *Actually*, she thought, *except for the excruciating hour at Quentin's table, I've kind of had a good time this evening*. Her frog legs were exquisite, and she'd really enjoyed Cameron's company.

"Thanks for dinner," Elizabeth said sincerely as she and Cameron walked out of the restaurant.

"It was my pleasure," Cameron responded, taking her hand in his and kissing the back of it. Then he fingered the silver watch dangling on her wrist. "Hey, nice watch."

"Oh, I've had it forever," Elizabeth said. "I got it as a birthday gift from my grandparents years ago."

Cameron nodded, as if Elizabeth's statement confirmed something that he had been thinking. Then he took both her hands in his and leaned toward her.

For a moment, Elizabeth panicked. Was he going to kiss her? What should she do? She couldn't exactly push him away and run off. But he just smiled at her and kissed her lightly on the cheek. "Thanks for a lovely evening, *Elizabeth,*" he said.

Then he winked and disappeared into the night.

Elizabeth's mouth dropped open. How did he know she wasn't Jessica? Then it hit her. Her watch! She had forgotten that Jessica never wore a watch. Elizabeth sighed as she walked toward the Jeep in the parking lot. Jessica was going to kill her.

Chapter 9

"This is it," Jessica said, pointing to the Wakefield's split-level house on Calico Drive.

Quentin expertly pulled his silver Mercedes to a stop in front of the curb.

"Thanks for a lovely evening," Jessica said, flashing Quentin a fake smile.

"The pleasure was all mine," Quentin responded suavely.

Jessica put her hand on the door handle, anxious to get away from Quentin and his overblown ego. Not only had he talked about himself nonstop all through dinner, but all during the car ride home as well.

But Quentin reached over and took her hand in his. His other hand trailed slowly down her neck, sending a slow shiver of disgust down Jessica's spine.

"I like you, Jessica," Quentin declared. "You've got style and guts. I really think you're going to go places."

Now Quentin had her full attention. "You do?" Jessica asked, her blue-green eyes sparkling.

"I do," he whispered, kissing her softly on the cheek. He followed with a trail of soft kisses along her neck and ear. Then he leaned forward and captured her lips in his.

Jessica closed her eyes and returned his kiss, trying to lose herself in the moment. But all she could think of was Cameron. She pictured his laughing brown eyes and the dimple in his chin. She thought of the last time he had kissed her— unexpectedly—in the mail room, and of the sparks of lightning that had coursed through her entire body. She moaned and wrapped her arms around Quentin, kissing him harder.

"Mmm, Jessica," Quentin murmured, increasing the pressure on her lips.

Jessica spoke to Cameron in her mind. *Cameron, it's almost like I'm kissing you. Are you thinking the same thing while you're kissing—*

Jessica shivered suddenly and pulled out of Quentin's grasp, hit by a horrible thought.

"Jessica, are you OK?" Quentin asked.

Jessica nodded, feeling the blood rush out of her face. "Yeah, sorry, I just got a sudden chill. It must be the night air."

"Well, let me take care of that," Quentin said,

turning on the engine and rolling up the window. He wrapped both his arms around her and rubbed her back slowly.

As Quentin held her in his arms, Jessica fixated on Elizabeth and Cameron. She only hoped that Elizabeth wasn't receiving a passionate kiss from Cameron at the moment. But if Cameron believed Elizabeth were Jessica . . . Jessica pushed the thought away. The thought of Cameron kissing her sister made her skin crawl.

Finally Jessica pulled out of Quentin's arms. "I better go in," she said, leaning over and giving him a peck on the cheek.

"Sleep well," Quentin said. Then he winked. "After all, you want to look your best tomorrow."

Jessica turned the handle and pushed the door open. But then she stopped and faced Quentin again. "Do you really think I have a chance to end up in the magazine?" she asked.

Quentin nodded. "Don't worry," he assured her. "I'll make sure of it."

"See you tomorrow," Jessica said, hopping out of the car.

It's all worth it, she assured herself as she hurried up the front walk. Quentin was the key to her career. He was going to make her a supermodel.

Late Friday night, Todd lay in bed fully dressed, listening to the sounds of the sleeping house. He could hear the dishwasher humming in the kitchen and the whirring of the heat vents. But otherwise, the house was silent. His parents had gone to bed an hour ago.

Todd glanced at his alarm clock—eleven P.M. It was time to go. He slid soundlessly to the ground and slipped his feet into his waiting shoes. He carefully picked up his brown leather jacket from the chair and stuffed his wallet into his pants pockets. Holding his breath, Todd stood perfectly still, listening. But nothing stirred in the house.

Todd padded soundlessly down the hall and listened at the door of his parents' room. He could hear his mother's even breathing and his dad's snoring. Then he inched his way down the hall and tiptoed down the winding staircase. A wooden step creaked, and Todd stopped. He strained his ears, breathing a sigh of relief when he could make out the faint sound of his father's snoring. Todd continued down, remaining close to the wall to prevent the steps from squeaking.

He carefully pulled open the front door and crept outside, slowly shutting it behind him.

The night was clear and cool, and Todd pulled his jacket on, taking deep breaths of the balmy air. A feeling of freedom surged through him as he headed for his BMW across the street. Todd pulled the door open and slid in, closing it quietly behind him.

As he turned on the accelerator, Todd felt heady with excitement. It was eleven P.M. and he was on his way *out*, heading to downtown L.A. for a date with a gorgeous supermodel. He couldn't wait to tell Aaron and Winston all about it. They would turn green with envy.

Glancing in the rearview window, Todd turned up the collar of his jacket and fluffed out his hair. He looked cool and dark, he thought in satisfaction. He would fit in perfectly with the late-night Los Angeles crowd. Todd flicked on the radio and turned the knob, stopping at a techno station. The pulsing beat filled his body, and a jolt of adrenaline coursed through him.

This night is much more exciting than making out with Elizabeth at Miller's Point, Todd thought to himself. If he'd gone out with *her* tonight, he'd already be in bed by now.

Elizabeth was too uptight anyway. After all, Simone wouldn't make such a big deal about it if he kissed someone else.

Elizabeth is just a girl, Todd decided. *Simone is a woman.*

Jessica burst into the house with one thought on her mind—Elizabeth and Cameron. She hadn't even thought about the goodnight kiss before. If she had, she would have rethought the whole evening. She might share dates with her sister, but she didn't share kisses.

Jessica bounded up the stairs two steps at a time and burst into Elizabeth's room. Nobody was there. She flicked on the overhead light, blinking as she adjusted to the glare. The bed was still perfectly made like Elizabeth left it every morning.

Jessica began to panic. What if Elizabeth and Cameron had gone out afterward somewhere? What if they had gone to Miller's Point? What if Elizabeth really liked him?

Jessica, calm yourself, she told herself sternly. *Elizabeth would never do that to you. She would never steal a boyfriend from you.* But then Jessica thought of Elizabeth's secret affair with Ken Matthews. When Jessica and Ken were going out, Elizabeth had pulled a twin switch and had gone on a date with Ken to see if she still had feelings for him. And she had kissed him.

Jessica's feeling of foreboding burst into full blossom and she flew down the steps. "Liz, where are you?" she called.

She ran into the kitchen and turned on the light. The cheery copper-colored room was empty and spotless. "What is this, a ghost house?" she muttered.

Jessica hurried into the living room, her panic mounting. Then she heaved a sigh of relief. Elizabeth was curled up under an Afghan blanket on the sofa. "There you are!" she said in relief, sinking into the armchair in the corner.

"Huh?" Elizabeth asked in a groggy voice, opening her eyes to slits.

Jessica couldn't stand one more moment of waiting. She drummed her fingers on the arm of the chair. "So, did he kiss you goodnight?" she asked.

"What?" Elizabeth asked, wrapping the blanket around her shoulders and pulling herself up to a sitting position. She ran her fingers through her disheveled hair.

"Cameron," Jessica explained impatiently. "Did he kiss you?"

Elizabeth rolled her eyes. "You're welcome, Jessica," she said. "It was a pleasure for me to cover for you." Then she smiled devilishly. "Did you enjoy your meal?"

Jessica scowled. "Very funny, Liz. Yes, it was delicious. Now, you could please just answer the question?"

A strange glint came into Elizabeth's eyes. "Of course he kissed me," she said. "Do you really think Cameron would go out on a date with you without kissing you goodnight?"

A horrified chill crept slowly down Jessica's spine. "Did you kiss him back?"

Elizabeth shrugged, yawning. "Well, I didn't want to, but I had to. You know. So he would think I was you."

Jessica was furious. And hurt. Elizabeth had actually betrayed her. "I can't believe you kissed my date! What a disgusting thing to do!"

"Well, you don't want him to think you're a bad kisser, do you?" Elizabeth asked, her face all innocence.

Jessica stared at her opened mouth. She couldn't believe Elizabeth would do this to her. Her own sister. Her *twin*.

"Jess, he's a great kisser," Elizabeth said in a dreamy voice. "He's tender, but passionate at the same time." She sighed and snuggled into the Afghan. "I can see why you like him so much."

Jessica stood up, staring at her sister in horror. Had Elizabeth become an alien being? Had she transformed into psycho twin? Jessica threw up her arms. "Look, I don't want to hear another word." With that, she stomped up the steps.

She heard the sounds of Elizabeth's footsteps behind her and hurried more quickly down the hall.

"Wait, Jess —" Elizabeth said from behind her.

"Leave me alone," Jessica said, slipping into her bedroom and slamming shut the door behind her.

But Elizabeth just opened the door and followed her anyway, a slight grin on her face. "Do you know how many *l*'s there are in the word *gullible?*" she asked.

"Elizabeth, don't talk to me," Jessica said, storming into the bathroom and slamming the door behind her. Her whole body was heated up, and she was trembling slightly. Jessica wrapped her arms around her body. She couldn't believe that Cameron would kiss her sister. And that Elizabeth would betray her like that. She leaned her head against the door, feeling totally defeated. Then Elizabeth's words penetrated her consciousness.

Jessica quickly pushed open the door. Elizabeth was sitting against the wall on Jessica's bed, casually thumbing through a fashion magazine.

"What did you say?" Jessica asked.

"I asked you how many *l*'s there were in *gullible*," Elizabeth said with a smile.

Jessica heaved a sigh of relief and flopped down on the floor, pushing a pile of clothing out of her way. "So you didn't kiss him," she said.

"Of course not, silly," Elizabeth affirmed.

Jessica collapsed dramatically onto the floor. "What a relief!" she said. Then she sat up again, her good spirits quickly restored. "Well, it all worked out perfectly," she said. "Now I'm going to get my shoot with Quentin and go out with Cameron as well—"

"Not quite," Elizabeth said, cutting her off.

This time Elizabeth's face looked serious.

"Oh, no, what happened?" Jessica asked.

"The jig is up, Jess," Elizabeth said. "Cameron figured out that we pulled a twin switch." Elizabeth grimaced. "He noticed my watch."

"Drat," Jessica muttered. And it had all been going so well. *But then,* she thought diplomatically, *it could have been worse.* The most important thing was that Cameron didn't kiss Elizabeth goodnight.

Jessica shrugged. "Oh, well," she said. "I guess I'll just call him tomorrow and apologize. I'm sure he'll understand."

Elizabeth shook her head. "Jessica Wakefield, some times you are just too much."

Jessica gave her a dazzling grin. "I am, aren't I?"

Chapter 10

Elizabeth sat at a stool at the kitchen counter on Saturday afternoon, furiously chopping up vegetables for dinner. All day, the only thing she had been able to think about was Todd and Simone. She had woken up thinking about them, they had plagued her mind all morning, and now here they were again, tormenting her. She was beginning to see red. *Think of something else,* she commanded herself. *Think of Jessica and Cameron.* But as she viciously whacked a yellow squash, she couldn't help envisioning Simone's head.

The phone rang, and Elizabeth rushed to get it, grateful for a distraction from her disturbing thoughts. She wiping her hands on a dishrag and then picked up the receiver from the phone on the wall. "Hello?" she asked.

"Hello, Elizabeth, is that you?" a deep female

voice asked. Elizabeth recognized Leona at once.

"Hi, Leona!" Elizabeth said, surprised to hear from her on the weekend. She cradled the receiver in the crook of her neck and walked back to the kitchen counter, setting out a red and a yellow pepper on the cutting board. "So, are congratulations in order?"

"Not yet, but I'm working on it," Leona responded. "In fact, I had an inspiration last night. I'm going to lure Sam to a romantic weekend skiing in Lake Tahoe. I'm sure that once he's away from the city, he'll propose."

Elizabeth sliced through the red pepper. "Why don't you just ask him?" she suggested. "After all, he obviously appreciates liberated, independent women. I'm sure he'd be flattered."

Leona laughed, and her hearty voice came through the line. "Elizabeth, he would be terrified. And he would run for the hills. Believe me, men may put on a macho act, but inside they're like little boys. If a woman is *too* strong and independent, they get scared away. You see, essentially I'm asking him. But I'm letting him *think* he asked me."

"I see," Elizabeth said, not sure if she was convinced by Leona's logic. She scraped the slices of red and yellow peppers into a wooden salad bowl.

"I'm going to take Monday off as well," Leona asked. "If anybody asks, just tell them I'm sick."

"Uh, OK," Elizabeth said slowly.

"Thanks Elizabeth. You're a doll," Leona said. Then the phone clicked off.

127

Elizabeth hung up the phone slowly, feeling weird about the prospect of lying for her boss. Leona might be strong and independent, but she didn't seem to have much of a work ethic. Or a personal ethic either.

And that's why she's successful, Elizabeth thought in a moment of sudden clarity. *That's why she's on her way to the top.* People like Elizabeth—*nice* people—wouldn't get anywhere. They just would be betrayed and walked on.

Elizabeth sunk down in a chair at the kitchen table, feeling as though she had been cheated. She had always thought her ideals and integrity would get her somewhere. But, obviously, they were only in her way.

You're so naive, Elizabeth berated herself. *So, so naive.*

"My entire body hurts," Lila complained, sitting up in the chaise longue and stretching out her neck. It was Saturday afternoon, and Jessica and Lila were laying out by the pool in the Wakefield's backyard. Jessica was wearing a sleek new white one-piece bathing suit and Lila was outfitted in a floral bikini with a matching sarong.

Jessica raised an eyebrow. From the way Lila had been going on about her internship at Fowler Enterprises, you'd think she was doing manual labor, not working the switchboards.

"Must take a lot of effort to answer the

phones," Jessica said wryly, sitting up as well and reaching for a glass of iced tea on the side table between them.

"You have no idea," Lila said in a snooty tone. "I have to sit at the receptionist desk for eight hours a day, working the switchboard, directing clients, and answering phones. By the time five o'clock rolls around, I feel like I've been through a battle."

"You should try doing some *real* work," Jessica said. "Like moving fake boulders and lugging buckets of water around." Jessica picked up a bottle of sunblock, squeezed a bit on her palm, and began smoothing it on her face.

"At least you've got a *real* internship on a *real* fashion magazine," Lila responded. "I'm nothing more than a glorified secretary—for my *father*." Lila scowled as she picked up the bottle of sunblock. "No, I take that back. I'm not even glorified." She squeezed some of the lotion onto her palm, but then she dropped the bottle as if it were on fire. "Sunblock number 45? Jessica, are you crazy? What's the point of laying out if you block out *all* the rays?"

"The sun is good for your overall health," Jessica said pointedly. "But I have to protect my skin if I'm going to be a fashion model." She rubbed the rest of the lotion on her arms and shoulders.

Lila shook her head. "You got any baby oil around here?"

Jessica laughed and threw her a bottle of suntan oil.

"That's better," Lila said, sitting up and smoothing the oil on her golden-brown legs.

Jessica felt around the ground under her chair, searching for her tube of lip balm. "Well, if you hate it so much, why don't you ask your father for more responsibility?" she suggested, pursing her lips and running the lip balm along them. Jessica smacked her lips together, blanching at the coconut taste.

Lila looked at her aghast. "You mean, *work?*"

Jessica shook her head. "No, you're right. You might break a nail."

Lila sighed. "Actually, my father wants this to be a learning experience for me—he wants me to learn what it's like for the rest of the world."

"And have you learned anything?" Jessica asked.

"Definitely," Lila asserted, pushing her sunglasses on and leaning back in the chaise longue. "I am definitely meant to be rich and idle." She picked up her glass of iced tea and took a sip.

"I, on the other hand, am meant to be rich and working," Jessica said.

"Hmm?" Lila asked. Her eyes were closed and her face was lifted to the sun.

"Quentin promised to get me into the magazine," Jessica said.

Lila snorted. "I'll believe that when I see it."

"Don't worry, Lila. I'll still be your friend when I'm rich and famous," Jessica offered generously, lowering the chaise longue and laying her head back. Jessica closed her eyes, enjoying the luxurious feel of the hot sun beating down on her body.

"Thanks, Jess," Lila said flatly. "So does that mean you blew off Cameron?"

"Well, not exactly," Jessica said. She swung her feet off the chaise longue and sat up. Then she told Lila about the Cameron debacle of the night before. Jessica sighed when she was finished. "So, I guess I'll have to weasel my way out of it on Monday."

Lila turned her face to Jessica, covering her eyes from the sun. "Jess, if you really like this guy, I wouldn't wait until Monday."

"You're right," Jessica decided, jumping up. "I'll call him right now."

Jessica pushed open the sliding glass door and ran into the kitchen. A few minutes later, she reappeared, carrying a cellular phone and a telephone directory.

Jessica plopped down on the chair with the big white telephone book on her lap, leafing through the pages until she got to the S's. "Lila, there are like a thousand Smiths in here," she said in dismay.

"His last name is Smith?" Lila asked. "That's so stupid."

Jessica shook her head. Sometimes Lila's twisted logic defied a response. She ran a finger slowly down the dense column, peering at the small print. "Cagey, Caitlin, Caliban, Callum, Cary—Lila, there's no Cameron."

"I'll take care of this," Lila said. She picked up the cellular phone and pressed 4-1-1. "Yes, I'd like the number of a Mr. Cameron Smith, please." She admired her long shell pink manicured nails as she waited. "No, are you sure? OK, thank you."

Lila hung up the phone. "He's not listed. How strange," she said. "He must be too poor to have a phone."

Jessica frowned. "I guess that means I'll have to talk my way out of this mess at *Flair* on Monday." Then she shrugged. "Oh well. I'm sure it'll work out."

But somehow she had a feeling that Lila might be right. Monday might be too late. Jessica sighed. Maybe she really had blown her chances with Cameron after all.

Todd woke up late on Sunday morning. Feeling groggy, he sat up in bed rubbing his eyes. The sun was streaming through his window, and he could hear his parents downstairs talking over brunch. Sunday brunch was a tradition at the Wilkins's home. Todd stood up and picked up a crumpled pair of black jeans and a wrinkled wine-colored T-shirt from the floor, pulling them on quickly.

But then he ripped them off again. He went out to a club again Saturday night, and the cloying smell of cigarette smoke was in his hair and on his clothes. He threw on a navy blue bathrobe and hurried to the bathroom down the hall.

Ten minutes later, Todd headed down the steps, whistling to himself. He was wearing a clean pair of sweatpants and a T-shirt, and he was freshly shaven. He was beginning to enjoy this routine of going to bed late and getting up late. He couldn't believe how easy it was to sneak out. The night before he and Simone had gone to a trendy jazz club downtown, and he had actually enjoyed himself for the first time. He was getting to know some of the people in the model crowd she hung out with, and they seemed to like him.

"Good morning," Todd said cheerily as he walked into the kitchen.

"Morning, dear," his mother said with a smile. She was dressed casually, in jeans and a blazer, and her auburn hair was tied up in a green scarf.

"Mmm, looks great," Todd said, gazing appreciatively at the Sunday-morning spread. A large platter of scrambled eggs stood in the middle of the table, with a basket of homemade blueberry muffins next to it. His mother had fixed a fresh fruit salad as well, with cantaloupe, honeydew melon, and kiwi.

Todd sat down at his table and filled his plate.

"You're up late," his father remarked, looking up from the newspaper on his lap.

"Yeah, I was studying for a history test last night," Todd said, thinking quickly. He shrugged. "Since I couldn't go out, I figured I'd make the best of my time."

Todd could feel his face flushing and stared at his plate. He wasn't used to lying to his parents like this. But then, what was he supposed to do? If they were going to insist on imposing absolutely ridiculous rules, then he was going to have to find a way to get around them.

"Good thinking," his father said. The Italian coffeemaker began to hiss, and Todd's father stood up and went to the stove. He returned a moment later with two cups of espresso, setting one down in front of Mrs. Wilkins.

"I'm sorry we were so tough on you, Todd," his father said when he sat down. "But it's important for you to learn responsibility at a young age."

Todd nodded. "Don't worry, there are no hard feelings," he said. "I understand." But his father's kind words just added to his guilt, and now Todd really felt like a heel. His stabbed at the eggs on his plate with a fork, concentrating on his food. He felt his dad's piercing eyes on him, but he kept on eating steadily, trying to seem unconcerned.

"Would you like some more eggs, dear?" Mrs. Wilkins asked.

"Sure, thanks, Mom," Todd said, reaching out a hand for the platter.

"What's that?" Mr. Wilkins asked suddenly.

"What's what?" Todd asked, his heart began to sound a drumroll in his chest.

"That, the red stamp on your hand," Mr. Wilkins said, pointing at the back of Todd's right hand.

Todd looked down at his hand and gulped. The stamp from the club last night hadn't washed off in the shower. "Oh, that's nothing," he said quickly. "Just, just something from school on Friday."

Mr. Wilkins voice was cold. "You didn't have school on Friday."

Todd swallowed hard. "I meant last week—"

But Mr. Wilkins cut him off. "Don't bother, Todd. You didn't have a stamp on your hand yesterday." Mr. Wilkins frowned, disappointment marring his features. "It's from a club. You obviously snuck out last night."

Todd didn't respond. For a moment, there was total silence in the room. Todd sat perfectly still, waiting for his punishment. What were they going to do, ground him for the rest of his life?

When Todd's father spoke again, his voice was quiet and resolved. "Todd, I want you to listen to me. If you cross the line one more time, you're going to be in big trouble." He looked Todd straight in the eye. "Is that understood?"

"Yes, perfectly," Todd muttered, his face heating up in anger. He stared at the table, biting back a response. He felt guilty for lying to his parents, but he was also fed up with the way they were treating him. They were acting like he was an infant.

He felt as though the whole world had been dictating his actions lately. Elizabeth went nuts just because he had kissed Simone, and his parents were trying to completely control him. It wasn't as if he was doing anything wrong. He was just going out dancing at night. Simone was right. If he didn't assert himself, they'd always treat him like a child.

Todd stood up and threw down his napkin. "I think I've lost my appetite," he said. "Do you mind if I leave without finishing my breakfast . . . or won't I get any dessert?"

"Todd!" his mother exclaimed, looking shocked.

"Watch it," his father warned. "You're pushing it."

Todd shrugged, stalking out of the room. He grabbed his basketball and headed for the front door. He needed to work off some steam.

Chapter 11

"Where in the world is Simone?" Quentin demanded, throwing his hands in the air. He had been repeating the words like a mantra for the past two hours. He kicked at a rock in frustration, sending a cloud of dust in the air.

On the set, Jessica winced, holding back a cough. It was late Monday morning, and Quentin was totally stressed out because Simone was hours late and no one could get in touch with her. The morning's shoot was a Roman ruins scene, and the set was fully constructed. Big gray rocks stood in front of a crumbling acropolis, and five black cats were running around the ruins. The lights were ready as well, and everybody on the art crew was standing around, waiting for Simone.

Quentin stalked back to his camera and peered through the lens. "Isn't somebody going to adjust those lights?" he roared, pointing to a blue lighting fixture strung up in the corner.

"Yes, sir, Mr. Berg," responded an assistant quickly, hurrying over to the light.

"Uh-oh, looks like Quentin's on the warpath," Shelly whispered to Jessica.

"I think we better stay out of his way," Jessica whispered back.

Quentin looked at his watch for the hundredth time. "This is an extremely important shoot," he ranted to everybody and nobody, "and we've only got this morning to shoot it."

"*Mrrrw!*" screeched a skinny cat, jumping from the wall of the acropolis onto Quentin's shoulder.

"Would somebody *please* take care of these animals?" Quentin shouted, flinging the cat off his shoulder. The cat yowled and went flying to the ground.

"Here, kitty," Jessica called, quickly gathering the animal up in her arms. "C'mere, kitties," she said, clucking her tongue as she poured dry cat food into a plastic blue bowl. The four other cats quickly ran to her, rubbing against her leg. "OK, there's enough for all of you," she said soothingly.

Shelly joined her quickly, filling a couple of bowls with milk.

"Why are there cats on this set, anyway?" Jessica asked her.

"Quentin's trying to capture the look of ancient Rome. Apparently, the ruins are overrun with stray cats," Shelly explained.

"Well, it will certainly look authentic," Jessica said, placing the bowl on the floor. The five cats scrambled to get at the food.

"*Sss!*" hissed the biggest cat. Soon all of the cats were yowling and clawing at each other. Jessica quickly grabbed the bowl of food from the ground, and the cats all clambered around her, meowing loudly.

Quentin glared at them. "What is this, the set of *Cats*?" he burst out.

"Oh, boy," Jessica muttered under her breath. "Do we have any more bowls?"

Shelly handed her a stack of bowls, and Jessica lined them up on the table, quickly filling them up with food.

"Oww!" Quentin yelped suddenly. Jessica looked over and saw Quentin rubbing his thigh on the set. He had obviously walked into a fake boulder.

"Jessica, what's that rock doing in the middle of the floor?" Quentin yelled.

Jessica sighed. Quentin was definitely losing it. The rock was right where he had told her to put it five minutes ago. "I'll get it in just a sec," she said, pushing back a strand of dirty hair.

"Get it *now*," he barked out.

"Fine," Jessica responded angrily, placing all the bowls of food on the floor and heading to the set. She was just about at her wit's end. She had spent the last few hours pushing around piles of rocks, and now she had to push them back. Her arms were killing her from lifting the heavy boulders, and she was hot and dusty from building the framework of the acropolis.

Quentin's obviously forgotten about our date last night, Jessica thought as she eyed the huge gray rock. He was so stressed out about Simone that he had been screaming at Jessica for the past two hours. But Jessica had managed to keep her cool. She was hoping that Simone wouldn't show and that Quentin would use Jessica in her place.

Jessica picked up the boulder with both arms and staggered to the right, dropping the boulder on the edge of the set. A cloud of sawdust rose in the air and Jessica coughed, choking in the dust.

"I can-not be-lieve this," Quentin yelled, looking at his watch. "It's not possible." He charged from one end of the set to the other like a hungry lion. Then he sunk down into a low director's chair and dropped his head in his hands. "How am I going to get another model on such short notice?" he moaned.

Jessica took that as her cue. She didn't look much like model at the moment—covered from head to toe in particles of dust—but that couldn't be helped. Now was her chance, and she had to grab it.

Smoothing her hair down, Jessica headed in his direction. "Um, Quentin," she began. "If you'd like, I would be happy to—"

But just then Simone breezed in, looking

entirely unperturbed. "Good morning, everybody," she said cheerily. Despite her chipper tone, she looked exhausted. Her skin was pale and wan, and her eyes were sunken into her face. *Probably from dancing all night with my sister's boyfriend*, Jessica thought in disgust.

Quentin flew out of his chair at the sight of her. "Simone, do you know what time it is?" he demanded, practically purple with rage.

Simone looked at her watch. "Eleven o'clock," she responded sweetly.

Quentin shook his head. "I'm not even going to be able to develop this film myself. I'm going to have to FedEx it to New York at lunchtime, and they'll have to turn it around there."

Simone shrugged. "So?"

Quentin looked like he was about to explode. "*So?* So—you aren't the only model in this industry. Maybe you should think about that the next time you decide to show up two hours late!"

"Humph," Simone pouted, swiveling on a high heel and waltzing away. "I'll be in wardrobe."

As Jessica listened to the angry exchange, a brilliant idea popped into her head. Maybe she would get her chance to stand in for Simone after all. . . .

"Hello, Leona Peirson's office," Elizabeth said into the phone on Monday morning. She was sitting behind Leona's desk, up to her elbows in work. She was doing research for an article on life conditions of women in ancient Greece and fielding Leona's calls as well.

"Yes, this is Rupert Perry," said a deep male voice. "I'd like to set up a meeting with Leona for early next week."

"Uh, just one moment," Elizabeth said, frantically running a finger down the office directory for his name. Then she found it. Rupert Perry was the head of marketing.

Her screen beeped, indicating that her Library of Congress search was complete. "Five articles found," it read. "Continue searching?" it prompted. Elizabeth pressed "y."

"What day would be good for you, Mr. Perry?" she asked into the phone.

"Just a moment. I need to check my schedule," he responded.

There was a sharp knock on the door, and Anne, the receptionist, popped her head in. "Is the report for the meeting ready?" she mouthed.

Elizabeth nodded and held up an index finger. Cradling the phone on her shoulder, she clicked the mouse and switched windows on her computer screen. The editorial board was meeting to go over the report Leona had dictated to Elizabeth on Friday, and Elizabeth had typed it up. She scanned the screen and printed it out, handing it to the receptionist.

"Thank you," Anne said.

Elizabeth nodded, turning her attention back to her call.

"How is next Thursday at two o'clock?" Mr. Perry was asking.

Elizabeth flipped through Leona's desk calendar. "That's fine, Mr. Perry. I'll just pencil you in."

Just then, the other line buzzed. Elizabeth ran her fingers through her hair, feeling frazzled. She didn't know how Leona managed to juggle so many things at once.

"Hello, Leona Peirson's office," Elizabeth said.

"Hello, Leona Peirson," said a familiar female voice.

"Leona!" Elizabeth exclaimed. "I'm so glad you called. It's been total chaos here, and I had to make some executive decisions for you. I typed up our notes from Friday for the board meeting today—is that OK?"

"That's perfect," Leona reassured her. "That's exactly what I was going to ask you to do. It looks like you can do my job as well as I can."

Elizabeth laughed, feeling relieved. "Not quite. I think one day is about all I can handle." She swiveled Leona's armchair around and leaned back.

"Well, actually, Elizabeth, I've got some bad news for you," Leona said. "I broke my leg skiing."

"Oh, no!" Elizabeth exclaimed, sitting up straight. "How awful. Is it serious?"

"Well, not really," Leona responded. "But I'm in traction for the moment, and I won't be able to move for a few days."

"I'm really sorry," Elizabeth said sympathetically.

143

"Me too," Leona said. "I'm itching to get to work."

"Well, I'll be happy to help you in any way I can," Elizabeth offered.

"Great," Leona said. "Have you got a pen on you?"

Elizabeth grabbed a yellow legal pad and pen. "Shoot," she said.

"OK," Leona said. "I need you to sit in on the meeting today and present our report. Get everybody's input and make any corrections you think advisable, and then circulate a memo to the entire editorial department—and circulate a copy to the heads of the other departments as well. Then I need you to thoroughly research our three feature articles on the Library of Congress database and Lexis/Nexis. Do a complete printout and article summary. Make sure you proofread and fact check any stories that come in as well. . . ."

Elizabeth's eyes widened. This was enough work for an entire department, not one person. In fact, Leona wasn't asking her to assist her—she was asking her to *replace* her.

Five minutes later, Leona got to the end of her list. Elizabeth shook out her wrist, which was tired from all the writing, and stared at the page, wondering how in the world she could possibly accomplish everything on it.

"Did you get all that?" Leona asked.

"Yeah, I think so," Elizabeth said slowly.

"Don't worry, Elizabeth, I've got the greatest confidence in you," Leona said.

"Thanks, Leona," Elizabeth replied, swallowing hard. She just hoped she wouldn't disappoint her.

"Oh, and can you take care of a few personal things as well for me?"

Elizabeth stared at the phone in consternation. This was going too far. "What did you have in mind?" she asked cautiously.

"Just a few errands, but make sure you make a note of them," Leona said, speaking quickly. "I need you to water my plants, pick up my calls, open my mail, respond to any invitations by phone or mail, and feed the cats."

Elizabeth's mouth dropped open. She had expected Leona to ask her for a few personal things to take care of at *work*, like watering the drooping plant on her desk. After all, she was an *intern*, not a personal assistant. And besides, didn't Leona have any friends who could take care of her personal life for her?

"I keep an extra pair of house keys in the right drawer of my desk," Leona added. "You can use those."

Elizabeth opened her mouth to suggest that a friend stay at the house when Leona spoke up again. "Listen, the doctor's here. I've got to go. Cover for me at the office, OK?" she said. "Just say I'm working at home. I don't want anyone to know that I took off to go skiing."

"Uh—uh, sure," Elizabeth stuttered.

"Thanks, Elizabeth. You're the best," Leona

said. "Oh, and don't forget to pick up my dry cleaning. And you might want to vacuum as well while you're there. Bye, love!" Then she hung up.

Elizabeth dropped the receiver with a clatter. First her boyfriend dumped her for a supermodel, then the editorial board rejected her idea. Now she was picking up her boss's dry cleaning. Was there some kind of curse on her life? How much worse could things get?

"Jessica, get me some water," Simone ordered. "My skin is getting completely dehydrated under these bright lights." She was standing in front of the ruins dressed in an emerald green sheath. With her slanted eyeliner and gold eye shadow, her face had the same mysterious appearance as the cats around her. A number of extremely good-looking Italian male models were posing in the background.

"I think her brain is dehydrated," Jessica whispered to Shelly by the makeup table.

Shelly shook her head. "I think her brain is *fried.*"

"Jessica, did you hear me?" Simone repeated in a shrill voice.

"I'm sorry, did you shriek?" Jessica responded. But then she stood up and walked out of the room before Simone had a chance to reply. Just last week Jessica had brought up an entire case of mineral water, but Simone had already gobbled it all up. *The skin is the key to beauty,* Simone was fond of repeating. *And water is the key to the skin.*

Jessica pressed the button at the elevator bank, glad to get away from the dynamic duo for a few minutes. Quentin had been shooting Simone for the last hour, and she had been whining and complaining nonstop. Quentin was getting testier and testier by the minute, a sure sign that the shots weren't going well.

Fifteen minutes later, Jessica returned, lugging another case of French mineral water in her arms, as well as a basket of vegetables and dried fruit. She dropped everything in the wardrobe room and stretched out her aching neck. Then she took out a bottle of water and filled up a plate with celery sticks.

When she returned to the main studio, Quentin was kneeling in front of the camera, and assistants were running around adjusting the lights for the next shot. Simone was pacing impatiently along the set.

"Here you are," Jessica said sweetly, handing her a bottle of water and a glass of ice. "And look," she said, holding up the plate of celery sticks, "a yummy treat as well!"

"Quentin, can't you do anything about the insolent interns?" Simone complained.

Quentin glanced around the camera. "Can't you do anything about your incessant whining?" he responded.

Jessica grinned, scoring her first victory for the day.

"Humph!" Simone pouted, setting the glass down on a rock and pouring the effervescent water into it. One of the cats leapt onto the rocks and stuck his head into the glass, sniffing at the contents.

"Oh, how disgusting!" Simone complained. She held the glass at arm's length and held it out to Jessica. "Replace this immediately."

"My pleasure," Jessica said, handing her another glass. She had brought out a double of everything, anticipating Simone's every request.

"Thank you," Simone said tightly, taking a delicate sip.

"Hey, Jess, can you give me a hand over here?" Shelly called from the makeup table.

"Sure," Jessica responded happily, hurrying over to join her. Shelly was in the process of making up Antonio, a striking male model with dark features and an aquiline nose.

"What can I do for you?" Jessica asked.

Shelly waved a hand in the air. "Oh, I just wanted to get you away from her highness."

"Shelly, you're the best," Jessica said gratefully. She took a seat on a stool and opened a jar of base, trying to look occupied.

"Shelly says you're the one who put together the set," Antonio said to Jessica with a smile. "And from the looks of you, that's obvious."

Jessica glanced down at her dust-covered body ruefully. "Yeah, by the time I get done every day, I look like more like the ruins then the set."

"Well, your efforts have certainly paid off," Antonio complimented her. "You've really done a professional job."

"An-ton-io!" Shelly complained in exasperation. "One more word out of you and I'm going to paint your face instead of your lips."

"Sorry, Shelly," Antonio said docilely.

"Shh!" Shelly instructed. She looked carefully at his coloring, then chose a compact. "Now close your eyes," she directed, covering his face with beige powder.

Suddenly Jessica heard a yowl and looked over at the set. One of the cats had ducked behind Simone's rock and another was circling the boulder. Suddenly the bigger can pounced on the smaller one. Soon the two cats were snarling and hissing.

"Uh-oh," Jessica said to Shelly. "I think Simone's getting caught in another cat fight. I better go break it up."

"Would somebody please control these felines?" Simone snarled.

Jessica jumped and hurried over to the refreshment table to distract the cats. She grabbed a box of dry cat food from the counter and knelt down, shaking the box hard. All of the cats came scampering over.

Quentin clapped his hands together. "OK, everybody take their places," he called. "The shot's ready." Quentin peeked into the lens of his camera, then stood up. "Simone, I want you front and center. Antonio, Marco, and Stefan, spread out and lean against the acropolis. Nice. Good. Simone, I want you sulky. Male models, you're expressionless. Jessica, get the cats on the set." Jessica quickly jumped up and hid behind one of the borders on the set, throwing pieces of food onto the floor. The cats quickly ran between the boulders, adding a mysterious feel to the setting.

"Great! Perfect!" Quentin breathed, taking the shot. Then he adjusted the lens and clicked the camera a few more times. "Thanks guys, that's it for you," he told the models.

The guys headed for wardrobe, and Simone followed quickly behind. "Wait, Simone, I'm not done with you," Quentin ordered.

Simone gave him an exasperated look and returned to the set. "I want some close-ups of you," he said, picking up the camera hanging around his neck. Kneeling down, he zoomed in with the telephoto lens. "Give me expression. I want passion, anger, frustration."

Simone stared blankly into the camera.

"*Expression*, Simone," Quentin repeated.

"Arggh," Simone grumbled, shooting him an annoyed look.

"Great!" Quentin said, taking the shot.

Simone put her hands on her hips and pouted.

"Nice!" Quentin yelled, clicking the camera again.

"I have had enough of this!" Simone declared, her eyes shooting sparks.

"Perfect!" Quentin breathed, moving in close to her and taking shot after shot.

Simone crossed her hands over her chest, her face was practically purple with rage.

Quentin stood up and rewound the film. "That's a wrap," he said.

"I am going directly to a spa at a location I have no intention of disclosing," Simone announced. "No one should even *try* to track me down, since I will be totally out of reach." Then she stomped out.

Jessica's ears perked up at Simone's words. With Simone out of the way, she might finally get a shot at modeling herself.

Quentin sunk into a chair. "Well, I'm glad I got at least one good roll of film. For the first several rolls, Simone looked so tired that I thought I was going to have to pour chicken noodle soup over her head."

What a great idea! Jessica thought.

"If anyone needs me, I'm in the darkroom," Quentin said, standing up.

Jessica watched Quentin walk away, and a devious idea popped into her head. She waited until he had disappeared into the darkroom, then she looked around surreptitiously. Everybody was engaged in an activity—the assistants were taking down lights, Shelly was packing up her tray, and the set designer was gathering the cats together.

Her heart pounding in her chest, Jessica walked

nonchalantly toward the camera. Then she clicked open the back of it, exposing the film. Holding her breath, she quickly shut it again. She glanced around the room quickly and let out her breath in a rush. Nobody had even noticed.

Jessica rubbed her hands together, unable to believe her luck. If everything went according to plan, she was on her way to stardom.

Todd screeched into the parking lot of the Mode building and jumped out of his black BMW. He knew Simone had a photo shoot this morning, and he was hoping to catch her before she left for the day.

He hurried through the revolving doors when he caught side of a tall, slim figure stalking out the opposite entrance. It was Simone, and she looked like she was in a hurry. She was still dressed in her modeling attire—a long, shimmering green dress—and she wore a determined look on her face.

"Simone!" Todd called, running after her.

Simone stopped, an annoyed expression on her perfect features.

Todd jogged up to her, his heart thumping nervously against his rib cage. Even though he had spent every evening with her this weekend, her presence still intimidated her. Especially when she was wearing four-inch heels that made her taller than he was—and when she had the blasé look on her face that she had on now.

"Oh, hi, Todd," Simone said when her reached her.

"Hi," Todd said. "Listen, I—" He ran his fingers through his hair nervously, suddenly embarrassed at what he had to say.

"Yes?" Simone prompted him, tapping a high heel on the gravel.

Todd clenched his jaw and forged on ahead. "Well, my parents found out that I went out with you, and I'm in a lot of trouble at home."

Simone rolled her eyes. "This again!" she said, throwing up her arms. "Really, Todd, aren't you a bit *old* to be getting in trouble? Believe me, you'll never get anywhere at this pace. If you want to make it in this business, you've got to be independent. You've got to be your own man."

Todd swallowed hard, feeling more like six years old than sixteen. "I know," he said quickly. "I've tried to explain that to them, but they don't seem to understand. So, I wanted to know if you'd like to come to dinner tonight. You see, maybe if my parents meet you—" Todd blushed. "And see how wonderful you are—they'll be more understanding about the time we spend together."

Simone had been steadily tapping her heel on the ground as he spoke. Now she glanced at her watch. "I'm sorry, Todd, but I can't make it tonight. Maybe another time."

Todd felt a pang in his chest, feeling hurt by her casual words and disparaging tone, but he tried not to let it show. "Sure, no problem," he said in a nonchalant voice. "I'll call you tomorrow, then."

Simone shrugged. "Fine, whatever," she said.

Then she turned and strode away.

Todd just looked after her, feeling younger than ever.

Jessica crouched down in a corner in the main studio, filing negatives in a photo box. Quentin had been ranting and raving for the past half hour, and Jessica was trying to remain as inconspicuous as possible. He had discovered his film had been exposed after returning to the main studio and was yelling generally at everybody for incompetence. Fortunately, Quentin thought it was a fluke and didn't assume that somebody had tampered with his camera.

Jessica wasn't the only one laying low. The lighting assistants were pretending to be busy with some lights in the back, and the set workers were all sitting along the wall, whispering among themselves. Michael and Shelly were standing together at the makeup table, quietly putting away beauty supplies.

Quentin raked his fingers through his scruffy blond hair. "Now we can't get the shoot done," he shouted. "Do you know what this means?" He didn't wait for an answer. "This means the layout will be delayed. Which means the entire issue will be held up. Which means I'll lose my job. Which means my career is *ruined*."

The set designer clicked open the back door, and a couple of assistants followed him, carrying lights in their hands. Then Michael headed quietly to his salon. Shelly pushed open the door of wardrobe a few minutes later, a huge makeup case in her hand. Jessica hunched over her work, trying to concentrate on arranging the negatives.

When Jessica looked up, she swallowed hard. It looked like everybody had slowly managed to slip out of the room. Now it was just Quentin and Jessica. Quentin was slumped over a table, holding his head and moaning to himself.

Jessica gathered together her courage and stood up. Now was her chance, and she had to grab it. Jessica walked over to him and laid a comforting hand on his arm. "That's really tough," she said softly. "There's no way we'll will be able to get another model here in time."

"I know," Quentin said in despair. He stood up and began pacing around the room agitatedly. "There's got to be *something* we can do," he said.

"Well, if you'd like, *I* could fill in for Simone," Jessica suggested.

Quentin hesitated, and Jessica held her breath.

"All right," he said finally. "We'll give it a go. After all, we don't have a choice, do we?"

Jessica shook her head quickly.

"OK, go directly to hair and makeup," Quentin ordered. "We have no time to spare." Quentin opened the door of the side room and yelled. "Hey, you guys, bring those lights back in here! We've got another model on board."

Jessica hurried out of the room before Quentin could change his mind. As she slipped into Michael's hair salon, her heart began pounding in excitement. Her career was about to be launched!

Chapter 12

"Ninety-one, ninety-three, ninety-five. . ." Elizabeth said, reading the house numbers aloud as she drove slowly down Ocean Lane during her lunch break. "Ninety-*nine*. That's it." Elizabeth pulled the Jeep to a stop in front of Leona's condominium, pausing for a moment to admire the idyllic setting. The apartment complex was surrounded by beautiful cherry trees, and it was located only a mile from the ocean.

Elizabeth fitted the key in the lock on the second floor and pushed open the door. "Wow," she exclaimed, whistling under her breath at the sight that greeted her. The apartment was a huge airy space with light wood floors and high cathedral ceilings. If it weren't for the separate rooms, the condo's interior would have resembled a loft.

Elizabeth set down her bag on a small, round, wrought iron table, taking in the stylish decor of the living room. Two black leather couches were arranged perpendicularly in the middle of the room, with a big glass table in front of them. A blue art deco clock hung on the wall, and shell pink Tiffany lamps added a hint of color to the stark room. But most spectacular of all was the view. The far wall of the living room was made entirely of windows, and the foamy, blue-green Pacific Ocean sparkled in the distance.

The apartment is just like Leona, Elizabeth thought. *Sleek, modern, and fashionable.*

"Mrrw!" meowed a cat, prancing into the room. Soon two identical Persian cats were rubbing against her leg.

"Hey, you guys must be hungry, huh?" Elizabeth said, leaning down and stroking their fur.

Elizabeth hurried into the kitchen and rummaged through the cabinets, finally finding a stack of canned cat food. One of the cats leapt onto the counter and the other clawed at Elizabeth's leg impatiently, meowing incessantly. "OK, OK, just a minute," she berated them, lifting the cat off the counter and dropping him on the floor.

Elizabeth opened a can of food and divided it between the two bowls, and then she filled up another bowl with fresh water. She took a quick look in the refrigerator, wondering what Leona ate. *Evidently not much,* Elizabeth thought, staring at the empty fridge. All that was in the refrigerator was a bottle of diet Coke and a half-eaten grapefruit covered in aluminum foil. She shook her head. If a starvation diet was how Leona managed to keep so thin, then Elizabeth didn't think it was worth it.

Elizabeth caught sight of a big blue watering can on a high shelf and remembered the plants. She reached up for it and filled it with lukewarm water. Returning to the living room, she carefully watered the giant rubber plants in the corner. Then she headed back to the kitchen, pausing to pick up a frame from the bookshelf. It was a shot of Leona with a tall, dark guy. *Hmm,* Elizabeth thought. *That must be Sam.*

Elizabeth put her hands on her hips and surveyed the space. *Leona really has everything,* she thought in admiration. Independence, success, a cute boyfriend. . . . *Someday,* Elizabeth thought, *this is exactly what my life will be like.*

Driven by curiosity, Elizabeth explored the rest of the apartment. She peeked into the bathroom and found a clawfoot tub and a whirlpool. The bathroom was done in lime green, with painted Spanish tiles on the floor and an elegant pink marble sink against the wall.

Then she checked out the bedroom. Unlike the rest of the apartment, the bedroom was soft and romantic, with delicate ivory linens on the bed and long white curtains that swept the floor. Elizabeth pulled open the door to the walk-in closet and gasped. It looked like Leona had more clothes than Lila Fowler. Her suits were arranged by color, creating a rainbowlike row. And on the door hung pairs and pairs of shoes. Elizabeth flipped through the suits, fingering the rich materials and admiring the soft colors. She stopped as she came upon an exquisite ivory-colored suit with big round pearl buttons. Unlike most of Leona's ensembles, this one had a short-cropped jacket that was to be worn buttoned-up.

Elizabeth lifted out the suit, wondering how she would look in it. Did she dare? She looked around quickly, but only a fluffy cat was in sight, curled up contentedly at the base of the bed. Then Elizabeth shrugged. Why not? After all, if Elizabeth wanted to be just like Leona, then she had to *feel* like Leona. Trying on her clothes would only help Elizabeth to emulate her.

Elizabeth quickly pulled off her own skirt and jacket and slipped into the luxurious woven silk. Pulling on a pair of Leona's beige pumps, she stood in front of the full-length mirror. Elizabeth gasped at her reflection. She looked professional, yet stylish. She turned, admiring the sharp cut of the suit. No wonder people said clothes make the man—or the woman.

Pretending she was Leona, Elizabeth strode into the living room and took a seat on the leather couch. The cat padded after her, jumping up and kneading her lap with his paws. "Hello, kitty," she said in Leona's deep modulated voice. She picked up a note pad from the glass coffee table, and pressed the play button on the answering machine. "Leona, it's your sister, Terri . . ." came the first message.

"Your sister Terri," Elizabeth scrawled, running a finger through her hair like Leona did. Ten minutes later, she had gotten to the end of the messages. Elizabeth set the pad on the table and stood up graciously.

She paused in the middle of the floor, feeling regal in her elegant surroundings. "Now what?" she said to herself, placing an imagined French-manicured hand on her cheek. "Oh, yes, the mail." Elizabeth picked up the pile of letters she had brought in and carried them over to the sleek black desk in front of the window. Perching on the chair, Elizabeth crossed her legs and slit open the first one with a gold letter opener. "Now what's this?" she asked. "Ah, an invitation to a runway show. Hmm, I'll have to check my calendar." The rest of the mail contained personal letters and bills. Elizabeth left the letters on the desk and tucked the invitation into her bag. She would have to compose a response at work.

Elizabeth stood up and stretched in the sun, looking in wonder at the beautiful blue-green ocean right in the backyard. She was having so much fun she almost didn't want to take off the suit and go back to work. She walked through the living room, fingering knickknacks and looking at photos.

Then a tape recorder on the side table caught her eye. "Hmm, I wonder what that's for," Elizabeth said aloud. She sat down on the couch and picked it up, looking at it curiously. She was about to press "play," but then she stopped herself, feeling a twinge of guilt. It was one thing to try on Leona's suits, but it was another to invade her privacy.

Then Elizabeth shrugged the feeling away. Leona had no right to make Elizabeth her personal slave. If she was going to have to come here every single day to take care of Leona's life, she might as well learn all she could.

Elizabeth leaned back into the plush leather couch and pressed "play." Leona's deep voice came through, dictating letters. Elizabeth listened as Leona read a letter to Rupert Perry, the head of marketing. She yawned as Leona went through a long list of marketing possibilities for the Greek and Roman antiquity edition.

Oh well, I've heard all this before. Elizabeth picked up the tape recorder and searched for the stop button, but then she paused suddenly at Leona's next words. "Letter to Gordon Lewis," Leona was saying. Gordon Lewis was the hotshot new publisher of *Flair* who had brought the magazine to L.A. a few months ago. "Note to myself," Leona said. "This letter is not to go through Elizabeth."

Elizabeth's eyes widened at the mention of her name, and she listened closely, pacing the carpet

162

and holding the tape recorder in her hand. "Dear Gordon," Leona said in a crisp, clear voice. "As you suggested, I would like to formally submit the idea we discussed on the phone. It's actually quite simple and has the benefit of bringing *Flair* into the age of interactivity. I propose a column tentatively titled "Free Style," a one-page article written by a *Flair* reader with her ideas on fashion. The column would of course conform with the theme of the magazine, and submissions would be accepted, thus guaranteeing the high quality of writing that we depend on at *Flair*. I would be happy to discuss my idea at the next editorial board meeting. With best regards—Leona."

Elizabeth was stunned. She rewound the tape and played it back again. Then she fell back hard on the couch and clicked off the tape. Slowly, the significance hit her.

Leona had never pitched the idea at the meeting. In fact, she had stolen it from Elizabeth. And now she was taking full credit for it. Elizabeth couldn't believe what she'd just heard. She dropped her head back on the couch, staring up at the high ceiling. Leona had been her idol.

Elizabeth felt a knot twist slowly in her stomach. She felt entirely betrayed. And devastatingly disappointed.

Jessica walked carefully down the hall to the main studio after lunch, her hips thrust forward in an imitation of Simone's walk. She was wearing Simone's green dress and four-inch platform heels. The art director had frantically hemmed the dress and taken it in at the sides, and Shelly had made up her face in glamorous golden tones. Jessica's blue-green eyes were accentuated with shades of green eye shadow, and mauve blush with hints of gold brought out her cheekbones. Michael had twisted her hair into long, golden curls that bounced lightly around her face as she walked.

Jessica paused at the door of the photography studio, suddenly hit with the enormity of what was happening. She was actually about to be photographed by Quentin Berg for the hottest magazine in the fashion industry. She wasn't just fooling around with Lila on the beach with a camera. This was for real. She had entered the big league. Jessica's tongue turned dry, and a thousand butterflies began flitting around her subject. Was she crazy? She didn't know anything about modeling.

Jessica closed her hand around the doorknob and squeezed her eyes shut, forcing herself to take long, deep breaths. *One, two, three,* she counted slowly, trying to regain her composure. She felt exactly like she did when she was about to go onstage. She had the same tightening in her chest and the same queasiness in her stomach.

Get into the part, she told herself. When she was nervous before a show, she calmed her anxiety by losing herself in her role. Now she tried to assume the part of an ancient goddess. Closing her eyes, she pictured a dusty acropolis in ancient Rome. She was Athena, and she had descended from Mount Olympus to find the man with whom she had fallen in love. He had dark curly hair and piercing brown eyes. Even though he was just a mortal, he looked like a god.

Feeling calm at last, Jessica opened her eyes. She straightened her back and held her head high, walking serenely into the main studio. Assistants were frantically assembling bluish lights, and Quentin was hunched over the camera. But the action stopped when she walked in, and all eyes turned to her. Jessica sucked in her breath, feeling suddenly nervous again.

Quentin whistled when he saw her. "You—look—*fabulous!*" he exclaimed.

Shelly grinned from the make-up table, giving her a thumbs-up sign.

Jessica let out her breath in a rush.

Quentin stood up and looked at his watch. "We've only got time to redo the last roll," he told Jessica. "We're just taking shots of you."

Jessica nodded, her heart hammering in excitement.

Quentin frowned. "If we had the time, I would go through the basics of movement with you. Why don't you just walk around the set for a few minutes to get warmed up? I'm going to follow you with the lens and get the camera in focus."

Jessica nodded and walked onto the set, taking her place in front of the ruins. Moving gracefully, she threaded her way carefully amid the fake rocks, her back squared and her head held high. When she reached the end of the stage, she lifted her arms up in the air and stretched, trying to relax all the muscles in her body. Leaning down and grabbing onto the edge of a rock, she slowly stretched out her vertebrae one by one. Then she walked back in the other direction.

Suddenly she noticed the camera was clicking. She turned quickly toward Quentin, a long golden curl falling over her eye. *Click*, went the lens.

"Great!" Quentin exclaimed. Then he jumped onto the set. "I'm going to position you for the next shot."

Quentin moved Jessica to the center of the set directly in front of the ruins. Then he lifted her left arm in the air and set it at an awkward angle above her head. Jessica quickly shifted her weight, adjusting her arm to a more comfortable position.

Quentin sighed. "Jessica, don't move. You've got to do remain exactly as I put you. OK?"

"OK," Jessica said, grimacing. Quentin put both her arms in the air above her head and joined her hands together. Then he turned her face way back so her chin was jutting out. Quentin stepped back to get a better look. "Now cock your hip far to the right."

Jessica did as she was told. Quentin made a diamond with his fingers and looked through it. "Perfect!" he breathed.

Is he kidding? Jessica wondered, desperately trying to keep still. She felt like some sort of ridiculous contortionist.

"OK, Jessica, hold that pose," Quentin said, taking his place quickly behind the camera. He fiddled with the lens and took the shot.

Jessica quickly let her hands down and stretched out her neck. All her muscles ached already.

"Now we're going to take a few close-ups," Quentin explained. He knelt down and adjusted the telephoto lens. "Listen to me carefully," he directed. "You're in Rome, and it's hot. Think passion, sparks, fire."

Jessica closed her eyes and imagined the dusty smell of a hot, dry ruins. She jutted out a hip and stared sultrily into the camera.

"Great!" Quentin said, clicking the camera.

"OK, now put your right leg out and your hands on your hips. You're ancient royalty, a Roman empress."

Jessica gazed regally out at the camera, and Quentin took a number of shots.

Quentin paced a few feet, his eyes narrowed in thought. Then he nodded to himself and turned back to her. "Jessica, get in front of the acropolis," he directed. "Guys, I want rain!" he yelled out.

Rain! Jessica thought. She looked on worriedly

167

as Nick Nolan and the set assistants hastily constructed an artificial rain machine. One of the assistants set up a window fan on the floor, and another lugged buckets of water onto the set.

"Ready!" Nick called a few minutes later.

"OK, Jessica, let's have a smile," Quentin directed from behind the camera. "Guys, action!"

Jessica stared at the camera, a terrified smile frozen on her lips. Suddenly the fan turned on and drops of ice cold water sprayed over Jessica's body. Jessica gasped and recoiled instinctively.

"Jessica, don't react!" Quentin ordered. "Hold your head high and keep your body perfectly still. And keep gazing straight at me, right through the spray." Jessica stared at the camera and forced a shaky smile on her face, trying not to blink as cold drops of water cascaded over her head.

"OK, fan off," Quentin instructed quickly. The water stopped abruptly, and Jessica shivered, shaking out her hair and wrapping her arms around her body. "Shelly, we need wind," Quentin said.

Jessica looked on in horror as Shelly came onto the set with a huge hair dryer in her hand. The next thing she knew she was being blow-dried by the makeup artist.

"Nice," Quentin said, moving in close. "Jessica, look straight at the dryer and throw your head back." Jessica's hair flew back in the wind and a gust of warm air hit her cheeks. She trembled at the sudden change in temperature.

Finally Quentin took the last shot. "Thanks everybody! That's a wrap," he called out.

Jessica breathed a sigh of relief and collapsed onto a rock. Grabbing a towel, she wrapped it around her body, not sure if she was hot or cold. She shook her head ruefully. Modeling was more work than she had realized.

Jessica sailed into the mail room late that afternoon, a Federal Express package in her hand. She felt like she was walking on air. Even though the shoot had been difficult, it had gone without a hitch. With the talented photographer behind the camera, she was sure she was going to look great. Quentin had sent her down to the mail room right after she had changed. He wanted her to FedEx the negatives to New York to be developed.

Jessica stopped at the desk in the front room, surprised that Cameron wasn't working behind the counter. A lanky guy she didn't recognize was in his place, throwing boxes onto the loading dock.

The guy heard her approach the counter and turned around. He had longish red hair and watery blue eyes. "Can I help you?" he asked.

"Yes, I'm Quentin Berg's assistant," she said. "We need to FedEx this package to New York for an immediate turnaround." She handed the guy the Federal Express package. "It's extremely important," Jessica added.

The guy nodded. "Tell Mr. Berg not to worry. I'll take care of it myself."

"Thanks," Jessica said, turning around to go. Then she paused in thought. Since she was in the mail room, she might as well find Cameron. After all, today was clearly her day. She was sure Cameron would forgive her for her little twin switch.

"Do you know where Cameron Smith is working today?" Jessica asked. She hoped he wasn't off somewhere delivering a package in the building, because then she'd never be able to find him.

The guy's forehead creased in thought. "Today's Monday, right? He should be at the computer, keying in our weekend deliveries."

"The computer?" Jessica asked.

The guy nodded. "There's a computer alcove behind the shelves in the main room. You can't miss it."

"Thanks," Jessica said, hurrying around the counter. She walked through the dark halls of the cluttered mail room until she came to a set of standing wooden bookshelves. She looked around them. Sure enough, there was a small workspace set up, and Cameron was hunched behind the computer, peering at the screen.

Jessica's stomach fluttered at the sight of him. He was wearing a red plaid denim shirt and a blue baseball cap, with a few dark curls peeking out. He looked cuter than ever.

Cameron looked up as she walked in the doorway, scowling when he saw her.

But Jessica breezed in, undaunted. "Hi!" she said, flashing him one of her best smiles.

Cameron barely looked up from the keyboard. "Don't bother with the cover-girl charm, Jessica," Cameron said in disgust. "I'm not crazy about being yanked around like a puppet." Cameron scraped back his chair and stood up, ripping a long list out of the printer. "You may be able to get away with pulling stunts like that with other guys, but I'm not going to be anybody's second choice."

Jessica felt as though the floor had dropped out from under her. For a moment, she was speechless, surprised at how devastated she felt by Cameron's brush-off. Her good mood was totally gone. Suddenly the photo shoot didn't seem to matter at all.

Staring into his angry brown eyes, Jessica had a startling revelation—she was in love with Cameron Smith. And now that she'd gotten what she wanted from Quentin, there was nothing to stop her from going out with Cameron.

"Please, Cameron, just give me a chance," Jessica begged, tears coming into her blue-green eyes.

But Cameron wasn't moved. "A chance to what?" Cameron spat out. "To yank me around again?"

"A chance to explain," Jessica said softly.

Cameron crossed his arms across her chest. "Fine, say what you have to say."

Jessica took a deep breath, finding telling the truth a lot harder than inventing a story. "Well, I talked Elizabeth into doing a twin switch on Friday night because, because—" Jessica hesitated.

"Because?" Cameron repeated sharply.

"Because I had a date with Quentin as well," Jessica said in a rush. "And I didn't know how to get out of it."

Cameron's face darkened. "Mail-room guy not good enough for you, huh?" he spat out.

"No, that's not it at all," Jessica protested. "Cameron, I promise, that's—"

But Cameron held up a hand. "Look, Jessica, I think I've heard enough. You're a lovely girl, but unfortunately your beauty is only skin deep." He shook his head in disgust. "I'm sure you'll make a great model," he said bitterly. "You've certainly got what it takes."

And with that, he turned and stomped off.

Jessica stared after him, tears springing to her eyes. Now what was she going to do? She heard the back door open, and she jumped as it slammed shut.

Then Jessica turned and ran after him. Cameron was the one she really loved. Now she knew that for sure. She couldn't let him leave like this.

Jessica ran through the dark corridor, dodging packages, until she came upon a pair of big red double doors. Swinging through them, Jessica found herself in the back lot of the Mode building. She blinked in the sunlight, looking around for Cameron. Then she saw him, sitting on a bench. *Their* bench—the bench where they had shared their first lunch together.

Jessica approached him slowly. "I didn't realize you were eating at Chez Bench today," she said. "Is there room enough for two at your table?"

Cameron didn't crack a smile.

"All right," Jessica said, walking in a small circle in front of him. "You don't have to say anything. Just listen, OK?"

Jessica drew a haggard breath, summoning up her courage. "You see, Quentin asked me out before you did, and I didn't think I could break it off with him." She kicked at the gravel. "He is my boss, after all, and I guess I wanted to get a chance at modeling." Jessica looked down. "I know that's not a good reason, but that's the only reason. I promise."

Jessica paused for breath. "And I didn't think you'd understand," she finished softly. Jessica sat down on the bench, looking deep into his eyes. "I know now for sure that I'm not interested in Quentin. And I promise that from now on you'll be the only guy for me." Jessica looked down at the ground. "That is, if it's not too late."

Cameron frowned. "I've got to think about it, OK?"

Jessica swallowed hard and nodded, trying to hold back her tears. "OK," she whispered.

She stood up to walk away, but suddenly Cameron grabbed her and pulled her back onto the bench. Then he wrapped his arms around her and brought his lips to hers, kissing her so passionately that Jessica's breath was swept away. Jessica closed her eyes and kissed him back with all of her pent-up emotion, feeling shocks of sparks spread through her entire body.

"I've thought about it," Cameron said, laughing as they pulled back. "And I've decided to give you one more chance. On one condition."

"Anything," Jessica said breathlessly.

"That you go out with me tomorrow night," Cameron said.

Jessica happily agreed. "OK, but this time it's my treat. And we're having burgers and fries."

"What? No frog legs?" Cameron asked with a grin.

Jessica shook her head vehemently.

"But just one more thing," Cameron said, waggling a finger at her. "Tomorrow night, I don't want to go out with any split personalities. You got that?"

"Got it," Jessica said happily.

Enid rushed into her house after work, flying high from her internship at Morgan Agency. They were shorthanded at the literary agency today, so she got to do some real editorial work—which meant talking to a few authors directly and proofreading a manuscript. It had been thrilling to be so involved in making a book. Plus, she had made a suggestion to the literary agent about editorial changes to an autobiography, and the editor had loved the idea.

Enid took the steps upstairs two at a time and ran into her bedroom, throwing her backpack on the floor and flopping down on her bed. She flipped on her side and picked up the phone, instinctively punching in Elizabeth's number. As the phone rang, Enid waited in anticipation, excited to share her news. But then she heard the phone pick up and she hung up quickly. She had forgotten. Elizabeth wasn't her friend anymore.

Enid stood up and kicked at a T-shirt on the blue carpet. She caught it in her hand, and threw it on the bed. Then she slumped down in a chair, feeling a gnawing sense of emptiness inside of her. Her life wasn't the same without Elizabeth in it.

Feeling restless, she picked up the phone again and dialed Maria's number.

Maria answered on the first ring.

"Hey, it's Enid," Enid said. "Listen, have you heard anything from Elizabeth?"

"Not a word," Maria said. "Why, have you?"

"No, nothing," Enid said.

"Well, that's just as well," Maria said. "We can have more fun without her."

"That's true, I guess," Enid said slowly.

"Just look at what an awesome time we ended up having on our horrible date. We don't need

Elizabeth *or* dopey guys to have fun," Maria insisted.

"Right," Enid said softly.

"Right," Maria answered.

Enid hung up the phone slowly. She knew that she and Maria had fun on their date, but she couldn't seem to recall the feeling. And she knew Elizabeth had been a bad friend, but somehow she didn't feel angry anymore.

Enid walked slowly across the room, deep in thought. Enid and Elizabeth had been best friends for a long time. And that should count for something. After all, for Elizabeth to have a total personality transformation must mean that Elizabeth wasn't doing well.

Maybe Elizabeth's not the one being the bad friend, pondered Enid. *Maybe I am. Maybe she needs me now.*

Chapter 13

Tuesday morning, Elizabeth lay comatose in bed, staring at the ceiling. After her horrible discovery at Leona's yesterday, she had gone straight home. Then she had sat in front of the TV watching reruns for eight hours. What was left of her spirit was totally sunk. She decided she'd spend the rest of the week at home. In bed. She had no will left to go to work. Everything was meaningless.

Elizabeth had been awake since nine A.M., and she had been staring at the ceiling for three hours. She had now memorized every crack and every shadow.

Elizabeth's stomach growled, but the idea of food made her nauseated. And the concept of standing up and going all the way down the steps was unthinkable. In fact, she didn't feel like she'd ever have the energy to move again. She was utterly disillusioned.

Now she realized that everything she thought had value was all bogus. Work was bogus—having ideas and working hard didn't get you anywhere. All that counted was money and power. Relationships were bogus—being a loyal girlfriend and a good person didn't matter. All that mattered were long legs and fame.

Elizabeth followed the crack on the wall to the corner, feeling as though that's where she had ended up—in some corner at the end of a blank wall. Ethics and ideals didn't matter at all. People who followed their beliefs just ended up where she was—alone and a failure. Her life had no purpose.

The phone jangled loudly and Elizabeth didn't pick it up. It rang five times. Then the person called back. Elizabeth sighed, wishing that everybody would leave her in peace. Finally she reached out a lead-weight arm and brought the receiver to her ear.

"Yes," she said in a monotone voice.

"Elizabeth, it's Reggie," said a female voice.

"Hi, Reggie," Elizabeth responded flatly.

"Why aren't you at work?" Reggie asked, her voice full of concern. "Are you sick?"

"You could say that," Elizabeth said, flopping over on her side and holding the phone to the ear. The position was uncomfortable and she sat up, twirling the phone cord around her fingers.

"What's wrong? Do you have a flu?" Reggie pressed.

"No, just have a small case of disillusionment," Elizabeth answered wryly. "I'm sure it'll get better in a few years."

"Uh-oh," Reggie said. "Did something happen with Todd and the Fashion Witch?"

Elizabeth sighed and stood up, cradling the phone in the nook of her shoulder. "I don't want to talk about it." She dragged the phone across the room and curled up in her refurbished velvet chaise longue chair in the corner.

"OK, I understand," Reggie said. "Then how about lunch? It will do you good to get out of the house. I don't know what's bothering you, but I know for sure that your bed is not going to help."

"No, thanks, Reggie, I don't have the energy," Elizabeth said, laying down flat on her back on the chaise longue. She studied the lines on the ceiling, noticing that the shadows were different from this angle.

"OK, then, I'll drive out to Sweet Valley and we'll go someplace near you," Reggie suggested.

Elizabeth's eyes widened. Why wouldn't Reggie accept no for an answer? "Listen, I appreciate the offer, but I have no appetite," Elizabeth said. And the idea of getting up and getting dressed seemed to demand an infinite amount of energy.

"Nope, I insist," Reggie said in a firm voice. "Café Felix in Sweet Valley at one o'clock."

"But —" Elizabeth protested, sitting up quickly.

"And if you're not there, I'm going to come over and drag you out of bed," Reggie warned. Then the line clicked off.

Elizabeth groaned and fell back in the chair.

"Mmm, this is *luscious,"* Maria said, taking a big bite out of the pizza she and Enid were sharing.

Enid and Maria were at Guido's Pizza Palace in Sweet Valley for lunch on Tuesday. Enid had called Maria that morning at work and asked her to meet her there to discuss something important: *Elizabeth.* After talking to Maria last night, Enid was convinced they were being bad friends. Something told her Elizabeth needed them now.

"Want a bite?" Maria asked, offering Enid her slice.

Enid shook her head, making a face. "Are you kidding? Pineapple and tomato? I think I'll stick to my side of the pizza—mushrooms and eggplant. It's a lot safer."

"C'mon, just try it," Maria urged.

Enid picked up the pizza cutter and cut off a tiny end of Maria's slice. Then she nibbled at it cautiously. The pineapple was sweet and juicy, and it brought out the flavor of the pizza.

"Hey, this is great!" Enid exclaimed. She took a whole slice and put it on her plate.

Maria laughed, taking a long draw on her lemonade. "See? What'd I tell you?"

Enid took a big bite of pizza. *"Mrmph mrmm mm mmrph."*

"You can say that again," Maria said with a chuckle.

Enid swallowed and wiped off her mouth. "I said, I'll never doubt you again."

Enid lapsed into silence after that, unsure as to how to broach the topic. Maria seemed adamant about ignoring Elizabeth until she apologized for her behavior. Enid was worried that Maria would convince her that was the best way. Or that Maria would feel betrayed. After all, if Enid started talking to Elizabeth and Maria didn't, then that would put a serious wrench in Enid and Maria's friendship. The last thing Enid wanted was to have to choose between Maria and Elizabeth.

Finally Maria pushed away her plate. "So, you said you wanted to discuss something important?" she asked.

"Yeah, actually, I did," Enid said slowly. "It's about Elizabeth. I've been thinking about the situation a lot, and I think we should reconsider our position. After all, we've both been friends with Elizabeth forever. She's been one of your best friends since second grade, and she's been my best friend all through high school."

Enid stopped for air. She had been hesitant to speak, but now the words were coming out in a rush. "Elizabeth's always been a wonderful friend," she continued. "She's always been loyal, considerate, and there for us. This is one of the first times she's actually let us down. And it's not really that big of a deal," Enid took a deep breath, but forged on ahead. "I think we should give her another chance," she finished. "I think she needs us now."

Enid looked at Maria nervously, worried that she would think she was abandoning her. But Maria was nodding her head. "I know," she said. "I completely agree with you. In fact, I was thinking the same thing."

Enid brightened. "You were?"

Maria nodded. "Yeah. Even though we've been having a wonderful time hanging out together, something isn't right. Something's—missing."

"Elizabeth," Enid supplied.

"Exactly," Maria confirmed. "I don't think either of us have totally honest with ourselves—or with each other."

Enid breathed a sigh of relief. "Boy, am I glad to hear you say that," she said. Then she leaned forward. "So it's agreed? We're going to give Elizabeth another chance?"

Maria smiled and nodded. "I think she's learned her lesson by now."

"Elizabeth, you showed up!" Reggie exclaimed happily as Elizabeth walked into Café Felix in downtown Sweet Valley. The tiny restaurant was packed, and Reggie was standing at the front of the line at the hostess's podium.

"Well, you didn't give me much of a choice," Elizabeth said, joining her in line. Actually, she was glad Reggie had dragged her out of bed. She felt better now that she'd showered and gotten up.

"You know, for someone who's in a state of depression, you look pretty good," Reggie said. Elizabeth was just wearing faded blue jeans and a pale yellow sweater, but she had washed her hair and put on some lipstick.

Elizabeth shrugged. "That's because I slept for about fifteen hours last night."

"Ms. Andrews?" the hostess asked.

"That's us," Reggie confirmed.

"Right this way," the hostess said, leading them to a small round table out on the terrace. The restaurant overlooked a quaint old street in Sweet Valley, and the calm blue ocean shimmered in the distance.

"The office has erupted into chaos without you and Leona," Reggie said as they sat down.

"Oh no! What do you mean?" Elizabeth asked in alarm.

"Well, I guess Leona's been getting a million calls about the report that you typed up yesterday— you know, suggestions and stuff. And Anne's been pulling her hair out trying to field all the calls."

Elizabeth grimaced, but refused to let herself feel responsible. "Well, this time Leona's going to have to bail herself out of her own mess," she asserted.

Reggie gave her an odd look, but then the waiter appeared. "Are you ready to order?" he asked.

"Actually I'd just like a salad," Reggie said. "What do you have?"

"Chef's, *niçoise,* Caesar, Caesar chicken, goat cheese, and arugula," recited the waiter.

Reggie laughed. "I guess you get asked the question a lot," she said. "I'll just have the chef's salad."

"Me too," Elizabeth said. "And a glass of mineral water as well, please."

"Coming right up," the waiter said, picking up their menus and walking away.

Reggie looked at Elizabeth with curiosity. "So I guess all this has something to do with Leona?"

Elizabeth turned around to make sure the waiter was out of earshot. Then she leaned in across the table. "Listen, Reggie, this is strictly confidential. If I tell you the story, do you promise not to breath a word of it to anybody?"

Reggie nodded. "On my honor."

Elizabeth took a deep breath. "OK. Well, it all started last weekend when Leona took off work to go skiing in Lake Tahoe. She asked me to cover for her at work on Monday."

Reggie lifted an eyebrow. "I'm not surprised. That woman is complete devoid of ethics."

Elizabeth nodded, giving Reggie the whole story of Leona's betrayal—from Leona's broken leg to her request that Elizabeth take care of her personal life to the incriminating tape that Elizabeth had found in her house.

The waiter appeared and the girls quieted down as he set their salads in front of them.

"So that's the whole story," Elizabeth said when he'd left. "The upshot of it is that Leona stole my idea and is trying to take all the credit for it." Elizabeth picked up her fork and took a huge bite of salad, suddenly feeling her appetite return. She hadn't eaten anything since dinner the night before. Just sharing the story with Reggie had raised her spirits considerably.

Reggie shook her head in disgust. "I wouldn't have thought that even the dragon lady would do such a despicable thing." Reggie had been negative about Leona ever since she had met her, and now Elizabeth could see why.

Reggie's eyes narrowed in thought. "Do you have any proof that the idea is yours?" She buttered a piece of warm French bread and took a bite.

Elizabeth pondered that one. "Well, I did write up a lot of notes," she said, but then her face fell—"and gave them all to Leona." Elizabeth shook her head sadly, spreading out her hands in a wide gesture. "Reggie, it's hopeless. I don't have any proof at all."

"Wait, don't give up so fast," Reggie countered. "We don't even know if she's sent out the letter yet. Who did she address it to?" Reggie took a last bite of her salad and mopped up the dressing with a piece of bread.

"Gordon Lewis," Elizabeth said.

Reggie whistled under her breath. "Gordon Lewis!" she exclaimed. "Leona sure goes right to the top, doesn't she?"

The waiter picked up their plates, and Reggie ordered two coffees.

Elizabeth drummed her fingers on the table, deep in thought. "I wonder if there's any way we could schedule a meeting with him," she said.

"Well, you know I'm all for that," Reggie said with a grin. "I'd give anything to meet him—and to put Leona in her place."

Reggie had a wild crush on Gordon Lewis, and Elizabeth had no trouble understanding why. The girls had caught sight of him one day at the Mission Café in L.A., and Elizabeth had to agree with Reggie that he was one of the handsomest men she had ever seen. He was tall and distinguished-looking, with longish brown hair, bright blue eyes, and chiseled features.

The waiter set down their coffees in front of them, and Elizabeth poured a sugar packet into hers. She stirred it slowly, her mind clicking as she tried to think of a way to catch Leona in her own trap. She took a sip of coffee, and suddenly it hit her. Elizabeth practically spit out her coffee.

"What happened? Did you just get hit with inspiration?" Reggie asked.

Elizabeth nodded and grinned an evil grin. "Reggie, let me ask you something. How far would you be willing to go to accomplish both of your goals?"

Reggie's dark brown eyes glinted. "I'd go all the way."

"That's great!" Elizabeth breathed. She felt as though a huge burden had been lifted off her shoulders. Suddenly she had all her energy back. It wasn't true that ethics never won out. Sometimes you had to fight for them, that was all.

Elizabeth hunched over the table and spoke in a whisper. "If the two of us work together, we can teach Leona a lesson she'll never forget. We'll put the plan into action ourselves. And you just might get your shot with Gordon."

"I'm in," Reggie said with a smile.

"But remember," Elizabeth said. "This is top secret."

"Highly confidential," Reggie agreed solemnly.

They shook hands on the deal.

Tuesday night, Todd pulled into the driveway of his house in a foul mood. After Simone had blown him off that afternoon, he had decided he was sick of being pushed around. So he decided to find her. After all, Simone clearly appreciated aggressive, masculine men. Todd wasn't going to sit around any longer and let her call all the shots.

But he couldn't find her anywhere. He had

gone to all her favorite spots, but she wasn't anywhere to be seen. Then he had done the circuit of all the dance clubs they had frequented, but most of them were closed. Finally, he had driven to her apartment. Only Celia, her roommate, had answered the door, and she had told him abruptly that she didn't know where Simone was. But she did mention—before she shut the door in Todd's face—that Simone had left that afternoon with two full suitcases. Todd scowled. He couldn't believe she left town without telling him.

Todd sighed as he pushed open the front door, expecting an explosion. His mother had made a special dinner tonight, and he had promised he'd be there for it. He had meant to call home to say he would be late for dinner, but he had gotten so caught up in his search that he had forgotten all about it. Now he was going to have to endure another lecture from his parents.

"Hello, Todd," his father said as he walked in. He had a serious look on his face.

"Hi, Dad," Todd responded tentatively.

"Why don't you take your coat off?" Mr. Wilkins said with a sigh. "I think we have to talk."

Todd gulped as he took off his jacket and followed Mr. Wilkins into the kitchen. His dad didn't sound mad—he sounded resigned. That was a bad sign. A very bad sign.

Mr. Wilkins sat down in a chair, and Todd took a seat opposite him, slinging his coat over the back of it.

Mrs. Wilkins brought a coffee pot to the table and joined them. "Did you have a nice evening, Todd?" she asked.

Todd swallowed, feeling guilty. "I'm really sorry about dinner, Mom. I meant to call." Todd raised his shoulders. "I guess I just lost track of the time."

Todd's mother patted his hand. "That's all right, dear," she said.

Now Todd was really worried. His mother wasn't angry either. Something ominous was definitely brewing in the air.

Mr. Wilkins poured some coffee into his mug and took a sip. "Well, Todd, you're obviously not concerned about following the rules of the household," he said. "When you didn't show up for dinner tonight, we were worried sick."

Mrs. Wilkins nodded. "We didn't know what had happened to you. We called Aaron and Winston and Bruce, but nobody knew where you were."

Todd could feel the heat rising in his body. He couldn't believe his parents had called all his friends. They were acting like he was in third grade. He was glad they didn't have school tomorrow, because his friends would be sure to tease him about it mercilessly.

"Even Elizabeth had no idea what you were doing tonight," his mother added.

At that, Todd practically exploded. His parents *knew* he and Elizabeth had broken up, and they knew he was going out with Simone. How could they call her? Didn't they have any tact? Did they want to rub the fact of their breakup in Elizabeth's face? Todd twisted his fingers together in his lap, forcing himself to remain quiet. He was obviously in enough trouble as it was.

"So, your mother and I have had a talk," his father said.

Here it comes, Todd thought, bracing himself for the worst.

"Todd, we've given you all our support with this modeling thing," his father began. "We agreed to let you quit Varitronics and take a shot at modeling, but clearly it's turning your head around." His father sighed. "We've tried everything we can. We tried grounding you, we tried scolding you. . . ."

Todd stared at his parents in horror. "What are you getting at?" he interrupted.

"Todd, I'm afraid you're going to have to give up modeling," Mrs. Wilkins said softly.

"What?" Todd protested. "No way. That's— that's ridiculous! Modeling doesn't have anything to do with this."

"Oh yes it does," his father replied. "Modeling has *everything* to do with it. Before, you were a normal teenage kid. Now you think you're some kind of superstar who can make his own rules."

Todd stared at his parents in shock. He couldn't believe they would dictate his life—and his career—like this.

Todd scraped his chair back and stood up, over-whelmed by shock and hurt. And in the back-ground Simone's words echoed in his head. *Are you a man or a mouse, Todd? Are you a man or a mouse?*

I'm a man, Todd decided.

Todd folded his arms across his chest. "Well, I refuse to give modeling up," he said calmly. "You can't force me."

His father's voice turned stern. "Todd Wilkins, as long as you live under our roof, you're going to have to abide by our rules—and that means giving up your modeling career."

Todd faced his parents calmly. "Fine," he re-sponded. "Then I won't live under your roof." He grabbed his jacket from the chair and shrugged it on. "I'll move out."

Chapter 14

Wednesday morning, Jessica arrived at work early, hoping to catch Quentin alone. He was supposed to have met with the editorial board late yesterday afternoon to go over their photo shoot, and Jessica was anxious to get the results. In fact, she was so nervous that she had barely slept at all the night before. When she finally did fall asleep, she just relived the shoot in her dreams. She felt like she had never left the Mode building.

As Jessica rode the elevator up to the eleventh floor, her heart pounded in anticipation. Even though Jessica was sure the shots would be fabulous, she was still nervous. After all, she wasn't quite tall enough to be a model. Plus, she was just an intern. She didn't know if the magazine would accept using her as a model. Not to mention that Elizabeth appeared to be on some kind of work strike, which wasn't going to help matters.

When Jessica walked into the photography studio, it was entirely deserted. She flicked on the lights and walked around the room, looking for some kind of sign—the photographs or a report or a note or something. But she didn't come upon anything out of the ordinary—just the usual jumble of cameras and costumes and props.

Jessica's stomach fluttered nervously. This was it—the big moment. It was all or nothing. With Simone safely on vacation, now was her chance to make it as a model. If they liked her, they could use her for another shoot. But if they didn't like her . . .

Banish the thought, Jessica commanded herself. *Think positive.* She paced around the room, her imagination soaring. She pictured herself on the cover of *Flair* in her emerald green dress, her blue-green eyes dazzling as they stared at the camera. Then she saw herself in quick succession on the cover of every other big fashion magazine— *Ingenue, Fashion Forward, Bella.* . . . Jessica Wakefield would be plastered all over the newsstands—the newest and hottest supermodel ever. She envisioned important parties, gallery openings, runway shows . . . and everywhere she went, Cameron would be at her side, driving all her fans wild with jealousy.

Quentin walked into the room. "Ah, just the face I was hoping to see," he said.

Jessica popped out of her reverie and her mouth turned dry. She turned to face Quentin, but found that she had lost her powers of speech.

"Well, I've got good news for you," Quentin said. "The magazine loved your photos. If I want, I can use you for another shoot."

Jessica felt the blood rush to her ears, and she felt faint. Was it possible? Was she actually going to be featured in *Flair* magazine? It really was a dream come true.

But she played it cool with Quentin. "Naturally, you'll want to," she said coyly.

"I think I might need some convincing," Quentin said in a low voice. He grabbed Jessica in his arms and pressed his lips to hers, kissing her passionately.

"*Mmph!*" Jessica protested, placing her hands square on his chest to push him away. But then she heard someone clear his throat from behind them.

She turned around quickly and gasped. It was Cameron, and he was staring at her, his face a mask of stone.

Then he turned around and walked out without a word.

Jessica chased after Cameron, leaving a baffled-looking Quentin behind.

Panting, she caught up with him at the elevator.

"It's over, Jessica," Cameron said, his brown

eyes devoid of expression. "No more chances." Cameron stepped smoothly into the elevator.

"Cameron, wait—"

But the door of the elevator closed, and Cameron was gone.

Hot tears slid down Jessica's cheeks. *What have I done?*

Elizabeth sat in front of her computer at home, aggressively clicking away at the keys. She was composing a letter to Gordon Lewis, and she was creating a masterpiece. Elizabeth skimmed over what she had written, smiling in satisfaction.

Then she leaned back and went over the steps of her and Reggie's plan in her mind. Switching screens with her mouse, she quickly outlined the plan on the computer. Then she read through the scheme. *It's perfect,* she breathed. Their strategy was foolproof. It was simple, but effective—and sure to expose Leona Peirson for the fraud that she was.

Elizabeth drummed her fingers on her desk, anxious to put their plan into motion. For the first time in days, she was brimming with energy. She was sick of lying around feeling sorry for herself. She was ready to take action.

It's not true that ideals don't count, Elizabeth thought. But sometimes you had to fight for them. And fight she would. It was time to march into battle.

As she thought for the millionth time about Leona's deception, Elizabeth's blood began to boil. She picked up a pencil from her desk and snapped it in her hand.

Elizabeth's eyes narrowed. *I'm going to get revenge on the woman who betrayed me,* she vowed silently. *If it's the last thing I do. . . .*

FASHION VICTIM

Written by
Kate William

Created by
FRANCINE PASCAL

BANTAM BOOKS
NEW YORK · TORONTO · LONDON · SYDNEY · AUCKLAND

To Anita Anastasi

Chapter 1

"Cameron, wait!" Jessica Wakefield pleaded as she watched the mirrored elevator doors slide shut, separating her from the guy she loved. She was left standing alone in the ninth-floor hallway of the Mode building, her heart sinking. *What have I done?* she asked herself.

Silence surrounded her like a thick, suffocating cloud. Most of the employees who worked in the chic Los Angeles high-rise wouldn't be arriving for hours.

Jessica had come in early, eager to catch a few minutes alone with her boss, Quentin Berg, to discuss the results of the photo shoot they'd done the previous day. Quentin was a world-famous fashion photographer, and even though Jessica was only a high-school intern, he'd allowed her to model for a very important fashion layout.

Not that he had much choice, Jessica thought

smugly. She'd worked *hard* to get herself into that shoot.

Quentin had previously shot the layout the day before using Simone, a supermodel with a super-obnoxious personality, who also happened to be Quentin's former girlfriend. Part of Jessica's job—the *worst* part—was having to put up with Simone's temper tantrums and constant demands for French mineral water and raw vegetables.

Jessica had taken the internship at *Flair,* the hottest new fashion magazine owned by the Mode Corporation, with only one thought in mind—to launch her modeling career. So yesterday, after Simone had left for the day, Jessica had discreetly opened Quentin's camera, exposing the film. There hadn't been time to call in another model, so Jessica had gladly stepped in to take Simone's place.

Only a few minutes ago she'd been happy enough to touch the stars. Quentin had just told her that her photographs had received a thumbs-up from *Flair*'s editorial board. Then he'd kissed her . . . at the very instant Cameron had walked into the studio!

Jessica slumped against the cold marble wall next to the elevator and closed her eyes. Hot tears streamed down her cheeks. *Talk about rotten timing!* Jessica thought. Cameron Smith, who worked in the mail room, was one of the sweetest guys she'd ever met. He was also gorgeous—with curly brown hair, impressive muscles, and big brown eyes. Unfortunately *he* wasn't the world-famous photographer

2

who could help her launch her career at *Flair*.

Jessica opened her eyes and pressed her fists against the smooth fabric of her turquoise pants. *Why did that jerk Quentin have to kiss me anyway?* she fumed. Aside from being a talented photographer, Quentin was an egotistical creep. He probably thought any girl would be thrilled to kiss him.

Fresh tears streamed down Jessica's cheeks as she recalled the expression of hurt and anger on Cameron's face as he'd gotten into the elevator. His features had appeared as if they'd been cut from stone, and his brown eyes had been glassy and cold. His parting words rang her in her ears: *It's over, Jessica. No more chances.* The memory felt like a hot knife tearing through her heart.

Jessica pressed her fists against her eyes. *Why can't Cameron understand how important my career is?* she wondered bitterly.

Jessica knew most people—even some of her teachers at Sweet Valley High—assumed that she wasn't serious about her future, that all she cared about were boys, shopping, and cheerleading. They seemed to think that her identical twin, Elizabeth, had inherited all the genes for logical thinking, maturity, and hard work.

But they were wrong. Granted, Elizabeth was clearly the more serious-minded twin. Older by four minutes, she was hardworking and reliable. She got straight A's in school, kept her room impeccably neat, and always remembered to do her

3

chores around the house.

Elizabeth hoped to become a professional writer someday and spent most of her free time writing for the *Oracle*, Sweet Valley High's student newspaper. Her idea of "fun" was to curl up with a book, organize her closet, or hang out with her boring friends, Enid Rollins and Maria Slater.

A bright spot in her sister's life—in Jessica's opinion—was Elizabeth's recent breakup with Todd Wilkins, one of the dullest guys in Sweet Valley. He'd started modeling for Quentin and was now dating Simone, but that didn't change Jessica's opinion of him. OK, *yes*, Todd was handsome, Jessica had to admit that. But he was still as boring as dry toast. She only wished Elizabeth would hurry up and get over him.

The differences between Jessica and Elizabeth were enormous, despite their identical appearance. They both had clear blue-green eyes, silky blond hair, and slim, athletic figures. In the past Elizabeth had usually worn her hair in a ponytail or braid, while Jessica had preferred to leave hers loose. But now even that small distinction was gone. Both sisters had recently gotten their hair cut to shoulder length, angled longer in front for a more stylish, modern look.

Jessica believed in living life to the fullest. Wild colors and loud music suited her best. Each day was a great adventure and much too precious to waste worrying about schoolwork. As long as her grades

4

were high enough to maintain her position as co-captain on the cheerleading squad, she was satisfied.

Compared to her sister, Jessica hardly fit the image of a serious, ambitious, and intelligent six-teen-year-old girl—but that's exactly what she was. She dreamed of becoming a glamorous celebrity someday, and she was just as determined as her twin to achieve success.

Jessica sniffed and stood in front of the elevator. Pushing back her hair from her damp face, she stared at her reflection in mirrored door panel. Her eyes were red and puffy from crying. *I'm a mess!* she thought.

Jessica dabbed her fingertips under her eyes, careful not to mess up her makeup. She'd carefully selected her outfit that morning—slim-fitting, turquoise satin pants with a matching tunic and a pair of funky seventies-style platform sandals. The look was designed to make her appear taller. Jessica realized her height of five feet, six inches, was the biggest obstacle to her career since suc-cessful fashion models were closer to six feet tall.

I'm going to make it anyway, Jessica vowed. *I'll do whatever it takes.* Her internship would end in a few days, and she wasn't about to leave without achieving a strong foothold in the business.

But a small voice in her head asked doubtfully, *Even if it means giving up love?* Jessica groaned to herself. She would just have to find a way to make it up to Cameron, to make him understand that she wasn't interested in Quentin at all.

Jessica stiffened as she heard footsteps coming down the hall. She knew it was Quentin by the distinct sound of his designer boots. Forcing her attention back to the present, she put on a cheerful smile and turned to face her boss.

In his early twenties, Quentin Berg was tall, with broad shoulders, mysterious gray eyes, and shaggy, reddish blond hair. As usual he was wearing faded jeans, today topped with a black T-shirt and a pale khaki vest. Jessica considered him fairly good-looking in a rumpled artist sort of way. Too bad he was a totally conceited jerk.

"What was that all about?" Quentin asked, his light brown eyebrows raised in question.

Jessica swallowed hard. "It was nothing," she lied. "The mail-room guy was just upset because I forgot to put a return address on a package."

Quentin smirked. "What a loser."

Seeing the smug expression on Quentin's face, Jessica was tempted to tell him the truth—that kissing him was the biggest mistake of her life. Then she remembered the photo shoot . . . and the fact that he might use her for another layout. She felt torn. She didn't want to blow her chances with Quentin, but her heart ached over what had happened with Cameron.

"Guys like that don't understand how meaningless their jobs are," Quentin said, his voice dripping with disdain. "I could have him fired, but what's the use? Another loser would just come along and take his place."

Jessica nodded, pretending to agree. But inside she knew Cameron was anything but a loser. She vowed to herself that as soon as her career took off, she'd drop Quentin and concentrate on getting Cameron back into her life. But until that time Jessica was stuck with the number one creep of the fashion-photography field.

"So Quentin," Jessica began, hugging his arm as they walked back toward the studio, "when is my next shoot?"

Quentin chuckled. "I'll have to think about it."

"What's to think about?" Jessica asked, batting her eyelashes up at him.

"I'm not sure you're ready for a full-fledged modeling career," he told her. "The fashion world is rough, Jessica. Modeling is more than a job—it's a lifestyle. We're talking lots of hard work . . . *total* commitment, with cutthroat competition every step of the way."

They'd reached the studio and were standing in the doorway, facing each other. "I know all that," Jessica insisted. "Believe me, I'm not afraid of hard work, and I'm one hundred percent committed. I know I have what it takes to make it as a supermodel."

Quentin gave her a long, measuring look. "Maybe you do." Then he pushed open the studio door and went in.

"I *definitely* do," Jessica countered as she followed

him through the main area of the studio, a huge, cavernous room strewn with ladders, lighting fixtures, small tables, and various props. "As a matter of fact, I think I'd be great in the swimsuit layout we're shooting tomorrow," she declared, even though she knew Simone had already been lined up for the job.

Quentin stopped at the door of his private office, one of the smaller rooms off the main area, and turned to Jessica. "You're certainly ambitious," he said, chuckling.

You have no idea how *ambitious,* Jessica thought wryly. She wasn't afraid to go after what she wanted. By taking advantage of every opportunity that came along, Jessica created her own good luck. She was determined to move in on Simone's position as a top supermodel—no matter what it took. *I'll even suck up to a total jerk if I have to!* Jessica thought.

Jessica stepped closer and gently placed her hand on Quentin's elbow. "I'm a lot easier to work with than . . . *some* models. More fun too," she added suggestively, trailing her fingers up his arm.

Quentin stared at her hand, then at her. "You're something else," he said wryly.

"How sweet of you to notice." Jessica draped her arms over his shoulders and flashed him a saucy grin.

Quentin leaned back, as if to put distance between them, but at the same time brought his hands up to frame the sides of her face. "What's going on here, Jessica? A few minutes ago I got the distinct impression you weren't interested in this sort of . . . extracurricular activity."

Jessica shrugged. "You caught me off guard, that's all."

"I see," he whispered, moving in for a slow, smooth kiss. Jessica closed her eyes, willing herself to respond as much as she could—or at least not to recoil from him.

When the kiss finally ended, Jessica exhaled with relief. "I should start getting the sets ready," she offered, looking for an excuse to avoid another kiss.

Quentin winked, obviously unaware of how she really felt about him. "If you're going to be a fashion model, we're going to have to work on your image . . . get you seen in the right places, with the right people." He paused. "I'm going to take you to the Edge tonight. That place is always good for a photo op."

A flash of excitement shot through her. The Edge was a very exclusive hot new techno club in downtown L.A.

"I'll pick you up at nine," Quentin said. "Be ready." Abruptly dropping the subject, he glanced at his watch and let out a low whistle. "Time's flying, babe," he said, snapping his fingers. "I'll be in the darkroom for a few hours. If Gordon Lewis calls, put him through. Otherwise take messages. There's a list of supplies we need on my desk. . . ."

Lost in her thoughts, Jessica nodded absently as Quentin barked out a few more orders. Excitement surged through her like electricity. *A photo op with a world-famous fashion photographer and my very own layout . . . I'm about to become a bona fide supermodel!* she mentally cheered.

Sitting at her desk in her bedroom, Elizabeth pushed up the sleeves of her pale blue sweater as she reread the last few sentences on her computer screen. *This plan just might work!* she thought, pleased with what she'd written. Her internship at *Flair* had turned out to be a disaster, but she was ready to fight back. At lunch the previous day she and her friend Reggie Andrews, an assistant fashion editor at *Flair*, had come up with an idea to help Elizabeth get revenge for the terrible way she'd been treated during her internship.

Elizabeth hit the command to print the document, then stretched her arms high over her head. Her neck, shoulders, and back felt painfully stiff. She glanced at her wristwatch and was surprised to discover that it was nearly four-thirty in the afternoon. She'd been sitting at her desk since early that morning, totally absorbed in her writing.

Elizabeth got up and began pacing across her room. As part of a new career-education program, Sweet Valley High students had been given the opportunity to work as interns during the school's two-week miniterm. Elizabeth had been thrilled to land a position in the editorial department of *Flair*.

From the start she had given her all to her work, putting in extra hours and sacrificing her personal life when necessary. Although many of her assignments had been dull, routine chores such as filing and opening the mail—"scum work," her boss had called it—Elizabeth had also been allowed to do some higher-level tasks. She'd proofread articles, drafted a letter to a writer, and researched various topics. She'd felt driven to prove herself capable to her boss, Leona Peirson, whom she'd idolized.

Leona had appeared to be exactly the kind of woman Elizabeth hoped to become someday—bright, ambitious, energetic, and assertive. Her respect had meant everything to Elizabeth. When Leona had implied that her look could use some improvement, Elizabeth had dipped into her savings for a fashion makeover.

Besides all that, Leona had often encouraged her to share her thoughts and ideas for the magazine. Elizabeth had been determined to come up with at least one brilliant idea during her internship, something that would really impress her boss.

She had put together a proposal for a new column to be written exclusively by *Flair* readers. But Leona had treated Elizabeth's hard work as if it were nothing more than a toddler's scribbled crayon drawing.

And then, to top it all off, Elizabeth had been devastated to discover that Leona was planning to propose the new column to the publisher, Gordon Lewis, and *Flair*'s editorial board as her own idea!

I wish I'd listened to Reggie sooner, Elizabeth reflected. Her friend had tried to warn her about Leona's true nature—*nasty.*

Elizabeth stopped pacing and sat down on her bed, drawing her knees up to her chin. Leona was a cold-blooded snake. But even if Elizabeth did manage to get back at her—then what? *My life still won't be perfect . . . or even as good as it used to be,* she realized dejectedly. She pressed her forehead against the soft fabric of her faded blue jeans. She knew she couldn't blame all her problems on Leona Peirson.

Elizabeth's own self-centered ambition had caused her to sacrifice her relationship with her two best friends, Enid Rollins and Maria Slater. Her boyfriend, Todd, had started getting resentful because she didn't have any time to see him. And he'd walked out of her life after he'd been "discovered" by Quentin Berg. Now he was working as a fashion model—and dating one. Elizabeth groaned as she remembered the time when she'd walked in on Todd kissing Simone in the photography studio at the Mode building. The memory sent a sharp pain right into the pit of her stomach.

Elizabeth lifted her head and pushed her hair back from her face. She needed her friends more than ever. Although Reggie would certainly be a sympathetic listener, Elizabeth didn't think she'd understand. Reggie was much older—in her twenties. And she didn't know Todd. Elizabeth longed to share her sorrow with Maria and Enid, her best friends in the world. She knew that having them around would make everything seem . . . less horrible.

I've been such a jerk, she told herself, her heart sinking as she remembered how badly she'd treated them. Elizabeth now realized that some things were more important than getting ahead in the business world. She wondered if they'd ever forgive her.

"I'm going to find out right now," she resolved, reaching for the telephone next to her bed. Just as she was trying to figure out what she would say to them, she heard a soft knock on the door.

Assuming it was her mother or father, Elizabeth softly answered, "Come in." The door opened, and Elizabeth's jaw dropped.

Enid and Maria were standing in the doorway, each holding a small paper bag. Elizabeth stared at them, speechless . . . and incredibly happy.

Dressed in a calf-length burgundy skirt, matching vest, and deep blue blouse, Enid had obviously come straight from her job at the Morgan Literary Agency, where she was doing her internship.

Maria was spending the miniterm working backstage at the Bridgewater Theatre in downtown Sweet Valley. Although she'd "retired" from her successful career as a child actor when she was twelve, she still had the look of a star, with smooth ebony skin, large brown eyes, and a tall, elegant build. Maria's outfit—wide-leg jeans and a pale yellow, hippie-era smock top—reflected her eclectic, slightly offbeat style.

"We come in peace," Enid said.

13

"And frozen yogurt," Maria added, waving her bag.

Elizabeth swallowed hard, feeling a lump in her throat. "Can you guys ever forgive me for being such a jerk?"

Enid and Maria looked at each other and shrugged. "Of course," Enid said. "That's what friends are for, right?"

Maria chuckled. "OK, now that we've settled that, let's get to the serious stuff. We've got some important decisions to make, girls."

"Like what?" Elizabeth asked.

"Like what flavor we should start with," Maria replied. "Pineapple coconut or fudge ripple?"

Elizabeth laughed. "Pineapple coconut first, fudge ripple for dessert. You guys are the best," she added. She ran downstairs to the kitchen for bowls and spoons, then joined her friends for a frozen yogurt picnic on her bedroom floor.

Elizabeth was helping herself to a generous scoop when she noticed Maria and Enid exchange concerned looks. "What's the matter?" she asked them warily.

"Liz, we heard that Todd moved out of his house Tuesday night," Enid told her. "He's staying at Ken Matthews's."

Elizabeth felt a sharp ache squeeze her heart. Although she was terribly angry at Todd for cheating on her with Simone, the news saddened her. "That's too bad," she replied softly.

"Time for dessert," Maria announced as she

opened the carton of fudge ripple frozen yogurt. "How's everything at *Flair*, by the way? It's strange not to hear you rattling on about your internship," she teased.

Elizabeth groaned. "Please don't remind me how stupid I've been!" Enid and Maria stared at her with matching looks of astonishment.

"What happened?" Maria asked.

"I found out that it was all a big lie, that's what," Elizabeth replied. "I was completely wrong about Leona, about everything. . . ." She took a deep breath and told them all about her column proposal and Leona's condescending response. "When I was at Leona's condo on Monday, I found a tape recorder with a letter she'd dictated for herself, proposing *my* idea and passing it off as her own." Elizabeth remembered how angry she'd been at that moment, when she'd realized how Leona had betrayed her. "She'd actually inserted a note to remind herself not to let me see the letter!"

"That's terrible!" Enid cried.

Maria nodded. "But what were you doing at her condo?"

Elizabeth rolled her eyes. "Leona broke her leg skiing in Tahoe last weekend. She asked me to do her personal errands, water her plants, feed her cats, and cover for her at work because she doesn't want anyone to know she went skiing."

"So what are you going to do?" Maria asked.

Elizabeth flashed a mischievous grin and told

15

them about the plan she and Reggie had devised. "We're going to present the proposal ourselves," she explained. "Reggie is going to help me set up a meeting with Gordon Lewis, the hotshot new publisher of *Flair* magazine. If everything goes according to plan, my proposal will go to the board before Leona gets back."

Maria covered her mouth and pretended to gasp as though she were shocked at Elizabeth's scheming, and then she smiled. "That's brilliant!"

"I sure wish I could be a fly on the wall when you meet with Gordon Lewis," Enid said.

Why not? Elizabeth wondered as a marvelous idea popped into her mind. Smiling, she asked, "How would you guys like to get into the fashion industry?"

Chapter 2

Todd could barely keep his eyes open as he rode along the Santa Monica Freeway with Howie Kurtz, the real estate agent he'd called that morning. He was desperate to find an apartment after spending two sleepless nights on the lumpy couch in Ken Matthews's room.

"So . . . you're modeling for *Flair* magazine?" Howie inquired.

Todd nodded, then covered his mouth to stifle a yawn.

"How soon do you need an apartment?" Howie asked.

"Immediately," Todd answered. He slumped down into the seat and crossed his arms. He couldn't believe how messed up his life had gotten in such a short time. Elizabeth had been so caught up in her internship, she'd forgotten about what was really important—like making time for them to be together. One evening, when he'd gone to pick her up at *Flair,* she'd insisted he go wait for her in the photography studio where Jessica was working.

Todd had known Elizabeth was just trying to get him out of her hair because she had work to do, but he'd gone to the studio anyway. That was the event that had changed his life. He'd met Simone that day and had stepped into a modeling career.

Todd inhaled deeply and let his breath out slowly. Simone had captured his attention immediately. Tall, slim, with gorgeous ice blue eyes and incredibly long legs, she was one of the best-looking girls he'd ever seen—especially dressed as she had been, in a tiny white bikini.

Then Quentin Berg had asked him to pose for a few test shots with Simone. Although Todd had felt embarrassed and self-conscious at first, he had gradually relaxed enough to enjoy the experience. Quentin had invited him to come back and model for an actual fashion layout. Todd had happily quit his boring internship at Varitronics, his father's company, and began hanging out with Simone every night at the best hot spots in L.A.

Todd rubbed his hand over his mouth and stared out the window, bleary-eyed. He missed Elizabeth more than he could stand. He had gone to her office at *Flair* last Friday to try to apologize. Not only had she refused to see him, she'd humiliated him by announcing it over the intercom.

Todd had been sitting in the crowded waiting area, holding a bunch of red roses, when Elizabeth's voice had come blaring out of the phone speaker on the receptionist's desk: *Please inform Mr. Wilkins that I never want to see him again.* Todd cringed inwardly, waves of embarrassment crashing over him all over again at the memory.

"I'm going to take you to Manhattan Beach first," Howie was saying. "I have several listings over there that I think you'll like."

"Sounds great," Todd murmured. He closed his eyes and couldn't help nodding off.

He awoke a short time later, just as Howie was pulling up to a beautiful condominium complex. "Sorry I fell asleep." Todd yawned as he sat up straighter and rubbed his eyes.

"No problem," Howie replied breezily.

Todd gazed out the window, impressed by the manicured lawns and the expensive, late model cars in the parking lot. "Wow, this is great!" he exclaimed, suddenly feeling energized.

"This place has everything you requested," Howie said as he led Todd to a door on the east side of the building. "Pool, air-conditioning, sauna, whirlpool bath, microwave . . . I think you'll like it." He stepped back and let Todd enter first.

I'll say! Todd thought excitedly as he walked in. The apartment was huge, with a brick fireplace and a walk-out patio in back. Todd could already picture the parties he'd have. They could set up a barbecue grill on the patio . . . then head over to the pool for a late night swim. . . . *And no curfews,* he reminded himself.

"There's only one bedroom," Howie explained. "But a larger unit will be opening up at the end of the month."

"This is perfect," Todd said. "I'll take it."

"Great." Howie shook his hand. "The rent isn't too bad for Manhattan Beach." He named a price, then added the amount required for a security deposit.

Todd blanched. One month's rent would clean out his entire savings account. "There's no way I can afford that much," he admitted.

Howie looked at him with a bemused expression. "I figured that as a model working for *Flair* . . . "

"I'm just starting out my career. I've only been at it for a week," Todd explained, feeling rather foolish all of a sudden.

Howie's eyebrows drew together, as if he were deep in thought. "How much *can* you afford?" he asked.

Todd shrugged. "A few hundred a month, I guess."

Howie grimaced. "Come on, let's go," he said, heading for the door. "We're in the wrong neighborhood. With a few hundred dollars a month, you can't rent a toolshed around here."

Crestfallen, Todd followed. It seemed his modeling money wouldn't go as far as he'd thought. *I wonder if it's too soon to ask Quentin for a raise.*

*   *   *

Jessica felt her heart pulsing excitedly with the beat of the techno music blaring through the speakers when she and Quentin arrived at the Edge that evening. *This is fantastic,* she thought, her eyes wide as she gazed around the club. The tables were stark white, the floors shiny black, and a shimmering disco ball hung over the dance floor. A flashing red neon light surrounded the walls, casting a dazzling glow on the ultramodern decor. The club was packed with a hip L.A. crowd, and the party atmosphere seemed to crackle with electricity.

Jessica felt totally alive and excited. Her ice blue silk dress glimmered in the neon lights. She'd gone home from work earlier than usual that afternoon to give herself extra time to get ready. And although Quentin hadn't said much about her appearance after he'd picked her up that evening, Jessica felt extremely pleased with herself.

Quentin looked great too. He'd traded his everyday rumpled-artist clothing for a black retro dress jacket, a white button-down shirt, and black jeans. Jessica noticed lots of girls eyeing him openly and flashing him flirty smiles.

"Let's get closer to the dance floor," Quentin told Jessica. "Okay!" she readily agreed. With her hand loosely on her hip, she strutted after him toward the dance floor. But before they'd reached it, Quentin stopped abruptly and led Jessica away to a nearby table.

"Why do we have to sit?" she asked, disappointed.

Quentin turned his chair so that he was facing the dance floor. "Look around, Jessica," he replied. "We're here to be seen . . . and this happens to be the best spot in the whole place."

Jessica nodded mutely and took the chair next to his. Although she would've preferred to dance, she figured she should take his advice seriously. After all, the only reason she was out with Quentin was because he could help her career.

"This is the driving force of the fashion industry, Jessica," Quentin declared. "The L.A. scene, where celebrities, models, and fashion designers come together to make it happen."

Jessica nodded again, then sat up straighter as she noticed supermodel Tina Baker approaching the table. The striking brunette moved with an easy grace, her short black beaded dress and heavy silver jewelry shimmering in the neon lights. Jessica had long admired her and had even met her briefly some time ago, the day her best friend Lila's parents had remarried.

Tina enveloped Quentin in a hug, then turned to Jessica with an open, friendly expression. "Didn't we meet at the Fowler wedding in Sweet Valley?"

"That's right," Jessica responded, flattered that the famous model had remembered her.

"Would you like to join us?" Quentin ask Tina.

"Just for a minute." Tina sat down next to Jessica, chuckling. "I have friends waiting for me across the room, but first I have to find out what a nice girl like you is doing here with this character," she said jokingly.

Jessica giggled. "I'm working as an intern at *Flair*, as Quentin's assistant."

"You poor kid," Tina responded with mock horror, then smiled. "An internship at *Flair* sounds interesting. Are you interested in a career in photography?"

"Modeling," Jessica replied immediately.

Tina Baker nodded thoughtfully, narrowing her eyes as she gazed at Jessica with a measuring look. "I can see it. You have great eyes."

Jessica grinned broadly. "Thanks."

They talked for a few more minutes, then Tina announced she had to go meet her friends. "It was great seeing you again, Jessica. Lots of luck with your internship and modeling." She blew a kiss at Quentin and walked away.

"She's really nice," Jessica marveled, feeling incredibly pleased.

"Don't tell me you fell for her act." Quentin snickered, shaking his head. "Poor Jessica. You'll have to get used to people kissing up to you just to get to me. It'll happen all the time."

Jessica rolled her eyes, amazed at Quentin's arrogance. *He really is a jerk!* she thought. But as tempted as she was to tell him off, she held back. She still needed Quentin's help to establish herself as a model.

Quentin moved closer to her. "Look. Here

comes André Marceau of Marceau designs. Smile and wave, Jessica."

Jessica automatically obeyed, following his gaze to a tall, skinny man with waist-length gray hair. The man glanced over at her and Quentin and returned their greetings with a slight flick of his wrist as he walked by.

"André and I go way back," Quentin told Jessica. "I remember a layout I did for him last year. We were shooting in Chile, right on the coast. Suddenly, halfway through the day, the clouds came rolling in off the ocean.

"I slowed down the shutter speed and switched to black-and-white film." He flashed Jessica a sideways grin. "Everyone thought I was nuts, but those shots turned out incredible."

"That's great," Jessica responded politely.

"Believe me, 'great' is an understatement," Quentin replied. "It's no surprise that I won the VH1 award for best fashion photographer. There's no one else out there in my class."

Jessica sighed wearily and lowered her eyes. *I'm happy being here,* she silently told herself as she studied her silver-lacquered fingernails. *Even if Quentin is a totally self-centered, arrogant creep.*

Jessica noticed a red-haired guy wearing a forest green jacket standing over to her right, talking to the people at the next table. The conversation appeared to be lively and animated, though she couldn't hear a word of it over the loud music.

Jessica's eyes nearly popped out of her head as she recognized him. "Is that really . . . ?" she choked.

"Eddie Rook, the drummer from Nuclear Hearth," Quentin provided.

"Oh, my gosh . . . *Eddie Rook*," Jessica exclaimed, her sullen mood forgotten. "I *love* Nuclear Hearth. I have all their CDs!"

A tall blond girl in a sleeveless black leather jumpsuit rushed over and gave the rock star a big kiss.

"That's Sophia Tolland," Quentin whispered in Jessica's ear. Jessica nodded. She remembered seeing the model's face on a recent cover of *Mirabella*.

Jessica studied the couple intently as they lingered at the other table. Eddie Rook was standing behind Sophia Tolland, his arms around her slender waist and his chin resting against her hair.

Jessica smiled softly. There seemed to be something special about celebrities, as if they were surrounded with a glittering, magical aura. She was thrilled to know that someday soon, she too would become part of the magic. *No matter what it takes, I'm going to make it as a supermodel . . . and world-famous celebrity*, she vowed. Even if it meant spending her evenings with a jerk like Quentin Berg.

Just then Sophia Tolland turned her head. "Quentin!" she shrieked, her eyes wide. Obviously thrilled, she led Eddie Rook over to Jessica and Quentin's table.

I can't believe this! Jessica thought, her stomach fluttering excitedly.

Quentin rose to his feet and exchanged double-cheek kisses with Sophia, then shook hands with Eddie Rook. Sophia held out her hand, showing off a huge solitaire diamond on her finger. "We're officially engaged," she announced.

"That's fantastic," Quentin replied enthusiastically. "I wish you two all the happiness in the world."

As the three stood chatting for a few minutes Jessica noticed Eddie and Sophia glancing down at her, as if wondering who she was. *Why doesn't Quentin introduce me?* she wondered hotly. Finally she stood up and looped her arm around Quentin's, hoping he'd get her unspoken message—*I'm here and I won't be ignored!*

Quentin flashed her a tight grin. "This is Jessica," he said, making it sound like an offhand remark.

Jessica stiffened at the vague, unflattering introduction. But she wasn't about to let Quentin's bad manners ruin the thrilling moment for her. "I'm so pleased to meet both of you," she said sincerely, trying not to sound like a dithering, starstruck fan.

"We're headed over to the bar," Eddie Rook told them. "Some of the guys from my band are throwing us an engagement party, and they've posted bodyguards to keep all the paparazzi away from our table. You two are welcome to join us."

Jessica's heart leaped to her throat. *A party with Nuclear Hearth!* she silently shrieked, fighting the urge to jump up and down. She imagined her friends' reactions. *Lila will be totally jealous. . . .*

Then she noticed Quentin was shaking his head. Jessica froze. *He can't possibly be turning down the invitation?* she thought, questioning his sanity.

"You *have* to come celebrate with us, Quentin," Sophia pleaded, batting her incredibly long eyelashes at him. "After all, the photographs you took of me for the Chanel layout are what made Eddie fall in love with me."

Her fiancé laughed. "I carried a crinkled-up magazine page in my pocket for months before I got the nerve to call her," he admitted. "So you really should come to the party."

Of course we should! Jessica's mind shouted. She held her breath, wishing she could plant the right words in Quentin's mouth.

"Thanks, but maybe some other time," Quentin finally replied, draping his arm around Jessica's shoulders. "I've got to stay here and baby-sit my underage date."

Jessica reeled back, blazing. Heat rose in her cheeks. *How dare Quentin humiliate me like that!* she raged silently, her fists clenched at her sides.

Eddie chuckled, and Sophia shot her a sympathetic smile.

Jessica grinned tightly and said nothing, though her face felt as if it might crack under the pressure. She would have loved to scream at Quentin at that very moment, but she didn't want to embarrass herself even more than he already had.

27

Jessica waited until Sophia and Eddie left, then turned to Quentin. "That was a terrible thing to say!" she spat out furiously.

Quentin patted her shoulder. "You seem to be in a bad mood tonight, Jessica."

"I am now!" Jessica snapped, shrugging off his arm.

"I don't see what you're so mad about," Quentin complained. "It hardly makes sense to join Eddie and Sophia at a paparazzi-free table since we're here to be seen. And besides, you *are* underage." He combed his fingers through his shaggy, reddish blond hair and flashed her a condescending smile. "I was only thinking of you, Jessica."

Jessica's temper flared hotter. "Thanks for the favor," she retorted bitingly.

As the evening dragged on, a sharp headache began to throb in the middle of her forehead. Jessica sat glumly, ignoring Quentin's cues to "smile and wave" at the celebrities who passed by. *I'm bored,* she realized, somewhat amazed. *I'm sitting in L.A.'s hottest new club, with a world-famous fashion photographer, meeting celebrities . . . and I'm totally bored!*

"Quentin, can't we get up and dance for a little while?" Jessica pleaded.

"No, the dance floor is too crowded," Quentin declared, shaking his head. "I don't want to give up this table just to get lost in that mob." He moved his chair closer to hers and pointed to someone across the room. "That's Jeffrey Lee, the model who's doing the Quest jeans commercials. I once worked with him on a fabulous layout for *GQ*. . . ."

Jessica slumped back in her chair as Quentin continued his boastful monologue. A moment later she caught herself counting the tubes of neon lights on the ceiling. *Some date,* she thought, reaching her limit of tolerance. She wasn't sure what would happen if she spent one more minute sitting with Quentin. *I'm either going to explode . . . or fall asleep!*

". . . then I took some shots with the mountain peaks in the background," Quentin was saying.

Jessica rose to her feet. "I think I need some fresh air," she announced.

Quentin looked up at her and nodded. "You do seem worn out," he remarked. "Maybe you should touch up your makeup a little too."

Jessica drew her lips in a tight smile, holding back the nasty response bubbling in her mind. She headed for the closest exit, her head high and her back straight. "What a creep," she mumbled under her breath.

Outside, the pounding techno music had faded to a muffled, rhythmic sensation beating through the walls of the club. She breathed the cool night air deeply and exhaled with a sigh of relief. She began walking. A soft breeze fluttered in Jessica's hair and along the bottom hem of her silk dress. The constant hum of city traffic surrounded her, punctuated with blaring car horns and the occasional roar of a motorcycle. Across the street a

29

high-rise building spelled out its address with lighted windows against a dark background.

Jessica knew that being a successful model would require hard work and sacrifice. But she hadn't expected such torture. Aside from being a talented and famous photographer, Quentin Berg was a jerk and total bore.

Jessica walked around the corner toward the front entrance of the Edge. *If only I were here with Cameron tonight,* she thought sadly. She stopped and closed her eyes for an instant, picturing his gorgeous brown eyes, his soft lips. . . . *But what about your career?* a pesky voice in her head demanded.

"It's so unfair!" Jessica groaned to herself. She wished more than anything that Cameron and Quentin's positions were reversed—that Cameron was the famous photographer and Quentin was the nobody.

Jessica continued walking farther up the block, passing the line of people standing at the entrance of the Edge. She imagined the fun she might've been having at that moment with Cameron as her date. The evening would be absolutely fabulous. They would have danced together, no matter how crowded the dance floor was. When people stopped by their table, Cameron would introduce her respectfully. He'd want everyone to know how special she was, how deeply he cared for her.

Jessica smiled softly. With Cameron she still might have chosen to slip out of the nightclub—but certainly not by herself . . . and *not* because she had a headache.

Jessica's mind spun a delicious fantasy of herself and Cameron sitting in the Edge, their eyes locked in silent communication. Finally their longing desire for each other would become overpowering . . . and they'd have to steal a few private moments together. . . .

She reached the end of the block and turned around, slowing her pace to an easy stroll. She wasn't in any hurry to get back to Quentin.

Jessica noticed a white Porsche pulling up in front of a restaurant a few doors away. Despite her pensive mood, she couldn't help admiring the car's sleek, gleaming exterior.

When the Porsche stopped, a female valet in a fancy gray uniform, matching cap, and white gloves hopped out of the car. Her double-breasted jacket had gold braided ropes draped over the shoulders.

Jessica watched the entrance of the restaurant, hoping to catch a glimpse of the car's owner. *Someday I'll be able to drive a car like that,* she assured herself.

A guy with curly brown hair, wearing a dark tuxedo, came forward to take the keys from the valet. Jessica's heart skipped a beat. She stopped in her tracks and gaped at him. *Cameron?* she thought, stunned. She continued staring as the car pulled away from the curb and disappeared into the stream of heavy traffic.

But it couldn't have been him, Jessica reasoned. She didn't think Cameron could easily afford a meal at such a fancy restaurant, let alone a Porsche. But the guy had looked so much like him. . . .

A sharp ache pierced her heart. Tears pooled in

her eyes, blurring her vision and creating halos around all the lights. *I miss Cameron so much,* she realized sadly. Jessica decided it had been her own wishful thinking that had conjured up the vision of him in the Porsche. But even if he couldn't afford to drive a fancy car, Cameron was the guy she truly loved.

She recalled how angry he'd looked when he'd walked in on her and Quentin that morning. *What if I've lost Cameron forever?* she wondered, choking back a sob.

Jessica vowed to make it up to him as soon as possible. She'd go down to the mail room tomorrow and force him to listen to her explanation. *I'll bring him a nice lunch,* she planned.

Jessica dabbed her fingertips across her face, brushing away her tears. It was time to go back to Quentin and his dull version of partying.

The following morning Maria and Enid accompanied Elizabeth to the Mode building. Elizabeth had talked it over with Reggie the night before, and they'd both agreed that it would be useful to more have players involved in their plan.

Elizabeth felt a weird sensation as she stepped into Leona's office. The black lacquered desk was completely scattered with stacks of unopened mail, papers, magazines, and file folders. The computer was still on, the screen-saver program flashing white stars on a dark background. "I feel like she's going to walk in any minute," Elizabeth murmured as she lowered herself into Leona's leather chair.

Maria curled up in the chair on the other side of the desk. "Don't worry, Liz. Leona is miles away, with a broken leg."

Maria's outfit of a cashmere sweater and slim-fitting black moleskin pants, with silver hoops in her ears, was much too artsy and unique for the editorial department. But that didn't matter, because Maria was going to stay behind the scenes for most of their plan.

Enid walked over to one of the large windows on the far wall. "What a view!" she exclaimed. She was more conservatively dressed, in a black calf-length wool skirt with a cream-colored vest over a burgundy silk blouse.

"Will you get back here and pay attention!" Maria scolded jokingly. "We have business to conduct."

"I'll call Reggie," Elizabeth replied, picking up the phone.

Reggie joined them a moment later. "You've brought the reinforcements," she said, walking into the office with a welcoming smile. Elizabeth quickly made the introductions.

"OK, where do we start?" Reggie asked, tucking her hands into the pockets of her blue blazer. She was wearing a matching tailored skirt that was the same length as the jacket. "I have a meeting this morning, but it shouldn't take more than an hour."

"No problem," Elizabeth assured her. "We can handle setting up the meeting with Gordon Lewis."

Reggie's face brightened at the mention of *Flair*'s handsome, dynamic publisher. Elizabeth knew her friend had a secret crush on Gordon Lewis.

"Everyone know their lines?" Maria demanded after Reggie left for her meeting. Maria had been unanimously elected to be the director of this morning's caper because of her vast acting experience. As a child, she'd starred in a science fiction movie and several television commercials. And as she was rounding out her dramatic experience through her internship as a set designer at the Bridgewater Theatre company in Sweet Valley, everyone figured she was the perfect choice.

Maria pushed up the sleeves of her violet cashmere cardigan and began coaching them on the roles they would play. "Remember, Elizabeth, you're a *newly* hired assistant editor. Any questions you can't answer, go back to that point—you haven't been here long enough to know everything.

"And Enid," Maria continued. "You're supposed to be a secretary, not a jack-in-the-box. Tone down the enthusiasm. Put a hint of boredom into your voice."

Enid stuck out her tongue as soon as Maria turned her back.

Elizabeth snickered. "No matter how this turns out, I want you guys to know that I think you're the best friends in the whole world," she declared. "I don't know how to thank you."

"Next time *you* buy the frozen yogurt," Maria quipped. "Now let's get this show rolling." She clapped twice. "Places, everyone!"

Enid and Elizabeth's "places" were the two chairs on either side of Leona's desk. Elizabeth opened the Mode phone directory and scrolled down to Gordon Lewis's extension.

"And . . . *action!*" Maria ordered. "Be sure to lower your voice and pronounce each word clearly, especially the endings. It'll counteract the squeaky babbling effect of being nervous."

"Thanks for the tip," Elizabeth replied dryly. "But what if my mind completely blanks out?"

Maria picked up the spiked message holder on Leona's desk and aimed the point threateningly. "I'll figure out a way to make you snap to attention," she said, laughing.

Elizabeth dialed the number to Gordon Lewis's office and tried to put the call on speaker phone so they could all listen.

Maria frowned. "Why can't we hear anything?"

"Oh, no!" Elizabeth whispered harshly. "I think I pushed the button for the intercom." She dialed again, grabbed the handset, and handed it to Enid. "I'm too nervous for high tech. Let's just do this the old-fashioned way."

A moment later Enid perked up. "Yes, hello. Ms. Wakefield would like to speak to Mr. Lewis," she said with authority.

Maria gave Enid a thumbs-up sign, then cued Elizabeth to take the phone. Elizabeth took a deep breath as she waited for Gordon Lewis to pick up

35

the call. The instant he came on the line, he asked, "Who is this?"

"Elizabeth Wakefield," she told him. "I'm a new colleague of Leona's at *Flair.*"

"I wasn't aware they'd hired anyone new," he replied. "How long ago did you start?"

Elizabeth blanked out for a second, but Maria's encouraging expression snapped her out of it. "I was hired by . . . Mr. Jowerininerskily, last . . . um, month," Elizabeth answered.

"While I was on vacation?" Mr. Lewis asked sharply.

Elizabeth nodded, which was stupid, since Mr. Lewis couldn't see her. "That's right, during your vacation," she told him hastily.

"Figures they'd increase the editorial staff when I'm out of the country," he grumbled. But he seemed to accept Elizabeth's status. "What can I do for you, Ms. Wakefield?"

"I have an idea I'd like to discuss with you," she said, pleased with her confident tone. "I think it could bring in a lot of revenue for *Flair.* Actually I've been meaning to call you for some time, but I haven't because, well, you know how busy—"

Maria signaled with a finger dragged across her throat.

Elizabeth gulped, realizing she'd been babbling. She swallowed hard and forced herself to get back in control. "When would it be convenient for me stop in at your office and show you my idea?"

"Today's out." He paused, as if he were flipping through the entries in his appointment book. "And most of tomorrow too. I have a meeting across town in the morning. Why don't I stop in when I get back to the building, say around eleven?"

Elizabeth's jaw dropped. "Oh, you want to come *here?*"

"That would be easiest. But I'm afraid I don't even know where your office is," Mr. Lewis said. "I assume you're on the eleventh floor, right?"

"That's right," Elizabeth managed to choke out. "The eleventh floor. My office is . . . I'm in Leona's office—her *old* office. She's somewhere else." She caught a glimpse of Maria rolling her eyes.

"OK, I'll see you tomorrow around eleven, Ms. Wakefield," he said.

"I'm looking forward to it," Elizabeth replied. She hung up feeling scared but triumphant.

The girls exchanged high-five slaps. "We did it!" Enid cheered.

"You guys were great," Maria commented. "A few rough spots, but you handled them well."

Enid and Elizabeth grinned. "Hey, Liz. Who's Mr. Jowerin . . . whatever?" Enid asked.

Elizabeth laughed. "Beats me. I purposely made up an unpronounceable name that Mr. Gordon couldn't easily remember."

"That was smart," Maria said. "Now we have to get ready for act two—The Meeting."

Elizabeth nodded, her eyes wide. Suddenly the

impact of what she'd just done—and was *about* to do—hit her full force like a bucket of ice water splashed in her face. "I've got a meeting with the head of this company!" she shrieked. "Oh my gosh, I have to make this office look like it belongs to me." She jumped up and began frantically scooping up the papers on Leona's desk. "How am I going to pull this off?"

"You're just nervous, Elizabeth," Enid said reassuringly. "Which is perfectly normal under the circumstances."

Elizabeth uttered a hysterical-sounding laugh. "*Normal?* I must be totally *insane!* What if Gordon Lewis sees right through me?"

"Just relax and breathe deeply," Maria instructed.

"I can't relax. I have to *think!*" Elizabeth picked up Leona's brass cube paperweight and passed it nervously from hand to hand. "Let's see. . . . The presentation is ready to go, although it could use a bit of polishing. The materials are in Reggie's office. I hope Reggie doesn't have anything important scheduled tomorrow at eleven."

Elizabeth set the paperweight down and immediately picked it up again. "When are we going to practice for our meeting with Gordon Lewis?"

"I'll pick up Enid after I'm done at the theater and we'll come back here," Maria assured her, glancing at Enid with a questioning look.

"Sounds fine with me," Enid added.

"Thanks. I just hope I'm done in here by then,"

Elizabeth replied, gazing around the office. She spotted items that shouted "Leona Peirson works here!" everywhere she looked: an engraved plaque in the bookcase behind the desk . . . an old postcard pinned to the bulletin board, probably addressed to Leona . . . a personalized memo pad with Leona's name on every page. . . .

Elizabeth sighed wearily. "Finding and removing all traces of Leona is going to be an enormous task."

"We'll check it over when we come back," Maria offered.

As Elizabeth gathered up Leona's unopened mail a small, glossy envelope caught her eye. Curious, she ripped it open, then glanced at her friends. "It's OK for me to open Leona's mail," she remarked defensively. "She asked me to, so it's part of my job."

Maria and Enid both chuckled. "Don't worry, we won't turn you in for tampering with the U.S. mail," Maria said wryly.

"Even though it *is* a felony," Enid added.

Elizabeth pulled out a printed card and read it to herself. "It's an invitation to a party at the Bel Air hotel tonight. I've heard some of the editors talk about this. All the bigwigs in publishing are sure to be there—including Gordon Lewis." Elizabeth smiled brightly. "What luck!" she exclaimed.

"We're going?" Enid asked innocently.

Maria tucked her arm around Enid's elbow. "You have a lot to learn about subterfuge," she teased.

"I have to talk to Reggie about it," Elizabeth murmured, thinking aloud.

Elizabeth leaned forward and snapped her fingers. "Ms. Rollins, get Reggie Andrews on the phone and set up a lunch meeting next door at the Mission Café," she barked at Enid. "Then bring me a cup of herbal tea."

"Wow, Liz! You're more than good," Maria proclaimed. "You're *dangerous*."

All three girls laughed.

Chapter 3

I will make *Cameron listen to me,* Jessica vowed as she rode the elevator down to the lobby of the Mode building at lunchtime. She planned to surprise him with a gourmet meal, hoping to catch him off guard so he'd listen to her apology.

Jessica glanced down at the brown paper bag she held in her hands, in which she'd packed a loaf of fresh bread, assorted cheeses, strawberries, chilled sparkling cider, and chocolate cookies she'd baked herself. *How can he resist such a romantic lunch?* she thought, smiling.

When she reached the lobby, Jessica paused to check her appearance in the mirrored doors of the elevator. She'd worn a black leather miniskirt and deep purple satin jacket with black leather trim. The look was everything she'd wanted—elegant, fun, and sexy. *Perfect,* she silently congratulated

41

herself. A wonderful feeling of anticipation tingled up her spine as she went off to search for Cameron.

Cameron usually spent his lunch hour outdoors, in the central courtyard of the Mode building, which he'd jokingly named "Chez Bench." Before stepping outside, Jessica hastily finger-combed her hair and took a deep, bracing breath.

Shading her eyes from the glaring sunlight, Jessica scanned the area. He wasn't there. *Maybe he couldn't get out for lunch today,* she reasoned, swallowing her disappointment. She hoped that if Cameron had to work during his lunch hour, he'd be extra grateful to her for bringing him such a marvelous lunch.

Jessica smiled brightly as she strolled into the mail room. Unlike the posh lobby and high-tech photography studio, the mail room was a shabby maze of cluttered storage nooks, sorting areas, and loading docks. A guy with long blond hair, wearing a faded flannel shirt, was stacking boxes in a corner. "Can I help you, miss?" he asked.

"I'm looking for Cameron," Jessica told him. "Do you know if he went out for lunch?"

The guy shrugged. "I'm the only one here right now. If Cameron is the guy who used to work here, he's gone. I took his place."

A thick, cold feeling sank into the pit of her stomach. "Gone?" she echoed.

The new mail clerk nodded. "He quit. Is there anything I can help you with?"

42

Jessica tossed the guy her bag of her food and ran out of the room. She'd suddenly lost her appetite.

Later that afternoon Elizabeth returned to Leona's condo with Enid and Maria. "This won't take long," Elizabeth said as she unlocked the front door. She wouldn't have come back at all if it weren't for the cats. It wasn't fair to let them starve just because their owner was a lying snake.

"This really is gorgeous," Maria remarked as she followed Elizabeth inside.

Elizabeth shrugged. Leona's condo was breathtakingly beautiful, with high cathedral ceilings and pale wood floors. The living room was a huge open space; the far wall was made entirely of windows, and the colors of a spectacular sunset flooded the room. Over to the left two black leather couches were arranged perpendicularly around a glass table. A blue art deco clock hung on the wall, and shell-pink Tiffany lamps added a softening touch to the stark decor. "Leona has good taste," Elizabeth stated blandly. "I have to give her that."

"I think your customers have arrived," Enid said as two Persian cats came rushing into the room. She bent down to pet one, then jerked back her hand. "Ouch, he bit me!"

"They must be *so* hungry," Elizabeth said, feeling a pang of guilt for having neglected them for two days. She hurried into the kitchen, with the two cats yowling at her feet.

"I know, it was terrible of me not to come sooner," Elizabeth apologized as she opened a can of cat food. She was about to scoop it into the two ceramic cat dishes on the floor when an impish idea popped into her head. "I think you guys deserve better."

Elizabeth went into the formal dining room and opened the black china closet. "I think Leona's cats should dine in style tonight," she announced cheerfully as she removed two elegant white dinner plates rimmed with gold.

In the kitchen Elizabeth piled a large heap of cat food on each plate. *"Bon appétit,"* she said, setting them on the floor.

Pleased with herself, she returned to the living room. Maria and Enid were sitting on the black leather couches, their stocking feet propped up on the glass table. Maria's cashmere cardigan was bunched up behind her head as a pillow, and the shirttails of Enid's burgundy blouse were sticking out of her black skirt. "I see you've made yourselves right at home," Elizabeth remarked, chuckling.

Her smile froze on her face as she noticed the small tape recorder on the side table, right where she'd left it Monday. "I want you both to hear this," she told her friends. She turned on the recorder and Leona Peirson's deep, brisk voice filled the room.

"Letter to Gordon Lewis," Leona was saying. "Note to myself. This letter is not to go through Elizabeth."

Enid gasped and Maria bolted upright, but neither uttered a word.

"Dear Gordon," the recording continued. "As you suggested, I would like to formally submit the idea we discussed on the phone. . . . I propose a column tentatively titled 'Free Style,' a one-page article written by a *Flair* reader with her ideas on fashion. . . . I would be happy to discuss my idea at the next editorial board meeting. . . ."

Elizabeth slumped down next to Enid on the couch. Even though she knew the contents of the letter and could probably recite most of it from memory, hearing it again left Elizabeth feeling as shocked as when she'd first discovered the recording.

"That woman is *vile!*" Maria declared after they finished listening to the recording.

Enid agreed. "She even used *your* title for the column!"

Elizabeth plunked her feet up on the couch and grinned. "Leona will soon get exactly what she deserves."

"That reminds me," Maria said, jumping to her feet. "We need to go over the fine points for your meeting with Gordon Lewis tomorrow." She began pacing around the room. "It's the small details that can make or break a convincing performance."

She turned to Enid. "Remember to address Elizabeth as Ms. Wakefield at all times," Maria instructed. "You'll have to serve coffee when Gordon arrives. I suggest you bring cups and saucers from home so you'll be sure to have them ready. Bring a tray too."

Enid gave her a stiff, military salute. "Yes, ma'am."

"And remember, Elizabeth, as a corporate

executive, you never 'use' anything—you *utilize* it," Maria continued. "Actually you should tack on an *ize* to as many words as you can. It'll make you sound more convincing."

"Got it," Elizabeth replied. "And now if you two will excuse me, I've got some houseplants to *waterize*."

"And I have to *telephonize* my mother and let her know I'm going to be home late," Enid said.

Maria shook her head, laughing. "You two are hopeless."

In the kitchen Elizabeth turned on the sink and filled the blue watering can she'd used the last time she'd been there. Glancing down at the cats, she giggled. They seemed to be thoroughly enjoying their elegant dining experience.

"Reggie seems really nice," Enid commented when Elizabeth returned to the living room. "But isn't it possible that she's just as ruthless as Leona?"

"No, Reggie isn't like that at all," Elizabeth insisted. "She's really a sweet person."

Maria snorted. "How could anyone working in the Mode empire be *sweet?* Look what working there did to *you* in just a few days."

Elizabeth flinched as if she'd been stung. "I suppose I deserved that."

"I was just teasing," Maria insisted.

"But getting back to Reggie," Enid interjected. "What if she's just another Leona in training? She might be trying to claw her own way up the corporate ladder."

"No way," Elizabeth replied. "Reggie's career is important to her, but it's not her whole life. She wants to get married someday and raise a family." Elizabeth reached up to water a hanging ivy plant. "Reggie's been in love with Gordon Lewis for ages. But she's never had the courage to speak to him."

"That's sort of cute," Enid said.

Maria nodded. "Yeah, it is. Maybe there's something we can do to help. At the very least we can push them together tonight," she suggested.

"We'll make her look absolutely irresistible," Elizabeth added, another great idea taking shape in her mind. "Not that Reggie isn't already beautiful. But we have to find something absolutely stunning for her to wear. And I know exactly where to look. . . ."

"I like the idea, but we still have to drive back to Sweet Valley and get ourselves dressed up for the party," Enid pointed out. "We don't have time for an emergency shopping trip to search for an *absolutely stunning* outfit for Reggie."

"Just leave it to me," Elizabeth said. "I'll call Reggie and tell her to come over right now."

"Oh, sure, and maybe we can hold a quick bake sale or a car wash to pay for her stunning outfit," Maria remarked sarcastically.

Elizabeth shook her head. "We're not going to *buy* anything, just . . . borrow. Leona has tons of stuff in her closets. We can all get ready for the party right here."

47

Enid and Maria looked at her with matching dumbfounded expressions.

"It'll be fine," Elizabeth assured them.

Maria turned to Enid. "I *told* you she was dangerous."

"Trust me," Elizabeth insisted. "Leona won't be back for days, maybe weeks. And by the time she does get back, a few extra wrinkles in her fancy outfits will be the least of her problems."

They went upstairs and searched through the huge walk-in closet in Leona's bedroom. "Let's concentrate on finding something for Reggie first," Maria suggested, "since she's the leading lady of tonight's performance."

Elizabeth flipped through a few outfits. "I just found it," she announced, pulling out a short black dress with a deep neckline and suede trim. She carried it on its hanger to the bed and laid it out for her friends to see. "It's a Lina Lapin design," Elizabeth explained.

Maria looked it over and nodded. "It's sensational. Gordon Lewis won't know what hit him!"

Enid inhaled deeply and sighed. "I feel like a fairy godmother."

"This is it," Todd announced as he and Ken pulled up in front of an old Victorian house in an older neighborhood near Hollywood.

Todd stepped out of his black BMW and gazed at his new home. He was surprised at how shabby the place appeared. The drab gray paint was cracked and chipped, the front porch sagged, a broken window on the second floor was pieced together with duct tape. Howie had shown Todd the apartment the night before, but it had been dark outside and the house hadn't seemed so . . . *ugly*.

"It's huge," Ken commented. The guys each grabbed an armload of boxes and duffel bags from the trunk of Todd's BMW.

"It's divided into apartments," Todd explained as he led the way to the front entrance. There was a gaping hole in one of the door panels. "I guess the super must be on vacation," he mumbled dryly. Inside, the hallway smelled like old cabbage and wet dogs. "What's it like to be going out with a big-time model?" Ken asked as they climbed the stairs to Todd's fourth-floor apartment.

"Simone is awesome," Todd answered automatically. "A few nights ago we went to the Edge, a techno club downtown. There was this crowd of like a hundred people at the door, trying to get inside. Simone and I went right up to the front of the line, and the bouncers waved us right in."

"Must be great." Ken sounded impressed.

"It's amazing," Todd agreed, forcing himself to sound more enthusiastic than he actually felt. "The real exclusive places have a list of the people they'll let inside, like rock stars, famous actors, billionaires, and"—he paused for effect—"top fashion models."

"What's it like inside those places?" Ken asked.

Todd shifted his duffel bag to his other hand. "Like the best party you've ever been to, times a thousand."

Ken chuckled. "That good, huh?"

"Out of this world," Todd said. "Great bands, beautiful girls everywhere you look . . ." He didn't add how much he missed Elizabeth, how empty his life felt without her.

At door of his apartment Todd reached into the front pocket of his jeans and took out his keys. "It's not too big, but it's all mine," he declared triumphantly as he unlocked the door.

Todd walked into his apartment, and his heart sank. Like the exterior of the house, the place looked a lot worse than it had the night before. The living-room carpet was a grungy, sickly orange color, worn thin in spots. The walls were stained with brown streaks, and a thick, dark spiderweb draped down from the ceiling.

"It'll look a lot better once I get my stuff in here," Todd said, trying to sound cheerful. "Maybe a little paint on these walls . . . it'll be great."

Ken leaned back against the living-room wall and folded his arms, his expression grave. "Make that *lots* of paint."

"Okay, lots of paint," Todd returned bitingly.

Suddenly Ken jumped forward, shaking his arms. "I felt *something*," he muttered. "Look, there it is!"

Following Ken's gaze, Todd saw a huge centipede dash up the wall and disappear into a crack in the woodwork. "Cool. I even get to trap my own dinner," he joked, gulping down his revulsion. Ken wandered over to the tiny kitchen off the living room. "Don't bother," he called a moment later.

"With what?" Todd asked.

"They've already left dinner for you."

Bemused, Todd went over to investigate. The kitchen was every bit as ugly as the living room, with cracked linoleum on the floor and ratty old curtains in the window above the sink. A cheap white plastic patio table and chairs were set up in the corner. The kitchen appliances were probably older than Todd.

Ken opened the refrigerator and a nasty, sour stench wafted into the room. "Old milk and shriveled-up pizza," he said.

"Sounds delicious," Todd replied sarcastically. "You can close the refrigerator now."

Todd peered into the oven. It appeared to be standard quality, with a broiler and two racks. Everything was coated with a thick layer of dark grease, but Todd figured he could take care of that with some detergent and steel wool. *This is really mine,* he realized, a tiny flicker of interest springing to life inside him.

Ken ambled over to the table and sat down in one of the plastic chairs. "So Todd, now that you're busy with Simone, would you mind if I asked Elizabeth out?"

Todd felt as if he'd been punched in the stomach. Then a sudden, bone-chilling anger gripped his heart. He slammed the oven door shut and slowly turned around. "Ken . . . ," he began, his voice smooth and steady as a steel knife, "if you go anywhere near Elizabeth, I'll break your nose."

Ken raised his hands and laughed. "I was just kidding. One Wakefield twin was enough for me." He and Jessica had dated steadily for some time until she'd cheated on him with a guy from a rival school. Todd knew that Ken wasn't completely over the ordeal.

"Really, I was kidding," Ken assured him.

"You'd better be," Todd warned. But he remembered that Ken and Elizabeth had had a brief, secret fling when Todd had temporarily moved to Vermont. What if she and Ken decided to pick up where they'd left off?

Todd opened and closed kitchen cupboards, absently noting their contents. But all he was aware of at that moment was his stomach twisting into knots. Elizabeth was a great girl—and now she was free. Even though Ken was only kidding, Todd knew it wouldn't be long before some guy did ask her out. *It's my own fault,* Todd thought, mentally kicking himself for losing her.

Suddenly a burst of angry shouting erupted in the apartment next to Todd's. Something crashed against the wall, the force of the impact strong enough to shake Todd's stove and refrigerator. A stream of curses, male and female, followed the crash. "Live entertainment," Ken quipped.

"Great," Todd uttered dryly. "Since I don't have a TV yet . . . or a phone."

Ken pushed his hands deep into the pockets of his denim jacket and glared at him. "Todd, this place is a dump."

"It's not *that* bad," Todd argued weakly. "With a little fixing up, it might be OK."

Ken's lips twisted in a sarcastic grin. "Yeah, *right*. And with a little intense psychotherapy your neighbors might be OK." He shook his head. "You don't have to live here. You can stay at my place until you find something better," Ken suggested.

Todd was tempted. Just thinking of having to clean out the smelly refrigerator made him sick. But he remembered the looks on his parents' faces when he'd stormed out of the house Tuesday night, when he'd finally had it with their attempts to control him. *They think this is all a childish prank,* he told himself. *They're waiting for me to fall flat on my face and come running back to Sweet Valley.*

Todd refused to let that happen. Even if his parents had zero confidence in his ability to make it on his own, Todd believed in himself. And he was determined to prove it to his parents.

Todd sat down across from his friend and flattened his palms against the table. "I appreciate your offer, Ken, but finding a better place isn't the problem. Right now I can't afford a fancy apartment . . . or even a decent one," he admitted. "But soon I'll be getting more modeling jobs and making big money."

"I can't believe you're serious about living in this dump," Ken argued.

Todd looked him straight in the eye. "I'm going to live here," he replied. "And I'm *very* serious."

"Oh, wow!" Elizabeth breathed, her eyes wide as she walked into the party at the Bel Air hotel with her friends that evening. The air seemed to crackle with energy. The room was filled with lavishly dressed people talking in small groups and sipping champagne. Elizabeth recognized several famous faces from photographs in magazines and on book jackets.

Waiters wearing red tuxedo jackets and balancing trays of champagne glasses over their heads wove through the crowd. A buffet had been set up along the far wall, with a huge, spiral-shaped ice sculpture in the center of the table. On the other side of the room a string quartet was performing on a raised dais, the strains of classical music just loud enough to be heard above the muted buzzing sound of the many conversations among the guests.

"Wow, *everyone's* here!" Reggie whispered.

"Shouldn't we mingle?" Enid asked.

Elizabeth shook her head, gripped with panic. *I'm not ready for this,* she thought. Even in a glamorous opal chiffon dress—a Pierre Jové original—and silver high-heeled sandals, she felt as if the words *sixteen-year-old impostor* were tattooed on her forehead. "What if they throw us out?" she murmured.

Maria squeezed her hand. "Why would they? Are you planning to start a food fight?"

Enid and Reggie chuckled, but Elizabeth just

stared straight ahead, too nervous to appreciate her friend's attempt at humor. "What if everyone figures out that we're teenagers crashing the party?"

"Come on, Elizabeth," Maria gently chided. "We look just as grown-up and snazzy as everyone else here."

Elizabeth exhaled slowly. Maria was right. She had used her stage makeup skills to make herself, Elizabeth, and Enid look older. And they all *did* look fabulous—thanks to the outfits they'd "borrowed" from Leona's closet. The black Lina Lapin dress was a perfect fit for Reggie. It showed off her slim figure and long legs to perfection, as if the designer had created it with her in mind. Leona's clunky silver earrings and chain necklace added the finishing touches.

Enid looked incredible in a shimmering lime green velvet gown, with silver mesh earrings and matching bracelet. Maria had chosen a long, floral print silk skirt and a tailored black leather sleeveless jacket with gold buttons. A matching leather bag hung over her shoulder.

"We all look wonderful," Reggie said.

"Now, are we going to get this show on the road, or what?" Maria asked impatiently.

Elizabeth took a deep breath and let it out slowly. They'd come to this party to set the stage for her meeting with Gordon Lewis the following day—and to help get him and Reggie together. Elizabeth wasn't about to give up, no matter how many butterflies fluttered in her stomach. "It's now or never, I guess," she said, steeling her courage.

Maria pushed the strap of the leather bag farther up her shoulder. "Reggie and I will look around for Gordon. Elizabeth and Enid, you two should probably find a corner and hide for a while."

"Gee, thanks," Enid grumbled.

Maria pursed her lips. "We don't want Gordon to see you or Elizabeth until the meeting tomorrow. But I promise we'll come tell you as soon as we've spotted him."

Elizabeth nervously rubbed a fold of her gray chiffon dress between her fingers. "Where should we wait?" she asked.

"There aren't many people around the banquet table," Maria observed. "Let's meet there."

Reggie pressed her bottom lip between her teeth and rolled her eyes. "I still can't believe I'm doing this," she whispered as she and Maria turned to go.

Elizabeth and Enid exchanged furtive looks and headed toward the banquet table. Unaccustomed to wearing such flimsy, high-heeled shoes, Elizabeth took small, slow steps to avoid losing her balance. *Please, don't let me fall on my face,* she silently prayed as she eased her way through the crowd.

When she finally reached the buffet, Elizabeth gripped the edge of the linen-covered table and breathed a sigh of relief. Enid wobbled up next to her. "They should put a warning label on these ridiculous shoes," Elizabeth grumbled.

Enid took two plates from a stack next to the

ice sculpture and handed one to Elizabeth. "As long as we're here, we might as well enjoy ourselves," Enid suggested. She helped herself to some black caviar from a crystal bowl on ice.

Elizabeth selected a bite-size pastry shell filled with pâté and truffles, then added some shrimp cocktail and a small serving of spinach salad to her plate. Just as she popped the flaky pâté tart into her mouth, a woman with short-cropped dark hair, wearing a glittery white beaded dress, came up to her. "Excuse me, didn't we meet in Milan last spring?" she asked Elizabeth.

Startled, Elizabeth shook her head.

"I'm positive we did," the woman insisted. "You're with *Vogue*, right?"

"You must have me mixed up with someone else," Elizabeth replied. "I'm not . . ." Suddenly she felt some crumbs brushing against her lips, falling to her chin, and she realized she was talking with her mouth full. Totally embarrassed, Elizabeth clamped her teeth together and pressed her fingers over her lips. Her face felt as though it were on fire.

Enid stepped in to help. "Liz decided not to go to Milan this year," she told the woman in a casual tone. "But she went lots of other places. Because she's a very important fashion editor . . . but not at *Vogue*."

The woman gave them a strange look and walked away, shaking her head.

"That went well," Enid muttered sarcastically.

Elizabeth swallowed, then drew in a shaky

breath. Just then she saw Reggie and Maria hurrying toward them.

"He's in the bar," Reggie announced, choking out the words.

Maria glared at Elizabeth's plate with a look of horror. "Liz, please don't tell me you're eating that salad."

Elizabeth frowned, bemused. "I haven't yet. What's wrong with it?"

Maria grabbed the plate away from her. "What's *wrong* is that we don't have any dental floss with us. Once you speak to someone with spinach stuck in your teeth, you'll lose their respect *forever.*"

Enid giggled. "That's quite profound, Maria." But Elizabeth mentally swore an oath never to eat in public again.

Maria and Reggie led the way to a circular alcove on the other side of the private banquet room. Standing near the entrance, Elizabeth peered inside. A polished oak bar dominated the area. Black tables were arranged along the perimeter. Elizabeth spotted Gordon Lewis sitting alone at the far end of the bar. Tall, with bright blue eyes, brown hair, and chiseled features, he was one of the handsomest men she had ever seen. She pointed him out for Enid.

Enid's eyes widened. "He's *gorgeous!*" she exclaimed.

"*I* think so," Reggie added. She drew in a

shaky breath. "What if I go up to him and he brushes me off?"

"Have you seen yourself in a mirror lately?" Maria questioned. "In *that* dress you should worry that he might fall off his seat and hurt himself."

Reggie uttered a shaky laugh. "I'm so nervous."

"Use your feelings," Maria advised her. "Acting is about honesty."

Enid wrinkled her nose. "What are you talking about? Acting is about making believe."

Maria glared at her. "Excuse me, who's the director of this show?"

"Director?" Enid asked pointedly. "Or *dictator?*"

Maria shrugged. "They mean the same thing." She turned to Reggie. "Gordon is a bigwig in the company you work for. It's perfectly natural to feel a bit jittery. Let it be part of your act."

"What if I'm so nervous, my voice chokes up and I can't speak?" Reggie asked.

"Too bad we're not doing a musical," Enid interjected. "Then you could burst into song whenever you got too nervous."

The others groaned. "I can teach you some of the tunes from *Evita*," Maria joked. It was the musical she was working on at the Bridgewater Theatre company.

"Okay, this is it," Reggie declared softly. "Watch for my signal." With her shoulders back and her head held high, she glided over to the bar.

Holding her breath, Elizabeth waited to see if the encounter would go according to plan.

Chapter 4

Standing between Enid and Elizabeth, Maria watched Reggie glide over to Gordon Lewis, her arms gracefully at her sides and her chin raised just enough to project self-confidence. The stool next to his was vacant, and Maria wondered how Reggie would handle it.

Don't sit down immediately, Maria thought, wishing she could send telepathic stage directions to Reggie. *Make him think you might walk away any minute.*

Reggie rested her arm on the bar—and remained standing. "Yes!" Maria breathed, clenching her hand into a victorious fist. Gordon and Reggie began talking. "I wish I knew how to read lips," Enid whispered.

"Read their faces," Maria replied. "Gordon's blue eyes are flashing with enough electricity to light up three city blocks."

Enid giggled. "Handy guy to bring along on camping trips."

"They do seem to like each other," Elizabeth remarked.

"It's so *romantic*." Enid sighed. "They make such a beautiful couple."

A tall, stunning woman with chin-length blond hair walked into the room. Wearing a shimmering deep green beaded dress and diamond jewelry, she sparkled with countless dots of reflected light. "There's another one to invite on your next camping trip, Enid," Maria joked.

"I love her dress," Elizabeth murmured.

Suddenly the woman rushed over to Gordon Lewis and they exchanged a warm hug. Maria gasped. Enid and Elizabeth uttered strangled sounds of horror.

"Tell me this isn't happening," Enid whispered.

"Poor Reggie," Elizabeth said woefully. "This was supposed to be her big chance with Gordon."

"Do you think we should go in there and rescue her?" Enid suggested.

"She's not being held prisoner," Maria pointed out.

Suddenly Elizabeth turned her head sharply to the side and did a double take. Her gaze seemed to be focused on a brown-haired guy in a tuxedo who was walking out of the room. "Cameron?" Elizabeth blurted incredulously.

Nonplussed, Maria stared at her. "Cameron who?" she and Enid asked in unison.

Elizabeth shook her head. "Never mind. I just

61

caught a glimpse of someone who reminded me of the guy from the mail room at the Mode building," she explained. "Jessica has been seeing him. But it couldn't have been him."

"Not likely, if he works in the mail room," Enid replied.

Maria saw Reggie rubbing the side of her nose. "There's my signal," she said, reaching into her leather evening bag. She took out the compact cellular phone that they'd "borrowed" from Leona and dialed the number for the local hot line that played a continuous recording of weather information.

"Break a leg, Maria," Elizabeth said.

Maria chuckled. "I'm wearing a long silk skirt and five-inch-heel shoes, so I just might."

"If that happens, you can call Leona and commiserate together," Enid joked.

"Doesn't that sound like fun," Maria replied dryly over her shoulder. Strolling into the bar, she eased herself into character. She was playing the role of a freelance writer who'd worked often with Reggie and Elizabeth.

"Maria," Reggie called, her eyes projecting a look of delighted surprise.

Maria approached the bar, giving Gordon and the blond woman a brief smile before turning back to Reggie. "Reggie Andrews, you're *just* the person I wanted to see," Maria told her. "I have Elizabeth Wakefield on the phone. She's been trying to reach you all evening."

Reggie took the cellular phone from Maria and smiled apologetically at Gordon and the other woman. "Excuse me, but I really do have to take this call." She held the phone up to her ear. "Elizabeth, I thought you'd be here hours ago. . . . You're *where?* . . . That's incredible . . . and he's giving us an exclusive? . . . No, I promise I won't breathe a word of it. . . . *Really?* . . . His designs for the Paris show? . . ."

Pressing her bottom lip between her teeth, Maria closely observed Reggie's performance. *The monologue is bit rushed . . . but her facial expressions are superb,* she thought. She spotted Elizabeth and Enid standing outside the bar, watching anxiously. Maria secretly gave them a brief, hopeful smile.

Reggie ended her "call" and folded up the compact phone. "Thanks, Maria," she said, handing it back to her. "I'm glad Elizabeth was able to reach me."

"You're very welcome," Maria replied, slipping the phone back into her bag. "I know with Elizabeth it's always something vital."

Reggie introduced Maria to Gordon and to Geneva Clark. "Geneva is a painter and sculptor," Reggie said. "She just arrived a little while ago from a two-week trip to London."

Maria shook hands with them, then glanced at Reggie, trying to understand exactly what was going on with her. Reggie seemed to like Geneva Clark, and Maria was almost positive it wasn't an act.

"Elizabeth Wakefield. What a coincidence,"

Gordon commented after the introductions had been made. "I just spoke with her this morning."

Reggie smiled. "She's fabulous, isn't she? Everyone says Elizabeth is the hottest new voice in the fashion industry. And from working with her, I have to agree."

"I've never met her," Gordon said. "But I have a meeting with her tomorrow."

Geneva Clark reached over and daintily picked out a cashew from the crystal bowl on the bar. "I know an *Alice* Wakefield," she mentioned casually. "I wonder if they're related."

Maria blanched at the mention of Elizabeth's mother's name. "Distantly, maybe," she uttered in a strangled voice. *As in the distance between L.A. and Sweet Valley,* she added silently.

Geneva Clark pulled the nut bowl closer. "Gordon, you remember Alice Wakefield, the designer who decorated my loft last year? I'm having her redo the beach house."

"Vaguely," Gordon replied.

Maria nervously fingered the clasp of her leather bag. *That woman is going to ruin everything,* she worried.

Gordon turned to Reggie. "Elizabeth Wakefield wants to tell me about an idea she has for *Flair.* Do you know anything about it?"

"No, I don't," Reggie replied brightly. "I've been assisting her on several different projects—it could be any one of them. But I'll give you a tip,

Gordon. If Elizabeth Wakefield offers you an idea, you should grab it. Other magazines have been clamoring to recruit her away from *Flair* since the day she arrived."

"Interesting," Gordon replied, cupping his chin with his hand. "I'm looking forward to meeting her."

OK! Maria cheered silently. Elizabeth would finally get to present her idea for "Free Style" to someone who took her seriously.

"Thanks for your advice, Reggie," Gordon said. "Meeting you may be one of the best things that ever happened to me. For several reasons," he added in a low, sexy voice.

Maria glanced at Geneva Clark to see her reaction. To her surprise, the woman seemed totally oblivious. She was munching salted nuts with a perfectly contented look on her face.

Just then she stood up and smoothed her hands over her exquisite green dress. "I'm going to go check out the buffet," she announced. "After two weeks of that ghastly British cuisine I'm *starving.*"

"That's a great idea," Maria blurted.

Geneva winked, then shot Gordon a teasing look. "I'd better get my fill now because I know there won't be anything good to eat in your apartment."

His apartment? Maria silently shrieked.

"You're right," Gordon said, chuckling as he rose to his feet. "I'll go with you." He invited Maria and Reggie to join them, but Reggie declined for them both.

The instant Gordon and Geneva left, Elizabeth and Enid came rushing over to the bar. Reggie slumped onto the barstool and burst out laughing.

"What's so funny?" Maria demanded.

"*You,*" Reggie gasped. "You should have seen your face when Geneva said that Gordon didn't have any food in his apartment." She started laughing again. "Geneva Clark is Gordon's twin sister."

Maria folded her arms and shot her a pointed look. "Why didn't you tell me?"

"I'm sorry about that," Reggie said. "But right before you came in, Geneva was complaining that everyone at this party considered her to be nothing more than Gordon Lewis's sister and that she was tired of being introduced that way."

"What about you and Gordon?" Elizabeth asked.

Reggie smiled brightly. "Well . . . it's still too early to know for sure, but I have a good feeling about us."

"All right!" Maria exclaimed.

Todd felt like a zombie when he arrived for his photo shoot with Quentin Berg on Friday morning. Although the bed in his apartment was an improvement over Ken's lumpy couch, Todd's neighbors had kept him awake all night. The shouting next door had continued until four A.M. Five minutes later country western music had started blaring from the apartment below his. *But I'm here on time,* Todd congratulated himself.

After his sessions with the makeup artist and hair stylist, Todd went to the wardrobe room to change into his first outfit for the day: bright orange moleskin pants topped with a royal blue velvet jacket and a paisley ascot tied at his throat. *What kind of guy would dress like this?* he asked himself incredulously.

Todd returned to the main area of the photography studio. Everyone was rushing around, preparing for the shoot. "Where's Simone?" Todd asked one of the technicians working the lights.

"Good question," the man replied. "She's lucky Quentin had a meeting this morning. But would you mind stepping just a few feet to the left? You're blocking our mark."

"Sorry," Todd mumbled.

He ambled over to the couch in the corner of the studio, where he wouldn't be in anyone's way.

An hour later Todd was still sitting there. Simone hadn't arrived yet, and Quentin had called to say that his meeting was running late. The whole crew was freaking out about being thrown off schedule. Todd wished he could take a long nap, but he knew he'd be in big trouble if he messed up his appearance.

Finally Simone strutted into the studio with her hand on her hip, looking very sexy in a skintight, shiny green jumpsuit and black leather boots. She struck a pose and pivoted in a complete circle, her black hair swirling around her face.

But watching her, Todd felt a slight twinge of disappointment. He recalled the delight of seeing

Elizabeth each morning at school . . . in the hall outside the *Oracle* office . . . at her locker. . . . *But Elizabeth isn't my girlfriend anymore,* he reminded himself with a swift mental kick. *Simone is.*

Todd rushed over to her, but before he could kiss her, she turned away.

"Time for that later," Simone said. "First, will someone please get me a mineral water!"

Just then Quentin and Jessica walked in, laughing at some inside joke.

Todd caught a glimpse of the sudden fierce look in Simone's eyes just before she grabbed him and planted a big, sloppy kiss on his lips. He tried to respond, but he was haunted by the suspicion that Simone was only putting on a show for Quentin and Jessica. The thought gave him a cold, hollow feeling in his gut.

When the kiss was over, Simone smiled sweetly at Todd and wiped a spot next to his mouth with her fingertips. "I think I've just messed up the makeup artist's hard work," she said, giggling.

Todd returned the smile, pushing aside his doubts. He didn't want to believe her affection was just an act. "I moved into my own apartment yesterday," he told her. "We'll be able to see each other whenever we want."

Simone wrapped her arms around his neck. "That's great, Todd."

He felt reassured by her reaction. "How about coming over for dinner tonight?" he suggested.

Jessica chuckled. "Quentin and I would love to come," she interjected, flashing Simone a catty look. "But we're already committed to another engagement."

"Well, *I* wouldn't miss dinner at your place for anything," Simone told Todd. "By the way, you look really hot in that suit. I think I'll buy it for you to wear next time we go out." Then she gave him another big kiss.

Sitting behind Leona's desk, Elizabeth waited for Gordon Lewis, who was due to arrive any second. She was wearing a pale gray skirt and matching vest with a pink, short-sleeved blouse. Elizabeth thought the outfit gave her a polished, professional image. *But what if Gordon takes one look at me and guesses I'm only sixteen?* she worried.

Elizabeth realized her hands were shaking. "Slow, deep breaths," she told herself, trying to calm her shaky nerves.

At the sound of the buzzer she jumped. Enid's voice came over the speaker. "Gordon Lewis is here to see you, Ms. Wakefield."

Elizabeth took one last calming breath. "Show him in, please," she answered. She dried her clammy palms on the front of her skirt and rose to her feet.

The moment the door opened, Elizabeth put on her best version of a self-confident smile. "Good morning, Gordon," she said, stepping out from behind the desk. "I'm so pleased to meet you at last." She shook his hand firmly.

Gordon raised his eyebrows in a look of mild surprise. "The pleasure is mine."

Elizabeth slipped behind the desk again and gestured toward the chair across from hers. "Please, have a seat. Would you like some coffee?"

Gordon sat down and linked his fingers across one knee. "Thanks, I would."

Elizabeth pressed the phone intercom button. "Enid, two coffees, please." She sat back and braced her elbows on the arms of the chair. "It'll just be a minute."

"You're much younger than I'd expected," Gordon commented.

Elizabeth chuckled good-naturedly. "Child prodigy," she replied. "That's what Leona calls me."

The door opened and Enid came in, carrying a tray with a pot of coffee, two china cups, spoons, cream, and sugar. Elizabeth thought she looked totally convincing as a secretary, wearing a dark blue dress and loose-fitting jacket, with a burgundy scarf draped around her neck.

After Enid served the coffee, she turned to Elizabeth and winked discreetly. "Will there be anything else, Ms. Wakefield?"

"Thanks, that'll do for now," Elizabeth answered.

"I'm surprised Leona hasn't approached me about this idea of yours," Gordon said, eyeing her over the rim of his coffee cup. "That is the usual way things are handled around here."

Elizabeth swallowed hard. "Yes, well . . . Leona

had some other matters to attend to and insisted I handle this project on my own."

Gordon seemed satisfied with her answer. Relieved, Elizabeth picked up the phone, pressed the numbers for Reggie's extension, and asked her to come in.

"He's there?" Reggie gasped.

Elizabeth smiled evenly. "And please bring the materials we went over this morning."

Reggie entered a moment later, carrying large boards with blown-up versions of the sample readers' columns Elizabeth had written. Even dressed in neutral colors—a dark brown silk blouse and skirt and a long tan jacket—Reggie seem to project a bright, colorful image.

Gordon smiled warmly as he shook Reggie's hand. Elizabeth noticed he held it a second longer than professional courtesy would require. "It's nice to see you again," he said.

Reggie nodded and smiled, as if she didn't trust herself to speak. She helped Elizabeth set up the boards, then took a seat next to Gordon.

Elizabeth briefly presented her idea. "'Free Style' would be a monthly column, selected from reader submissions. We'll announce a monthly theme in a prior issue and invite readers to share their thoughts on the subject." She glanced at Gordon Lewis, trying to gauge his reaction. He seemed to be listening attentively, but his serious, thoughtful expression gave no hint to his feelings.

"These are examples of what we expect to print," Elizabeth continued, pointing to her samples. "We want our readers to feel that *Flair* is their magazine, the source they turn to—and trust—for the latest fashion and beauty information. And the best way for us to develop loyal readership is to allow *them* to become part of *us*." She paused. "That's the reasoning behind 'Free Style.'"

Elizabeth finished making her presentation and turned to Gordon. Squeezing her hands together behind her back, she waited for him to say something. He was silent for a moment, and her heart started sinking. *He hates my idea,* she thought.

"I love it," Gordon said finally.

Elizabeth's eyes widened. "You do?" she squeaked. She cleared her throat. "I mean, I thought you would appreciate the concept."

"Absolutely," Gordon said. "And since it comes from you, who by all accounts represent the future of the fashion world, I'm sure it'll be a hit."

Elizabeth and Reggie exchanged victorious looks.

"There's a board meeting scheduled this afternoon at four o'clock," Gordon told them. "I'd like you both to be there." He shook hands with Elizabeth, then turned to Reggie. "Do you have a minute?" he asked.

"Sure," Reggie answered hesitatingly. She walked out of the office with him.

Elizabeth sat down heavily and closed her eyes. *We did it!* she realized. She was finally going to get the chance to present her idea to the board.

A moment later Reggie waltzed back in, her brown, almond-shaped eyes glittering. She closed the door and leaned back against it. "He asked me out for dinner Saturday night."

"That's fantastic!" Elizabeth cheered. She rushed over and gave Reggie a big hug. "But I'm not surprised," she added.

"At last my life is coming together," Reggie said dreamily.

"Jessica, where's my mineral water?" Simone screeched from the makeup table.

On the other side of the main studio area Jessica sighed wearily and brushed the sand off her hands. She was setting up a fake beach scene for the next layout and resented having to stop to cater to the impossible brat. But Simone's cries were too loud and shrill to ignore. She'd been in an especially nasty mood ever since Todd had left the studio a few hours earlier.

Jessica stepped out of the huge sandbox and went over to the cooler in a corner of the room. She'd stocked the cooler with mineral water and celery sticks in anticipation of Simone's constant demands. *I'll have to remember to treat my underlings with more class when I'm a supermodel,* she thought, squeezing the neck of a water bottle as if it were Simone's skinny white throat.

Shelly Fabian, the makeup artist, was an easygoing woman with smooth ebony skin, ample hips, and long skinny braids woven with colorful glass beads. She flashed a grateful smile as Jessica approached the table.

Simone was sitting with her legs stretched out in front of her, her arms folded tightly across her chest and her bottom lip curled in a sullen pout. Jessica thought she looked like a bad-tempered string bean. "Will there be anything else, Simone?" she asked, her voice dripping with sarcastic sweetness.

"I'll let you know," Simone replied snidely.

Shelly snorted. "Now, maybe I can get this eyeliner on your face before it goes out of style?"

Simone flashed her a nasty look, then grabbed the plastic bottle from Jessica's outstretched hand. "This is the wrong brand!" Simone complained, throwing the bottle on the floor. "Jessica, I know you're not the brightest kid in the world, but you can't be *that* dumb!"

Standing behind Simone, Shelly rolled her eyes.

Jessica stifled a giggle. "That was the only kind they had downstairs today."

"You're lying," Simone spat accusingly.

Jessica shrugged. "Call down to the cafeteria and ask them yourself if you don't believe me."

"Can I please get back to work?" Shelly asked impatiently, a cosmetic brush poised in her hand.

Simone pursed her lips and raised her chin. "No," she snapped. "Not until I get my mineral water."

"But the girl said they don't have it," Shelly argued, clearly losing her temper.

Simone sneered condescendingly. "This is a very big city. I'm sure they have my French mineral water *somewhere*. Go out and buy the *right* brand," she ordered Jessica. "And please try not to mess up again."

Quentin came over and gave Jessica a kiss on the cheek. "The beach set looks great," he commented. "You did a nice job. The red and blue towels were a perfect choice."

"Thanks," Jessica said, giving him a big smile. She glanced at Simone and was incredibly pleased with the look of pure venom in the model's eyes. Even though Jessica wasn't really in love with Quentin, she did love the effect their relationship had on Simone.

"OK, let's hurry up over here," Quentin said. "We're on a tight schedule this afternoon and already running late."

Simone crossed her arms and shot him a defiant look. "We're going to be running a whole lot later if Jessica doesn't figure out how to *read*, because I'm not moving from this chair until I have my mineral water."

Quentin exhaled loudly. "We don't have time for this, Simone," he warned. He turned to go.

"Well, I'm on a tight deadline too," Simone announced. "I need to get ready for my dinner with Todd, so you've got until four o'clock to finish this job."

Quentin stiffened. He turned around slowly, his eyes narrowed and shooting sparks at Simone. Jessica noticed Shelly moving away cautiously.

"What did you say?" Quentin demanded, his voice steady and cold.

"You heard me," Simone shot back.

A hush came over the studio. All work stopped. Jessica noticed the wary looks being exchanged among the crew members.

An angry red flush rose in Quentin's face. "OK, Simone. Have it your way. If you're in such a hurry, why don't get out of here *right now?*"

Simone blanched, obviously thrown off guard by his anger. "That's OK," she murmured defensively. "I signed on to do this shoot, and I'll do it."

"You don't understand," Quentin spat, emphasizing each word, "so let me make it clear. We won't be needing you after all, Simone."

Simone gaped at him, visibly alarmed. "But the shoot . . ."

"You're free to go, Simone," he stated evenly. "Jessica can do the shoot."

Yes, yes, yes! Jessica silently cheered.

"Quentin, I won't forget this . . . *ever*," Simone growled, her nostrils flaring.

"See that you don't," he replied smoothly.

Simone shot Jessica a look of pure loathing. Then she executed a perfect catwalk turn and stormed out of the studio.

Jessica watched her go, savoring the delicious victory. This was an even better break than she'd dared hope for!

"Back to work, everyone," Quentin barked. "Let's get you to wardrobe, Jessica."

"You bet!" Jessica replied eagerly, her heart leaping.

A short time later Jessica strutted into the main area of the studio, wearing a shimmering blue maillot with a long, diaphanous cover-up wrapped loosely around her hips. No one paid much attention to her except for a harried technician who called out to everyone that they were ready to begin the shoot.

Across the room someone replied, "Finally!"

Jessica was undaunted by everyone's apparent lack of appreciation. She'd studied her reflection in the dressing-room mirror and knew without a doubt that she looked totally fantastic. Filled with self-confidence, she made her way through the maze of equipment and cables to the beach set she'd helped create.

"All right!" Quentin cheered as he strolled into the studio. "Thanks to Jessica, we just might get this shoot finished in time. Who's working the breezes?" he asked.

A lanky, gray-haired technician jogged over with a small, battery-operated fan in his hand. "Right here, Quentin."

"Keep it soft to start," Quentin told him. "I want enough to flutter the hair around her face without pushing it back."

"You got it," the technician responded.

Quentin shot orders to the lighting crew, snapped his fingers at the guy operating the sound system, and winked at Jessica. "Let's begin!" he announced.

To the driving beat of techno music on CD, Jessica posed and preened for the camera. Quentin kept a running monologue going, directing her moves and calling for her to express various emotions as he snapped photo after photo. ". . . Now step to the left . . . sideways . . . flash me that gorgeous, sexy smile . . . and those eyes . . . I'm drowning in those ocean blue eyes. . . ." At one point his compliments were so outrageous, Jessica tipped her head back and burst out laughing.

"Beautiful!" Quentin exclaimed. "Laugh for me again, baby."

Jessica giggled, then whirled around and gave him a saucy look over her shoulder, her movements in sync with the music.

Quentin whistled. "You're beautiful!"

Jessica tucked her arms behind her back and tipped her head, letting the breeze from the fan blow her hair across her face. Quentin moved closer for a few shots, then slowly circled to the side of the sandbox for different angles.

This is what I was meant to do, Jessica realized. Modeling was more than fun. Being in front of the camera made her feel joyously alive, filled with pure energy. When Quentin called for a break, she was surprised to find that they'd been shooting for two solid hours, minus a few minutes here and there for wardrobe changes.

Quentin gave her a kiss on the cheek. "Good work, Jessica. I'm proud of you."

Then one of the crew members handed her a bottle of cold mineral water. Jessica realized it had come from the supply she'd brought in for Simone.

Jessica grinned, her whole body radiating with the glow of victory. *Look out, Simone!* she thought, raising the bottle in a silent toast to her absent archenemy. *I'm moving into your top spot.*

That afternoon Elizabeth and Reggie exchanged nervous glances as they sat at the long conference table, surrounded by the members of the editorial board. Elizabeth's heart was firmly lodged in her throat, and her whole body was shaking. Even the decor of the executive meeting room was imposing, with dark wood paneling on the walls and crystal chandeliers hanging from the ceiling.

Gordon stood at a podium at the head of the table, calling the meeting to order with an air of supreme authority. Elizabeth had been intimidated that morning when she'd faced him in Leona's office, but this was a million times worse. Everything about him shouted "power," from his dark pinstriped suit to his deep, steady voice. *What am I doing here?* Elizabeth thought, panic rising within her.

Gordon briefly introduced the idea of the reader column, then glanced at his watch. Obviously annoyed, he turned to Elizabeth. "It's after four-thirty. I don't know how much longer we can wait for Leona."

Elizabeth gulped. "Leona?"

"You did inform her of this meeting?" he asked, pinning Elizabeth with a sharp look.

Elizabeth nodded, her eyes wide. "Yes . . . but Leona had an emergency to take care of this afternoon," she improvised. "She said she'd try to get back in time for the meeting, but if not, we should go ahead and present the proposal to the board." Elizabeth held her breath, waiting for his next move. *What if he throws us out of the meeting?* she worried.

But Gordon seemed to accept the explanation. He introduced Elizabeth and Reggie, then turned the meeting over to them.

Elizabeth felt strangely lightheaded as she and Reggie stepped up to the podium. The reality of the situation pressed down on her with terrible force. Her legs were like rubber, her throat dry, and for one long, horrifying moment, her mind went completely blank.

Then Reggie discreetly pinched her arm, and the stinging pain jolted Elizabeth out of her daze. "Good afternoon," she said, her voice trembling slightly. "I'm here to tell you about 'Free Style,' an exciting new concept for increasing *Flair* readership through maximized reader loyalty."

As Elizabeth gave an overview of her idea, her confidence increased. It gratified her to see the attentive expressions around the table. The sample columns and promotional copy she'd written seemed to go over particularly well. "'Free Style' will be the bridge between the real woman and the fashion fantasy," Elizabeth declared, her voice clear and strong now. "But of course, a new idea must also be measured by its bottom-line projections." She turned the presentation over to Reggie.

"We fashion editors face a daunting challenge in presenting today's look to today's woman," Reggie began, gripping the sides of the podium. "Reader loyalty is our strongest weapon in a fiercely competitive market. We estimate 'Free Style' will increase *Flair* readership by twenty to thirty percent over the first three years of implementation." Reggie paused. "But unlike other promotional programs, 'Free Style' will utilize resources that are currently available or that can be acquired with minimum expense."

Elizabeth felt giddy with relief when the presentation was over. She and Reggie thanked the board members for their time and offered to answer any of their questions or concerns about "Free Style."

"I think this is a marvelous project," one woman commented. "Have you considered targeting various age ranges of readers?"

"No, we haven't," Elizabeth replied. "But that's a good idea. It would be interesting to look at a similar theme from the thirty-year-old, twenty-year-old, and teen points of view."

Others offered their opinions and suggestions, and a lively conversation developed around the table. It was obvious that "Free Style" was a hit. Elizabeth felt a rush of pleasure swelling inside her. *The editorial board of L.A.'s hottest fashion magazine is discussing my idea,* she marveled to herself.

"I think we're ready to go for a vote on this

matter," Gordon said, stepping up to the podium.

Elizabeth held her breath. *It's really happening!* she thought. She glanced at Reggie, who smiled back with a look of excited anticipation in her eyes.

Suddenly the double doors flew open. Elizabeth turned to see what had happened—and froze, her heart in her throat.

Leona was standing in the doorway, braced with crutches, her brown eyes flashing with rage.

Chapter 5

A hush fell over the conference table as Leona limped into the room. Despite the crutches she looked as sharp and polished as usual, in a short-skirted herringbone suit with black suede trim. A taupe silk blouse, gold knot earrings, and a gold chain necklace complemented the outfit. Her hair was impeccably arranged in a sleek, straight style, not a single dark blond strand out of place.

Leona was dressed for battle.

What is she doing here? Elizabeth wondered. A cold feeling of dread enveloped her, weighing her down until she felt as if she might sink into the plush gray carpet under her feet. Next to her Reggie uttered a soft groan.

"Sorry I'm late," Leona stated evenly as she lowered herself into a chair at the end of the table.

Gordon stared at her incredulously. "What happened? Were you in an accident?"

"Yes, but lucky for me I'm back in time for this meeting." She fixed Elizabeth with a piercing glare.

Elizabeth swallowed hard and lowered her eyes. *How did Leona find out?* she wondered.

"We're just about to vote on the proposal for 'Free Style,'" Gordon told Leona. "Your child prodigy has handled the presentation admirably," he added.

"My child prodigy?" Leona shrieked. "Not in this lifetime! After all I've done for you, Elizabeth! How could you turn on me like this?"

Elizabeth gulped. She wanted to say something in her own defense, but her throat felt like stone. All she could do was shake her head mutely.

Leona turned to Reggie. "And you! You're never going to get away with this! You can kiss your career good-bye. I'll see to it that you never work in fashion editing again."

Gordon raised his hands, his expression grave. "You'd better explain yourself, Leona," he demanded.

"That girl is an *intern!*" Leona responded, pointing at Elizabeth. "She's a high-school kid and a conniving, no-good thief. With Reggie's help she stole *my* idea for 'Free Style'—along with most of my proposal."

"These are very serious accusations," Gordon challenged. "You'd better have proof."

"Of course I have proof," Leona replied. "Memos, copies, computer files—I have tons of documentation."

All of it false! Elizabeth's mind screamed.

"*You* stole the idea from Elizabeth," Reggie accused hotly.

Leona shot her a withering look. "Is that what she told you?" She uttered a quick, nasty laugh. "Elizabeth seems to be an accomplished liar. She managed to fool me and apparently everyone else," she said, gazing at the others around the table.

Facing the icy stares of the board members, Elizabeth opened her mouth to protest, but only a strangled sound came up from her throat.

Gordon looked directly at Reggie, his blue eyes filled with accusation. "You knew Elizabeth was an intern," he charged.

Reggie nodded solemnly. "But I can explain—"

"Never mind," he said tersely, cutting her off. "The situation is painfully clear."

"Gordon, if you'd only hear me out," Reggie pleaded.

His expression hardened. "This meeting is adjourned. You're both fired. I'll phone security and have them send someone up to escort you out of the building."

Elizabeth reeled back as if she'd been socked in the face. Her legs felt unsteady, and bright colors swirled before her eyes. She clutched the back of a chair to keep from crumpling into a heap on the carpet.

I was so close, Elizabeth thought, her heart sinking. But she felt even worse for Reggie, whose dream of finally being with Gordon seemed shattered beyond hope.

Todd swiped the back of his hand across his sweaty forehead as he scanned the directions on the box of scalloped potatoes mix. "Where am I going to get a two-quart casserole pan?" he wondered aloud, frustrated.

Todd desperately wanted this dinner to turn out perfect. He'd invited his parents and Simone and was eager to prove to all three that he could make it on his own. He'd bought a ton of groceries and a cookbook and had spent hours preparing the main course—marinated pork roast with garlic and peppercorns.

With the roast baking in the oven, Todd was concentrating on the side dishes. "A two-quart casserole, huh?" he grumbled. "Let's see what we've got." He knelt in front of the cavernous bottom cupboard and searched through the kitchen paraphernalia that had come with the apartment. "What junk!" he muttered, pulling out a greasy, stained plastic bowl. He found a bread pan with a hole rusted through the bottom, tons of mangled spoons and forks, assorted parts to an electric coffeepot, and a mass of tangled extension cords—but nothing even close to a two-quart casserole pan.

Todd noticed everything in the cupboard was sprinkled with what looked like black grains of wild rice or caraway seeds. *I guess a gourmet slob used to live here,* he thought.

As he was tossing the stuff back into the cupboard he smelled something burning. "What the—," he began, springing to his feet. A veil of smoke was seeping out from around the oven door.

"My roast!" he moaned. Todd reached for the chrome handle on the oven door, which was as hot as a sizzling frying pan. "Ouch!" he yelped, jerking his hand away. He grabbed a thick wad of paper towels to use as a makeshift potholder and yanked the oven door open.

Clouds of smoke billowed out, choking him. Todd held his breath as he lifted the smoldering pan out of the oven and dumped the whole thing into the sink. The tender, juicy, flavorful pork roast of his dreams had turned into a shriveled-up, smoldering black lump.

"No problem," Todd told himself, trying to pretend he was calm. He went around the apartment, opening all the windows to let in some fresh air. So he'd change the menu; big deal. *To what?* he wondered.

Todd returned to the kitchen and surveyed the contents of his refrigerator. He'd thoroughly washed the interior before putting away the groceries, but the faint odor of sour milk still lingered. "Chicken," Todd said, sighing with relief. He'd bought a stuffed, precooked chicken that only needed to be heated for twenty minutes. It even came with its own disposable baking pan. *Am I prepared or what?* Todd mentally congratulated himself.

Todd peeled off the plastic wrapper. He figured after the chicken was done, he could use the same pan for the scalloped potatoes. *My dinner is saved,* he thought. He popped the chicken into the oven, then set about to clean up the evidence of his pork disaster.

After dumping the roast into the garbage, Todd tried to wash out the pan. The black gunk that coated the bottom was baked on solid. He was tempted to throw the pan away too, but it had come with the apartment. Todd's lease specified that if anything was missing when he moved out, he'd have to forfeit part of his security deposit.

Todd decided to let the pan soak for a few days, hoping some of the mess would dissolve. But he didn't want to leave it in the sink where his parents would see it.

After considering several hiding places, Todd carried the pan into his bedroom and pushed it under his bed. While he was there, he noticed more of the black sprinkles he'd found in the kitchen. *That's strange,* he thought. He picked up a few between his fingers and spread them out on his palm for a closer look.

Todd suddenly realized what they actually were. Disgusted, he shook his hand vigorously. "This place is covered with mice droppings!" He groaned as he rushed into the bathroom to scrub his hands.

A few minutes later, as he was changing into a clean pair of jeans and shirt, Todd realized that the odor of burned food was still pretty strong, even with all the windows open. Actually it seemed to be getting *worse.*

He stopped in the middle of buttoning his shirt and sniffed the air. "No!" he shouted, bolting out of the room. "Not my chicken too!"

Again the kitchen was filled with dense gray clouds. Holding his arm across his face to cover his nose and mouth, Todd groped his way to the stove. When he opened the oven, gusts of pungent smoke billowed out.

Todd dumped the smoldering chicken into the sink and turned on the faucet. "Now what?" he cried, totally discouraged. Obviously there was something wrong with the oven—which meant the scalloped potatoes were off the list too. That seriously limited his options for dinner.

He waved a damp towel in the air to move the smoke toward the open kitchen window. Then he searched through his stock of food for something else to cook. He'd wanted to serve something fancy, impressive—but it seemed his choices were limited to buttered toast, canned soup, macaroni and cheese, or peanut butter and jelly.

He settled for macaroni and cheese and toast. *Pasta and bread won't be so bad,* Todd assured himself. After all, lots of fancy restaurants served meals that were basically nothing more than pasta and bread.

Preparing the toast was a bit tricky because the old toaster didn't push the bread up when it was done. The first slices he tried added more smoke to the gray haze that still lingered at the ceiling. He had to watch over the toast as it browned, then pull it out with wooden tongs.

Todd dragged the small kitchen table into the living room and set it with the mismatched plastic plates and cups he'd found in the cupboards. After he laid out the food, he stood back and frowned. "This is pathetic," he said.

He considered running down to the gas station on the corner to use the pay phone to call out for pizza or Chinese food. But at that moment the doorbell rang. Todd gulped. It was too late to change the menu.

This is it, he thought, bracing himself as he opened the door. His parents were standing there . . . and right behind them was Simone.

Lying in a patio chair in her backyard, Elizabeth felt totally drained. Scenes from her disaster that day kept flashing through her mind: images of Leona's rage . . . accusing looks from the board members . . . Gordon Lewis's cold expression as he'd called for a security officer to escort Elizabeth and Reggie from the building. . . .

But worst of all was the visible heartbreak on Reggie's face. Elizabeth squeezed her eyes shut and groaned softly. No matter how much it hurt, her brain kept rehashing the horror of those final minutes of the board meeting.

At first she'd been in a state of shock. During the bus ride home from Los Angeles that afternoon, she'd felt completely numb. The depression had set in a short time later, pressing down on Elizabeth as though she were carrying a ton of granite on her head.

Elizabeth shifted her position in the chair and gazed absently into the crystal blue water of her family's pool. She'd come outside that evening with the intention of swimming laps, hoping the exercise would help stop the mental torture for a while. But now she couldn't force herself to move from the chair. She had no energy for swimming. She wondered if she'd have enough to get herself back into the house.

I lost everything, Elizabeth realized. Not only had her plan backfired, destroying her career opportunities at *Flair* and at every other magazine owned by Mode, but she'd also ruined the life of her only friend in the company. *Poor Reggie would've been better off if she'd never met me,* Elizabeth thought sadly.

"Hey, Liz!" Jessica called as she bounded outside and ran over to her twin. "You'll never guess what happened today. I—yes, me, Jessica Wakefield—will be appearing in a huge swimsuit layout in next month's issue of *Flair!*"

She plunked herself into a lawn chair and scooted it closer to Elizabeth. "It was fabulous!" Jessica gushed, leaning back and kicking her legs in the air. "I can see why everyone thinks Quentin is such great photographer." She bolted upright and giggled. "Because he really is. He's a great artist, but he also makes the work fun. He had me laughing. . . ." She sighed dreamily.

Elizabeth forced herself to smile.

"But that's not the best part," Jessica added. "Guess

why I'm going to be in the layout—instead of Simone."

Elizabeth shrugged. "Haven't got a clue."

Jessica crossed her legs and grinned smugly. "Simone was acting like the biggest brat in the whole world today, worse than usual. She came in *hours* late, for starters, wearing a green satin jumpsuit that looked like it had been painted on. Then after lunch, while the rest of us were working our heads off to get everything set up for the shoot, she decided that mineral water from Maine wasn't good enough for her."

Seems Simone's day was almost as bad as mine, Elizabeth thought dryly as her twin filled her in on the details of her victory.

"It was so wonderful, Liz," Jessica said. "Quentin just kicked her out and put me in. Then she stormed off in a huff, and I swear, her skin looked as green as her outfit! He's taking me to a celebrity party at Planet Hollywood tonight," she added excitedly.

"That's great, Jess," Elizabeth responded, genuinely pleased that things had worked out so well for her twin.

"This internship is turning out better than I'd dreamed," Jessica declared. "But the best part of it is that you and I are doing it together."

Elizabeth exhaled a shaky breath. "Together," she repeated.

"Wouldn't it be wonderful if you and I both ended up working at *Flair* permanently?" Jessica asked dreamily.

Elizabeth caught her bottom lip between her teeth as she tried to control the flood of despair washing over her. But her sister's words had broken down the last of her defenses.

Powerless to stop herself, Elizabeth burst into tears.

Jessica was startled by Elizabeth's sudden reaction. "Liz, what's wrong?" she asked. "Is it Todd?" *Did that jerk do something else to twist the knife in her back?* she wondered hotly.

Elizabeth opened her mouth as if to speak, but she was sobbing too hard to answer.

Jessica reached across the gap that separated their chairs and hugged her sister. "He's not worth it, Liz," she whispered soothingly as she patted her twin's back. "Believe me, dating Simone is the perfect punishment for a guy who—"

Elizabeth shook her head. "No, not Todd," she sobbed.

Jessica leaned back and looked at her directly. "What is it, then?"

"Everything!" Elizabeth wailed. "I got fired."

Jessica's jaw dropped. "From *Flair?*" she asked in disbelief.

Elizabeth nodded as a flood of fresh tears streamed down her face.

"Why? What happened?"

Elizabeth drew a shaky breath. "It all started with an idea I'd had for the magazine . . . ," she began.

Jessica's reactions went from concern to bewilderment to pure hot anger as she listened to her sister's story. "Leona Peirson actually took your idea and passed it off as her own?" she raged.

Elizabeth nodded. "I might have never known about it if I hadn't listened to the tape recorder I found in her condo."

Jessica raised her eyebrows. "Her condo?"

Elizabeth laced her fingers around her raised knee. "Leona asked me to take care of her personal errands while she was recuperating in Lake Tahoe. She keeps a spare set of keys in her office."

Jessica exhaled sharply. "Leona stabs you in the back, then expects you to be her *maid?* What a snake!" she cried.

Elizabeth's lips twitched as if she were trying to smile. "That's exactly what I think of her." She went on to explain how she, Enid, Maria, and Reggie Andrews had tried to get back at Leona. "But the whole thing fell apart when she burst into the board meeting this afternoon," Elizabeth said, choking back a sob.

"How did Leona know you and Reggie would be there?" Jessica asked.

Elizabeth shrugged weakly. "I wondered that myself. But I guess it doesn't matter now."

"It's so *unfair!*" Jessica exclaimed. "That witch should've been the one to get fired—not you!"

Elizabeth sniffed. "*Fair* doesn't seem to mean much in the world of high-fashion publishing." She brushed the back of her hand across her damp cheek. "We gave it our best shot, though. I'm just sorry I've ruined Reggie's life in the process."

"Your plan wasn't half bad," Jessica admitted, impressed with her twin's daring creativity. "But you should've come to *me* in the first place." She gently squeezed Elizabeth's hand. "Enid and Maria may be good friends, but trust me—they're not too swift when it comes to being devious and manipulative. Those are *my* specialties."

Elizabeth sniffed and cracked a slight grin. "I'll keep that in mind."

"You do that," Jessica replied.

"I'm just glad it's over," Elizabeth breathed.

Jessica squeezed her bottom lip between her teeth. *No, it isn't over—not by a long shot,* she vowed to herself. *Leona Peirson is going to get exactly what she deserves.*

After all the times her older sister had come to her rescue, Jessica decided it was her turn to do the same for Elizabeth.

Chapter 6

"Did you enjoy working in Paris?" Todd's mother asked Simone during dinner.

Simone wrinkled her nose at the food on her plate. "Not really," she answered without looking up. "What's in this orange slop?"

Todd breathed an exasperated sigh. "I already told you," he reminded her. "Macaroni and cheese."

"It's very creamy," Mrs. Wilkins commented. "What brand did you use?"

Simone rolled her eyes and mumbled something under her breath.

Todd cringed, then turned to his mother. "I'm not sure what kind I bought," he answered. He'd already thrown away the box. And besides, he knew his mother had only asked to be polite.

"I think I'll have more of this toast," Mr. Wilkins announced as he added a few more slices to his plate. "It's delicious. Just the right amount of butter." When he tried to pass the serving platter to Simone, she waved it aside.

"Oh, please!" she whined, fingering the stiff collar of her bright blue dress. "The day I resort to eating buttered toast . . ." She didn't finish the sentence, but her sentiments were clear—she'd have to be desperate to eat the meal Todd had prepared.

Todd admitted to himself that the dinner was an unqualified disaster. His parents were trying too hard to be gracious, and Simone had been wearing a look of utter disgust since the moment she'd first walked into the apartment. Todd's one lucky break was that his shouting neighbors weren't home.

"I must admit buttered toast is one of my weaknesses," Mrs. Wilkins said, helping herself to another piece. "What are your favorite foods, Simone?"

Simone braced her elbows on the table, her hands under her chin. "Carrots, celery . . . I stick to fresh vegetables most of the time," she replied in a haughty tone. "Even if I weren't a top model, I'd still watch my weight. There's no excuse for a woman letting herself go."

Todd hadn't considered that she might be referring to his mother—until Simone turned to Emily Wilkins with a snide look and added, "No offense."

A bright red flush rose in his mother's face, her deep green eyes simmering. For a long, tense moment no one said a word. Todd shifted uneasily in his seat. The only person who didn't seemed to be

in a state of shock was Simone. She studied her fingernails, which were painted the same blue shade
as her dress. Finally Bert Wilkins broke the silence.
"So Todd, are getting yourself settled in?" he asked.

Todd shrugged. "I want to fix up the place a little."

"That would be nice," Emily Wilkins commented, pushing her short auburn hair behind her
ear. "Some fresh paint . . . maybe a few colorful
throw rugs . . ."

Simone snorted loudly. "A bulldozer would be
your best bet."

"I know this isn't the best apartment in the world,
Simone," Todd responded defensively. "I'm planning
to move to a nicer place as soon as I can afford to."

"I'll visit you when that happens, Todd,"
Simone replied coldly as she got up from the table.
"But in the meantime this place is giving me the
creeps." She pushed her fingers through her short
dark hair, then lowered her hand to her hip. With
her shoulders pressed back, hips jutted forward,
and nose stuck in the air, Simone sauntered out of
the apartment, slamming the door behind her.

Todd lowered his eyes, his face burning with
humiliation as he and his parents sat in awkward silence. Again it was his father who spoke first.
"Simone seems like a spirited girl," he remarked.

Mrs. Wilkins smiled wryly. "She certainly is."

Todd felt the macaroni and cheese sitting heavily in his stomach. He knew his parents were trying
to show their support for him, even though it was

obvious that he'd made a huge mistake—*several* huge mistakes.

Todd absently chewed off a corner of cold, greasy toast. *Man, do I miss Elizabeth!* he admitted silently. He decided it was time to tell Elizabeth the truth— that he still loved her and probably always would.

But before Todd could go to Elizabeth and beg her to forgive him, he first needed to break things off with Simone.

In the middle of the night Elizabeth was jostled from a deep sleep. She opened her eyes and saw her sister's shadowy form standing over her bed.

"The keys," Jessica whispered urgently, shaking Elizabeth's shoulders. "Wake up!"

"Stop it," Elizabeth groaned. Jessica shook her harder, nearly rattling her twin's teeth.

"All right, I'm awake!" Elizabeth muttered in self-defense. She sat up and pushed her hair back from her face. "What's wrong?"

"What did you do with Leona's keys?" Jessica asked.

Elizabeth exhaled wearily and glanced at the lighted digital display on her clock radio. "It's two o'clock in the morning," she whined.

Jessica sat down on the edge of the mattress. "Do you still have Leona's keys?"

Elizabeth nodded, yawning. "I never got around to putting them back in her desk."

"Yes!" Jessica cheered softly.

"Can I go back to sleep now?" Elizabeth grumbled as she lowered her head to her pillow.

"No way. Get up and put these on," Jessica ordered, dumping a few articles of clothing on Elizabeth's face.

Elizabeth shoved them aside and sat up again. "Maybe you should tell me what's going on, Jess."

"I've come up with a brilliant plan that might help prove the magazine idea was yours. But we really have to hurry," Jessica urged. "I'll fill you in about the details on the way."

Twenty minutes later Elizabeth was sitting in the passenger seat of the twins' Jeep, staring incredulously at her sister as they headed along the interstate toward L.A. "*That's* your brilliant plan, Jess? To sneak into Leona's condo and steal her tape recorder?"

Jessica shrugged. "Sure, why not? That tape is what clued you in to Leona's dirty dealing in the first place. Maybe when Gordon Lewis listens to it, he'll have a few doubts about her himself."

"I should have guessed," Elizabeth muttered, glancing at the black jeans and sweatshirt her twin had ordered her to wear. Jessica was dressed the same, and two black ski masks and four black leather gloves lay in a single heap between their seats.

Jessica shifted lanes to pass a slow-moving van. "What other choice do we have?" she asked.

"I don't care," Elizabeth replied tersely. "Turn around at the next exit because we aren't going through with it. Breaking and entering is a serious crime."

"You're absolutely right about that," Jessica said breezily. "But thanks to you and Leona's keys, we won't be *breaking* and entering—just entering."

"I think it's called 'illegal trespassing,'" Elizabeth retorted.

"Leona Peirson *invited* you to let yourself into the condo, right?" Jessica said.

Elizabeth folded her arms. "What's your point?" she asked wryly.

"Well," Jessica began, "Leona never actually *uninvited* you, did she?"

Elizabeth glared at her. "Jessica, she *fired* me."

Jessica shrugged. "It's not the same thing," she countered.

"It's close enough." Elizabeth turned toward the window and stared into the darkness. She thought back to Thursday afternoon, when she'd played the tape for Enid and Maria in Leona's condo. *Why didn't I grab it when I had the chance?* she wondered, mentally kicking herself.

"How can you possibly sit back and do nothing?" Jessica demanded. "Leona Peirson stabbed you in the back, and you're the one who's going to have to pay for it, Liz."

Elizabeth absently toyed with a loose thread on her sleeve. "I just want to put it behind me," she said tiredly.

"What about your plans of getting a summer job at *Flair,* maybe working as an editor someday?" Jessica asked pointedly. "Do you want to put all that behind you too?"

101

"I don't know." Elizabeth leaned her head back and sighed. "Having that tape might help clear my name, but it's so risky. . . ."

Jessica smiled broadly. "It would be so easy to sneak into her condo and get it. Leona wouldn't even know we were there." She giggled. "And even if she did wake up, she can't exactly chase us down on crutches."

Elizabeth nervously chewed her bottom lip. "It's totally crazy."

"Look at it this way. . . . What if you'd left your backpack at Leona's, with your all your school stuff," Jessica began. "And let's say you had a very important test tomorrow and you absolutely needed your books. Leona is sound asleep with a broken leg, and you have her keys."

Jessica tipped her head questioningly. "Would you rudely wake Leona up and ask for your bag, or would you politely let yourself into her condo and get the bag without bothering her?"

Elizabeth frowned, bemused. "I have no idea what you're talking about," she said.

"Pretend the tape recorder is your backpack and we don't want to disturb Leona while she's sleeping," Jessica explained breezily.

Elizabeth rolled her eyes, amazed at how far her twin's logic could stretch. "The tape recorder might not still be on the side table."

"It's worth a look," Jessica insisted.

Elizabeth pictured the side table in the living

room where she'd left the tape recorder. It wasn't too far from the front door, only five or six feet . . . just a few quick steps . . . a matter of seconds. . . . Elizabeth stiffened, shocked at the direction of her thoughts.

Then she recalled how devastated she'd been when Gordon Lewis had called security to have her and Reggie escorted from the Mode building. And she remembered Reggie's miserable expression. . . . Elizabeth squeezed her eyes shut and took a deep, shaky breath.

Jessica drummed her fingers on the steering wheel. "We're only minutes from L.A.," she pointed out. "It would be a shame to have come all this way for nothing."

Maybe if Gordon heard Leona's tape, he'd understand why Reggie helped me and would forgive her, Elizabeth thought. She caught her bottom lip between her teeth and gazed out the window. "Jessica, take the Ocean Lane exit and turn left at the first light," she whispered.

"All right, sis!" Jessica cheered.

Elizabeth nervously wrung her hands together, her stomach flipping and turning. *We have to at least try to get back that tape,* she reasoned. *There's no other choice.*

Chapter 7

When the twins arrived at Leona's condominium complex, Elizabeth was dismayed to see how well lighted the area was. Floodlights shone over the entrance to the main driveway, as if standing guard against trespassers. Ground lamps seemed to have been planted everywhere else.

But the cherry trees that surrounded the complex provided a solid trail of shadows. *This will work,* Elizabeth thought, willing herself to feel strong and confident—despite the nervous fluttering in her gut and the squeezing sensation in her throat.

Wearing black ski masks and gloves, the twins followed the shadows of the cherry trees around to Leona's building. The windows of her condo unit were completely dark. Elizabeth hoped it meant that Leona was sound asleep.

Elizabeth clenched her fist around Leona's keys to

keep them from jingling as she and Jessica stalked up to her second-floor condo. *This will work*, Elizabeth chanted over and over. She unlocked Leona's door and pushed it open, holding her breath. Jessica squeezed her hand as they tiptoed into the foyer.

Jessica kept watch at the entrance to the hallway that led to Leona's bedroom while Elizabeth slipped into the living room and carefully picked her steps toward the seating arrangement. Pale moonlight shone through the glass panels on the far wall, allowing her to make out the shapes of some of the furniture and miscellaneous objects among the shadows in the room.

Feeling her way with her hand along the back of the couches, Elizabeth located the side table. Immediately her fingers curled around a small, rectangular object. Elizabeth sighed with relief. Crouching down next to the table, she took out her flashlight and risked a quick peek to see that the tape was still in the tape recorder.

Yes! she silently cheered. Anxious to get away with her prize, Elizabeth hurried toward the doorway.

But as she crossed the room Elizabeth tripped over an unexpected suitcase lying on the floor and fell flat on her face with a heavy thud. Still clutching the tape recorder, she froze.

Suddenly Jessica was there, dragging her up by the arm. "Leona's coming!" she hissed.

Elizabeth's heart jumped to her throat. She grasped Jessica's hand and whispered, "Out the back!" They dashed into the kitchen, where a small light above the sink had been left on. The clop-thud pattern of footsteps sounded from the foyer. *Leona's right behind us!* Elizabeth's mind screamed. Gripped with panic, she raced to the sliding glass doors that opened to the second-floor deck. Her hand shook uncontrollably as she fumbled with the latch.

"Hurry!" Jessica urged.

Elizabeth tugged on the door, but it wouldn't budge. The clop-thud footsteps moved into the living room, drawing closer.

Elizabeth uttered a strangled groan from deep in her throat. Then Jessica crouched down and reached for a brass latch near the bottom of the door that Elizabeth hadn't noticed.

As the twins rushed outside, several outdoor lamps flashed on. The entire deck, including the stairs to the ground level, was caught in the bright, glaring light.

"This way," Jessica hissed. She swung her leg over the railing and lowered herself down the other side.

She'll break her neck! Elizabeth worried as she watched her twin shinnying down one of the support posts. Then she heard a sound at the door. In the space of a heartbeat Elizabeth shoved the tape recorder into her back pocket and leaped over the deck railing herself.

Gripping the post with her arms and legs, she inched downward. When her feet finally touched the ground, she and Jessica dove into the shadows.

Elizabeth glanced back and saw Leona standing on her deck, wearing a long white satin robe that shone in the light. Elizabeth's heart stopped for an instant, then she and Jessica took off running.

When they finally reached the Jeep, a Doberman pinscher with a bloodthirsty gleam in his eyes was standing next to it, blocking their path. The girls stopped for a moment, then gingerly stepped closer.

"Nice puppy," Elizabeth cooed, holding out her hand to let him sniff it.

The beast bared his teeth and growled.

"This is totally ridiculous," Jessica declared. She waved her fist at the dog and growled back. "We don't have time for this, so beat it!" she commanded.

To Elizabeth's surprise, the Doberman ducked his head and skulked away.

"What a way to start the weekend!" Jessica exclaimed as they jumped into the Jeep. She pulled off her ski mask and laughed. "We even had a wild animal to spice up the adventure. Do you think Leona recognized us?"

Elizabeth gulped. "I hope not." She peeled off her own mask and shook out her matted hair.

Jessica started the engine and headed back toward the interstate. "OK, let's check out the prize," she said. "I want to hear the tape."

Elizabeth pressed the play button and adjusted the volume. Leona's crisp, all-business voice filled the cab of the Jeep. Recognizing the letter to the head of marketing, Elizabeth fast forwarded the tape for a second, then let it resume playing.

"Letter to Jonah Hall, advertising," Leona was saying.

Elizabeth frowned. The incriminating memo that referred to her should have followed Leona's letter to the marketing department. "It's gone!" she cried. "The letter to Gordon about 'Free Style' isn't here anymore. Leona taped over it!"

"Let's listen to the whole tape," Jessica suggested. "Maybe you don't have the right place."

"No," Elizabeth argued. "I remember exactly where it was, right after the letter to Rupert Perry in marketing."

"Are you positive?" Jessica asked.

Elizabeth nodded, tears pooling in her eyes. "I guess it's really over now. Without that memo I don't have any evidence against Leona—and no hope of proving my innocence."

Todd knocked on the door of Simone's apartment Saturday afternoon, feeling confident that he'd made the right decision. They didn't belong together at all. If he'd needed any more proof of that fact, all he had to do was remember last night's dinner.

The door flew open and a tall, thin girl with bright red hair came bounding out, nearly bumping into him.

"Oh, hi!" she gushed, her blue-green eyes wide with surprise.

Todd realized that the girl's eyes were the same color as Elizabeth's, and a sharp, longing pain sliced through him. "I'm here to see Simone," he told her.

"I'm her roommate, Cecile," the girl said.

Todd nodded. He remembered speaking to her over the phone when he'd tried to reach Simone a few days earlier.

"Sorry I have to rush off," Cecile said, already stepping away as she spoke. "Simone's on the phone, but go in and make yourself comfy."

Todd thanked her and entered the apartment. Following the sound of Simone's voice, he walked into a huge living room with a high ceiling and lots of windows. Simone was sitting on the floor, leaning back against a pile of large cushions in a corner. She was wearing bright pink boxer shorts that showed off her long, shapely legs and a white cropped T-shirt that showed off quite a bit too.

"Todd, *darling*," she gushed loudly, clamping her hand loosely over the telephone mouthpiece. "It's so great to see you. I was getting so lonesome. Kick off your shoes and get comfy." She blew him a pouty kiss. "I'll meet you on that nice, soft couch in just a second—as soon as I finish taking care of a little business matter."

Todd shifted uneasily as she resumed her phone conversation. He suspected this wasn't going to be as easy as he'd hoped. Feeling incredibly out of place, he paced around the room, tapping his fingers against the sides of his thighs.

He'd never been in Simone's apartment before. Todd wondered how long it would take before he could afford something as nice. Her living room alone was more than twice the size of his place.

Todd tried not to eavesdrop on Simone's conversation, but she was practically screaming into the phone. He quickly realized she was talking to Quentin and that their "business matter"—whatever it was—wasn't going too well.

"Yes, that's right—Todd!" Simone was saying. "Todd is here. I'm thrilled. And no one cares what *you* think about it!"

Todd cringed. He didn't like the sound of that at all. The last thing he needed was to have Quentin mad at him. Without the support of the famous photographer, Todd knew his chances of making it big as a fashion model were dismal. He could be stuck in his dank, disgusting apartment, living with rodents and cockroaches, for a long time.

Simone cursed, then uttered a bitter laugh. "Yeah? Well, I think *you're* a dirty, rotten, scum-of-the-earth jerk!"

She slammed down the phone. "Quentin Berg can be such a creep."

Todd didn't know how to reply, so he simply shrugged.

Simone stood up and pushed her hands through her hair. The motion caused her T-shirt to slip higher, revealing more of her smooth white skin.

Todd stared at her blankly. Everything about

Simone—her body, her clothes, her expressions, the way she moved—was incredibly sexy. But seeing her now, Todd was surprised to realize that he felt absolutely no attraction to her.

Simone jutted her hip sideways and looped her thumbs into the waistband of her boxers. "You're standing there like you're ready to bolt," she pouted.

Todd rubbed his hand across the back of his neck. "Actually," he began, "I'm sort of in a hurry—"

"I'm really glad you're here," she interrupted, flashing him a sweet smile. "Now sit down, kick off your shoes, and relax. I'll be right back."

"No, wait," he protested.

Simone giggled. "I love it when you're eager. Don't worry, I'll just be two seconds." She disappeared through a set of swinging double doors, leaving him feeling utterly exasperated.

Maybe I should've broken up with her in a letter, Todd grumbled to himself as he sat on the edge of the couch. He glanced down at the toes of his basketball sneakers. *And I'm definitely keeping my shoes on!*

Nearly twenty minutes went by before Simone returned, carrying a tray of raw carrot sticks, two cartons of low-fat yogurt, and a large bottle of mineral water. "Here we are, sweetheart," she announced. "Lunch." She set the tray on the coffee table in front of the couch.

"Looks filling," Todd muttered sarcastically.

Simone giggled. "It's what models eat, Todd. Join the club."

"Thanks, Simone, uh . . . I didn't come here for lunch," he muttered awkwardly.

Simone snuggled up next to him on the couch. "I know, but it's the least I could do after you went to the trouble of preparing a home-cooked dinner last night." She leaned forward and picked up a carrot stick. "I had such a good time. Your parents are really nice," she added sweetly.

Todd gaped at her, bewildered by her sudden change of attitude. She had to be one of the weirdest girls he'd ever known. *Why was I even attracted to her in the first place?* he wondered. He remembered thinking she was gorgeous, an exotic combination of pale skin and black hair, with luscious full lips and a long, lean body. But now, watching her gnaw on the tip of a carrot stick with her pointy front teeth, she reminded him of a rodent. *She's freaky looking,* he thought. He was more anxious than ever to get out of there.

"Simone, we have to talk," Todd began evenly.

Simone rested her head on his shoulder. "I love these quiet times together, don't you?"

Todd shrugged away from her, putting distance between them. "It's over, Simone. I came here to tell you that I don't want to see you anymore."

Simone's sweet expression vanished and was replaced with a hateful stare. "Just like that?"

Todd nodded. "We've had some fun times, but it would never work between us in the long run. We'll both be happier if we go our separate ways."

112

"Save the sappy lines for your high-school girls!" Simone retorted. She jumped up and began pacing.

Todd rose to his feet. "Good-bye, Simone."

She whirled around and faced him with a fierce look in her eyes. "Fine, Todd, if that's what you want. But you can kiss your modeling career good-bye."

That stopped him. "What do you mean?" he asked, all of his nerves on alert.

Simone let out a nasty laugh. "I'm going to make you pay for this, Todd," she growled, stabbing the air between them with her carrot. "By the time I'm through with you, the closest thing you'll get to a modeling gig is if you become an escaped felon and they hang your picture up at the post office." With that, Simone stormed out of the room.

Todd's mind was reeling as he left her apartment and got into the elevator. He was glad that his relationship with Simone was finally over. But the notion that he'd just ended his career as well filled him with panic. He slumped against the elevator wall and hung his head. *Without modeling jobs my new independent lifestyle is going to be totally miserable,* he thought.

"I can't believe how much has happened in the past two weeks," Jessica commented to Amy Sutton and Lila Fowler that evening as she floated around her family's backyard pool on an inflatable raft.

Amy was lounging on a patio chair in a blue bikini. "I'm ready to go back to my own life," she said. "But I

113

really enjoyed working with my mom." Dyan Sutton was a sportscaster at WXAB, the local TV network where Amy had served as a production assistant.

Sitting on the edge of the pool in a white maillot, with her feet dangling in the water, Lila sighed wearily. "I'm just glad it's over," she proclaimed. "One more day of that internship, and they would've had to rush me to the hospital for exhaustion."

Jessica rolled her eyes. She knew that to Lila, "exhausting" meant having to answer phones while you were trying to touch up your manicure. Lila hadn't taken the internship program seriously from the start and had settled for a boring position as a receptionist at Fowler Enterprises, her father's computer company.

"My internship turned out great," Jessica said. "Quentin says I have what it takes to be a supermodel."

Lila snorted. "Yeah, right."

Jessica giggled. Besides being her best friend, Lila was also her biggest rival. "When we were at Planet Hollywood last night, he introduced me to some people from the Carlmary modeling agency," Jessica bragged. "And two nights before that I met Eddie Rook."

"Whoopee," Lila drawled, kicking droplets of water on Jessica.

"I also saw Tina Baker at the Edge," Jessica told Lila. "She remembered me from your parents' wedding."

Amy raised her knees and wrapped her arms

around her legs. "What's it like, going out with a guy that old?"

Jessica chuckled at the strange question. "He's in his early twenties," she countered. "I wouldn't call that old. Quentin is sort of a jerk, but he can help me get my career going, and that's what matters." She sighed. "I just wish it hadn't cost me my relationship with Cameron." Jessica closed her eyes as a pang of regret sliced through her heart like a knife. It hurt even to think about him and what might have been. . . .

"The guys at school are *so* boring," Amy complained.

"Most guys are," Lila replied, with a bitter edge in her voice.

"What about the one you met at camp?" Amy asked. "You haven't talked about him for a while."

Jessica shifted onto her side, dipping the float. She realized that Lila hadn't gushed over Bo Creighton, her long-distance boyfriend from Washington, D.C., for some time. "Amy's right," Jessica said. "It's strange not to hear you say 'Bo this' and 'Bo that' every time you open your mouth."

Lila shrugged. "Bo is fine," she said wearily. "I'm just getting tired of dating over the phone."

"Isn't it weird for us to be sitting like this on a Saturday night?" Amy wondered aloud. "I mean, here we are, three of the most popular girls at SVH. . . ."

Jessica slipped off the float and swam to the

edge of the pool. "You're absolutely right," she declared. "In two days we have to go back to school. I say we should hit the beach disco right now and celebrate our last weekend as working women."

Curled up in her chaise longue, in her most comfortable faded jeans and a loose-fitting white sweater, Elizabeth was writing in her journal. Jessica and her two best friends, Lila Fowler and Amy Sutton, were outside in the pool, the faint sounds of their splashing and laughter drifting through the open window. *I wish I could stop thinking about Todd,* Elizabeth wrote. *I guess I am because it's Saturday night. My brain seems to be lagging behind reality because it still can't figure out why I'm not on a date with him tonight. Enid and Maria will be coming over in a while. I think they're trying to keep me from getting too depressed.*

Elizabeth paused, tapping her pen against her chin as she thought. She heard Jessica and her friends running upstairs and into Jessica's room. A moment later rock music blasted through the walls, loud enough to set Elizabeth's teeth on edge. She thought of getting up to complain, but then the volume dropped to a more reasonable setting.

Elizabeth read what she'd written and grimaced. *I'm drowning in self-pity!* she chided herself. Suddenly Jessica, Amy, and Lila burst in through the door of the bathroom that connected the twins' bedrooms, all three of them wrapped in damp towels.

"Where's your tan leather belt?" Jessica asked, already digging through Elizabeth's closet.

Elizabeth sighed wearily. She didn't even have the energy to protest.

"We heard what happened at your internship," Amy said as she towel-dried her blond hair.

Lila sat down on Elizabeth's bed. "I think it's just awful what that woman did to you."

Just then the phone rang. Jessica grabbed the extension on Elizabeth's nightstand. "No, this is her sister, Jessica," she told the person on the other end. "Who may I tell her is calling?"

A wide-eyed look of shock came over Jessica's face. She handed the phone to Elizabeth and whispered, "It's Leona Peirson."

Chapter 8

Elizabeth gulped in a quick breath of sheer panic. Her hands trembled as she took the phone from her sister. "Hello?" she murmured, lowering herself to the edge of her bed. She presumed Leona was calling about the stolen tape recorder.

"I'm sure you didn't expect to hear from me, did you?" Leona asked.

Elizabeth mumbled a vague response.

"We parted on such bad terms. I just can't let things stand as they are between us," Leona explained. "After all, things were terrific at the start. You're a very bright and talented young woman."

Elizabeth wrapped the telephone cord around her finger as she listened incredulously. Jessica, Amy, and Lila were crowded around her with rapt expressions on their faces.

"I want you to know that I have a lot of respect

for your ability," Leona continued. "You really surpassed my expectation of an intern. I know you'll go far in the business world."

"Thanks," Elizabeth muttered dryly. "But what you did was so unfair!"

Leona chuckled. "Elizabeth, you're naive. It happens all the time in the corporate world. Remember what I told you at the very beginning, the day you first showed up at my office?" she asked. "Talent, skill, and hard work are the minimum expectations. Getting ahead takes a whole lot more. And sometimes people get hurt." She paused. "I'm sorry it had to be you."

So am I, Elizabeth added silently.

"But I think you've learned an important lesson—and you can thank me for that," Leona stated evenly.

Elizabeth exhaled sharply. "Gee, *thanks*, Leona," she retorted sarcastically. "I guess having my idea stolen, my proposal plagiarized, getting fired, and being thrown out of the Mode building was all worthwhile."

"OK, we both know 'Free Style' is a fantastic idea," Leona admitted. "But let's be realistic. You don't have the experience and finesse to pull off a project of that scope—yet."

"That still doesn't make it right for you to reject my proposal and then pass it off as your own," Elizabeth argued. Jessica gave her a thumb-up sign. Amy leaned over to whisper into Lila's ear, jostling the bed.

"Try to understand, Elizabeth. This project is

worth much more to me than to you. Its value to you might be what—an A-plus on your report card?" Leona asked snidely. "For me 'Free Style' means more of the two things that make this world go round: power and money."

Elizabeth rolled her eyes, sending Jessica, Amy, and Lila the silent message, *This woman is too much!*

"You're a very intelligent girl," Leona said. "I won't insult you by saying that what I did was right. But I'll make it up to you someday."

"Don't bother," Elizabeth snapped. The door-bell rang at that moment; Jessica gestured for Amy and Lila to answer it.

Leona laughed. "You have a lot of spunk too."

Elizabeth clenched her jaw. Leona's conde-scending tone made her blood boil.

"We need to put some closure on this whole thing," Leona said. "Let me take you to lunch to-morrow. There's a fabulous little French café in Flora Beach that I'm sure you'd enjoy."

Isn't she gracious! Elizabeth thought sarcasti-cally.

"Is twelve-thirty OK for you?" Leona pressed.

Elizabeth squeezed the corner on her bottom lip between her teeth as she considered the invita-tion. A heart-to-heart talk with Leona over lunch might be just the perfect solution to her dilemma. *Especially if I get the whole thing on tape!* Elizabeth reasoned.

Amy and Lila returned to the room, followed

by Maria and Enid. "What's going on?" Maria asked in a stage whisper. Jessica hissed at her to be quiet, and everyone sat back down on the bed. Elizabeth shifted sideways as the mattress dipped.

"OK, Leona." Elizabeth cleared her throat. "I'll meet you for lunch tomorrow." Ignoring the collective gasp of surprise from the other girls in the room, she took down the directions to the restaurant.

By the time she hung up the phone, Elizabeth felt incredibly energized. "Hi, guys," she greeted the new arrivals. "I just lined up a power lunch."

"I can't believe you want to go out to lunch with *her*," Lila said, wrinkling her nose.

Elizabeth grinned. "I wouldn't miss it for the world."

"Did she give you a reason why she wanted to see you?" Enid asked.

"Closure," Elizabeth replied. "She says she wants to put closure on this whole ordeal—and I plan to do just that. I'm going to gather enough evidence over lunch to fix her once and for all!"

Beaming, Jessica gave her a hug. "That's my twin!" she said proudly.

Todd turned up the volume on his car radio as he drove toward Sweet Valley on Sunday morning. The traffic on the interstate highway was heavy, probably from people trying to escape the hot, sweaty city for the day. In the rearview mirror Todd could see a gray haze over the L.A. skyline.

He tried to imagine what Elizabeth was doing at that very moment. *Having brunch with her family?* he thought. *Maybe swimming in her pool?* Todd sighed. He recalled Sunday walks on the beach with Elizabeth, her hand in his as they side-stepped the waves. Sometimes they'd drive to Secca Lake for a picnic. . . .

Todd wondered how he could've risked all that he'd had with Elizabeth—for a girl like Simone. Looking back over the past two weeks, he seemed to have made some of his stupidest moves of all time. "What was I *thinking?*" he asked himself aloud.

The drive seemed to take forever, but finally he reached the exit that led to Sweet Valley. Todd suffered a pang of homesickness as the familiar sights of the town came into view. But most of all he was eager to see Elizabeth. He couldn't stand to be apart from her, knowing how badly he'd hurt her.

Heading toward Calico Drive, Todd got caught at every single traffic light, each one raising his frustration level a notch.

Finally! he silently cheered as he turned onto Elizabeth's street. But as he neared the Wakefields' house he saw the twins' Jeep pulling out of the driveway. *Let it be Jessica,* Todd hoped.

He got there just as the Jeep cleared the driveway and took off down the street—with Elizabeth at the wheel. Todd honked his car horn, but she didn't look back.

"Elizabeth!" he hollered uselessly, watching

as the Jeep turned left at the end of the block.

Todd tightened his grip on the steering wheel and followed. He *had* to speak to her. He couldn't put off his apology any longer.

So tell me, Leona . . . have you decided what to call the readers' column? Are you planning to use my original name for it? Elizabeth mentally rehearsed as she drove along the coastal highway. *Do you feel the budget projections* Reggie *came up with are realistic?*

Elizabeth chuckled softly. She was surprised to find that she was actually *enjoying* herself. Even the drive was turning out to be pleasant. The day was sunny but not too hot, and although the traffic was heavy, it was moving at a steady pace.

I'm not sure if the blowups of the sample columns I *did were striking enough. If you* had *done them, would you have used a colored border?* Elizabeth imagined herself asking. She was sure her lines would get Leona talking.

Following the directions Leona had given her, Elizabeth got off the highway and turned onto a county road that meandered along the cliffs overlooking the ocean. The sharp, winding turns forced her to drive slowly, but Elizabeth didn't mind because it allowed her to better appreciate the breathtaking scenery.

Elizabeth realized that she wasn't at all nervous about meeting Leona—probably because she was so well prepared. She'd been coached for hours the night before by her friends, her twin, and her twin's friends. Enid and Maria had teamed up against Jessica, Lila, and Amy to argue the best way to entrap a guilty person. The debate had generated lots of great ideas and a complete script of questions and comments to get Leona talking about "Free Style."

Elizabeth touched the small tape recorder in the pocket of her ivory linen blazer and smiled. Her plan was going to be sweet irony—Leona would be caught with her own equipment.

There wasn't much traffic on the county road, but after she'd driven a few miles, Elizabeth became aware of a black pickup truck following close behind her. Assuming its driver wanted to pass, Elizabeth touched her foot to the brake to slow down, hoping to make it easier for the truck to get around the Jeep.

But when she checked the rearview mirror, the truck was still cruising close behind. A blond-haired man with a thick mustache was at the wheel. Elizabeth stuck her left arm out the window, waving for him to pass. *What is he waiting for?* she wondered when he didn't take the hint.

Elizabeth tried to increase the distance between their two vehicles by speeding up a bit, but the other car stayed with her, moving closer until it was right on her tail. She glanced in the rearview mirror and saw that the driver was laughing. "What a creep!" Elizabeth muttered heatedly.

Just then she felt a *thump* from behind. The sudden impact caused her to jerk the steering wheel. The Jeep glided across the center median into the left lane before she could bring it back.

Shaken, Elizabeth pushed down on the gas pedal, desperate to get away from the crazy driver. But like an evil shadow, the truck clung to the back of the Jeep. As they whipped around a sharp curve, tires squealing, he hit her again. The Jeep swerved dangerously close to the edge of the cliff.

Horrified, Elizabeth struggled to maintain control of the Jeep. *Is he trying to run me off the road?* her mind screamed. The answer became obvious as the truck slammed her again.

Elizabeth gripped the steering wheel with both hands and pushed down on the gas pedal. The truck also picked up speed. It shifted to the left lane and pulled up right beside her.

"Hey, gorgeous!" the driver yelled to her. "Blow me a kiss!"

Elizabeth faced forward. She felt beads of sweat dripping down her face as she concentrated on maneuvering along the twisting, narrow road. Suddenly the black pickup sideswiped the Jeep.

"Stop!" Elizabeth screamed, her eyes blurred with hot tears. The driver honked his horn and hit her again.

Elizabeth held her breath as she pushed the gas pedal down all the way. Terrified, she fishtailed around the next sharp curve, her tires screeching.

Before she managed to straighten out the wheel, the crazy truck bumped her again from behind. Elizabeth's heart jumped into her throat as the Jeep swerved close to the edge of the cliff—close enough for her to catch a glimpse of the shimmering blue water far below.

Chapter 9

Where did she go? Todd wondered as he drove along a narrow mountain road in the middle of nowhere. He'd followed Elizabeth out of Sweet Valley but had lost sight of her in the heavy traffic on the interstate. Some time later Todd had caught a glimpse in his side-view mirror of a black Jeep driving off the highway. Hoping it was Elizabeth, he had gotten off at the following exit and back-tracked to the ramp that the Jeep had taken.

Now, after driving along the twisting path high above the ocean, Todd wished that he'd stayed on the interstate. He hadn't seen any other vehicles for some time and he had no idea where he was going.

Looks like I made another big mistake, he assumed, reproaching himself. It seemed his only option was to head back to Sweet Valley and wait for Elizabeth at her house. *I'll wait as long as it takes,* he vowed.

Just as he was about to pull over and turn around, he spotted a black Jeep in the distance—and a black pickup truck following on its tail. All of a sudden the truck rammed into the Jeep, sending it fishtailing into the left lane.

A fist of cold panic squeezed Todd's gut. "Elizabeth!" he cried, his foot pushing down heavily on the gas pedal. Todd felt absolutely certain it was her Jeep—and that she was in grave danger.

Todd had no idea why someone was trying to hurt Elizabeth, but he knew he wouldn't let it happen. He whipped around a sharp curve without braking, fishtailing more than ninety degrees before he was able to straighten out the wheels. Pushing his BMW to faster and faster speeds, he raced forward. Within seconds the black truck was just ahead—still riding dangerously close to the Jeep's back bumper.

Todd glanced at the license plate and repeated it silently to himself over and over, committing it to memory. Suddenly the truck lurched forward and bumped into the Jeep.

Horrified, Todd cursed loudly. The Jeep swerved onto the shoulder of the road, then jerked back onto the road too far, veering into the left lane.

Keep it steady, Elizabeth! Todd's mind screamed. He held his breath as she straightened the wheels.

Quickly devising a plan, Todd moved into the

left lane and pulled up alongside the truck. He caught only a brief glimpse of the driver, but in that moment of fear it was as if Todd's brain had snapped an instant photo of the man's short blond hair, flat nose, bushy mustache, and flabby chin.

Todd pushed forward ahead of the truck and slowly began steering his car to the right, his fingers gripping the wheel so hard, they felt numb. The guy was honking his horn crazily, but Todd kept moving over, trying to wedge his way in behind Elizabeth's Jeep, forcing the other driver to slow down.

Elizabeth steered around a hairpin curve, then ventured a glance in her rearview mirror. "Todd!" she screamed. Seized with panic, she pulled over to the narrow shoulder of the road and jumped out of the Jeep. Todd had been right behind her a second ago, with the crazy truck bearing down on *him*.

Elizabeth started running, terrified at what she might find. She imagined Todd's BMW lying in a mangled heap at the bottom of the cliff. . . .

Elizabeth stopped short as she came around the bend in the road. Just a few yards ahead Todd was standing next to his BMW, shading his eyes with his hand. Both he and his car appeared to be in great condition. Farther down the road she spotted the black truck driving away.

Elizabeth uttered a cry of relief and rushed into his arms. They held each other wordlessly for a long moment.

"I've never been so glad to see you in all my life!" Elizabeth said finally, still trembling in the aftermath of her harrowing experience.

Todd continued to hold her tightly. "I'm just glad I got here in time. Oh, Elizabeth, if I had lost you . . ."

She nodded and rested her head on his shoulder, letting his warm strength soothe her frazzled nerves. He smelled of sunshine and spicy aftershave. Elizabeth almost wished she could stay in that very spot forever.

Suddenly her mind shot out a warning, just a name—*Simone*. Tearing herself away, Elizabeth stepped back, her heart squeezing painfully. No matter how much she still loved Todd—or how badly she wanted to stay in his arms—he wasn't hers anymore. *Simone is his girlfriend now*, Elizabeth reminded herself sadly. The fact that he'd just saved her life didn't mean that he wanted to come back to her.

Todd gently pushed a lock of her hair behind her ear. "I was so scared, Elizabeth," he said, his voice thick with emotion, "when I saw that truck hit the Jeep . . ." He drew in a shaky breath. "What was going on anyway?" he asked. "Do you know the guy who was driving?"

Elizabeth shook her head. "Some jerk playing games, I guess."

Todd muttered an oath. "This is a pretty stupid place for that sort of game. It's probably a four-hundred-foot drop to the bottom of the cliff."

"I know." Elizabeth closed her eyes, trying forget the sheer terror she'd felt when the Jeep had nearly skidded to the edge of the cliff.

"How bad did he damage your Jeep?" Todd asked.

Elizabeth shrugged. "I didn't even look. I just jumped out and came running to see if you were all right."

Todd squeezed her hand, then entwined his fingers with hers. "Let's go check it out," he suggested.

Hand in hand, they walked along the side of the road toward the spot where she'd left the Jeep. "I was on my way to meet Leona Peirson for lunch when that black pickup appeared out of nowhere," Elizabeth explained.

Todd's lips twitched. "Figures you'd be on your way to a business lunch on a Sunday afternoon," he gently teased.

A veil of tears blurred her vision. Elizabeth drew in a deep breath and told him everything that had happened at *Flair* between her and Leona over the past week. "But I can't prove any of this," she pointed out. "So I agreed to meet her today for lunch today, hoping she'd let something slip during the conversation—which I planned to record as evidence."

"Sounds like a great idea," Todd said.

When they reached the Jeep, Elizabeth was surprised to discover how little damage there was—nothing more than a few scratches and a small dent on the side. Todd pointed out the flecks of black paint from the other car.

131

Elizabeth cautiously opened the driver's-side door and peered inside the cab. Her bag had fallen off the seat, its contents strewn across the floor. But other than that, everything seemed perfectly normal.

"Would you like me to drive you to the restaurant?" Todd offered.

Elizabeth shook her head. "Thanks. But I'm too upset to go through with it now."

Todd smiled tenderly. "Then let me take you home. I'll make arrangements to get the Jeep back to Sweet Valley." He moved closer, as if to kiss her. "You're so special to me, Elizabeth," he whispered, his breath softly fanning her face. "I want to take care of you. . . ."

Elizabeth jumped back, even though she desperately wanted to kiss him. "I'll be fine, really," she responded, struggling to keep the ache in her heart from seeping into her voice. "I can get home on my own."

"But I want to help," Todd insisted. "You're still upset. I can tell."

Elizabeth swallowed painfully. "There's nothing more you can do," she said. Although she dreaded having to drive the Jeep all the way back to Sweet Valley, she felt too vulnerable to accept Todd's help. *Maybe Jessica, Enid, or Maria can come and meet me*, she thought hopefully.

"There's no way I'm going to leave you here alone," Todd declared, reaching for her hand.

Elizabeth drew back her hand. "Don't worry

about me," she replied. "My friends and Jessica will provide any help I need."

Desperate to escape before she broke down in tears, Elizabeth slipped behind the wheel, slammed the door shut, and started the engine.

Suddenly her whole body started shaking. She was terrified. She couldn't even make her foot move off the brake.

Todd started walking toward her. *I have to get out of here!* she told herself firmly. She put the Jeep in gear, then bent over the steering wheel, almost hugging it. Cautiously she slid her foot over to the gas pedal.

Todd leaned over the door and peered at her through the window. "Are you sure you're all right?" he asked.

"Never better," Elizabeth lied. Without looking him in the eyes, she shot him a quick, forced smile. Finally he stepped away from the Jeep.

Gulping down her fear, she inched the Jeep away from the shoulder and fumbled through a K-turn.

Elizabeth waved to Todd and drove away, forcing herself not to look back.

Jessica rushed into her house that evening, loaded down with shopping bags. Quentin had called her earlier and had *ordered* her to be ready by seven-thirty for a very important dinner party at Spago's, one of the most famous and elite restaurants in Los Angeles. Jessica had immediately flown into a panic over what to wear. Elizabeth had the Jeep, so Jessica had called Lila to arrange a trip to Valley Mall.

Jessica found two messages on the answering machine. One was from her parents, saying they would be home late that evening. The other was from Elizabeth: "Jessica, the mission was aborted. Call me at Reggie Andrews's."

Jessica frowned, wondering what had happened. But she didn't have time to find out just then. She ran upstairs to her room and dumped her packages on the bed. She'd found two spectacular outfits: a long, pale yellow silk sheath and a short deep green brocade dress with cutaway shoulders and a stand-up collar. She hadn't been able to choose between them, and since she was in such a hurry, she'd bought them both, along with a few accessories. She'd charged everything on her mother's credit card, which was supposed to be for emergencies only. But Jessica figured that looking good at Spago's qualified as an *extreme* emergency.

An hour later Jessica stood in front of her mirror, admiring her reflection. She'd decided on the long dress she'd bought at the Designer Shop. Its pale yellow shade brought out the sun-streaked highlights in her hair. The scooped bodice was adorned with delicate seed pearls sewn in vertical rows. Jessica also thought the body-skimming cut of the skirt showed off her lean curves to their best advantage.

Jessica turned her head slightly, loving the way

her hair moved with its new, stylish cut. *I look like a celebrity fashion model,* Jessica thought optimistically.

Although she knew her height was a mark against her, Jessica believed the dress made her look a bit taller, especially with the strappy high-heeled mules she'd bought at Kiki's.

Jessica pulled the cap off a lipstick tube. Just as she was about to smooth it across her lips, Cameron's words came back to her, hitting her like a bucket of cold water. *Too bad your insides aren't as attractive as your outside,* he'd remarked derisively.

"No!" Jessica snapped, trying to push away the painful memory. She tried to concentrate on her high hopes for the upcoming evening, reminding herself that Quentin would be arriving any minute.

Jessica gave up and tossed the lipstick into her evening bag. Forgetting Cameron was impossible. If he would give her another chance, she'd gladly break up with Quentin. Even if it meant giving up her chance to become the next supermodel of the fashion world. *Nothing is worth losing the guy I love,* Jessica decided.

She only wished she could tell Cameron how she felt. But she had no idea how to get in touch with him. Jessica had tried to find his number, but there wasn't a listing for a "Cameron Smith" in Los Angeles or any of the surrounding towns.

Jessica heard a car pull up in front of the house. She glanced out her bedroom window as the Corvette whipped into the driveway and noisily honked its horn. "How *charming*, Quentin," she grumbled.

She grabbed her bag and rushed downstairs. Although Jessica firmly believed in keeping a guy waiting, it didn't seem like a wise move to try with Quentin. He was enough of a jerk to drive off without her.

The moment Jessica got into his car, Quentin turned to her and asked, "How long were Todd Wilkins and your sister dating before they broke up?"

Jessica fastened the seat belt. "Cute opening line, Quentin," she muttered sarcastically. "But whatever happened to 'Hello, Jessica, you look lovely tonight'?"

"You do," Quentin responded automatically. He backed out of the driveway, then spared her a quick glance. "The dress was a good choice," he added, almost as an afterthought.

"I spent the entire afternoon at the mall and must have tried on at least a hundred different outfits," she said.

"Were they pretty serious?" Quentin asked, drumming his fingers on the steering wheel.

Jessica nodded. "Some of the dresses I found were way too formal looking for me. But I didn't want anything too sporty because—"

"I meant Todd and Elizabeth," Quentin clarified. "Were they serious about each other?"

Jessica glared at him resentfully. "Why do you want to know all this?" she demanded.

"I'm just curious," Quentin replied.

Jessica crossed her arms and exhaled sharply. "They were *too* serious, if you ask me."

Quentin nodded pensively. "I suppose Todd and

Elizabeth have a lot of things in common, huh?"

"Who cares?" Jessica snapped. If Quentin was trying to figure out a way to get back together with Simone, Jessica wasn't about to help him. But despite her efforts to change the subject, Quentin continued quizzing her about Elizabeth and Todd's relationship until they arrived at Spago's.

Jessica's spirits rose as she noticed the paparazzi hanging around the entrance, ready to snap their cameras at any celebrities who might appear. *I'm really here,* she marveled.

"This is a major photo op, so be sure to smile as we walk into the restaurant," Quentin instructed.

Jessica raised her eyebrows. "Oh, so you *do* remember why we came?" she asked pointedly. "I was afraid we would be discussing my sister's love life all night."

"And no sarcasm," Quentin returned dryly.

Jessica smiled brightly, too excited about the great possibilities ahead of her to remain annoyed with Quentin. She felt like a world-class celebrity as they strolled into the restaurant, with paparazzi cameras snapping their picture.

Jessica noticed a hot-looking guy in a dark tuxedo standing just inside the door. Something about him was familiar. . . . *A movie star, maybe?* she wondered. The guy turned slightly, and his gaze met Jessica's. With a start she realized it was Cameron. His gorgeous brown eyes widened, as if he were equally shocked to see her.

Quentin clasped Jessica's elbow firmly, but she shrugged her arm free and rushed over to Cameron. She didn't care if he was only a waiter; Cameron was the guy she loved, and she wanted him to know. "I can't believe it's really you!" Jessica exclaimed, her heart dancing joyfully. "You disappeared from *Flair*, and I had no idea how to get in touch with you."

Cameron rocked back on his heels, his hands deep in the pockets of his dark pants. "Well, here I am," he said dryly.

Jessica smiled brightly, exhaling a shaky sigh. Just standing near him made her feel as if she were riding an emotional roller coaster. Her mouth was dry, and a rapid pulse fluttered in her neck. There was so much she wanted to say, but the absent look in his eyes suddenly made her feel intimidated. "I'm glad you found another job, Cameron. This must be a great place to work," she commented.

Cameron narrowed his eyes. "What do you mean?"

"Don't tell me the hotshot people who eat here are lousy tippers," she said, laughing. "Aren't they afraid you waiters will leak it to the tabloids?" He gave her a strange look, as if he had no idea what she was talking about.

"You *do* work here, don't you?" Jessica asked.

Cameron looked away. "Yeah. Sure, whatever," he mumbled.

Jessica thought she knew the reason for his sullen reaction. "Cameron, I don't think any less of you because you're a waiter," she assured him honestly.

138

"Thanks," he replied bitingly. "But I'm in sort of a hurry." He turned to go.

Jessica winced at his brusque manner. "Please wait, Cameron."

"Your *date* is glaring at us," he said with a smirk, looking over her shoulder.

Jessica uttered an exasperated sound and signaled to Quentin that she would only be a minute. Then she turned back to Cameron and smiled softly. But there was no encouragement in his eyes.

Determined to make him understand, Jessica pressed on. "I love you, Cameron. Whether you believe me or not, it's true."

Cameron folded his arms and stared at her incredulously. "Those are nice words, Jessica. But it's hard to believe you, considering you're out with Quentin tonight."

"Forget Quentin," Jessica insisted. "I won't ever see him again if that's what you want." *After the swimsuit layout appears in* Flair, *my career will probably take off on its own*, she thought.

Cameron snorted. "Am I supposed to be flattered?"

"I don't care if you are or not," Jessica replied sharply. "But you know as well as I do, Cameron Smith, we belong together. Or are you too scared to admit it?"

Cameron was silent for a long moment. Jessica held her breath, hoping . . .

"Jessica, come on," Quentin called behind her.

She groaned and waved at him over her shoulder.

Cameron raised his eyebrows. "I think your table's ready, Jessica. As for me, my shift is over. See you around."

"Wait!" Jessica begged desperately.

As if he hadn't heard her, Cameron turned around and walked out of the restaurant.

Tears stung in her eyes as she watched him go. *Why won't he believe me?* she thought, her heart writhing in pain.

Chapter 10

"Are you feeling any better, Liz?" Enid asked as she scooped a spoonful of fried rice onto her plate and passed the carton to Maria. They were sitting in Reggie's living room, wearing jeans and sweatshirts, their plates balanced on their laps. Numerous white takeout cartons of Chinese food were lined across the coffee table.

Elizabeth had changed out of the linen suit she'd worn to meet Leona into comfortable jeans and a gray sweatshirt borrowed from Reggie. "I think I'm feeling better," she answered softly. Although she was still very upset, she was no longer trembling uncontrollably. After she'd driven away from Todd that afternoon, Elizabeth had quickly realized she was in no condition to be driving a motor vehicle. She'd pulled into a roadside gas station and called Reggie.

Reggie had insisted on coming to get her. She'd brought Elizabeth back to her apartment, then called Enid and Maria to help get Elizabeth and her Jeep back to Sweet Valley.

"Here, you have to keep up your strength," Reggie said, placing a waxed-paper-wrapped egg roll on Elizabeth's plate.

Elizabeth sighed. "What would I do without you guys?" she wondered aloud.

"Avoid greasy food?" Maria quipped, helping herself to more Szechuan chicken.

Reggie groaned. "I've been moping around, eating nonstop for the past two days," she admitted. "Tomorrow I'm going to put together my résumé . . . and get on with my life." A wistful look came into her eyes. Although Reggie hadn't mentioned Gordon's name, she was obviously crushed about what had happened between them.

"I'm so sorry things turned out so terribly," Elizabeth said. "It's all my fault."

"No, it's not," Enid countered.

Maria nodded. "You did what you thought was best."

"They're right," Reggie agreed. "This is Leona's doing. I've always sensed something off-balance in her." She lifted a neat pile of rice to her mouth with her chopsticks and chewed thoughtfully.

"You mean because she's such a workaholic?" Elizabeth asked.

Reggie narrowed her eyes. "No, more than

that." She tipped her head, her chopsticks poised in midair. "Elizabeth, where were you supposed to meet her for brunch?"

"Someplace called La Café des Crêpes," Elizabeth replied. "Why?"

"I've been there. It's in Flora Beach." A strange expression flickered across Reggie's face. "You were following the directions Leona gave you?"

Elizabeth nodded.

"What are you getting at?" Maria asked.

"I'm not sure," Reggie replied. She hesitated for a moment. "There are much easier ways to get to Flora Beach from Sweet Valley."

Enid gasped. "Do you think *Leona* is behind that stunt on the highway? That she actually planned to have someone drive Elizabeth off the road?"

Elizabeth shook her head. "It's not her style," she argued. "Leona Peirson is a white-collar criminal. I don't think she'd resort to hiring a hit man."

"I wouldn't be too sure of that," Reggie warned. "If Leona sees you as a threat, you could be in a lot of danger."

"What kind of a threat could I possibly be to her?" Elizabeth countered. "She's already fired me. I'm history as far as *Flair* and the entire Mode Corporation are concerned." As she spoke them, the words left a bad taste in Elizabeth's mouth. *Leona is the one who should be history,* she thought.

The girls finished eating and began carrying the

dirty dishes and debris into the kitchen. Elizabeth fumed silently as she rinsed the plates and stacked them in the dishwasher.

Finally something inside her snapped. Elizabeth clenched her fist and brought it down hard on the tiled surface of the kitchen counter. "I'm not ready to quit!" she proclaimed.

"There's a little Kung Pao shrimp left," Enid said, offering her a white carton dripping with brown sauce.

Elizabeth exhaled sharply. "I'm talking about *Leona*," she clarified. "The dishwasher is full, by the way."

"It's over," Reggie said firmly. She squeezed dishwasher detergent into the dispenser on the door and replaced the bottle in the cabinet under the sink. "It's time to move on."

"No, it's not over," Elizabeth argued. "We'll still bust Leona. And as soon as Gordon knows the truth, he'll forgive you."

Maria glared at her. "Are you crazy? Leona Peirson might be the one who tried to get you killed, Elizabeth."

"We don't know that for sure," Elizabeth pointed out.

"Drop it," Reggie advised. She patted Elizabeth's shoulder. "Leona is too dangerous to mess with."

"But we can't just let her get away with what she's done," Elizabeth cried. "It's not fair!"

"Neither would it have been *fair* if that guy managed to push you off a cliff," Maria countered. "I think this is one situation where you can be happy just to be walking away in one piece."

Enid and Reggie nodded solemnly. "It's not worth risking your life," Enid said.

A cold, prickling sensation crawled up Elizabeth's spine. *What if they're right about Leona?* she wondered. *And what if she tries it again?*

Todd arrived at the police station shortly after seven that evening, confident that he'd made the right decision in coming. He'd spent the day agonizing over what had happened to Elizabeth. *Someone tried to kill her!* his mind kept repeating. And that someone had nearly succeeded.

Todd's gut twisted into knots at the idea of Elizabeth getting hurt—or worse. Nothing in his life would ever seem right again. *Without her . . .* Todd shuddered at the cold, gray picture that formed in his mind.

He loved Elizabeth with all his heart. And he had resolved to do whatever he could to help her—even if she wouldn't have anything to do with him.

Todd walked over to the police officer sitting behind a sliding window. "I'd like to report an incident that happened this morning on one of the mountain roads," Todd said, aiming his voice through the small opening at the bottom of the glass pane.

The police officer pushed open the window. "An accident?"

"No, a *crime*," Todd insisted. He reached into the pocket of his jeans and pulled out the scrap of paper on which he'd written down everything he could remember about the black Toyota pickup truck and its driver. "A crazy driver tried to run my girlfriend off the road." Realizing what he'd said, Todd swallowed hard. "I mean, my *friend*," he amended with a pang of sadness.

"Come on in and we'll have someone take your statement," the officer said.

A few minutes later Todd was sitting in an office cubicle, telling a police detective named Shirley Wester what had happened to Elizabeth that morning. "I wrote down everything I remembered," he said, handing her his notes. "It was a black Toyota four-by-four. I wrote the license plate number at the top of the page. I also got a good look at the driver," he added.

Detective Wester nodded thoughtfully as she studied the paper Todd had given her. After a few seconds she rose to her feet. "I'll be right back," she said. "I'm going to run a check on this vehicle."

Todd drummed his fingers on his knee, then walked over to the narrow window behind the officer's desk. The sun had already set, but bright spotlights illuminated the area around the building.

Detective Wester returned and abruptly asked, "You're absolutely sure about this information?"

"Yes, I am," Todd replied.

She perched on the corner of her desk and crossed her arms. "You were pretty upset this afternoon. Maybe you got the license number wrong?"

Todd shook his head. "No, absolutely not. I mean—yes, I was upset. That was *why* I made a point of memorizing everything I could about the other car . . . in case something terrible happened and I ended up being the only witness."

Detective Wester stepped behind the desk and sat down. "And the driver? Could you pick the guy out in a lineup?" she asked.

Todd clenched his jaw. "I know I could."

"Sit down, Todd," Detective Wester said, gesturing toward the chair he'd occupied a moment ago.

Todd saw the grave expression on the woman's face. "What's wrong?" he asked as he sank into the chair.

The detective leaned forward. "The car you described belongs to a well-known thug. We've got a file on him thicker than the L.A. Yellow Pages. He freelances his services. At reasonable rates, I hear."

Todd felt the blood drain out of his face. "You think someone *hired* him to hurt Elizabeth?"

Detective Wester raised her hands in a halting

pose. "It's just a theory. We'll know more after we've questioned the suspect. But if you can identify him in a lineup, my job will be a whole lot easier," she told Todd.

"Don't worry, I will," he declared.

"OK," Detective Wester said, shaking Todd's hand. "Soon as we bring him in, I'll give you a call."

Jessica slumped in the passenger seat of Quentin's Corvette as he drove her home that evening. The glamour of Spago's restaurant had been lost on her—she'd daydreamed about Cameron during the entire dinner. She decided to break things off with Quentin once and for all. She knew she'd never be able to get Cameron back into her life if she didn't.

It's over between us, Quentin, Jessica silently rehearsed. *I appreciate all you've done for me. . . . I think you're incredibly talented. . . . I'm sorry it didn't work out for us. . . .* She wondered what Quentin's reaction would be to her decision. He seemed to be the kind of guy who would cover up his hurt feelings with a show of anger. *But artist types are so unpredictable,* Jessica thought. *I just hope he doesn't break down and cry.*

When Quentin pulled up in front of her house, Jessica inhaled deeply and braced herself for the plunge. "I don't want to keep seeing you," she announced.

Quentin gazed at her with a bemused look in his eyes for several seconds without saying a word. Then he shrugged and replied, "OK."

Jessica glared at him. "That's it?" she demanded. "Just 'OK'?"

"What's the problem?" he asked evenly.

Jessica leaned back against the car door and crossed her arms. "Aren't you the least bit upset?"

"Why should I be?" Quentin smiled and squeezed her hand.

Feeling insulted, Jessica raised her chin defiantly and pushed open the car door.

Quentin chuckled. "Get over it, Jessica. This is another one of those things you'd better get used to if you're serious about making it as a model. In the fashion business people come and go—professionally *and* personally."

"Thanks for the advice," Jessica snapped. She jumped out of the car and slammed the door shut. *What a total jerk!* she thought hotly. Without looking back, she marched up the front walk.

She heard Quentin drive away as she entered the house. "Good riddance!" Jessica muttered. She plunked herself down on the living room couch and breathed a sigh of relief. Then she started laughing. *I don't have a single reason to be mad,* she realized. *Everything turned out perfect!* She'd gotten exactly what she'd wanted from Quentin—a big layout in the upcoming issue of *Flair*, which would mean lots of publicity. *And I don't have to kiss up to the creep anymore,* she reminded herself.

Jessica smiled brightly. Now she was free to pursue Cameron, her real love.

"Thanks for helping me bring the Jeep home," Elizabeth told Enid and Maria later that night as the three of them stood in the Wakefields' driveway. Enid had driven the Jeep back to Sweet Valley for .Elizabeth, with Maria following them in her Mercedes.

"Are you going to be OK?" Enid asked.

Elizabeth nodded. "I'm planning on driving to school tomorrow morning."

Maria draped her arm around Elizabeth's shoulders. "Our own Miss Nerves-of-steel," she teased gently.

"I don't know about *that*," Elizabeth replied. "But I'm really anxious to get back to my normal life." She inhaled deeply and sighed. *As normal as my life can be without Todd,* she thought sadly. She wished there were a way for them to get back together, but she didn't feel even a shred of hope. *Todd obviously would rather be with a supermodel.*

Elizabeth's eyes watered, and for a moment she was afraid she was going to start sobbing. It seemed she'd lost so much over the past few weeks. Choking back her tears, she forced herself to smile. "You're the best friends in the whole world," she declared.

Maria pulled them all together for a group hug. "We're not too bad," she agreed wryly.

After they drove away, Elizabeth walked to the front door of the house. The instant she stepped inside, her twin came barreling down the stairs.

"Where have you been?" Jessica demanded.

"At Reggie Andrews's apartment for most of the day," Elizabeth replied. "Didn't you get my message?" She lowered her voice to a whisper. "Are Mom and Dad home?"

Jessica shook her head no. "Good," Elizabeth breathed. "I'm not sure I could face them right now. With any luck, they won't notice the Jeep when they come home." She began trudging up the stairs to her room. "Tomorrow will be soon enough to explain the damage."

"But not for me!" Jessica insisted. She followed Elizabeth to her room and sat down on the edge of the bed. "I want the explanation *now*, Liz! What happened? Did you have brunch with Leona?"

"I never made it to the restaurant," Elizabeth explained. Pacing back and forth across her floor, she recalled the entire harrowing ordeal for her sister.

"How horrible!" Jessica exclaimed.

Elizabeth shuddered. "I nearly drove off the cliff. I don't know what I would've done if Todd hadn't been there."

"Thank goodness for Mr. Boring-as-dry-toast," Jessica said. "But it does seem strange. . . ."

"What do you mean?" Elizabeth asked.

Jessica's eyes narrowed. "Leona knew the route you'd be following this morning. I'll bet she's the one who set up the whole thing."

Elizabeth stopped in her tracks. "That's exactly what Enid, Maria, and Reggie said." Then she waved her hand in the air as if to erase the notion. "I just can't see Leona doing something so drastic."

Jessica shrugged. "Maybe Todd set it up so that he could come out looking like a hero."

Elizabeth glared at her twin. "Now there's a *brilliant* theory," she uttered sarcastically.

"You're right," Jessica replied flippantly. "He's not creative enough to come up with a plan like that." She stretched out on Elizabeth's bed and tucked her hands under her head. "So that leaves only one other suspect—Leona Peirson. She must still see you as a threat. Maybe she's worried that you made copies of all your work."

"No, I'm history as far as Leona is concerned," Elizabeth argued. "Although I *wish* I were a threat to her. You can't believe how much I hate losing to that woman!"

Jessica flipped onto her side, facing Elizabeth. "I think it's time for you to back off and get on with your life, Liz."

"You really think I should let her get away with what she's done?" Elizabeth asked, surprised at her sister's reaction.

"Definitely," Jessica said. "Now that Todd is

gone, you can have so much fun. . . ." She swung her legs over the edge of the mattress and jumped up. "And speaking of fun, my photos for the swimsuit layout will be ready tomorrow. I'm going back to the studio first thing in the morning to check them out. I'm dying to see them!"

"What about school?" Elizabeth asked. "You *do* remember classes start tomorrow?"

Jessica shrugged. "Guess I'll have to skip for the day." She crossed the room and slipped into the connecting bathroom.

"Why don't you wait until after school?" Elizabeth suggested, raising her voice to be heard over the sound of running water.

"Can't," Jessica answered. She opened the door and popped her head back into Elizabeth's room. "I have cheerleading practice after school. I'll have to be back in time for that." With a giggle she ducked back into the bathroom.

Elizabeth shook her head, marveling at her twin's priorities. *But Jessica never lets anything stop her from chasing after her goals,* she admitted to herself.

Elizabeth curled up in her chaise longue and stared absently into space. *Did I give up too easily?* she wondered. Sure, she'd tried hard to get back at Leona—and had failed. But now what? Could she forget all that she'd suffered at *Flair* and just slip back into her normal life at Sweet Valley High?

Elizabeth sighed wearily. If she were half as

bold as Jessica, Leona Peirson wouldn't be getting away with all her dirty dealings. *I would go back to L.A. tomorrow and march right into the Mode building.* . . .

Elizabeth blinked. "That's it!" she cried, bolting to an upright position.

A surge of energy tingled through her body, pushing away her gloomy mood as a plan began to take shape in her mind.

Chapter 11

Elizabeth shrieked as Jessica whipped across two lanes of heavy downtown traffic Monday morning to snag a parking spot in front of the Mode building.

Jessica shot her a sideways glance, then backed the Jeep into the tight space. "I hope you haven't been permanently traumatized by what happened to you yesterday, Liz."

Elizabeth rolled her eyes. "If that didn't do it, your driving certainly will."

Jessica giggled, obviously undaunted by the insult. "This is going to be a fun day," she predicted. "We should skip school together more often."

"Thanks, but I'll pass," Elizabeth muttered dryly.

Jessica dropped her keys into her bag, her eyes glittering with excitement. "I shouldn't be more than an hour. Unless the layout is so fabulous that I can't tear myself away," she added, laughing.

Elizabeth smiled, trying to show enthusiasm for her twin's spectacular achievement. But inside, her heart was pounding like a kettledrum. She hadn't told anyone—not even Jessica—that her real reason for returning to the Mode building was to take one last stab at Leona. She'd made up an excuse about needing one more day to recuperate from her near-fatal brush with the black truck.

Jessica hopped out of the Jeep. "You're going to wait for me here, right?" she asked through the open window.

"Right," Elizabeth lied. "I've got a book to read."

"Sounds exciting," Jessica scoffed. "By the way, you look really great this morning. We even match—sort of. Is that a new outfit?"

"Actually, it's yours."

Jessica chuckled. "No wonder I love it. We should take a drive to Sunset Boulevard later and scope out the guys. Dressed like me, you're sure to find a new boyfriend."

Elizabeth exhaled slowly, waves of sadness crashing over her. She didn't want a new boyfriend. *I want . . . Todd,* she thought. "No thanks, Jess," she replied softly.

"Spoilsport!" Jessica shot back. She flicked her wrist in a jaunty wave and walked away.

Elizabeth waited for her sister to join the throng of people entering the Mode building. *Please let this work!* she hoped fervently.

Elizabeth suspected that her friends and Jessica were right—Leona was dangerous. But caught off guard, she probably wouldn't have anything devious planned. And maybe the surprise of seeing Elizabeth again would help loosen her tongue.

Elizabeth stepped out of the Jeep and locked it. The small tape recorder was in an outside pocket of her canvas bag, ready to pick up any shred of evidence Leona might let drop. *I hope she's in the mood to brag about what she did,* Elizabeth thought.

After having being escorted out by a security guard three days ago, Elizabeth felt nervous about returning to the Mode building. She tried her best not to look guilty as she walked across the lobby. If anyone stopped her, she was prepared to say that she was Jessica. But Elizabeth was relieved when she made it into the elevator without having to lie about her identity.

The ride up to the editorial department seemed to take forever. Elizabeth ignored the cold, measuring stares from the other women in the elevator. A week ago she would have withered under their scrutiny, but now she didn't care a bit if they found her short black skirt and purple tank top lacking in style. She'd selected her outfit carefully that morning, just in case she did have to impersonate Jessica to get into the building.

Elizabeth got off at the eleventh floor. Her legs were shaking, her palms were sweaty, and her heart throbbed as if she'd just run the eleven flights of stairs instead of riding up on the elevator.

For a moment she considered hopping into the next elevator going down.

No way! a strong voice in her head declared. Elizabeth clenched her fists. *I have to do this.* Determined, she headed down the hallway, forcing her legs to walk steadily.

When she reached *Flair*'s editorial department, Elizabeth was relieved to see that the receptionist was busy at the water cooler, her back turned.

Elizabeth quietly snuck past the receptionist's desk and hurried down the corridor toward Leona's office. Then she reached into her canvas bag and turned on the tape recorder. She took a deep breath. "I *can* do it," she whispered.

Holding her head high, Elizabeth burst into Leona's office.

I miss this place already, Jessica realized as she walked around the photography studio, looking for Quentin. The atmosphere seemed to crackle with energy as everyone rushed around amid the jumble of equipment and props.

Jessica finally located Quentin in one of the storage rooms. "Good morning," she said cheerfully.

He glanced at her, then pointed to a stack of boxes on the floor. "Carry this stuff down to my car," he ordered gruffly. "We're doing a shoot on location. You can ride with one of the tech crews or follow in your own car."

"My internship ended on Friday," Jessica informed him.

Quentin eyed her sternly. "So that means you can't carry a few boxes to my car?"

"It means I'm not your flunky anymore," Jessica replied. "I only came to see the swimsuit layout before it goes to print."

"On my desk," he grumbled. "At least make yourself useful and deliver them to the mail room. The issue is being printed tomorrow, and the photographs have to be messengered right away."

Jessica grinned. "I'd be delighted to help you out, Quentin."

"Great," he muttered. "And hurry up."

Thrilled, Jessica scurried over to Quentin's office and found the mailer containing the photos. "My ticket to the top," she murmured excitedly. She grabbed the package and rushed out of the studio.

As she headed for the elevator Jessica carefully pulled out the photographs. She took one look and stopped in her tracks. "*Simone?*" she hissed.

Jessica made a low, growling sound deep in her throat as she shuffled through the rest of the photos. She couldn't believe what she was seeing. The wicked witch appeared in every single shot.

Flames of hot anger blazed through Jessica. "He switched them!" she shrieked.

"Thanks for coming in this morning," a gray-haired police officer said as he ushered Todd into a darkened room. A glass panel spanned the length of one of the walls. Todd didn't have to be told that it was a one-way mirror.

He hadn't expected to be called back to the police station so soon, but he was relieved that the case was getting immediate attention. Todd knew he wouldn't be able to rest easy until they found the jerk who'd tried to hurt Elizabeth.

The officer gestured toward the straight-back chairs facing the one-way mirror. "Have a seat. Soon as you're ready, we'll begin. By the way, I'm Officer Troper," he added.

Todd sat down and mentally prepared himself for the lineup by picturing the driver of the black truck, trying to remember as many details as he could.

A few minutes later eight men filed in on the other side of the glass. "That's him!" Todd declared, immediately recognizing the guy's broad nose and fleshy chin. "Second from the right."

"Take your time, son," Officer Troper advised. "Look at them closely. Study their profiles." Over a telephone intercom he instructed the men to turn from side to side.

"I'm sure," Todd insisted, his hands clenched into fists. He wanted to strangle the creep.

The police allowed Todd to watch the suspect being questioned. Two detectives took turns asking the guy about his whereabouts the previous day. His lawyer, who was sitting next to him in the interrogation room, kept interrupting with objections.

At first the guy denied all the accusations against him. "I didn't even *see* a black Jeep yesterday," he claimed.

What a filthy liar! Todd thought, fuming. Sitting next to him in the observation room, Officer Troper snorted, obviously sharing Todd's opinion of the guy's statement.

Detective Wester slammed her notebook on the table and glared at the suspect. "We have an eyewitness who identified you," she countered in a threatening tone. "A *reliable* witness, who places you at the scene and who even remembered your license plate number. So let's drop the fairy tales right now before I lose my patience."

Todd heard Officer Troper mutter under his breath, "Go, Shirley."

As the interrogation continued, the guy's answers began to sound more and more shaky. His hotshot attitude disappeared, and he seemed to crumple in his seat.

Finally, with a nod from his lawyer, he gave up. "OK, I was there yesterday!" he shouted. "I bumped the Jeep, sideswiped it . . . but I'm not the real criminal. I only did it because I needed the money."

"You're saying someone *hired* you to go after that girl?" Detective Wester asked.

The guy nodded. "Yeah. It was supposed to look like a car accident."

Todd inhaled sharply. *If I hadn't gotten to Elizabeth's house in time to follow her, this creep would have killed her—and walked away free!* he thought hotly.

"Who hired you?" the detective asked the guy.

"First let's discuss the charges against my client," his lawyer interjected. "I think it would be appropriate to discuss a plea bargain in exchange for that information."

"Forget it," Detective Wester replied smoothly. "I can lock up your client right now, just on the basis of his outstanding traffic tickets—and you know it." She glared at the suspect. "Besides, the person who hired him might be someone out of his own imagination."

The guy raised his chin defiantly. "I'm telling you the truth now," he said. "It was a lady named Leona Peirson!" He went on to reveal the details of their deal.

Todd's blood turned to ice as he listened. *Leona Peirson wants Elizabeth dead.* The realization shot his panic level to new heights.

Next to him Officer Troper chuckled derisively. "These lowlifers will say anything to save their hides."

"I believe him," Todd said. He explained what had happened between Leona and Elizabeth over the past two weeks.

The officer picked up the phone and buzzed the extension inside the interrogation room. "The story checks out," he said. "Let's bring the woman in."

A flurry of activity erupted as several more police officers entered the observation room, followed by Detective Wester. "Thanks for your help, Todd," she said, dismissing him. She picked up the phone and gave the order for a police cruiser to be dispatched to the Mode building.

"What about Elizabeth?" he demanded. "She could still be in danger."

"You said she was back at school today, right?" Officer Troper asked.

Todd nodded. "Yeah, but Leona Peirson might have hired someone else to go after her in Sweet Valley."

Detective Wester placed her hand on his shoulder. "Don't worry, Todd. A school building away from the city is probably the safest place your friend could be right now," she told him. "As long as she isn't in L.A., I'm sure Elizabeth is fine."

As Todd drove away from the police station he impulsively decided to go to the Mode building. He wanted to be absolutely sure the police arrested Leona Peirson—so that he could tell Elizabeth she was safe again. It was the least he could do after the terrible way he'd treated her.

Leona appeared startled to see Elizabeth, but she quickly regained her composure. "I'm sorry," she said, folding her arms on her desk. "If you're looking for a job, we don't have any openings."

Seeing the smug expression on her former boss's face, Elizabeth's blood began to simmer, bolstering her courage. "I'm not here for a job," she retorted.

163

Leona raised her eyebrows. "You just happened to be in the neighborhood?"

Elizabeth slammed the door shut and leaned back against it. "I just want to get one thing straight between us, Leona. I want to hear you admit that it was *my* idea."

Leona smiled innocently. "What idea is that?"

"You know perfectly well," Elizabeth shot back.

"You poor, misguided kid," Leona drawled. "But in spite of what you did to me, I still believe there's hope for you, Elizabeth. You were one of the brightest interns we've ever had here at *Flair.*"

"Just admit it, Leona!" Elizabeth demanded tersely.

Leona grinned. "I'd be happy to discuss whatever you want to know"—she held out her hand—"as soon as you give back my tape recorder."

Elizabeth's jaw dropped.

Leona tipped back her head and laughed. "Did you really think you could get away with stealing it? I didn't get where I am by being stupid."

Elizabeth felt utterly defeated. She'd completely run out of ideas on how to prove her innocence. It seemed Leona had won after all.

"I want it back immediately," Leona said sharply. "Consider yourself lucky that I haven't had you arrested for trespassing and burglary."

Elizabeth slowly dragged herself forward. She placed the tape recorder on Leona's desk, then turned to go.

"Not so fast," Leona said. "We still haven't discussed what's on your mind."

Elizabeth stopped. The heaviness in her chest felt like a granite boulder. She sighed wearily and turned around, then froze in numb terror as she stared at the gun in Leona's hand.

"Sit down, Elizabeth," Leona ordered. "We're going to have a little talk. And when we're finished, you and I will take an early lunch together—someplace nice and secluded. . . ."

Elizabeth nodded automatically, her whole body in a state of shock. But a corner of her mind remained calm and acutely aware of what was going on while calculating and groping for a way out of the situation. A few hazy ideas popped into her head. . . .

"I said sit!" Leona raged.

Elizabeth winced as if she'd been slapped. Then, as she obeyed, she faked a stumble and landed with her arms stretched across Leona's desk. In the span of a heartbeat she reached out and secretly pushed a button on the phone.

"Were you always this clumsy?" Leona chided.

Elizabeth's pulse hammered fiercely as she lowered herself into the chair. "Sorry," she murmured. "I'm *scared*, that's all."

Leona appeared calm, even friendly. "I came back to town Friday morning and called the office," she explained. "As soon as I heard you'd already left for 'the meeting,' I knew exactly what was going on."

She shook her head woefully. "You were out of your league, Elizabeth. Granted, your idea for 'Free Style' was great—but it takes more than ideas to get ahead. You should never have tried to compete with me."

Elizabeth clutched the sides of the chair, her heart in her throat. "OK, fine, you win," she conceded in a thin, shaky voice. "You've gotten away with stealing my idea. Why don't you just let me go now?"

Leona shrugged. "There's nothing I'd like better. But unfortunately your little trick with Gordon Lewis brought the mess to a new level."

An uneasy sensation crawled up Elizabeth's spine. "What do you mean?" she asked.

"The trouble you've caused!" Leona rolled her eyes. "It's as if you'd swung a baseball bat at a wasps' nest. Gordon is completely bent out of shape. He's taking this whole thing much too personally, in my opinion. He's been running around here like a scorned man, ranting and raving. . . . He wants to prosecute Reggie for conspiracy."

Elizabeth gasped. "That's not fair!"

Leona sneered at her. "There you go again, you silly fool," she replied bitingly. "Fair doesn't mean a thing in the real world. Reggie Andrews knew that when she plotted against me. As for you— Gordon wants to make an example out of you for future interns." Leona exhaled with a forced sigh. "I tried to argue on your behalf, but the man is adamant. I'm supposed to be building a case against you . . . pressing charges . . . taking action to seek punitive damages. . . . Like I said, it's a real mess."

Elizabeth was stunned as she tried to make sense of what she was hearing. *Leona stole, lied, plagiarized my work—and now she's holding me at gunpoint. . . . But Reggie and I are the ones being prosecuted!*

"Gordon called me ten minutes ago and ordered me to contact your school and your parents today." Leona leaned forward and grinned. "But you and I know that would be a big mistake."

Elizabeth nodded mutely, her heart in her throat.

"I checked out your background," Leona continued. "How am I supposed to bring down a model student who also happens to be a hotshot lawyer's kid? But I hate loose ends, and since the jerk I hired for the job was a miserable failure . . ."

A cold fist squeezed Elizabeth's heart. "What do you mean?" she asked, fearing the answer.

Leona flashed her a crooked smile and winked. "I missed you at brunch yesterday. Those mountain roads can be treacherous, huh?"

"So it *was* you!" Elizabeth gasped. "You actually want me *dead?*"

"My career is everything to me," Leona stated with a nasty grin. "With Gordon pushing me against the wall, I don't have many options left."

Elizabeth stared at her, wondering how she could have ever admired such a cold-hearted monster. She realized that there always had been a hardness about Leona, a predatory gleam in her brown eyes. Reggie had warned her. But Elizabeth had been blinded to all that by her own ambition.

"It's time for us to go for our drive," Leona announced. She tossed a lock of her dark blond hair behind her shoulder and pointed the gun at Elizabeth's face. "Now move it!" Leona barked.

Chapter 12

Still holding the gun, Leona tucked her crutches under her arms and limped around the desk. A terrible look of violence sparkled in her eyes.

Elizabeth felt paralyzed with fear. A scream clawed in her throat.

"Let's go, *child prodigy*," Leona hissed, striking Elizabeth's leg with one of the crutches.

"No, please!" Elizabeth begged, tears spilling down her cheeks. "I promise not to cause you any more trouble."

Leona sneered and pushed the barrel of the gun against Elizabeth's neck. "It's too late for promises," she growled.

"It *isn't*," Elizabeth pleaded desperately. "I'll tell everyone that I'm guilty, that I tried to pass off your work as my own."

All of a sudden, two police officers burst into

the room. At that very instant Leona pressed the gun into Elizabeth's hands and sagged against her desk.

"Nobody move!" one of the policemen ordered.

Wearing an expression of relief, Leona turned to the officers. "Thank goodness you're here!" she uttered breathlessly, as if *she* were the one who was being threatened at gunpoint.

"Give yourself up," she told Elizabeth. "I know you really didn't mean to hurt me. You're just a mixed-up kid who needs help."

Elizabeth was stunned. Leona's act was absolutely flawless. She actually had tears in her eyes. But the police apparently weren't fooled. One of them approached her with a pair of handcuffs.

"What are you doing?" she asked tremulously. "*I'm* on crutches."

The other officer rolled the chair out from behind Leona's desk and gruffly ordered her to sit down.

"Leona Peirson, you're under arrest for the conspiracy to commit murder," the first policeman stated as they pulled her arms behind the back of the chair and fastened the handcuffs on her wrists. "You have the right to remain silent. . . ."

"You're making a big mistake!" Leona screamed. "You don't have a shred of evidence against me."

The police officer finished reading Leona her rights, then said, "Your scummy friend sang like a canary this morning."

"I don't know what you're talking about," Leona insisted.

The cop shrugged. "He seems to know about you. Says you hired him to do a nasty piece of work yesterday morning."

Leona's nostrils flared. "Obviously the guy is lying."

Gordon Lewis showed up at the door. "Tell them they're wrong," Leona pleaded with him. "They're accusing me without any proof."

"They're not," he replied evenly. "We have all the proof we need, thanks to your conversation with Miss Wakefield."

"And you believe her over me?" Leona retorted. "I don't know why you're turning on me like this, Gordon. You know that Elizabeth Wakefield is a vindictive liar."

Gordon's expression hardened. "Drop the innocent act, Leona. I'm talking about the conversation that took place in this office within the last ten minutes. Your intercom was on the whole time. The receptionist heard everything and called me."

"But how—" Leona turned to Elizabeth, her eyes blazing. "It was *you*, wasn't it? You turned it on!"

Elizabeth grinned. During one of her meetings with Leona, Elizabeth had used the intercom to tell Todd that she didn't want to speak to him ever again. "Guilty as charged," she responded.

Leona cursed everyone—especially Elizabeth—as the police took her away, chair and all.

After she was gone, Gordon turned to Elizabeth. "I owe you an apology," he said. "I'm so sorry for everything you've been put through because of your internship with us. I'd like to make it up to you if I can."

"I'm just glad the nightmare is over," she replied shakily.

"Leona was right about one thing—you are the best intern we've ever had." He reached out and shook Elizabeth's hand. "Anytime you want a job, you've got one," he said.

Elizabeth smiled. "I hope the same goes for Reggie Andrews."

"It certainly does," he said. "I'm going to call her right now and beg her to come back."

As they walked out of the office Elizabeth caught a glimpse of Todd slipping around the corner in the hallway. "What's he doing here?" she wondered aloud.

"You mean Todd Wilkins?" Gordon asked. "He's the one who led the police to Leona."

Elizabeth felt a surge of happiness—and hope. *Maybe Todd really does care about me after all,* she thought.

Jessica stormed back into the studio and confronted Quentin. "What's the meaning of this?" she demanded, waving the photos under his arrogant nose.

"Haven't you got those out yet?" he

complained. "I thought I told you to hurry."

"And I thought this was supposed to be *my* layout," she spat back at him.

Quentin crossed his arms and glared at her. "I'm the one who makes the final decisions around here," he reminded her pointedly.

"But it was settled," she argued. "You said the shots you took of me were fantastic."

"I changed my mind," he replied flippantly, as if it weren't a big deal that Jessica's hopes had been shattered. "Now, if you'll excuse me . . . I've got work to do." He began barking orders to the lighting crew.

Jessica's temper flared. "That's *it*, Quentin? You suddenly changed your mind?" she raged.

Quentin shrugged. "That's right. It's my job to choose the right model. And I decided Simone was better for the job after all." He reached out and gently squeezed her shoulder. "Thanks for stopping by, Jessica. It was nice to see you again. But we're running on an extra-tight schedule this morning, so if you don't mind . . ."

Jessica felt as if she were ready to explode with anger. "You're the biggest jerk I've ever met!"

"I've heard that line before," he quipped. He yelled at one of the technicians, then turned back to Jessica. "Listen, before you go, would you mind checking over the equipment list? We're really shorthanded today."

"I already *told* you, I'm not your flunky anymore," Jessica retorted hotly. "And I'm not leaving until we've settled our business. You promised me a layout in *Flair*, Quentin."

"It didn't work out," he said. "Deals fall through every day in this business."

Just then Jessica heard a familiar voice laughing behind her. Her anger blazed hotter.

Simone walked passed her and slipped her arm around Quentin's waist. "Jessica, you poor little thing," she drawled, pushing out her huge, silicone-filled lips. "Quentin never had any intention of putting you in *Flair*. He was just using you."

Jessica glared at Quentin. "Tell me she's lying."

Quentin ducked his head sheepishly and said nothing.

"You'd better start explaining," Jessica demanded fiercely.

"It was no big deal," he responded defensively. "Simone tried to make me jealous by fooling around with Todd. So I decided to give her a taste of her own medicine."

Jessica was speechless, her jaw hanging as she stared at the pair of them. *And I thought I was doing the using*.

Simone playfully elbowed Quentin in the ribs. "He's such a beast!" she chirped.

Quentin tweaked her nose.

They're a perfectly disgusting match, Jessica realized. *And if I don't get away from them immediately, I'm going to puke*.

Wanted: swimming pool attendant for upscale fitness club . . . minimum wage w/ weekend bonus. Apply in person: Hollywood Bod. Todd reread the ad and circled it. "Sounds interesting," he murmured.

Todd was sitting at his kitchen table Saturday afternoon, scanning the *L.A. Times* classified section as he ate his lunch of cornflakes and milk—his fourth bowl that day. If he didn't find a job soon, he knew he'd be living on cornflakes for a long, long time.

The past week had been dismal. The only bright spot had been Leona Peirson's arrest. Elizabeth was safe now. *I miss her so much!* Todd admitted to himself. He was aching to see her again. But until he got his life on track, he figured Elizabeth was better off without him.

Lack of money seemed to be the major factor holding him back. When Todd had phoned the photography studio at Mode to get his modeling schedule for the week, he'd been told that there were no sessions planned for him in the near future.

He'd tried contacting Quentin Berg several times since, but the photographer hadn't returned any of his calls. Finally Todd had tried setting up appointments with every modeling agency in the phone book, but no one seemed interested in helping him.

Todd suspected Simone had made good on her

threat to ruin his chances as a model. As much as it angered him, he was still glad he'd broken up with her. He'd walked out on his parents because they'd tried to control him. He wasn't about to put up with a vindictive, controlling girlfriend who was only using him anyway. He wished he'd seen her true nature at the very beginning. If he had, he would still be with Elizabeth.

Todd shook away the sad thought. At that moment his biggest concern was restocking his food supply and coming up with next month's rent. His savings were running out much faster than he'd planned. And since he could no longer count on modeling, it seemed he'd have to work a lot harder than he'd imagined in order to survive on his own.

Todd had planned to continue his education with the help of a private tutor, but that plan was out of the question now. He could barely afford milk to go with the cornflakes, so he certainly couldn't hire a tutor. His choices were to transfer to a Los Angeles public high school, where he wouldn't know a single person, or to drop out of school altogether. He wasn't happy with either option.

Todd scooped up another spoonful of cereal, chewing as he read. *Lawn maintenance assistant, Morgan Retirement Home* . . . He nodded. "An outdoor job," he murmured. "That could be fun."

Someone turned on the television next door and a commercial jingle blasted through the walls, startling him. He clenched his fist and pounded on the wall. His neighbor answered by shouting a string of colorful curses.

Todd rolled up the newspaper and threw it against the wall. *I didn't move to L.A. to live in a dump like this,* he thought, fuming. A cloud of despair swept over him as he considered the hopelessness of his situation. Even with *two* low-paying jobs he wouldn't be able to afford a nicer apartment.

"Stop it!" Todd ordered himself. "I *am* going to make it!" He was determined to show his parents that he could take care of himself—even without them hovering over him day and night, forcing him to obey their rules and curfews.

Todd picked the newspaper up off the floor and carried it back to the table. He spread it open and found his place. *Waiter . . . downtown luncheonette . . .* As he continued reading he heard a crunching noise next to him.

He looked up and saw a fat gray mouse perched on the rim of his cereal bowl.

"What the—," Todd shrieked, jumping up so abruptly that his chair toppled over backward. The mouse glared at him, as if he thought Todd was being terribly rude. Then he boldly reached down and clasped a cornflake between his paws. His cheeks puffed out as he nibbled his prize.

Todd grabbed a pot cover from the cupboard and stalked back to the table. "You've gone way too far this time, and you're going to be sorry," he warned.

Apparently dismissing the threat, the mouse continued munching. Todd wasn't surprised. The creature had been taunting him for days. It was obviously very brave, considering that it had no problem coming right up and challenging Todd to his face.

Todd stalked over to the table. Just as he brought down his makeshift trap the mouse scurried away.

Todd shouted a curse and jerked back his arm, accidentally knocking his cereal off the table. The plastic bowl bounced. Streams of milk and globs of mushy cornflakes shot across the floor.

And right in the middle of the mess the mouse resumed his meal.

"Stay right where you are, you fat ugly thing," Todd growled as he picked up the pot cover again. As he lunged across the floor he nicked his elbow on a piece of chipped linoleum. The mouse darted past him and slipped into a crack under the bottom cabinet.

"You can't run from me forever!" Todd yelled as he wiped drops of blood off his elbow. He'd been trying to corner that mouse for days. Sharing the apartment with it was bad enough. But eating together from the same bowl went way beyond gross. Todd had been pushed to his limit.

"I'm going to get that dirty stinker!" he vowed as he crawled nearer to the spot where the mouse had disappeared. "This is *war*. Man against beast!"

Suddenly he saw the mouse scurry out from

under the cupboard. Todd lunged again, with his bare hands this time, and managed to grab the creature by its tail.

"You're outta here!" he exclaimed victoriously.

Holding the dangling mouse at arm's length, Todd speed-walked out of the apartment and down the four flights of stairs to the front door. "And don't come back!" he grumbled as he set the mouse down on the ground.

Todd brushed his hands and was about to go inside when he happened to catch a glimpse of a man crossing the street toward him. Then he saw who it was, and his whole body stiffened. Mr. Wilkins hesitated at the sidewalk and stared back at Todd.

Not now! Todd moaned to himself. His kitchen was splattered with soggy cereal, and the employment section of the newspaper was scattered across the table. There wasn't any food left in the refrigerator. Todd's father would know immediately how bad things had turned out for him.

Todd stood his ground, his hands in the back pockets of his jeans as he waited. Suddenly Bert Wilkins began waving a white flag. Then Todd saw the moving van parked across the street.

Todd exhaled a long breath, his body nearly sagging with relief. He walked to meet his father halfway. Communicating without words, they exchanged a hug.

"Let's go get your things," Mr. Wilkins said simply.

Todd grinned. "Gladly."

When the last of his stuff was packed into the van, Todd felt better than he had in a long time. He'd finally gotten his life back in order . . . *almost*.

There was just one piece missing. Todd still had to fix the most important thing in his life—his relationship with Elizabeth.

Feeling miserable, Jessica was spending her Saturday curled up in front of the TV, channel surfing as she ate her way through a bag of nacho-cheese-flavored tortilla chips. She couldn't stop thinking of Cameron and of how badly she'd messed up their relationship. *I should have followed him when he walked away from me at Spago's last week. . . . Maybe he would have listened to me. . . .*

Elizabeth walked in, scowling with disapproval. "Jessica, it's two o'clock in the afternoon," she said in an irritating, bossy big-sister tone. "Don't you think you should at least get dressed?"

"I am," Jessica replied tersely.

Elizabeth exhaled sharply. "Oh, yes. White bathrobes are so very *in*," she drawled sarcastically. "I love the accessories too. Those fuzzy pink slippers are this season's fashion *essentials*."

Ignoring her, Jessica flipped to a different station and settled in to watch an infomercial about acne cream.

"Are you sure you don't want to come to the

Plaza Theatre with Enid, Maria, and me?" Elizabeth asked. "They're showing a double feature—two Bette Davis movies for the price of one."

Jessica grimaced. "Have fun."

"We could do something else if you want," Elizabeth offered. Jessica pressed the mute button on the remote control. "Liz, I know you're trying to be helpful, but you're really annoying me."

Elizabeth threw up her hands. "OK, fine—I'm leaving," she said as she backed out of the room.

Jessica turned the volume back up on the TV and changed the channel again.

"Good-bye, Jess," Elizabeth called out to her a few minutes later. Jessica heard the front door open and close, then the sound of the Jeep pulling out of the driveway.

"Alone at last." She sighed wearily. Her parents were also out for the day. Jessica reached into the bag for another tortilla chip.

Jessica had tried phoning Cameron at Spago's, but they'd told her they didn't have anyone named Cameron Smith on staff. She was convinced that it was a lie. After all, she had seen Cameron there with her own eyes.

Maybe Cameron told them to say it because he didn't want to talk to me, she thought sadly. *What if he never calls me?* Returning to school had been terrible. It emphasized the fact that her internship was completely over—and her experience at *Flair* had ended. But Jessica wasn't ready to put it all behind her and start over at SVH.

A tear rolled down Jessica's cheek. She wiped it with the back of her hand and sniffed loudly. "It's all my fault," she muttered. She'd spent her days at school that week in a daze, cursing herself for going out with Quentin when Cameron was the guy she loved.

Knowing that Quentin had been using her made her even more upset. All the time she'd spent putting up with his rude, arrogant behavior hadn't help her career a bit. Jessica remembered how excited she'd been when Quentin had photographed her for what she'd *believed* would be a dazzling swimsuit layout in *Flair*. But it had turned out to be nothing more than a cruel joke.

Jessica mentally kicked herself. *How could I have been so blind?*

The doorbell rang, interrupting Jessica's self-recrimination. "Go away!" she grumbled. It rang again.

"Can't a girl have a few minutes of privacy in her own home anymore?" she muttered as she dragged herself off the couch.

When she opened the front door, she was surprised to find a deliveryman standing there with an express package addressed to "Miss Jessica Wakefield."

Jessica eagerly signed for the package, her spirits somewhat lifted. She carried it into the living room and set it on the marble coffee table. But when she opened it, her heart sank. In it were the blue pages for the next issue of *Flair,* the one Jessica had *thought* she'd be in.

Her temper flared. *Someone sent this just to torture me!* she presumed. *Is this Simone's sick idea of a joke?*

Sobbing, Jessica threw the pages across the room. "I never want to see a copy of *Flair* magazine again as long as I live!" she raged. "And as for this box of *garbage* . . ."

She decided she would take the nasty little "surprise" out back and burn it. But as she bent down to pick up the blue pages, one of the photographs snagged her attention. Jessica looked closer . . . and saw *herself.* "It can't be," she murmured.

She sat down in the middle of the floor and studied the photo of herself wearing a belted maillot with a sheer cape billowing from her shoulders. The camera had caught her laughing, with her arms gracefully poised at her sides and her windblown hair framing her face.

"This is incredible," Jessica breathed. There was a ten-page spread of *her* looking absolutely gorgeous. She gazed at each photo, mesmerized.

I doubt Simone sent these, Jessica thought, giggling. Curious to know who did, she examined the package. She found a pale gray envelope tucked inside the box, with her name handwritten on the front, and quickly tore it open. It was a formal invitation to a dinner party at the home of someone named Mr. Edward McGee.

Jessica sat down on the couch, her gaze fixed on the embossed card. *Edward McGee,* she mentally repeated. The name was familiar. . . . She racked her brain, trying to remember where she'd heard it.

Suddenly the answer popped into her head. *"E. McGee!"* she exclaimed. "The man who owns *Flair* and the entire Mode Corporation! He wants *me* to eat dinner at his house?"

Jessica's hands trembled with excitement as she checked the date and time on the invitation. "Oh, my gosh, it's for *today!*" she cried. There was a note on the bottom of the card, saying that a limo would be arriving to pick her up at her home at seven P.M.

Jessica looked up at the wall clock and shrieked. "That means I have less than five hours to get ready!" She dropped the card and raced to her room.

Chapter 13

Jessica felt like a princess as she rode to L.A. in the back of a luxurious stretch white limo. She didn't know why Edward McGee had invited her to dinner, but she was positive something wonderful was about to happen.

She was certainly prepared for it, thanks to her recent trip to the Valley Mall. Smoothing the hem of her short, deep green brocade dress, Jessica congratulated herself on her foresight. Stocking up on fabulous outfits had proved to be a stroke of genius.

Jessica gazed out the window as the limo passed through the open gates at the entrance of a very long, winding driveway. Rows of tiny white lights illuminated it on both sides, creating the illusion of a silver-edged ribbon stretched across the sloping grounds.

At the end of the driveway the limo pulled up

in front of a huge Beverly Hills mansion. Jessica could hardly contain her excitement. *I'm going to a party at E. McGee's,* she happily chanted to herself. The driver stepped out of the car and opened the door for Jessica.

A uniformed butler greeted her at the entrance to the mansion with a stiff, formal bow. "Follow me, miss," he said with an equally stiff and formal English accent. He led her into an elaborate study, where a white-haired man was sitting behind a mahogany desk.

The elderly man rose to his feet. With a respectful bow the butler left the room, closing the doors behind him.

Jessica felt somewhat intimidated at first. Then the man smiled warmly, instantly putting her at ease. "Welcome to my home, Miss Wakefield," he said, coming forward to shake her hand. "I'm Edward McGee."

"Thank you, sir," she responded.

He gestured toward a leather chair across from his desk. "Please make yourself comfortable. The other guests won't be arriving for at least another half hour. I wanted an opportunity to meet with you privately."

Jessica couldn't imagine why. She sat down, burning with curiosity.

Mr. McGee returned to his seat behind his desk. "The blue pages of the new issue of *Flair* were sent to you," he said. "I trust you've received them?"

"Yes, I did," Jessica answered brightly.

"I'd like to congratulate you on the excellent job you did modeling. It's always gratifying to discover and develop new talent. That's a goal of all my companies."

Jessica felt a warm glow in response to his compliment. "Thank you," she replied sincerely. She didn't see the need to mention that she hadn't been the first-choice model for the layout or that she'd been "discovered and developed" because of her own conniving and the fact that Simone had thrown one of her nasty temper tantrums the day of the shoot.

"You're a very talented young woman," Mr. McGee remarked.

Jessica smiled. But as much as she was enjoying the conversation, her mind remained puzzled. "Is that why you invited me here tonight?" she asked bluntly.

Mr. McGee chuckled, apparently pleased with her direct question. "Partly," he answered. "But the main reason is that I wanted to introduce you to my son."

A blind date? Jessica groaned to herself. *All this—just to get fixed up with some geeky rich kid?*

"My son has been looking forward to this evening for some time," Mr. McGee was saying. "He's quite a fan of yours, Jessica. And now that I've met you, I can understand why."

Jessica tried to keep her outward expression

neutral, but inside she cringed. *Great. I get to spend the evening listening to a spoiled jerk bragging about daddy's millions,* she thought bitterly.

There'd been a time when she might have been impressed by a guy's wealth, but Jessica had learned from recent experience that no amount of money or power could make up for a no-spark romance. Although she didn't want to offend Mr. McGee, Jessica had no intention of going along with his plan. She wasn't about to repeat the same mistake she'd made with Quentin.

"I'm really flattered, Mr. McGee," she began hesitantly. "But you see—"

"I'll be right back," he said, cutting off the rest of her sentence. Before she could say another word, he slipped out of the room.

Jessica clenched her jaw, fuming. "I'm stuck!"

She stood up and began pacing across the room. *As soon as that man comes back I'm going to tell him flat out that I'm not interested in meeting his son,* she promised herself.

Moments later she heard the door open behind her. Thinking it was Mr. McGee, Jessica whirled around, prepared to deliver her speech. But to her amazement, Cameron Smith walked into the room.

Jessica gasped. "What are you doing here?" she asked as she looked around nervously. "You'd better leave!"

Cameron gave her a crooked smile. "Aren't you happy to see me, Jessica?"

188

"Thrilled," she responded. "But you're going to be in big trouble if you don't get out of here. Mr. McGee will be right back, and if he finds that a former mail-room clerk has crashed his dinner party, he'll have you thrown out for sure—and probably arrested too."

Cameron nodded pensively. "Will you come with me?" he asked her.

Jessica didn't hesitate for a second. She scooped up her evening bag from the leather chair and rushed over to take his hand. "Let's go!" she urged.

Cameron still didn't move. "You would actually leave with me?"

"We don't have time for this," Jessica warned, tugging on his arm.

"Let me get this straight," he said. "You would duck out of here with me—even if it means giving up a fancy dinner party with the top man at *Mode*?"

Jessica planted a swift kiss on his lips. "You're the one I want to have dinner with," she told him. "I might even have enough money in my bag to treat you to a pizza."

Cameron gazed into her eyes. "Thanks, Jessica. Maybe some other time." Then he started laughing and wrapped his arms around her.

Jessica pulled herself away and stared at him. "What is so funny?" she demanded. "Are you intentionally trying to get yourself in trouble with Mr. McGee?"

"It wouldn't be the first time," Cameron muttered wryly. He tucked a lock of Jessica's hair behind her ear and smiled tenderly. "Let me introduce myself . . . I'm Cameron McGee."

Elizabeth sat at her desk, staring at her computer screen. She'd been trying for nearly two hours to finish her "Personal Profiles" column for the *Oracle*, but her mind kept drifting off the subject. She had interviewed Aaron Dallas about his internship with the L.A. Lakers, and though he'd had lots of interesting things to say, Elizabeth was having a hard time putting any of it into coherent sentences. *Concentrate!* she mentally ordered herself.

She stiffened her fingers over the keyboard and forced her attention back to her work. "'The Lakers team is like a family,' Aaron says. 'A *real* family—with sibling rivalry and a weird uncle,'" she began writing.

An image of Todd's face floated into her mind. Jessica had told her that Simone was back with Quentin. *Does Todd still have feelings for her?* Elizabeth wondered.

She thought back to the last time she'd seen Todd, when she'd caught a glimpse of him in the Mode building after Leona had been arrested. *If he hadn't gone to the police, Leona might still be free,* she realized.

Elizabeth sighed deeply. She knew she'd be

forever grateful to Todd for his help, especially during that horrible episode on the mountain road. . . .

"Not again!" Elizabeth shrieked as she realized she'd slipped back into her daydreams. She banged her fist on the desk, rattling the pencils and paper clips that were scattered across it.

Elizabeth got up and began pacing across her bedroom. For the past few days she'd tried almost frantically to jump back into her old routine at Sweet Valley High—volunteering to do extra assignments for the *Oracle*, signing up to tutor students who were having difficulties in English class, hanging out at the Dairi Burger with Enid and Maria, going to movies, the beach. . . .

But nothing seemed *right* to her anymore. It was as if her world had been skewed a few degrees, throwing everything off-balance.

Elizabeth plopped down on her bed and stared at the ceiling. She was pleased with the way things had turned out at *Flair*. Leona was in jail, Reggie and Gordon were dating, and Elizabeth had received the credit she deserved for "Free Style" and had been promised a summer job in the editorial department if she wanted it.

But none of those things could fill the gaping hole in Elizabeth's heart. Tears pooled in her eyes, spilling down the sides of her face. *I miss Todd*, she silently admitted.

Suddenly Elizabeth heard music coming from outside her window. She recognized the Jamie

Peters ballad immediately. She and Todd had danced to it the night they'd pledged their love to each other. Elizabeth swallowed against the thickening lump in her throat. Hearing the song now made her feel as if she might drown in a flood of her own emotions.

Elizabeth sat up, her heart thumping wildly. *It could only be Todd,* she thought, laughing as tears streamed down her face. She grabbed a wad of tissues from the box on her nightstand and rushed across the room. She held her breath as she pushed aside her curtains and peered outside.

Todd was standing under her window, holding a portable CD player. He had a serious but hopeful expression on his face, as if he had something important on his mind. . . . *Like maybe our relationship,* Elizabeth thought longingly.

A feeling of glorious happiness leaped in her heart. She opened the window and leaned out. "Excuse me, mister," she called to him jokingly. "I don't seem to have any loose change right now—but I do have lots of stuff in my desk drawer . . . would you mind if I tipped you in paper clips?"

Todd barely cracked a smile as he continued gazing up at her with an intense look in his eyes. "Elizabeth, will you take me back?"

Elizabeth blinked back her happy tears. "I don't know," she gently teased. "I might say yes . . . if you can make it up to my window."

Todd flashed her a huge grin and darted around

the corner of the house. He came back carrying a tall ladder. "No problem," he said.

Elizabeth laughed heartily. A sense of peace and rightness came over her. She and Todd shared something almost magical, something much more important than any job. "By the way," she called down to him. "I love you."

Todd smiled brightly. "In that case I'd better hurry."

"You do that," Elizabeth replied. After being apart for so long, she couldn't wait another minute to feel Todd's arms around her again, his lips on hers. . . .

Then suddenly he was there, crawling into her room. He stood for a moment in front of the window, the curtains fluttering at his sides. Elizabeth gazed at him, taking in the sight of him standing so close . . . finally.

They moved toward each other, and at last she was in his arms. She wrapped her arms around his neck and closed her eyes, letting the glorious moment seep into her heart. "Elizabeth, I'm so sorry . . . tell me you forgive me," Todd whispered into her ear.

Tears flowed from her eyes as Elizabeth looked into his. "I do," she sobbed. Then their lips met in a deep, searing kiss.

Jessica sighed contentedly as she snuggled closer to Cameron on the couch in Mr. McGee's study. "This is the best dinner party I've ever been invited to," she murmured.

Cameron chuckled softly. "I think they started eating without us. But if you're hungry, I can find something for us in the kitchen."

"No way," she countered with mock indignation. "I've been agonizing for days over whether or not I'd ever see you again." She tightened her arms around him and flashed him a saucy grin. "Now that I've got you, I'm not letting you out of my sight."

Cameron gently stroked the side of her face with his fingertips. "Jessica, I'm sorry it took me so long to finally come to my senses. I must've picked up the phone to call you at least a hundred times—but I was afraid you'd hang up on me."

Jessica gaped at him. "Why would I do that?"

"It seemed whenever I was around you, I'd turn into an arrogant jerk," Cameron admitted. "When I think of some of the nasty lines that popped out of my mouth—'Too bad your insides aren't as lovely as your outside'?" He shook his head woefully. "And then that night at Spago's . . . the girl of my dreams tells me she's in love with me. And I respond with a don't-call-us-we'll-call-you brush-off. I think my only excuse is that I was jealous—and that's a new experience for me."

Jessica's heart melted at the sorrowful expression in his sexy brown eyes. "We've hurt each other a lot. I say it's time to kiss and make up," she said, ressing her lips against his. Cameron deepened the kiss, sending delicious tingles up and down Jessica's spine.

When the kiss ended, Jessica leaned back so that she could look at Cameron directly. "Now it's time for me to apologize," she said. "I'm sorry that I didn't stop seeing Quentin after I fell in love with you. But I never cared two cents for him, and that's the truth."

Cameron brushed his lips across hers. "I know. I was in the studio Monday morning."

Jessica grimaced, remembering her ugly scene with Quentin and Simone. "You heard it?"

"I heard it," he replied. "I was up in the executive suite when all that trouble broke out with your sister and Leona Peirson. Then someone happened to mention that you were also in the building." Cameron paused. "I wanted to see you again and figured the most likely place to find you would be in the photography studio."

Jessica took a deep breath and let it out slowly. "So how much of the fireworks display did you manage to catch?"

"Every word," he answered.

"Dazzling, wasn't it?" Jessica groaned.

Cameron rolled his eyes. "Quentin and Simone," he muttered. "What a pair . . . I wonder what they're saying now that they've seen the blue pages."

Jessica giggled. "I'm sure it's something loud

and vicious. But how did my photos get into the layout?" she asked. "I thought Quentin had the last word."

Cameron shook his head. "He only thinks he does. The final decisions are made by the executive board—and as a vice president of the company, I chose your photos for the layout."

Jessica digested that bit of information. "So not only are you the owner's son—you're also a *vice president?* Gee, that's a nice promotion for a mailroom clerk," she teased. "But I suppose you'll have to give up your job waiting tables at Spago's."

Cameron laughed. "We have a lot of misunderstandings to unravel, don't we?"

"Let's start with why you were working in the mail room as Mr. Smith," Jessica suggested.

"As a brand-new vice president, I wanted to get a feel for the company from the inside," Cameron explained. "I wasn't satisfied to do the usual executive tour where you go around to all the different departments, shaking hands, pausing for an occasional ten-second conversation if you're not running behind schedule. . . . I wanted to learn how things ran on a day-to-day basis, but I wouldn't have been able to work alongside our employees if everyone knew I was the owner's son. So I made up a fake name."

"No *wonder* I wasn't able to find you in the phone book," Jessica said. "That was very sneaky of you."

Cameron wrapped his arms around her. "I wanted to tell you the truth, Jessica. But after I realized how I felt about you, it became important for me to know that you care about *me,* not my money."

Jessica looked into his eyes. "And do you know it now?" she whispered.

"Absolutely," he replied, moving in for a long, burning kiss.

I've sure lucked out, Jessica thought happily. Not only had she gotten the guy of her dreams but *also* someone who could help her with her career. . . .

What a great internship! she silently cheered. And then she was lost in the warmth of Cameron's passionate kiss.

SWEET VALLEY HIGH™

Don't miss any of this summer's fabulous Sweet Valley High
Collections!

Double Love Collection

DOUBLE LOVE
SECRETS
PLAYING WITH FIRE

Summer Danger Collection

A STRANGER IN THE HOUSE
A KILLER ON BOARD

Château D'Amour Collection

ONCE UPON A TIME
TO CATCH A THIEF
HAPPILY EVER AFTER

Flair Collection

COVER GIRL
MODEL FLIRT
FASHION VICTIM